THE TENTH

WILL A DIVIDED AMERICA

SURVIVE?

Stone J. Seguin

Allegiance Press

ISBN-10: 061597905X
ISBN-13: 9780615979052

ACKNOWLEDGEMENTS

It is impossible for me to thank everyone who assisted me in so many ways in the concept and preparation of this book. At the risk of excluding someone, however, I will try. First is my Lord and Savior, Jesus Christ, for his unending love and countless mercies.

Next is my family. I would be nothing without you and I thank my parents and amazing sisters for always being there. I can't ever say enough about you. I also thank my brothers. I carry both of you imprinted on who I am. To my children, I adore all four of you and thank God in Heaven every day for you. IIC, thank you for being the mother of our children and all you have been to me.

To my LHR, thank you for always being supportive and encouraging and loving me even when I make it very difficult. Many nights you sat by patiently as I typed away, never complaining, and then were excited to be the first to hear what I had just written.

Next is FPM. You were the first to truly challenge me and thereby encourage me to see if I could actually pull this off. Then, you were a constant and enthusiastic advisor, editor, cheerleader, and kick-me-in-the-pants friend when I needed it.

To GF, CW, and TI, I thank you for giving endlessly of your time and sharing your knowledge, insight, and ideas. I also thank you for asking me tough questions and holding me accountable to develop a credible story.

I also thank JM and RE, my copyeditors, for your diligent work and attention to details I would never have caught. You made this book immeasurably better.

Last, but certainly not least, to my graphic designer, EH, for bringing it all together with your creativity and great work. This may be one case where I do hope the readers judge the book by its cover.

-Stone Seguin

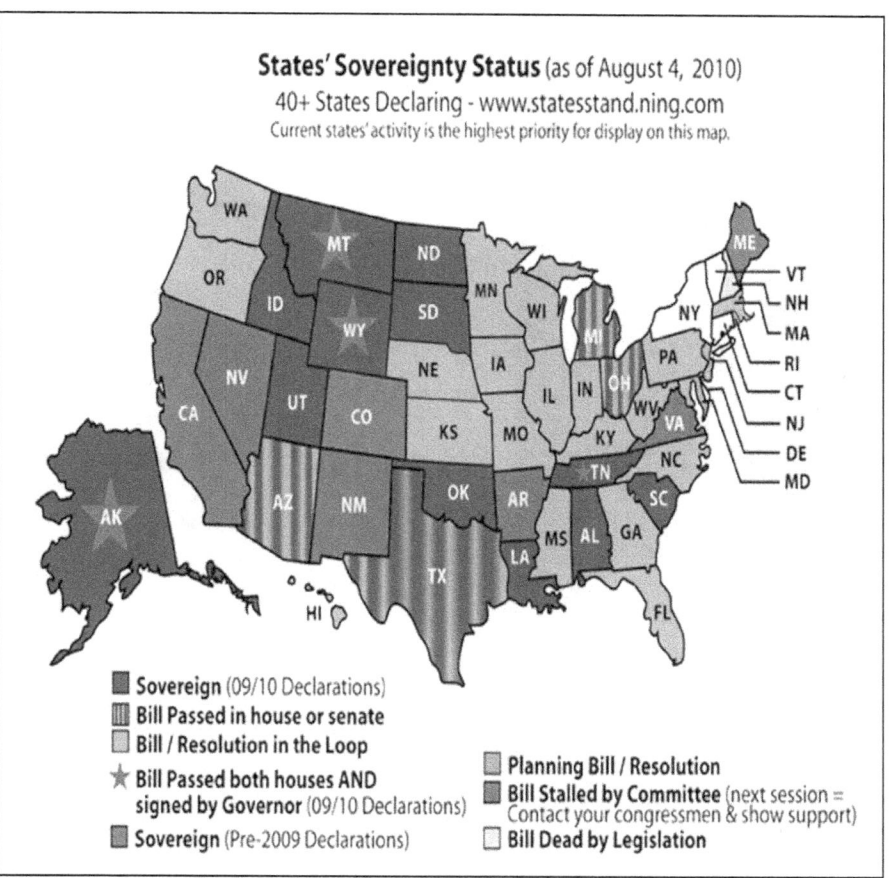

States' Sovereignty Status (as of August 4, 2010)
40+ States Declaring - www.statesstand.ning.com
Current states' activity is the highest priority for display on this map.

Sovereign (09/10 Declarations)
Bill Passed in house or senate
Bill / Resolution in the Loop
★ Bill Passed both houses AND signed by Governor (09/10 Declarations)
Sovereign (Pre-2009 Declarations)

Planning Bill / Resolution
Bill Stalled by Committee (next session = Contact your congressmen & show support)
Bill Dead by Legislation

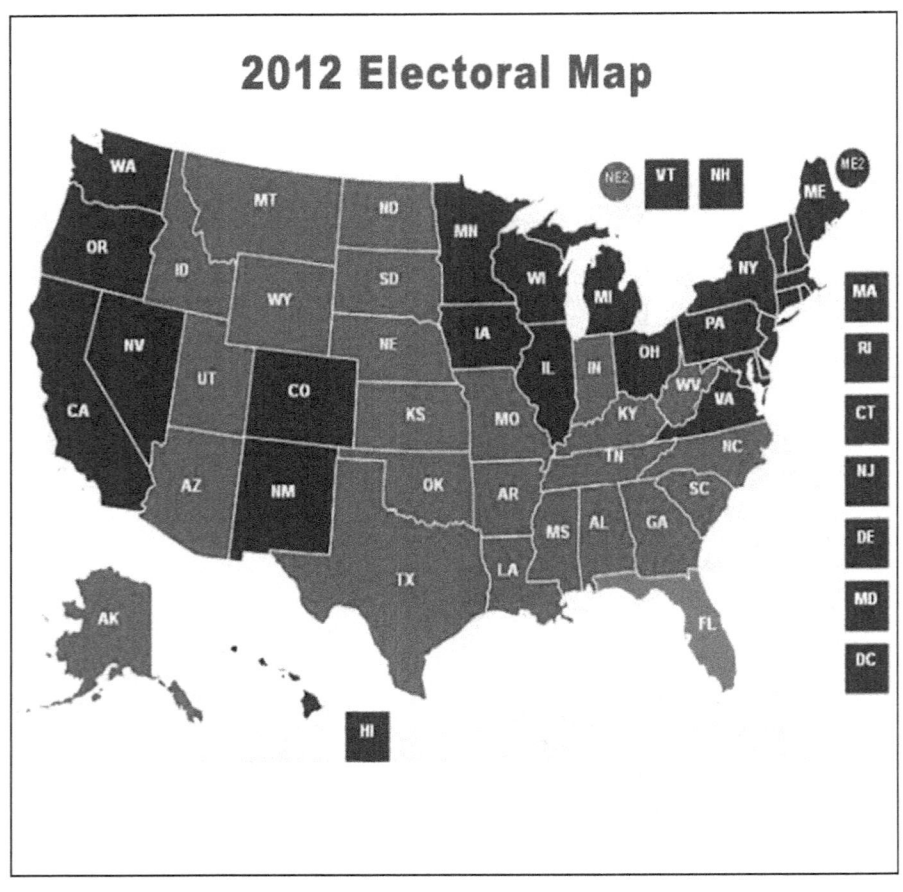

2012 Electoral Map

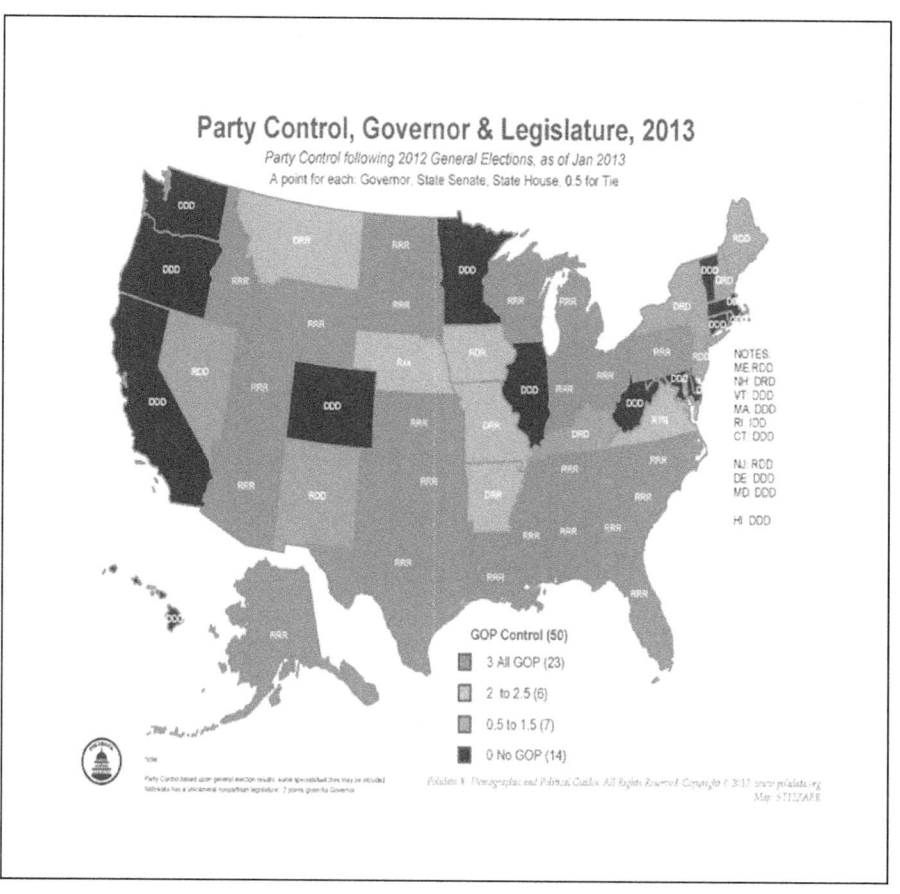

PROLOGUE

The Persian Gulf, the very near future

The crippled *Nimitz*-class aircraft carrier USS *Abraham Lincoln (CVN-72)* was making 14 knots on its way to Naval Support Activity (NSA) Bahrain where its damage would be assessed for repair. The Commanding Officer (CO) of the nuclear-powered ship, Captain James "Jimbo" Fisher didn't like the decision to keep his carrier in the Persian Gulf after the Iranian attack which had damaged his ship and two of her escorts twelve hours earlier. He didn't like the decision one bit. Fisher strode back and forth on the bridge as he cursed whichever spineless politician had made that decision. While the President was the ultimate arbiter of where his battle group went, he was surely being advised by one or more of his top staff. Here, in the Gulf and still damaged, the *Abe* made a tempting target. He was sure the Iranian mullahs and admirals were just contemplating their next move like a pack of hyenas circling a wounded lion. And, he could not believe that the President had forbidden American forces from fully retaliating by striking Iranian naval and air installations.

The official statement from Washington, D.C., read, "We will refuse to escalate the violence, especially since the Islamic Republic of Iran acted in self-defense after being attacked by Israel." Despite the vehement protests from pro-Israel circles, including many in the GOP, the Chief Executive had once again shown his true colors on the Middle East. He was no friend of Israel.

Regardless, American forces were once again forced to act with one arm tied behind their back by bureaucratic rules of engagement and could only act in self-defense and not fire unless fired upon. The fact that they had already been fired upon was notwithstanding. The thought that politicians could and should control a battle from some distant capital was ridiculous, but had been around for a very, very long time.

The Captain did not have to wait long.

"Bridge, Combat," came the call from his CIC Watch Officer.

"Go ahead," answered Fisher.

"Captain, we have numerous high-speed surface contacts approaching from the Northeast."

"Roger. Bosun, sound general quarters. Combat, Bridge. I'm staying here and taking the deck," said the Captain. "Mason, prepare for a mass surface boat attack," he said to his TAO.

"Roger, Captain. All weapons stations report manned and ready. *Ingraham* and *Ford* are in position to the Northeast and they are ready to intercept. *Halsey* is racing up from behind *Ford* and *Freedom* is also close by and is at flank speed to intercept the boat swarm," reported LCDR Mason Palmer from his station in CIC.

The Islamic Revolutionary Guards Corps Navy (IRGC Navy) had developed and practiced small boat "swarm" tactics since the end of the Iran – Iraq war in 1988. The Pasdaran (as the Guard units were known in Iran) found this form of asymmetric warfare particularly well-suited to the close confines of the Gulf. Dozens or even hundreds of cruise missile or other armed small boats would converge on a target from different directions to overwhelm the defenses. And the attack on this day would include the first-ever real combat use of wing-in-ground effect vehicles (WIG).

"Bridge, Combat. We have 90 plus high speed surface contacts approaching from 3 vectors. Speed varies from 45-55 knots. Designate raids 1-3. Range between 12 and 14 miles. CIWS and RAM mounts are on auto."

"Very well, Mase. Keep the updates coming," instructed the Captain.

"Bridge, Combat. New contacts, designate raid 4. Another 20 plus; range 10 miles. Raids 1-4 advancing on a threat axes spanning approximately 160 degrees. We are vectoring in our CAP to engage and have 2 more Hornets in bound from Bahrain, but it will be close."

"How are the CAP birds loaded out? Do they have anti-surface," asked Fisher anxiously.

"Affirm, Cap'n. Each has four Mavericks and two CBU-97 cluster bombs."

"I don't like those numbers, Mase. We have at least 80 widely dispersed boats heading our way and only 2 fighters for air support."

"We also have the Super Cobra we were able to embark on *Cape St. George*. That "Whiskey" Cobra will do some damage for us." The Captain used the nickname for the AH-1W Super Cobra attack helicopter on patrol with the ships.

Despite the optimism of his TAO, the Captain was right to be worried. Each of the four Maverick missiles carried by the two F/A-18E Super Hornets on Combat Air Patrol could easily destroy a small attack boat. And, each of the CBU bombs would disperse 40 sensor-fused munitions which could also destroy a small boat (or an armored vehicle as originally designed). But the over 80 boats were widely dispersed, limiting how many groups the Super Hornets could engage. Fisher figured that each F/A-18E would make one pass on each of two groups and kill many of the boats. But he could not count on all boats being neutralized. He would have to rely on his escorts and his own CIWS and RAM systems once again.

What the Captain did not know was that his injured ship was facing a far larger attack force. And, one that was coordinated. The surface search radars tracking the over 110 attack boats were not picking up the 10 semi-submersible Gahjae Class torpedo boats with each of the four flotillas. Based on the North Korean Taedong-C, the Gahjaes were advancing with the other Iranian craft and using the wakes to blend in with the surface clutter. Each Gahjae had two large torpedo tubes and was also laden with extra explosives. Like all the Iranian crews in the attack, they had volunteered with a willingness to martyr themselves while inflicting a humiliating defeat on the hated American infidels.

The last two components of the masterfully planned attack would come at the infidels from both above and below the waves. Mini-submarines were lying in wait to ambush the Americans even as their flying brothers in the new Bavar-2 ekranoplans closed in. Called

Wing-In-Ground effect craft in the west, the ekranoplans had been built from expertise acquired from their Russian allies.

The six Ghadir class mini-subs were staged along the expected path of the American carrier. Their orders were merely to drift quietly and wait for the American ships to come to them. And so they had. The steel monstrosity had steamed past the first 2 subs, positioning them in the perfect position to fire their Hoot supercavitating torpedoes along the wake of the ship. First developed in the 1970s by the Soviets, supercavitation torpedoes achieve their tremendous speeds by in effect "flying" in a gas bubble which is formed around the torpedo by the specially shaped blunt nose and gases vented from exhaust of their rocket engines. The bubble keeps the water from contact with the surface of the torpedo and this dramatically reduces drag and enables the tremendous speeds of over 200 knots.

"Are our escorts engaging with their 5 inchers?" demanded Fisher.

"No sir, they are in range, but there are a large number of civilian craft in the area. Merchants and fishing boats. We'll need to get positive ID," responded Palmer.

"ID hell," yelled the Captain. "Engage! All weapons stations engage!"

"Roger. All ships, weapons free. Engage. Say again, weapons free. Engage," said Palmer over the fleet radio link.

The 5"/54 caliber Mk 45 lightweight guns on the destroyers *Ingraham* and *Ford* began firing at the two groups nearest to them. The Republican Guards began to jink and maneuver their boats to avoid the incoming fire. The five inch guns were scoring hits, but not all of them were kills and the boat swarm came ever closer.

The Super Hornets arrived over two of the groups as they came within 6 miles. Of the 40 cluster bomb munitions dropped over the closest group, several homed in on the same target and only 16 boats were destroyed. For the next three passes, the strike fighters had similar success. The number of attacking boats was reduced by nearly half, but 61 boats continued to advance. And this did not include the 28 remaining semi-submersible boats.

Aboard the *Abe* the now familiar call of "Vampire, vampire," went out from the TAO. "New contacts, bearing 350 true, feet dry, still beyond the beach, but will be feet wet within a minute or two. Designate raid 5. Thirty-two missiles inbound. C-802 type."

"My God," thought the Captain. "And the tin cans?" he asked CIC.

"Destroyers are engaging the vampires now,"reported LCDR Palmer. And then, "Vampire, vampire. Contacts separating from raids 1 through 4. Short range missiles from the attack boats!"

Nineteen of the remaining Iranian craft were missile boats and these had now launched their missiles once inside the five mile range to the *Lincoln*.

"Combat, confirm this is a different set of vampires from the first," demanded Fisher.

"Confirmed two distinct sets of vampires inbound," said Palmer flatly as he continued to work the controls of his radar screen and strained to understand the reports flooding in from the escorting ships.

Eighty-three boats continued to advance and were now joined by 70 missiles. Meanwhile, the Super Hornets had come about and were now firing Maverick missiles at the lead boats. All 8 missiles found their marks and more attacking boats fell victim to the 5 inch guns from the destroyers and the lone Super Cobra attack chopper. All their missiles expended, the Hornets now swooped low to engage the attacking boats with their 20 mm multi-barrel Vulcan cannon. Fifty boats remained. Then 40. The AH-1W killed two more boats with Hellfires. But the boats weren't dying fast enough.

Four miles south of the fully engaged carrier, the Bavar-2 ekranoplans took off from the placid surface of the Gulf. They had been hiding behind two non-descript tramp steamers approximately 2 miles apart and taxied away from the *Lincoln,* continuing to use the steamships as cover. Once airborne, they quickly accelerated to their maximum speed of 120 knots. Half of the WIG craft swung northwest with the others turning northeast to approach the American ships from different vectors. The WIGs carried no weapons. They were the weapons and each carried 300 lbs of explosives and a single crewman as a pilot.

Made largely of fiberglass and flying a mere 15 feet above the waves, the ekranoplans were difficult for the American search radars to detect. Even worse, the fire control algorithms on the gun and missile systems evaluated the higher speed missiles as greater threats and continued directing the weapons systems to fire on them.

Onboard *Ingraham* and *Ford* the sailors manning port side .50 cal and 25 mm surface mounts began to shift fire from the surface boats to the low flying hybrid aircraft. Southeast of the *Abe*, the sailors on the *Cape St. George* did the same. The cruiser's SM-6 missiles and CIWS engaged the flying boats with some success. One Bavar somehow slipped past her defenses and crashed into her superstructure just below the bridge. The fireball was only the first.

"Explosions to the south," called out the *Lincoln's* port lookout. "They've hit the *Cape St. George.*"

"Damn it," swore Fisher. "Damn it!"

The *Cape St. George* had killed all but three of the 16 ekranoplans approaching her from the Southwest. One of the survivors had scored the hit on the cruiser while the other two continued on toward the carrier. While her bridge was almost completely out of action, *Cape St. George* was able to continue steaming and fighting from her CIC which remained intact.

Of the southeast group of WIGs, fully half of the 16 remained and pressed their attack.

To the north, one C-802 impacted the *Ingraham* along with a Bavar. Metal was ripped apart. Her entire superstructure seemed to be on fire. Meanwhile the *Ford* had been lucky and had only been struck by fragments of missiles destroyed close in by her CIWS systems. Her luck was not to hold, however, as she was struck almost simultaneously by two explosive laden boats. The first struck dead amidships. The second struck her hull aft, demolishing her screws and rudders. *Ford* seemed to leap out of the water before settling back and burning with smoke and flame pouring out of the two gaping holes in her side. Water flooded in and she quickly began to list to starboard as her damage control crews fought to save her.

Back aboard the *Lincoln*, her luck had run out as well. A single C-802 found its mark between the two forward aircraft catapults. Then, like wasps swarming much larger prey, the ekranoplans and attack boats closed in. A Bavar struck her flight deck on the port side while another flew into her number four catapult. A third flew into the island superstructure. On her starboard side, a single surviving surface fast attack boat struck her below her number 2 elevator. Worse, three of the semi-submersible boats had also slipped past the furious American defense and struck the wounded carrier. The powerful warship shuddered along her entire 1,092 foot length as explosions lit up the dark skies. Tongues of water leapt into the sky from the boat impacts at and below her waterline. She was burning from bow to stern.

On the bridge Fisher had been thrown about like a toy and lost consciousness temporarily. As he came to and regained his thoughts, all he could think to himself was how they had been like fish in a barrel. Their foes had laid this multi-layer trap for them and they sailed right into it. He had sailed his men right into it. He was sickened to the pit of his stomach as he struggled to his feet.

The final phase of the attack commenced. Each of the six Ghadir mini-submarines fired a single Hoot torpedo from ranges of between 1.4 to 2 miles. The torpedoes screamed through the water at the burning, stricken ship at almost 200 miles per hour. The ship's SSTDS torpedo defense system successfully neutralized four of the relentless killers. The other two ran straight and true into their target. The great ship shuddered again and more fires burned. Her keel was essentially broken in two locations and she started listing severely to starboard within minutes. Throughout the enormous ship, sailors and Marines were dead or dying. Many of the dead and dying were horribly burned. Dozens caught in the lower decks below the water line were drowned or drowning. Others were trapped in burning compartments and dying of smoke inhalation. Those blown apart from the impacting missiles and explosions or with their flesh literally shredded off their bodies from the jagged pieces of shrapnel suffered considerably less than their shipmates consigned to slow, agonizing deaths.

Above them, on the hangar and flight decks, some of the air wing crew was literally bathed in burning jet fuel and aviation gas. The horrible screams of the wounded were mixed with the deafening explosions. Other sailors, standing or working too close to the edge of the flight deck, were tossed into the air by the massive concussions only to plummet the more than 90 feet to the treacherous waters of the Persian Gulf. Hitting the water from that height was like hitting concrete. Most of those blown overboard hit the water awkwardly and died. A few lucky ones hit feet first and survived with broken legs and broken backs. These then faced their next struggle to survive in trying not to drown while dealing with their shock and injuries.

Within 20 minutes from the initial contact report, the great ship was a burning hulk, dead in the water. Not since World War II had the U.S. Navy lost a battle or a capital ship, let alone both.

WEST OF NATANZ, IRAN,

18 HOURS BEFORE

"Radar! Radar illumination," screamed Lt. Eddie Rozen, without meaning to, into his microphone from the backseat of his F-15SI Silent Eagle (Israeli version) all-weather, long-range strike fighter.

"They're just groping in the dark. They can't find us through our jamming and ECM," replied Major Moshe Alon, his pilot and the leader of the strike cell, in a reassuring tone. A veteran of Operation Orchard in 2007 and Operation Cast Lead in 2008, he was confident in the IAF's (Israel Air Force) ability to penetrate hostile air space, even without this newest fighter in the IAF, which the entire world didn't even suspect Israel had. With the new fighter they would certainly be able to enter the target air space. And officially, Israel did not possess the F-15SI. The modifications to the standard Israeli F-15I Ra'am (Thunder) were based on the "proposed" Boeing F-15 SE (Silent Eagle) which, as far as anyone knew, had not been produced. But even the major had to admit, to himself, that flying into Syrian airspace, or over the Gaza Strip was one thing. Flying against Iran's integrated air defenses, supplied mostly by their Russian allies, was something completely different.

"Bogeys, bogeys, rising to meet us," Rozen said, slightly more controlled this time.

"Their fighter radars have even less chance of finding us, concentrate on your weapons solution." The major was sympathetic, vividly remembering his first time in combat, flying over Syria in 2007 to destroy a secret nuclear reactor then under construction.

"Thank Heaven for the overcast sky," he thought to himself, since it further reduced the chance of detection by one of the biggest actual threats to his flight. The good, old-fashioned Mark I Eyeball.

His Silent Eagle was the lead plane in a 24 ship strike group of 12 F-15 SI's and 12 F-16I Sufa (Storm) fighters. Similar strike groups of various sizes were approaching other key sites of the Iranian nuclear program. The Bushehr nuclear reactor to the South, which was partially manned by Russian nuclear scientists, was targeted. Arak, a heavy water facility which they had bypassed to the south a short while ago was also to be hit, along with a half-dozen other sites, including command and control facilities, and key air defenses.

The Silent Eagles were in the lead, due to their reduced radar signature, and helping to clear the way for the very capable, but decidedly non-stealthy F-16Is. Although in truth, having to carry the massive bunker buster bombs, which was their primary payload on this cloudy night, externally (as opposed to internally) compromised most, if not all of the stealth gains. Nevertheless, the Silent Eagles were the most advanced warplane possessed by the IAF and were about to gauge if they were worth the massive investment made in them by their nation.

The Israelis had modified both the F-16I and F-15I (and later SI variant) with large conformal fuel tanks along the fuselage, which not only dramatically increased their fuel capacity, but actually reduced drag at certain speeds, thus boosting their range over the baseline models flown by so many other nations. The avionics and sensors suites were also substantially upgraded.

"Explosions to the south," reported Rozen dutifully.

"Must be cruise missiles from our submarines impacting the air defense sites." The Navy actually had the honor of firing the first shots, thought the major to himself. Dubious honor, he quickly corrected himself. In reality, the first "shots" had been fired by too-young looking technicians in non-descript office buildings back in Israel, which had launched a vanguard cyber-attack before the first naval cruise missiles were fired from submarines or the first fighters had blasted off the runways.

The Islamic Republic of Iran had already been the unfortunate target of the world's first coordinated multi-phase cyber-attack, which also included the first cyber super-weapon, the Stuxnet virus, beginning in 2010. Rumored to have been developed by either the U.S., Israel, or both together, the Stuxnet malware specifically targeted the Iranian nuclear program software. The cyber weapon would trick industrial process sensors and control systems not to shut down due to normal behavior, and even self-destruct. For instance, centrifuge controllers were given false normal readings even as the speed was increased to the point of self-destruction. At least one-fifth of the centrifuges which Iran needed to produce enriched uranium were destroyed in this manner.

Stuxnet had been preceded by another program called Duqu. This cyber-weapon took a type of reconnaissance by copying blueprints of Iran's nuclear program, thereby allowing Stuxnet to be tailored to its target. After Stuxnet came Flame, another malware reconnaissance tool. This one recorded emails, instant-messaging chats, images of users' computer screens, keystrokes, and network traffic. A compromised device didn't even need to be connected to the internet or a network since Flame would look for internet connected devices through local networks, or by looking for wireless devices such as Bluetooth. It could even remotely turn on microphones. The massive program also had the ability to wipe out hard drives, just as another program called Wiper had done to the Iranian oil ministries in the years and months before the physical attack. Even financial transactions had been targeted by a program named Gauss.

This time around, the cyber-attack tricked Iranian radars into seeing clear skies and then switched to show hundreds of aircraft approaching, thus leading their operators to think they were malfunctioning.

In the next phase of Operation Symphony, as the operation was called, air defense and command and control installations were the first to be physically targeted by heavily modified Popeye Turbo cruise missiles fired from one Dolphin class submarine in the Persian Gulf and two more in the northern Arabian Sea. Actually, the Popeyes and Dolphins were both modified. Four of the subs' torpedo tubes were enlarged to 650 mm from the standard 533 mm, while the SLCMs (submarine launched cruise missiles) themselves were stretched for greater range. The cruise missile attacks along with the cyber-attack effectively blinded the Iranian air defense forces. So although all critical nuclear sites were protected by Russian –made S-200 surface-to-air (SAM) systems and American-made Hawk missiles from the 1970s, their crews were firing without targeting solutions and hoping for the best.

Meanwhile, other Israeli aircraft and cruise missiles were attacking Iranian power lines and generating stations with special munitions that exploded to spread chemically treated carbon fibers on their targets. The fibers short-circuited the switching stations and transformers, causing havoc throughout the power grid, just as the demand was spiking due to the rapidly spreading reaction to the attacks.

The second wave of cyber-attack began at that moment. Cellular phone networks were flooded with false transmissions and began to overload and were then given false commands to shut themselves off. All Iranian ability to "see" or "hear," let alone react to what was happening to their country, was rapidly being severed. For good measure, a third wave was also set in motion by Israeli cyber assassins. The radio networks used by civilian first responders were similarly disrupted and then effectively shut down.

The power grid of the Islamic Republic of Iran crashed.

"Two minutes to release point, major."

"Let's pray our new innovation does the trick," replied the major, mostly under his breath.

"Don't you mean innovations, sir?"

The new innovation was two GBU-28 Paveway III laser guided bombs with BLU-122 warhead, 5,000 lb bunker buster bombs, one under each wing of the Silent Eagle, joined by a length of strong nylon rope approximately 225 meters in length. The "drag" bomb had small aerodynamic drag fins carefully engineered to have 5% additional drag than the normal bomb fins. This allowed the two bombs to fall at the precise separation, which allowed the first bomb to impact and detonate without destroying the drag bomb. This was a new take on the "tandem warhead" which had been used for years on anti-tank missiles. The hope was that the linked bombs would penetrate to the deeply buried and hardened bunkers in which the Islamic Republic of Iran was enriching uranium in thousands of centrifuges which had survived the Israeli cyber assaults.

Smart bomb technology could put multiple projectiles through the exact same point, as the world learned during the 1991 Gulf War watching bombs follow one another through windows or holes blown in walls by other bombs. But Israel was not the United States. Smart bombs, in reality smart bomb kits, which are then bolted on to "dumb" bombs, are expensive and time consuming to produce, especially for such a small country. So, to maximize the impact by the relative few bunker busters available, Israeli weapons designers came up with a simple, yet ingenious and effective solution: tie a conventional "dumb" iron bomb to a leading "smart" bomb. This served the dual purpose of getting two guided weapons for the price of one, and also ensured multiple, perfectly timed hits on target without risking another bombing pass by the same aircraft or a second sortie by another aircraft. And since rubble is easier to "bore through" than intact concrete or mountain rock, the follow-on weapon would be able to penetrate even further into the protected bunkers.

"Bombs away" said Rozen, with just a hint of exhilaration, even as he thought that he would soon be back over Iran, the campaign to destroy the nation's extensive nuclear weapons program being measured in days or weeks, rather than as the single raids that had destroyed Iraq's reactor in 1981 and Syria's in 2007.

In the front seat, the major could not stop himself from thinking about his son, try and try as he might. He knew that one and possibly two groups of paratroopers were already on the ground in Iran, attacking Fordo and perhaps one other installation. Even a major in the IAF was not told all of the details of such a secret and critical operation. It was strictly need to know, and he did not need to know. Nevertheless, it was crushing him. His oldest son was a paratrooper and was almost certainly part of the operation. He also knew that even at that instant, a volley of Jericho II and Jericho III missiles were being fired as the second wave (third wave, depending on one's point of view of the cyber-attacks). Next would come the huge Eitan ("Steadfast") Unmanned Aerial Vehicles (UAVs), each carrying multiple air-to-surface missiles, bombs, or electronic counter-measures (ECM) pods. These 737- sized UAVs, called Heron TPs in the West, would use their extremely long loiter time to continue attacking pre-selected targets and targets of opportunity, should they arise.

Alon and Rozen both expected to be back over hostile Iranian skies the following night, even before the Herons had departed.

"May G_d be with us all," whispered Major Alon to himself as he watched yet more eruptions light up the night sky, and knowing that the entire Middle East would now similarly erupt.

2

THE OVAL OFFICE, THE WHITE HOUSE

"Damn them," the President almost screamed. "They really did it? Just went and did it without our permission? Damn them!"

"Mr. President, they are a sovereign nation and we all *did know* that this was coming, sooner or later. Well, at least *most* of us knew," replied the President's National Security Advisor. Jack Darden squared his broad shoulders and looked his President and old friend directly in the eye.

Darden had played football at Northwestern University. As a pulling guard he specialized in opening holes for the guys carrying the ball. He still saw himself as having the same role for the Chief Executive of the land. Intensely loyal, almost to a fault, he had met the President when both were young professionals fresh out of college. He didn't always agree with his old friend, however. He typically took a more realistic view of the world and the Middle East. The President and others in the inner circle often called it a more pessimistic view.

For his part, as a Democrat from one of the most liberal states, the President had often been portrayed as not a friend of Israel. At least, the "right" wing media had tried hard to paint him that way, in his opinion. In reality, he merely wished to take what he considered a more pragmatic approach to nations such as Iran, Syria and North Korea. Labeling nations as members of an "axis of evil," for example, did not advance the diplomatic dialogue, in his opinion. Nor did Israel subjecting over a million Palestinians to a sort of apartheid and continuous aggression. No, peace would not be made by the blind, unconditional support of Israel which the U.S. had for so long practiced. A more balanced approach was needed to move Middle East peace forward, especially in the face of the ongoing conflagration in Syria and continued chaos in Egypt.

The President grunted and abruptly said, "Let's start the security briefing" with a distinct edge in his voice.

"Mr. President, ladies and gentlemen," began the National Security Advisor. "Here are the latest developments in the Persian Gulf. Early this morning approximately 110 Israeli aircraft struck at least 7 Iranian nuclear sites. The aircraft were preceded by massive and coordinated cyber attacks directed at Iranian early warning radar and air defense systems, energy infrastructure systems and the communication network. This was followed by cruise missile attacks launched by Israeli submarines in the Persian Gulf and Gulf of Oman. We believe that 2 or 3 submarines participated in the attacks. It is important to note that virtually no Iranian anti-aircraft activity was detected until just before the first air launched weapons began to impact their targets and this, in turn, was almost perfectly coordinated with the impact of the cruise missiles. In other words, the Israelis managed to get significant numbers of non-stealthy aircraft deep into Iran without detection."

"Didn't *we* detect them?" interrupted the President. "Isn't this why we have military assets all over the world and in space?" he demanded.

"Mr. President, we did detect over 150 of their aircraft lifting off from Israel and you were notified. The Israeli force included tankers, fighter escorts, UAV's, and other support aircraft. What were we supposed to do at that point? Threaten to alert our dear Iranian *friends* unless the Israelis agreed to turn back? It's probable that the Saudis may have also detected them and the Russians almost certainly did, but the Saudis probably gave them free passage over their air space and it appears the Russians were not able to communicate with their Iranian friends in any meaningful manner. This may be due to the cyber attack."

The President did not at all appear pleased by the explanation.

"In addition, as we all know, our signals and human intelligence have both taken severe reductions in capabilities due to budget constraints over the last few years, especially once the automatic spending restraints of sequestration fully took effect," interjected the Chairman of the Joint Chiefs of Staff, Air Force General Rick "R&R" Richardson.

"So, this is all because we didn't fully fund the Pentagon's wish list? Because we didn't buy every toy, bell, and whistle our uniformed friends asked for?" the President asked, his voice laced with sarcasm. Although he had hidden it remarkably well since assuming the office of Commander-in-Chief, the President's long-standing disdain for all things military was well known.

A palpable silence followed as all eyes fixed on the President. He furrowed his brow and asked for the briefing to continue.

"In short, the Israelis used more aircraft and penetrated further into Iranian airspace than even we had thought possible" reported Darden matter-of-factly.

"How did they get so many aircraft so far?" interrupted the President. "All of my intelligence experts said they didn't have the ability to do so."

"A couple of our estimates did include the possible use of buddy stores, in addition to all of their regular tanking assets. They probably also used some of their very large UAVs as tankers. We know they have been developing these capabilities."

"Buddy stores?" asked the Vice President quizzically.

"Large auxiliary fuel tanks with refueling hoses fitted to regular tactical aircraft," answered the CNO, Admiral Jankowski. "Allows fighters or attack aircraft to refuel other similar types of aircraft. Navy and Marine aircraft have used them for years. And frankly sir, isn't it a good thing that the Israelis were able to strike with such a large and effective force?"

The Admiral's response from the President and the Secretary of State were icy glares.

The NSA cleared his throat and then went on, "We believe the cruise missiles have primarily attacked command and control systems, air bases, and the Iranian power grid, which appears to be down in large sections around all nuclear sites, the capital of Tehran, and other key defense installations including air and naval bases. Not surprisingly, Republican Guard air defense and missile units appear to be particularly hard hit."

"Jesus," breathed General Richardson.

"There's more," continued Darden as he subconsciously ran his hand through his salt and pepper hair. "Just moments before beginning this briefing, I was informed that our strategic reconnaissance satellites detected no fewer than thirty ballistic missile heat plumes lifting off from southern Israel. These are almost certainly Jericho II missiles with a range of at least 1,400 kilometers and may also include Jericho IIIs with a range of at least 5,000 km, if you recall."

"My God," exclaimed the White House Chief of Staff, Joel Miller, himself Jewish by ancestry and faith. "Are they nukes?"

"We can't be certain but we don't believe so. Most estimates are that Israel would hold its nukes in reserve and only use conventionally armed ballistic missiles in the opening salvos, until and unless Israel itself were attacked with WMDs. In any case, the missiles should be impacting right about now, so we'll have confirmation," answered the DNI, the Director of National Intelligence.

"Why would they lead with aircraft if they planned to use ballistic missiles all along?" asked the Secretary of State.

"Surprise," answered General Richardson. "The Russians watch for the heat signatures of ballistic missile launches just as we do. Pretty hard to hide those and risk Ivan warning Tehran. In addition, large numbers of sudden ballistic missile launches would have also put the Russians, Chinese, Indians, and Pakistanis on alert. So, the aerial strike hit just minutes after the naval cruise missiles hit, and those in turn struck just after the cyber-attacks brought down the Iranian electrical and air defense grids. In any case, now that the Iranians are effectively blind, deaf, and dumb, they can't be warned."

"Correct, general," the NSA complimented Richardson. "In addition, the Israelis may be doing this as 'a time on target coordination' to take out scientists and technicians along with first responders rushing to the sites."

"General, please refrain from using that outdated, derogatory cold-war term for the Russians, however cute you think you are being," stabbed the Secretary of State. Richardson and the Secretary exchanged additional visual daggers.

Darden paused and drew a deep breath. "Lastly, ladies and gentleman, we also believe there are Israeli special operations teams on the ground in at least two locations."

"Are you *serious?*" interjected the President.

"Yes, Mr. President, I'm afraid I am. We've known of Israeli covert operatives as well as Special Forces teams operating inside of Syria and Iran for some time now. All those Iranian nuke scientists having accidental deaths the last few years haven't been a coincidence. Neither are Iranian armament shipments blowing up in Syria."

Knowing glances and nodding heads confirmed what everyone in the room already knew. Several Iranian nuclear scientists had met untimely deaths in the years and months during which the United Nations and the international community had attempted in vain to convince the Islamic Republic of Iran to abandon its nuclear weapons program. Bombs attached to cars by motorcycle riders in broad daylight was one of the more common causes of premature death for Iran's best nuclear minds.

"Is there *any* good news?"

"Well, we have not yet detected an Iranian response, at least none other than localized efforts to defend themselves within Iran itself."

"But we *know* there will be one," said the President. "So I'm not sure that really is good news." All the heads in the rooms nodded slowly and gravely in agreement.

The Persian Gulf

On board the supertanker MT *TI Europe*, the morning watch crew was looking forward to the end of their four hour watch which had started at 4:00 AM local time.

Known as an Ultra Large Crude Carrier, ULCC, the *Europe* was among the largest ships in the world. She carried 3.1 *million* barrels of crude oil just on-loaded at Saudi Arabia's enormous Ras Tanura refinery and terminal complex.

Even fully loaded and displacing over 500,000 tons, she was making a good (for her) 16 knots on the calm seas.

On the ship's bridge, the Third Mate scanned the blue, cloudless sky and drew in a deep breath. "Oh how I love smell of the sea," he thought to himself. A tall Norwegian with thick blond hair, he had grown up on the coast and had learned to sail in and out of the fjords from his grandfather practically from the time he could sit on his knee. He had sailed around the world several times during his merchant marine career and despite his good mood he did have to admit to himself that the Persian Gulf was his second least favorite place to sail, after the Straits of Malacca.

His pleasant reverie was shattered by the low rumble of a jet engine, distant at first, then louder and louder. The rumble became a scream which was immediately followed by a shattering blast. He was thrown back against the bulkhead and then he tumbled to the floor. Despite his disorientation, he fought to his feet and looked over his ship. Even as he looked at the fireball before his very eyes, he could not believe it. The ferocious concussion shook the massive ship along her entire 1,240 foot length. Fire alarm klaxons screamed and strained as smoke began to pour from the gaping wound amidships. He heard the screams of his crew as they raced to help their injured ship and shipmates. At sea, the culture is and always has been, "ship, shipmate, self."

"All engines stop!" he heard himself scream. "Please Lord, help us," he thought to himself urgently. He had not prayed to God since he was 14, but this seemed a good time to attempt a reconnection.

Despite the double hull safety design of the ship, oil gushed into the dark waters of the Persian Gulf as the *Europe* began slowing to a stop. A scant few minutes later and 200 miles to the East, another supertanker, this one having just entered the Persian Gulf, was also hit by an Iranian shore fired Silkworm anti-ship missile. By the time a fourth tanker was hit, this one still in the Gulf of Oman, 2 miles from the entrance to the Strait of Hormuz by a mine laid by an Iranian submarine, all non-military sea traffic within the Gulf and for fifty miles out had stopped. The flow of economically vital oil from the Gulf, upon which the entire world depended, had also stopped.

The missile and mine attacks in the Persian Gulf were only the first phase in the retaliation plan of the Islamic Republic of Iran.

Ras Tanura, Saudi Arabia

The senior shift officer yawned as he surveyed the massive wall covered with status boards. Mohamet Ibrahim had worked for Saudi Aramco, the state-owned oil company, for 18 years but was still awed by the gigantic size of his company's oil refining and export terminal complex. Among the largest in the world, the export terminals consisted of two piers and a chain of artificial, man-made sea islands with eighteen total ship berths. Each of the berths was able to accommodate the largest tankers in the world, up to 550,000 fully loaded deadweight tons. A nearby tank farm had a storage capacity of over 33 million barrels of oil and oil products.

Although Ibrahim's native kingdom had the largest oil export infrastructure in the world, he knew that the massive sizes driven by the quest for economy of scale efficiencies were also their Achilles heel. Few people outside of the kingdom or the oil industry knew that more than half of Saudi Arabia's vaunted oil reserves were in only eight fields, with the lion's share of *that* being in the two largest fields. Similarly, the single Abqaiq processing complex refined fully two-thirds of the kingdom's output. And, 75% of the total oil exports for the kingdom were loaded at Ras Tanura.

But the Iranians, centuries old antagonists of the Saudi royal family due to Shia – Sunni religious conflict, did know about the vulnerability of their Gulf rivals, as did their terrorist proxies inside the Kingdom. It was a little known fact in the Western world that although the ruling family was pro-Western and pro-U.S., the majority of the population of the Saudi kingdom was decidedly not. Many pro-Iranian terrorist cells existed inside the kingdom and were activated as soon as the first Israeli bombs and missiles exploded in Iran.

"Intruders," screamed the security officer standing a few feet away from Mohamet.

"Where? How far out?" he demanded.

"Inside the 2nd perimeter for certain," replied the diminutive security officer. "We are engaging."

"How many? What …" Mohamet never finished his sentence as his ears caught the sound of a sort of whistling.

"What is that," he thought to himself as the first mortar bomb exploded just feet away from the main control center. The concussion lifted him off his feet and slammed him against the bank of control panels. He shook his head, trying to clear his thoughts with his vision still blurry with the dust as more explosions shook the world around him. Now deafened, he could only feel, but not hear the blasts. "What in the world is happening?" he struggled as he saw the gaping mouths of his screaming friends, but could hear nothing. Blood was running from his burst left eardrum as well as from the back of his head where he impacted the control panels.

Two suicide terror squads had penetrated the first two of the three perimeter defense layers at the installation and set-up lightweight mortars before being detected and engaged by the facility's security police. The 82 mm 2B14 Podnos light mortars had been acquired from Russia and then given to the terrorists by their Iranian sponsors. Although able to be broken down and carried in four "man packs" these had been brought in on Aramco vehicles commandeered with the help of sympathetic employees.

As serious as this attack was, it was merely a feint to draw the eyes of the security forces inward, just as they should have been looking out. Out was where the three other terror cells were beginning to fire additional mortars even as they awaited the appearance of their airborne and seaborne comrades. The airborne allies soon arrived in the form of four ultra-light aircraft, loaded down with gasoline fueled IEDs. The two seat aircraft carried a lone pilot and 120 pounds of fuel and explosives. Each ultra-light angled for the largest storage tank visible and dove with screams of "Allau Akbar!"

The seaborne attackers came in on fast speedboats also loaded with explosives and bore in on the helpless tankers tied up at their berths. Explosion after explosion rocked the area and lit up the night sky.

The resulting fires were so large and intense that they were detected by the infrared systems of U.S. early warning reconnaissance satellites orbiting in geo-synchronous orbit, 22,000 miles above the earth's equator. Flash messages were sent from Buckley Air Force Base in Colorado (where the satellites were monitored) to NORAD headquarters in Omaha, Nebraska as well as to Washington, D.C.

The Middle East was now fully aflame, literally and politically, and the entire world would likely be engulfed along with it.

3

THE STRAIT OF HORMUZ

Aboard the *Nimitz* class aircraft carrier USS *Abraham Lincoln* (CVN-72), air operations had been at a frantic pace for the last four hours since word of the Israeli strike on Iran had first come into the communications center, known simply as "Radio." The "*Abe*" was the centerpiece of Carrier Strike Group Nine, which in turn was operating as part of the U.S. Fifth Fleet based in Bahrain in the Persian Gulf. Her escorting ships were arrayed around her, particularly to the North. Originally, the secretary of defense wanted to send the newly commissioned *USS Zumwalt* (DDG-1000) stealth destroyer through the straight, but the President said, "we need a bigger saber to rattle this time" – so, he sent in the *Abe*, against almost everyone else's recommendation.

Captain Jim Fisher was concerned as he looked out over the 4.5 acre flight deck from his perch on the bridge. He didn't like the idea of taking his precious ship with its priceless crew into such restricted waters. He knew that American aircraft carriers had been sailing in the Persian Gulf since World War II, but he still didn't like it. Here he couldn't maneuver freely. And here, he gave up one of the carrier's greatest strengths, the ability to keep potential enemies hundreds of miles away, while still being able to strike at them at the time and place of his choosing, should the need arise. Steaming in the "inbound" channel of the 21 mile wide strait, they were only eleven miles from Iran's hostile coast and the anti-ship missiles on that coast. Eleven miles is virtually instantaneous in flying time, especially when it comes to fast accelerating missiles. And Fisher truly didn't like the fact that his crew would have such a short time to react to any missile attack. In years past the Strike Group would have included three or four additional escort vessels. Ships which could be used as pickets to better defend his precious "bird farm." But, the last few years of budget cuts, sequestration, etc., had inexorably reduced the number of active duty navy ships leaving his beloved service stretched dangerously thin around the world. America's enemies, as always, had noticed and had become bolder by the day.

"All of the precautions have been covered," he thought to himself as he went through his mental list yet again. The ship's E-2D Advanced Hawkeye airborne early warning (AEW) aircraft was orbiting with its Lockheed Martin APY-9 radar that was able to "see" smaller targets and more of them at greater ranges than the older E-2C model it replaced. The rotodome contained the critically important, continuous, 360-degree scanning capability, along with the latest Active Electronically Scanned Array (AESA), which allowed operators to focus the radar on selected areas of interest.

Nevertheless, the athletic Floridian felt uneasy, and not just because he hadn't slept for the previous 18 hours. He just could not stop thinking about which and how many Russian, Chinese, or North Korean made anti-ship missiles the Iranians might truly have and what they might do with them.

"Bridge, Combat," he heard his CIC watch officer call.

"Combat, bridge. Go ahead," he replied.

"Captain, our surface search radar is picking up some activity on the coast, by Bandar Abbas, but nothing from the picket."

"Roger, I'm on my way," replied Fisher. As he opened the door of the Combat Information Center (CIC), the nerve center of the great vessel, he heard the call he had so dreaded and prayed fervently would never come.

"Vampire, vampire, bearing 021 true," came the shout from the primary air search radar operator just as the Hawkeye also radioed in the new contacts.

"All ahead full," commanded Fisher. "Unmask the starboard RAM and sea-whiz. Update number and speed."

"Forty-eight contacts sir, splitting into two groups. First group of 33, velocity is Mach 0.8. Profile suggests Noor missiles. Designate Raid 1. Second group of 15, speed is passing Mach 1.6. Profile suggests Sunburns. Designate Rai…"

"What?" screamed the captain incredulously? "Here? That fast? That *many?*"

"Sunburns," gasped the Tactical Action Officer (TAO) as he stared at his radar screen.

The SS-N-22 missile, NATO codename "Sunburn" was a nightmare for any sailor. Designed by the Russians specifically to destroy American aircraft carrier battle groups, they were rumored to have been supplied to the Iranians, but the rumors had never been confirmed. Until now.

The Sunburns' four powerful ramjet engines quickly accelerated them to their maximum Mach 2.5 speed for a blistering sea-skimming attack profile. In addition to their 750 pound warhead, their 9,000 pound mass traveling at such tremendous speed imparted enormous kinetic energy on any target struck. Designed specifically to defeat the U.S. Navy's vaunted Aegis radar system as well as the Close-In Weapons system (CIWS, commonly called sea-whiz), the SS-N-22s could fly as low as fifteen feet above the wave tops and perform violent, terminal pop-up maneuvers to avoid enemy missiles and gun systems just before striking their targets.

"Now it's all up to our Standards, RAM and sea-whiz," breathed the Captain.

"Let's hope God in Heaven also has something to say about the matter," said the TAO.

"Yes, yes indeed," agreed Fisher.

Unlike the CIWS, the RIM-116 RAM, or Rolling Airframe Missile system had been designed to defeat missiles such as the high speed Sunburns. But, they had never been tested in combat. The Block 1 version of the fire and forget missile system had infra red (IR) all-the-way guidance to its target and was an upgrade in capability over the CIWS gun system.

Steaming one mile to the north of the *Abe* to serve as a forward picket was one of her escorts, the guided missile destroyer *USS Sterett* (DDG-104). The sleek gray warship shuddered once, and then again as she began engaging the missiles screaming southward with her SM-2 Standard Medium Range missiles.

"Range twelve miles," called out the Lincoln's Tactical Action Officer as he stared intently at the radar screen," the palpable tension dripping from his voice.

"Nice coincidence," grunted Fisher.

As both groups of speeding "vampires" neared the RAM's eleven mile maximum range, the tongue of flame from the first of the 21 missiles in the launcher illuminated the night sky as it blasted free. With the Sunburns approaching at 1,100 feet per second, the American defenses had less than a minute to successfully engage all twelve remaining supersonic missiles even as their fire control computers and software attempted to sort out the subsonic Noors that were classified as lesser threats.

Aboard *Sterett*, the incoming Iranian missiles had closed the range and her own CIWS systems began to engage the flight. Four fell to her guns. But the numbers seemed too great and the time seemed too short. A first missile, a Noor, struck the ship forward of the superstructure where the SM-2's were exiting their Vertical Launch System tubes. The Iranian missile's warhead failed to explode fully, but an SM-2 just clearing the deck did. Further aft, a second Noor struck the side of the destroyer at its helicopter hangar.

"Explosions, explosions to the north" yelled the starboard lookout on the Abraham Lincoln. Despite the news, no one seemed to listen to him, much less acknowledge his report. Eventually, the Officer of the Deck did respond.

In CIC, all eyes stared anxiously at the screens as the arrow symbols representing missiles closed each other and then began to merge. The hostile dots were disappearing, but not disappearing quickly enough.

"Come on. Come on," said Fisher under his breath. "Please God, if you are real, if you are out there, we need you…only two more." He felt the pit of his stomach continue to tighten and thought of his wife, six year old son, and little girl, just entering the "terrible twos." "Please God…"

But on this day, it was not to be. A Sunburn slammed into the carrier's flight deck amidships, just forward of the island superstructure and next to elevator number two. The missile's hardened nose-tip burrowed through the flight deck, the hangar deck, and the third deck below before it's time delay warhead detonated. The mighty behemoth shuddered with the impact and force of the explosion. The fireball erupted skyward as sailors from her own crew and her escorts looked on in stunned disbelief. Further aft, a second Sunburn slipped through the defenses but mercifully struck only a glancing blow to the aft end of the flight deck, just behind elevator number three.

The expansive flight deck, covered as always with aircraft, fuel, sailors and ordnance, quickly became an inferno of explosions, shearing shrapnel, smoke and fire. An F/A-18E Super Hornet about to launch on catapult number three was shredded by shrapnel. Two 500 pound bombs hung on pylons under her wings detonated and added their roar of destruction to the firestorm. Hundreds of sailors and Marines died instantaneously. Hundreds more were grievously wounded and burned. Dozens of her 85 aircraft were destroyed. The rest of the 5,680 men and women aboard the vaunted aircraft carrier would now have to fight for their ship and fight for their lives. And, the attacks they suffered had just begun.

The Pentagon, E-Ring, Washington, D.C.

Lt. John Williams had only been assigned to the Pentagon for a month. And until a few days ago, he had loved his posting, particularly working in the outer "E-Ring," where all the big wigs had their offices with the outside views. Now, however, he dreaded his task of giving admirals with lots of gold on their sleeves and shoulders bad news. He took a breath, knocked on the door, and entered the office of his boss, Chief of Naval Operations (CNO), Admiral Mike Jankowski.

"Admiral, we have just received a Flash message from Fifth Fleet in Bahrain. The *Lincoln's* been hit."

"What? When? Did she hit a mine? A suicide boat? How bad is it?" The grizzled Navy veteran was struggling with his thoughts outpacing his words.

The U.S. Navy's eleven active supercarriers were unspeakably valuable and expensive. At the pinnacle of its World War II power, the U.S. Navy fielded 28 large aircraft carriers and 71 smaller ones. By the time of the Vietnam War, only 23 total carriers remained. The end of the cold war and continuing budget cuts reduced the force to 15 and then 12, and finally, the 11 that remained. Those eleven however, represented an almost unimaginable investment in national treasure and prestige, both in technology and the highly trained personnel.

"We don't know the details yet, sir, but it appears her battle group was hit with a mass missile attack from the Iranian coast just as they passed the strait's narrowest point. They report the attack was comprised of almost fifty Noor and Sunburn missiles. *Abe* suffered one major and one relatively minor hit from the Sunburns. The *Sterett* was also hit. She was hit by two Noors. Hundreds are dead or unaccounted for, and hundreds more are wounded. Both ships are fighting the fires. We don't have firm numbers on the casualties yet, but whatever they are now, they will go higher."

"My God," exclaimed Jankowski, making Williams wince. As a devout Mormon, Williams did not like the Lord's name to be taken in vain.

Jankowski saw Williams wince and immediately apologized. "Sorry, John. Just slipped out. But how could this have happened?"

"I understand sir. This is a huge shock. And admirals have no need to apologize to O-3s. In any case, we'll have to wait for the post action analysis, but obviously the distance and short reaction times played a part. In addition, the Iranians either got lucky or timed their attack exquisitely."

"Thanks. And how so?" asked Jankowski.

"The subsonic Noors arrived first and while they were being engaged by our systems, the supersonic Sunburns arrived and some got through."

"I see. Well, we'll go back and look at that some more later. So, what's her status?" asked the Admiral.

"Some of the fires are still burning but both reactors are intact and she is underway, making 9 knots. They think they can get to 12 knots if not more, very soon. At least 50% of her air wing was taken out, but it doesn't really matter since she can't carry out flight ops. The primary hit was almost dead center of her flight deck and the fires there and on the decks below are spewing heavy smoke. *Sterett* is dead in the water and also burning, but she may be able to get underway soon. Our damage control is the best, as you know. *Ingraham* and *Ford* are with *Sterett* and will take her under tow if she can't get underway. The other escorts are all with the *Abe*. We're flying CAP out of Bahrain and also have the escorts' Seahawks in the air providing a perimeter."

CAP, Combat Air Patrol, ensured that there was always a flight of protective fighters over the fleet at all times. However, this was of little help against a swarm of low flying cruise missiles, as the successful attack had just shown.

"Any further attacks from the damned mullahs?" questioned Jankowski.

"Not yet, but they're sure to try and finish them off if we give them the chance. We need to hit back and hard," Williams stressed. "We need to neutralize all shore and naval installations where further attacks against us can be launched."

"When is our next satellite pass?" asked the CNO.

"About 30 minutes, sir. We'll know more then," replied Williams with an optimistic tone.

"We need to brief the President and the Joint Chiefs, ASAP," thought Jankowski. And it was his turn to wince.

4

NEW YORK, NY, FOX NEWS
HEADQUARTERS

The camera centered in on the pretty blond news anchor as she arranged papers on the desk next to her open laptop. A street-view scene of New York City loomed through the panoramic window behind her. It certainly seemed that this particular network hired only pretty blondes as their female anchors, but it was one of the points the network's detractors loved to make.

The anchor, Sharon Smith, dressed in an attractive but professional blue dress to accent her blue eyes and snug against her shapely figure, began her report.

"Good Monday morning. I'm Sharon Smith reporting from New York. Here is the latest on the growing crisis in the Persian Gulf. Iranian shore based missiles believed to have come from mobile launchers have hit the aircraft carrier *USS Abraham Lincoln* and the destroyer *USS Sterrett* in the Strait of Hormuz. Hundreds of sailors on both vessels are dead or wounded and both ships are fighting large fires. Four oil tankers in the Persian Gulf and the Strait have also been hit by Iranian missiles and two more tankers have struck naval mines. A swarm of small boats manned by Iranian Revolutionary Guards attacked another tanker in the Gulf as well as two U.S. Navy destroyers and a frigate. One of the destroyers was hit by a homicide small boat laden with explosives and several sailors are reported dead or missing on that vessel. U.S. Navy and Air Force aircraft destroyed several small boats but have not retaliated against Iranian shore installations, to our

25

knowledge. All oil tanker traffic in and out of the Persian Gulf, almost 30% of the world's daily oil supply, has come to a standstill. Oil futures have almost doubled to $211 per barrel and Dow futures are in a free fall.

After the Israeli attack on Iran to stop that country's rapidly accelerating nuclear program, the Iranians have also responded with Shahab-2 and -3 short and medium range ballistic missile (SRBM and MRBM) attacks on Israel itself and on U.S. military installations in the region, including Iraq, Kuwait, Afghanistan, and Bahrain as many analysts expected. The next volley of Shahabs impacted the already burning Ras Tanura oil refinery and terminal complex in Saudi Arabia, as well as the major oil complexes of the other Gulf oil states. Over 1,000 rockets have been fired from Hezbollah controlled areas of Southern Lebanon into Northern Israel. Many missiles and rockets are reported to have been intercepted by Israeli anti-missile systems, but several also impacted Tel Aviv, Haifa, Rishon Le Zion, Beersheba, and smaller towns in the North. At least eighty civilians have been killed and over 200 wounded, Israel reports. The nuclear facility at Dimona was also hit by two missiles, which penetrated its defenses, but damage was light. In Jerusalem, a homicide bomber detonated a bomb belt inside the busiest shopping center and another bomber, this one reported to be a young woman, detonated her bomb in a crowded bus stop. At least 13 people have been killed in these two attacks and scores more wounded. Israeli security forces are on a full war footing and have foiled three other attempted bombings. Israel has called up 50,000 reservists and columns of troops and tanks have been seen moving toward the southern border with Gaza and the northern borders with Syria and Lebanon.

Israel is responding with massive artillery barrages and air strikes on Hezbollah positions in Southern Lebanon. No rockets or missiles have been fired from Hamas in the Gaza Strip or from the Palestinian controlled west bank as of yet. Israel has also attacked positions inside Syria, even though no attacks have come from that civil war wracked nation.

Unfortunately, the terrorist attacks have not been limited to over-seas locations. The violence has already come here, to the United States on our own soil. We now go to Jason Gilbert in our Washington bureau."

"Thank you Sharon. A little over 30 minutes ago multiple embassies and consulates here at home were attacked by suicide squads, some containing several terrorists. The Israeli embassy in Washington, D.C. has been attacked as have the Israeli consulates in New York, Chicago, Los Angeles, and Houston. Here in Washington, a massive truck bomb drove into the vehicle barriers and was detonated. Although the truck did not reach the embassy itself, the force of the enormous explosion did damage the main building. Within minutes, a van loaded with as many as six terrorists arrived and the terrorists fired at least two rocket propelled grenades (RPGs) into the crowd of first responders and victims. The other terrorists attacked by spraying fully automatic weapons fire and tossing hand grenades among the carnage. As you can see from the images, it is simply an incredible scene in our nation's capital. At least eight have died, including three capital police first responders and several more are wounded. Five terrorists were eventually killed by security forces from the embassy and police. One terrorist was wounded and is now in custody."

"Thank you for that report, Jason." The national anchor continued her report. "The attack here in New York was fortunately foiled with no loss of American life, although two NYPD officers and one FBI agent from the New York field office were injured. It is believed from the presence of the FBI agents that the agency, and perhaps other law enforcement agencies, had discovered this particular sleeper cell and were able to stop the truck bomb and van with the terrorists before they arrived at their destination.

Other terrorist cells were able to detonate car bombs at the consulates in Chicago, Los Angeles, and Houston. These terrorists attacked in the immediate aftermath with automatic weapons and rockets. Reports are still coming in, but it appears that those attacks have caused multiple deaths. And more reports are just coming in.

Israeli airborne forces have carried out a massive parachute drop into Southern Lebanon, along the Southern and Eastern banks of the Litani River. A large armored force is also advancing northwest into Lebanon from the Golan Heights in an apparent attempt to cut off Hezbollah forces from retreating to the North or to Syria. Heavy fighting is reported all along the line of the Israeli drop as well as on the border between Lebanon and Israel, as Israeli forces push north. This operation is reminiscent of the month-long war fought in 2006, but appears to be developing much more rapidly.

Also back here in the homeland, panic buying of gasoline and at grocery stores has already started, with massive lines forming even in cities not directly affected by the terrorist attacks."

5

SCOTTSDALE, ARIZONA,

THE GOVERNOR'S RESIDENCE

Sara Kay Doucet entered her private home office briskly but with her trademark friendly smile on her face, even with no one around. Her eyes, however, betrayed a hint of concern and her collapse on her overstuffed leather executive chair revealed her fatigue.

Arizona's governor arrived home well after 9:00 PM as was typical for her. She allowed herself to sit idly for a few minutes and stare off into space, rehashing the amazing events of the last few days. Then her mind suddenly flashed to her computer. Or rather, her mind flashed to what might be on her computer. With a sudden burst of vigor, she reached over and powered up her personal laptop sitting on her desk, next to her official tablet. She went quickly to open her private Facebook page, not the official Governor's Office page. She didn't want to seem too anxious, but she felt like a high school girl with anticipation all over again. The cursed computer wouldn't open the window fast enough! And then, there it was a new message from him! He was Jake Novack, her college sweetheart and hottest old flame. In fact, she didn't know if she believed in the term "soul mate," she knew she hated the overuse of the term, but if there were such a thing, Jake would be it for her.

They met during her sophomore year at Arizona State University while Jake was a junior. He was tall and with a swimmer's physique, dirty blond hair and dreamy blue eyes. They were both political science majors and had an electric attraction from the start. Their instant friendship rapidly became a torrid love affair full of fun, passion, and adventures of both a sexual and non-sexual nature. Sara was truly and totally in love with Jake, and Jake with her. Those two years were the happiest of her adult life. Unfortunately, Jake was from Ohio and felt obliged to return to join his father's successful political consulting business. For her part, Sara felt she could not leave her family in Arizona, so they reluctantly and painfully parted ways when Jake graduated.

Neither one was the type to think they could have a long-term, long-distance romance but they promised to remain friends; one never knew where life's journey would lead, after all.

For the first few years, they did keep in close contact and even managed to travel and see each other twice. The first such meeting was a wonderful week long cruise in the Caribbean. The second was an amazing ski trip to Colorado just before Christmas. But, with the inexorable march of time, each got busier and busier with their lives and careers and the contact became less and less frequent. Once Jake married, the contact became non-existent.

Sara had not realized how ardently she still loved Jake until he told her of his engagement. She cried herself to sleep that night and finally admitted to herself that she had been clinging to the hope that some way, somehow, they would still find a way to be together.

Eventually, in the due course of time, her wounded heart mostly healed and she went on with her successful and interesting life. Then she had met Tom and they hit it off, even though he intensely disliked politics and wanted to know nothing of it while Sara was a self-avowed political junkie. Their relationship grew and prospered along with Tom's real estate development business. Sara began her career as a high school teacher but after four years in the classroom she had become completely disenchanted. Between bureaucratic waste, centralized control, the powerful teacher's union and uninvolved or downright harmful parents, far more children were being harmed in the public schools than were being helped. Incompetent or even criminal teachers were not only protected by the union but even rewarded. In the face of falling test scores and a crisis in college preparedness, more and more states and districts adopted Common Core standards which in reality sought to lower standards. Four plus four would never, ever, equal nine regardless how many nice pictures were drawn or what kind of a "logic" reasoning story was offered! So, she decided to leave the classroom, as much as she loved working with "her" kids every single day run for the school board.

Her first foray into politics went down in a close defeat to a large, local political machine. Undaunted, she tried again and this time defeated her opponent; the same she had previously lost to. Sara went back to school and obtained a master's degree in Educational Administration while serving on the school board. After completing her graduate degree, she returned to the classroom, teaching at Pima Community College. She enjoyed the contact and discourse with the students immensely, but day by day felt that her true calling was higher political office. Tom, being a good and honorable man, was completely supportive all along her journey, despite his distinct and growing distaste for politics. Her marriage was good in every other aspect, but her political ambition (she considered it the Lord's calling as did her family and church family) was a constant underpinning of tension.

When Sara was elected to the state legislature, Tom was happy for her, but informed her that he could not leave Tucson, where they were both from and currently living, to follow her to the state capital in Phoenix. His successful business simply would not allow for him to reside in another city. But, trying to focus on the bright side, the proximity of the two cities would make it easy to see each other on weekends. And, it would be the perfect time to expand the business more aggressively into Phoenix, beyond the three small projects that he had already undertaken there. Sara understood and reluctantly agreed to live apart.

It was during these first few years living alone that Sara first began to feel lonely. She threw herself into her public service with abandon. She told herself that it was because God had confirmed her calling by blessing her with her seat in the legislature. And, while this was certainly true, she was gnawed, deep down, by the knowledge that there was another reason. She hated coming home to an empty house. She also hated her greatly diminished social life. She and Tom had always thoroughly enjoyed dining out, dancing (country and swing in particular), live theater, comedy shows, entertaining friends, and various other social activities. And while they still did such things on weekends (they alternated one weekend in Phoenix and one in Tucson) it was not the same, particularly during the long, lonely weeknights. During her first year apart from Tom, she had even twice become teary-eyed in front of her staff. After the second such near-breakdown, she chastised herself and grimly vowed to accept the consequences of her decision. From that point on, the loneliness subsided in its intensity, if not in its frequency. Her private life apart from Tom settled into a bearable routine and she was grateful that she found her time in the legislature fulfilling and even exhilarating.

And then Sara was practically drafted by the state GOP to run for Governor. She resolved to go to her husband for a very serious discussion about their future and she felt a lump in her throat as she realized it might determine whether it would be a shared future or not. To her surprise and immense relief, Tom had carefully considered this possibility far in advance of her and easily took the lead in the discussion. He would stand beside her and fully support a run for the governor's office. He would even move to Phoenix for the duration of her term, on one condition. She had to promise in no uncertain terms that she would not ever seek an office which would require her to leave the state, especially not to Washington, D.C. That he could not ever support and it would be the end of their marriage. Upon hearing this from her husband, Sara leapt upon him and enveloped her "big teddy butt bear" with her famous embrace and literally swamped him with kisses. The nickname was an inside joke which always drew puzzled looks from their children, even now grown.

Sara eagerly accepted the condition and explained that she had no desire to ever leave her beloved Arizona. Governor was the last office she would ever aspire to she promised Tom. Tom was relieved and elated as well. The night that followed was perhaps the best of their relationship.

That night seemed like only yesterday and also a lifetime ago at the same time. Where had the time gone? Where did it always go? She had been governor for five years and they had been five utterly amazing years. She was eternally grateful to Tom for making it possible. But, with time, her loneliness had returned and with a vengeance. Perhaps it was the end of the transition period of being governor which gave her a bit of time to think on such things. And worse, the loneliness had obviously hit Tom as well. It was rumors at first, that perhaps he was spending just a little too much time with his best client, the wealthy widow of a deceased real estate tycoon. When her fears were confirmed by a private investigator Sara was utterly devastated and angry, but primarily with herself. She knew that it was partly her fault. Her desire to serve as governor had driven her to reduce her marriage to a long-distance relationship. And, she was well aware of the weakness of so many men due to the experiences in her own family. Yet, she had gone off and made her husband and herself lonely for the sake of her political service. She could also blame him, but only partially. So, she never confronted him. She waited to see if he would come to her and he had not. With more time, however, their visits back and forth to be together became less and less frequent. Tom no longer protesting when another weekend passed alone only served to increase her guilt and her emptiness.

And now there it was. A message from him. Jake. That long-forgotten, tingly feeling was back and she felt re-born. But, the feeling was not due to her husband.

Fort Bliss, Texas

"Daddy, you can't be serious!" exclaimed Angelique Parker to her father while putting down her fork. "How can it be justified for Israel to bomb Iran and kill thousands of innocent people just because they want to? I know you're a soldier but even you can't agree with that. You always talk about how important it is to avoid civilian casualties and to what extraordinary lengths you and your guys always went to in Iraq to avoid them."

Major General Greg Parker, the commanding general of the First Armored Division, nicknamed "Old Ironsides," regarded his eldest daughter with a practiced patience.

"Yes, sweetheart, that is true. But, you also know that it is never quite that simple. The Iranian mullahs behind their nuclear program are not innocent. Far from it. They have been at war with our nation since 1979. And, they often purposefully choose to put military facilities right next to civilian areas to use them as human shields."

"Daddy, please! I don't think our government or your precious military would allow Iran or the U.N. or anyone for that matter, to tell us where to put our bases. Why should Iran be told what to do?"

"Penguin, you know you can't compare the Iranian government to ours. I don't even want to get into *that* debate. I know we raised you better than that."

"Enough you two, please! Can we save the political battles for some time other than dinner? It's the only time we are ever together anymore since you've been away at school, baby." Michelle Parker was growing tired of the constant ideological bickering between her husband and daughter.

"Actually, I think this is a good time. This is just a discussion and not a fight. No one is yelling. Well, your daughter's voice *does* tend to get louder."

"Ha ha, very funny dad. Dad changes the subject when he knows he's losing a discussion," Angelique chuckled.

"The difference is that the international community has decided that Iran, as a state sponsor of terrorism, could not be trusted with nuclear weapons. And, Israel has the right to self-defense."

"I'm sorry daddy. I must have missed the part where Iran attacked Israel. I must have missed it because they didn't," the daughter intoned with dripping sarcasm.

"Maybe you missed it because you aren't really paying attention, sweetheart," her father retorted with equal sarcasm. "Israel has been hit with literally thousands of missiles fired by Iran's proxies over the last decade. I don't suppose that counts as being attacked."

"So Iran is supposed to be held responsible for what private groups in Lebanon do? Really, dad?"

"Actually, when they supply those groups and call the shots for those groups, yes. But how about this, Iran's leadership has repeatedly vowed to destroy Israel, whom they call the "Little Satan," and America, whom they call the "Great Satan."

"Just political rhetoric. You all in the military say some things that would make people wonder. Particularly when running, right? Anyway, it's wrong what Israel does and gets away with it, all because they are protected by the mighty U.S. of A."

"I can't believe you've so thoroughly bought into the liberal nonsense they feed you at that school after only two short years," Greg observed. Every time that she came home from Columbia, she spouted more and more liberal points of view. And, nothing he did or said could sway her even remotely. She had also been accepted to West Point, like her father. With her stellar academic and athletic talents, she literally had her choice of schools. She had narrowed the choices down to the Ivy League school and his alma mater but ultimately rejected the military road.

Angelique stood up from the table, walked over to her father and leaned down to give him a kiss on the cheek.

"Daddy, you taught me to think for myself and that's what I'm doing. Maybe it's you that has bought into the nonsense for all these years."

6

NEW YORK STOCK EXCHANGE, NEW YORK, NY

O n the floor of the New York Stock exchange, Monday morning dawned ominously to match the gloomy, rainy weather outside. Traders had been flooded with sell orders even after the market opened down by over 180 points. The sell-off only accelerated as more and more bad news came in from the Middle East. The news of the oil tankers being hit and oil installation attacks was particularly devastating. West Texas Intermediate (WTI) oil, one of the major benchmarks, had shot up from $211 per barrel to $287 per barrel over night and continued to climb. North Sea Brent crude was up even more dramatically. By 1:30 pm, the Dow Jones Industrial average had dropped by almost 1100 points, just over 100 points shy of the first threshold for a trading halt. Mercifully, the market rebounded some on profit taking and closed down just over 900 points.

That night, in the over-night trading, the European markets were dragged sharply lower again. The Greek and Spanish stock markets in particular plummeted, leading financial analysts the world over to declare those economies in a full-blown collapse with Italy also teetering on the brink. The European Central Bank (ECB) had called an emergency session.

Black Tuesday, the second one in a mind numbing coincidence after the one in 1929, picked up where the previous day left off and spiraled out of control. By 11 am, the Dow was down 2600 points causing a trading halt of two hours. After the re-opening at 1:15 PM, the Dow fell another 285 more points to close down almost 2900 points for the day. Maalox, Prozac, and Tylenol packaging littered the trading room floor along with sell orders.

The impact on the global economy was stunning in its speed and scope. Huge portions of the logistics and transportation infrastructure simply stopped. Trucking companies cancelled contracts and deliveries. Grocery store shelves began to go bare. After all, the average American supermarket only had three days' worth of food in-stock once the deliveries stopped. And that's at normal consumption rates. With the onset of panic, stores in some areas were cleaned out in hours. Others lasted a day or two.

Desperation began to set in. Some people had taken to the streets. Then more and more citizens joined them. But despite the protests and government promises to "do something," deliveries of food and fuel became more and more scarce.

Los Angeles, CA (five days later)

The riots started, as they had in the past, in the Watts section of South-Central L.A. And, as before, they began as protests.

"My babies need milk," one woman shouted. "What are we supposed to do?"

"I bet the rich folks up in the Hills have plenty of food and milk," yelled another woman.

"Let's go see what they have. I bet they have all kinds of stuff."

Two days before, the protestors were angry over the skyrocketing price of food and gasoline. On this day, they were angry that there was no food available to buy and gas stations were starting to ration. This tinderbox situation was partly fueled by the lingering "Occupy Wall Street" anger over the exploitation of the masses by the super-elite 1%, which in turn drew on anger over double-digit unemployment rates which reached into the 40% range for minorities, reduction in welfare and food stamp programs due to empty government coffers, and a dozen other problems, depending on whom one spoke to. Then came the disastrous Obamacare program and the economy suffered more job losses and cutbacks. People were hanging on by an economic thread.

A tractor-trailer finally arrived at the Wal-Mart to replenish the mostly empty shelves, but it still did not open its doors. The manager had been directed not to open in the early evening, but to wait until morning due to the large number of restless people gathered. This did not go over well with the thousands of people wanting to fill their nearly empty shelves and refrigerators.

"Let's go see what the rich folks have. They can spare some," yelled a gang member who really didn't care about food, but was looking for an opportunity to loot stores and perhaps his next "ride."

"Yeah, let's go! Get the 1%! 1%, 1%!" the chant rose up sporadically from the crowd, but then grew louder. And then, "We are the 99%. Feed the 99%!"

A young man on a bike rode by and screamed "Police in masks are coming," and sped off, continuing to carry the message, like a modern day Paul Revere. "They're coming, they're coming. Police are coming! The heat's coming!"

Riot police did indeed arrive at the Wal-Mart, and although it was close to 100 police, they did not immediately move against the protestors, even though it was rapidly becoming a violent mob. The mob was taking on a life of its own and actually flowing away from the Wal-Mart.

A block away, a gang of youths took the "opportunity" to move against a liquor store. Windows shattered as rocks, bottles, a tire iron, and anything else that could be found was thrown at and through the windows. Then, in a scene eerily reminiscent of the 1992 Rodney King – L.A. riots, the Korean owner of the liquor store climbed on his roof and fired a warning shot into the air with his surplus, World War II- vintage, Russian-made Mosin-Nagant M44 rifle. The noise was deafening and the flash, a signature of the short-barreled model, readily visible in the failing light. Two gang members pulled out handguns, both Glocks, and fired at the roof. They missed their target, but the large .40 caliber slugs impacted the parapet and showered the shop keeper with fragments, cutting his face and eye. Enraged, he aimed and fired at one of his two assailants. The young African-American youth flew back, a gaping, sucking hole in his chest, blood spewing up and out.

A moment later, the first, warning, shot fired into the air by the shop keeper in defense of his livelihood, began its descent. It impacted on a woman swept up in the now violent mob, shattering the top of her skull with its tremendous terminal velocity as it fell. It was the same woman that minutes earlier had been asking for milk for her babies. The people in her immediate vicinity screamed for help.

"They shot her, they shot her," screamed a middle aged, out-of-work trucker.

"They're shooting at us," cried a teen-age mother who had also come out in search of formula for her three young children.

Back in front of the store, several gang members were now seeking to avenge their fallen friend and had taken cover behind cars, firing their handguns, holding them sideways, Hollywood style, at the shop owner, still on the roof. The shop owner's fourteen year-old son, tasked with keeping watch inside the store, heard the barrage of gunfire followed by screams and feared for his father's life. He grabbed the Mossberg Cruzer 12 gauge shotgun his father kept behind the counter and raced upstairs. His fear of finding his father shot proved true, he racked the slide, crept to the near corner of the parapet, raised the muzzle above the edge, pointed down, and fired. The roar of the shotty added to the firing Glocks and further convinced the mob that they were being fired upon by the shield-welding riot police.

Protestors-cum-rioters started yelling, "Fight back! We won't stop! They can't beat us! We'll never be defeated," as they surged toward the helmeted police.

"The people united can never be defeated! The people united can never be defeated" rose from the now-fully-enraged mob. Bottles and rocks were now being thrown at the police and the police were firing back with bean bag and tear gas cartridges.

The mob took on a life of its own, growing at a mind-numbing rate. People smashed the front doors of the Wal-Mart, even as others surged around the rear of the store and engulfed the laden tractor-trailer.

Another "protestor," a young black member of one of the Crips gangs, was struck in the head and began spewing blood. His older brother, the leader of that particular gang, ordered his "soldiers" to "take it to these damn pig cops for hurting our people, like my little bro." Within minutes, the riot police were being fired upon by dozens of rifles, shotguns, and handguns fired from side alleys, roofs, and from behind cars. Running gun battles between law enforcement, criminal gangs, opportunistic looters, and concerned citizens trying to defend themselves, erupted.

Similar urban battle scenes were being replayed in the Boyle Heights section of East Los Angeles, Compton, Santa Ana, Anaheim, and Oakland. By the early morning, the food and gasoline riots were spreading throughout the urban areas of Southern California and the San Francisco Bay Area often fanned by Facebook posts, Tweets, and Instagram, in addition to late night news reports. This continued the pattern seen ever since the Arab spring of 2012 and the ongoing Syrian Civil War with social media playing an increasingly large role in protests and movements. Now, protests could be organized or enflamed almost instantaneously.

By 3:00 AM, Pacific Time, three police officers and 27 civilians lay dead in the Greater Los Angeles area alone. Many more were hurt. Dozens of cars and buildings were burning. Tens of dozens of businesses had been looted or simply vandalized. Many of the civilians had been killed by other civilians, but this did not matter to a population that was already in despair, angry, and running rapidly out of food and gasoline. The populace burned with rage against the government that had failed to keep them fed and the police that had been killing them for merely trying to get food.

There was a brief lull as people returned to their homes to sleep, but the news of the riots flashed around the world on the 24 hour news cycle and also via social media. People "Facebooked," "Tweeted," and "Instagramed" pictures of their neighbors wounded and dying, and also of their own experiences in the riots. Millions could and did immediately sympathize. Millions of other people around the United

States woke to see the awful images of people dying on the streets of Los Angeles, as the city burned around them. The people in countless towns and cities saw the desperation in California and realized that their lot was not much better. The shortages that hit the big cities first were coming to the suburbs and smaller towns next. These people went to their local supermarkets and gas stations and found nothing but long lines or, worse, signs that read "Closed – No Gas" and empty food shelves. Throngs of people that had been relatively peaceful the last two days became unruly, and then violent, just as had happened in the big cities.

By 9:00 AM on the West Coast, angry and desperate people were beginning to flow back out into the streets. Fights broke out at gas stations. Looting began almost immediately, wherever there was food. People were stabbed for milk and bread. Roaming parties of heavily armed citizens and gangs began to defy police orders to return to their homes, wherever they were encountered. Police were being fired at from side alleys, upper floor windows, from behind cars, and the dozens of other places that the urban landscape offered as cover. Long seated dislike and even hatred of law enforcement and "the man" were boiling over, turning America's inner cities into war zones. And, as the Russians had learned in Chechnya and Americans had learned in Fallujah, the built up city landscape was a nightmare for any law enforcement or military force fighting against determined foes with countless places to hide, snipe, ambush, booby trap, and escape.

Soon the sheer numbers of armed and violent people on the streets of Los Angeles and Oakland overwhelmed the ability of local law enforcement and they were forced to abandon whole neighborhoods. The same thing happened in Chicago, Houston, Philadelphia, Miami, Atlanta, Boston, Detroit, Phoenix, Seattle and countless other cities. New York, however, with the exception of some unrest in the Bronx and Brooklyn, remained remarkably quiet.

Within hours, mayors began calling for governors to call out their state national guards and some were even asking for the federal government to declare martial law.

Throughout the nation, especially in the more rural areas of some states, hundreds of militia groups with tens of thousands of members viewed this as the beginning of the long-feared socio-economic collapse for which they had long prepared, and began to mobilize.

The actions of some state and federal law enforcement would only serve to reinforce their fears and spur the militias to accelerate their actions.

7

THE GOVERNOR'S MANSION, SACRAMENTO, CALIFORNIA

"We need to call out the Guard and we also need for the President to authorize regular US Army and Marines to help us stop these damn riots," said the Governor. In office less than a year, the first Hispanic governor of California, Eduardo Velazquez, was determined not to repeat the mistakes made during the 1992 "Rodney King" riots. He would not wait two whole days before activating the California Army National Guard and requesting federal assistance. The lesson from back then was that civil disturbances had to be nipped in the bud before they gathered momentum, took on a life of their own, and then truly got out of hand.

Velazquez bent his lanky, 6 foot 1 inch frame over his desk and pounded it with his fists. "We need to do something, don't we? We also have riots in Oakland, San Jose, Stockton, San Bernardino, San Diego, Fresno, and the Central Valley."

"Eddie, let's not overreact," answered his chief of staff. "We don't know that this is going to go down like in '92. Let's call up the Guard, but have them on stand-by. Or, we can have them move in with humanitarian help, but not yet try to enforce the law. Everything should quiet down if we can get food and gasoline to the folks that need it. We can also ask the President to have the Army and Marines ready, quietly, but let's not bring them into the cities yet."

"Fine," agreed the Governor. "Send the word out to have the military ready. But if this increases even one bit, *un poquito*, we are going to send them in and crush this. Decisively. And we have to do something about the guns. Starting now. I want door to door searches, on the spot confiscation. Anyone that gets pulled over has their vehicle searched for weapons. We can't have the wild west out here."

"Ok, '*mano*," his old friend reassured him by using the short version of "*hermano*," meaning "brother." "What about the legality of this? Will this stand up in court?"

"I think so," replied Velazquez firmly. The former Attorney General of the State of California often drew upon his vast knowledge of legal precedent often. "In 2005, in the aftermath of Hurricane Katrina, both Louisiana and Mississippi law enforcement conducted house-to-house firearms searches and confiscation due to the extreme nature of the emergency."

"Yes, I remember that Eddie. But I also remember that they were sued and had to return the firearms."

"Sure, of course, but years later. It took years for the cases to come up and eventually the law enforcement agencies did return the firearms, but after, well after the emergency was past. And while we are on the subject, we can search all vehicles crossing our checkpoints into and out of the cities for guns as well."

"And I suppose you have some legal precedent for this as well, *carnal?*" asked his friend, using yet another term, this one more slang, for brother.

"Does the Pope pray the Hail Mary?" the governor chuckled. "In 2002, during the Washington DC Beltway sniper crime spree, Maryland, Virgnia, and D.C. all enforced roadblocks and random searches for the snipers on the highways. There wasn't even a legal challenge on that one."

"So much for the Fourth Amendment..."

"Oh don't give me that. Don't even go there. We all know that everything is limited. There are no absolutes. Even for the Constitution," explained the governor.

"Right, right. We all know the example of the First Amendment not giving a person the right to yell 'fire' in a crowded theater."

"Exactly."

Although he wouldn't say it, the chief of staff couldn't help but think that this was different. A person who yelled fire in a crowded venue was clearly harming people willfully. But a person simply driving on the freeway or a city street was harming no one. Even a person carrying a firearm in a vehicle may only be taking reasonable self-defense precautions for his family, especially given the crazy circumstances in the world. "And what if the President is serious about wanting to declare martial law?"

"We'll cross that bridge if and when…but this may not be a bad thing."

Washington, D.C., the Oval Office

"Chicago and Detroit too?" asked the President exasperatedly. "I thought this was isolated to California?"

"No Mr. President." Joel Miller, the White House Chief of Staff ran his left hand through his graying and thinning hair. "The reports came in from Illinois and Michigan shortly after the first reports out of the West Coast, but you were already asleep and we didn't want to wake you. Still seemed like a matter for local law enforcement and maybe the National Guard."

"So how widespread is this thing?"

"What are you asking? How many riots are going on? In how many cities or states? How large are the biggest riots?"

"Well, yes, yes, and yes," answered the President. "What are we looking at? Give it to me straight, in its totality."

"As you know, food and gasoline shortages are widespread, along with power outages. In some places, grocery stores are completely bare. They have been picked clean and the companies can't tell us when they may get food there. The trucks can't roll without gasoline. In some cases there is no gasoline to be had. In others, there is gas, but the trucking companies don't have the money, the credit really, to buy the gasoline. So the food and gasoline are closely linked. With the power, it's different. In some places, there have been no disruptions. In others, there are rolling blackouts and brownouts continually. The deciding factor is the source of power. Places that get their power from hydro or nuclear have seen almost no interruptions. The problem is that most utilities rely on a mix. Some nuke or hydro and also some mix of natural gas and diesel. Natural gas has had some disruptions. The problem is diesel. Many utilities rely on diesel generators for their quick reacting peak demand. Diesel is suddenly in short supply so this is leading to widespread brownouts when demand peaks."

"So it's the oil companies that won't sell the fuel to the trucking companies? Damn it! I've had just about enough of those greedy big oil assholes!" the President exclaimed.

"I know what you mean, sir, but it's not that simple. Credit is freezing up. Some say it's largely frozen. So those that have fuel, and that have already spent the money to purchase it and or refine it, are understandably reluctant to sell it on credit if there is a feeling they many never get their money."

"Joel, don't give me that. Don't even give me that 'it's understandable,' crap. They are worried about their money while people are going hungry. Is that right? Women and children go hungry so some rich fat-cat can sit in his nice office and *not* have to worry about his future bottom line? Well it's not right I tell you and it won't continue on my watch. Not while the people are cold and hungry," the Chief Executive said with conviction.

Miller thought for just a moment to point out that summer was just barely giving way to fall and so there were very few places in the U.S. where people might be cold. But given his boss's evil mood, he thought better of it. So he continued with his planned briefing notes. "Almost every large city is experiencing *some* sort of social unrest. Long lines lead to fights and or protests. Some are relatively peaceful and small while others are large, violent, and growing larger. Several cities in California seem on the verge of going out of control, as do Detroit and Chicago. New York City, Boston, Philadelphia, St. Louis, Seattle, Baltimore, Atlanta, and Miami protests are still relatively smaller but may be getting ready to explode. And, what started out as food and gas riots are now becoming race-on-race violence. This is particularly disturbing. St. Louis and Chicago are seeing the most racial violence and that, too, is spreading at the gang level. Here in D.C. the presence of so much federal law enforcement seems to be helping keep a lid on things, but we definitely need to stay ahead of this and call out the D.C. National Guard. Maryland has already mobilized their Guard and I suggest we ask Virginia to do the same. The security of the capital cannot be risked."

The President was silent for an interminably long and uncomfortable time. "We have to do something," he said resolutely. "We will do something. I am invoking the National Defense Resources Preparedness order and declaring martial law before this gets any further out of hand. I'll give local law enforcement 24 hours to get things under control or we're going to regain control for them."

The two men strode down the hall on their way to the National Security briefing.

"Ah, Mr. President, I don't advise that. Only the Governors of New York and Illinois have requested federal troops and full declaration of martial law. Massachusetts and Maryland have endorsed the use of federal troops and martial law where necessary, but have not requested those yet for their states. The rest are still saying federal help is not needed yet. And then, there's California," the Chief of Staff trailed off.

"And what are our left-coast friends saying," replied the President sarcastically.

"The Governor called out the National Guard and although California has the most and biggest riots, all he is asking for is that we 'quietly move to have federal troops ready to help.' That's a quote."

"Well, let's give him what he wants. We will be ready to move. But we will *not* wait for their request. Like I said, 24 hours."

They arrived in the situation room and took their seats.

"Ladies and Gentlemen," began the National Security Advisor, "we begin today with the economic situation in the Eurozone. Spain and Greece are in total economic collapse and there is widespread rioting in their cities. Italy probably won't make it to the end of the week, and they also have widespread rioting. The European Parliament is convening an emergency meeting and will probably deploy elements of the Franco-German joint brigade to Greece and possibly also to Spain to help the security situation there.

The ECB, UN, IMF and China are calling for us to join them in a world-wide, coordinated rescue bailout. They are pointing out that we too have been hit with a stock market crash, rioting and signs of our own accelerating economic collapse."

"Are you suggesting that we give massive amounts of money to Europe? Money we don't have even for ourselves," asked the Secretary of the Interior incredulously.

"I'm not yet advocating a position," replied the NSA. "I'm merely reporting what they are saying. But they have been very clear that they will not act unless we join in the effort. They have also said that a portion of the money would be used here in the U.S. and we would also have any other assistance we need, including security assistance."

"Security assistance? Security assistance? What exactly does *that* mean?" demanded the Chairman of the Joint Chiefs of Staff.

The President jumped in, "it means exactly what it means. They are willing to provide us with whatever assistance we may need. It does not mean that NATO or Chinese troops are being airlifted here as we speak."

"Well, thank *God* for small favors," retorted the Chairman, barely able to hide his disgust.

The President glared at his top general. The icy cold stare that everyone knew meant he had crossed a line and would not be allowed to cross it again. The Commander-in-Chief cleared his throat before speaking. "We are a part of the global international community and we are going to be part of the solution. We are going to co-operate with our friends and allies. We are going to be part of the financial bail-out package for our European allies along with the IMF, ECB and China. We are going to bail out the states, which need help, and we are going to take whatever steps necessary to reassure anyone and everyone holding U.S. investments that we will restore order and stop this insane violence. The age of American jingoism and unilateral action is over."

The Federal government leviathan in Washington, D.C., reacted to the economic collapse and social unrest by passing massive bailouts for the states and for the Eurozone nations in conjunction with the International Monetary Fund. The other key players beside the United States were China and Germany, all under the auspices of the E.U. and U.N. Together, they crafted the International Monetary Stability Act for Financial Equality with the ridiculous English acronym IMSAFE, pronounced "I'm safe." In return for helping to stabilize the global economy as well as the American one, the international partners insisted on "measures that ensure our investments and assistance to the United States will not fall victim to the rampant social unrest and gun violence that seems to be spreading across this great land." To that end, they insisted that the IMSAFE be tied to security provisions including universal gun registration and "reasonable" gun ownership restrictions *inside* the United States. Under the emergency provisions of Patriot Act II, sweeping but "temporary" gun control measures were put in place by executive fiat of the President. All sales and transfers of semi-automatic rifles were banned, even small youth .22s. This ban even included private gun transfers between citizens not involving retail outlets.

Similarly, all sales and transfers of semi-automatic handguns were banned. Sale or transfer of any detachable magazine holding more than 7 rounds was also stopped "temporarily." All private ammunition sales, even for shotguns were halted "until the emergency subsided." Cities and states "particularly hard hit by civil unrest" were encouraged to undertake house-to-house, door-to-door searches and seizures of all firearms, even though no definition of "particularly hard hit" was given. These same governmental entities were also encouraged to establish "temporary" restrictions on the transport of firearms and enforce the same with roadside checkpoints. Private militias were to be outlawed, although no guidance was given as to what, exactly, constituted a militia. Did the members of a private shooting club qualify as a militia?

Any form of speech, including press and media, that might be construed as inciting violence or even protest was subject to be labeled as "hate speech" and the perpetrator arrested. Gatherings of more than 50 people were restricted without a permit until the "emergency has passed."

The international power brokers also insisted that the United States show "extraordinary restraint in not escalating the conflict in the Middle East, while recognizing every nation's inherent right for self-defense."

For millions upon millions of Americans, this surrender of national sovereignty and Constitutional rights was simply unacceptable, especially in such dangerous and uncertain times. For millions of these private citizen patriots, the implementation of such domestic and foreign policy measures was tantamount to a declaration of war.

8

CALIFORNIA STATE HIGHWAY 99, NORTHWEST OF FRESNO

The six Humvees (or Hummers as civilians called them) of the California National Guard's 1072nd Transportation Company had been sent out from the Fresno National Guard Armory two days earlier to help enforce the quarantine of the City. Fresno, like most other California cities, had been racked by riots for days. The economic crisis caused by the tripling of oil prices led to food and gasoline shortages. Shortages led to the protests, which then became riots, especially after local law enforcement intervened, often with heavy handed tactics. After the police and sheriffs proved unable to restore order, the Governor had ordered National Guard units to deploy and restore order by "all means necessary." This had translated into strict curfews, shoot-on-site for looters, and house-to-house confiscation of all privately owned firearms in a move reminiscent of the aftermath of Hurricane Katrina in 2005. The government security measures also included a total quarantine of those cities, with no civilian traffic allowed in or out without passing through checkpoints.

In the rural areas around Fresno, two local men had simply disappeared under suspicious circumstances. One man, the leader of the local Tea Party group, went missing from his home in the middle of the night. No one had any facts or evidence about wrong doing, other than his unusual and abrupt departure. The man was known to have family in Southern California and in Washington State, but this did not stop the rumor mill from operating at a high rate. Another man, the largely anonymous (known only to his members, or so it was thought) leader of a small militia group had been kidnapped while leaving a convenience store just outside of Fresno. This case was different. The newly installed security cameras at the store captured video of a power utility van that drove up behind the militia leader, the side door opened, and two men dragged him inside after delivering a crippling blow to the back of his neck. It just so happened that the employee on duty during the kidnapping was the younger brother of a militia member. These two incidents spread both concern and additional conspiracy theories through the local Patriot, militia, and Minuteman groups. Similar "reports" of missing militia, Tea Party, or other "anti-government" types began to circulate in multiple states.

In the Golden State, Lt. Joe Robles of the California National Guard had always enjoyed his military service, both active duty and now Guard. But, he did not relish this assignment. He could not escape the thought that he had not chosen to continue serving so he could operate against civilians in need, and instead wanted to help them. And to make matters worse, he knew that the Central California State Militia was extremely unhappy with the recent developments in Washington, Sacramento and locally. They had mobilized as soon as the social unrest started. He knew this because his older brother, nephew, and some neighbors were members of the local militia chapter. One person he knew actually belonged to two different militias! When asked why he belonged to two different groups, the former school mate had explained that it was important to be linked to as many like-minded people as possible. Although Robles agreed with most of their views regarding the growth of the Federal Government, the ongoing and worsening loss of liberty, and the inevitability of an economic collapse, he had never felt quite right about joining the militia, despite the open invitation from his family and friends.

The evening looked to be a bit chilly with partial overcast skies even as the twilight was failing into night. Robles and the other 14 men of his checkpoint were glad they brought their ponchos. It had been a long and tiring 48 hours but they were scheduled to be relieved and rotated back to the armory in the morning.

Three of their six M1114 HMMWVs (Humvees) had a single M2 HB .50 caliber machine gun. Known affectionately as the "Ma Deuce," the .50 cal or simply, the "fifty," had been around since the end of World War I. The combination of simple, rugged design coupled with devastating firepower had made it virtually impossible to improve upon the design, decade after decade. The M2 could reach out to an effective range of over 2,000 meters and dominate all but the most serious threats. Their company commander thought fifteen men backed up by three "fifties" would be sufficient to maintain the checkpoint for civilians. And, normally, he would have been right. But, these were not normal times.

They set up their roadblock checkpoint on highway 99, the "Golden State Highway," approximately midway between Fresno and Madera. Here, they could monitor all movement between the two cities. Two of the Ma Deuce Humvees flanked the highway while the third armed M1114 was thirty yards away to provide overwatch protection for any unexpected circumstance. The squad was in a three section watch of four on and four off, which meant that at any time, 5 of the men were on watch, manning the roadblock and overwatch Hummer while the other 10 men slept in their tents, ate, and maintained their equipment. Two county sheriffs were also supposed to be with the detachment at all times, but they were absent more often than not.

The day's traffic had begun with a largely normal stream but then grew with increasing numbers of vehicles loaded with people looking to "get out of dodge" in the city. Most of those evacuating or bugging out were going from the large city of Fresno toward Madera or the surrounding areas. But for some, shelter from the coming storm could be found in a larger city, or so they hoped.

Robles and his detachment thought nothing when the older, mid 1990's model Winnebago RV pulled off the north (west) bound lane with its hazard lights blinking. When they saw the pretty and curvy thirty-something year-old mother and her adolescent son get off the vehicle, they saw a chance to help a lady in distress, and perhaps get an email address or phone number in return as a reward.

"Corporal Smythe, why don't you and Private Hudgens go see about protecting and serving this young lady," said Robles slyly. In reality, he was extremely nervous and worried that his comrades would see the beads of sweat forming on his forehead. He had served with Smythe for three years and with Hudgens for just over a year. He did not want them killed. But, he also didn't want his fellow militiamen hurt either.

By the time the two Good Samaritan guardsmen had reached the RV, the pretty brunette had already popped the hood and was standing there with her son looking hopefully at the two approaching men. As soon as both guardsmen were peering into the engine compartment with their rifles slung, two armed militiamen rushed out from the RV, one holding an AK, the other an AR rifle. The guardsmen looked up in surprise only to hear the lady's voice behind them say "freeze and don't say a word" emphatically as she drew her own Glock 19 from its concealed position in the small of her back and pointed the pistol at them.

Thirty yards away, the two guardsmen manning the overwatch Humvee looked up in shock to see two men on mountain bikes only 10 yards away stop their bikes and aim AK rifles directly at them. The militiamen had approached undetected on mountain bikes from the opposite direction from the roadblock. The fact that the man not actually on the .50 caliber machine gun was reading a magazine had only made matters easier for the militiamen.

Four other militiamen on mountain bikes, along with Robles, similarly surprised the remaining 10 guardsmen in their tents. One of the guardsmen was shot in the shoulder by a militiaman as he reached for his rifle. The militiamen took the three highest ranking guardsmen (all corporals like Hudgens), including the one shot, into "custody," and then removed the remaining guardsmen's boots before tying them up, gagging them, and leaving them in their tents, but not before thoroughly searching the tents and removing any and all valuable equipment.

"Not a bad day's work, ladies and gentlemen," Robles announced as he leaned over to kiss his wife and hug his son. "We captured 14 men, 6 Hummers, 3 ARs and 3 fifties for the Central California Militia, and all without loss of life, praise God. Let's get out of here and get back to base camp."

I-80, 5 miles north of Rocklin, California

The men and women of Charlie Company, 1st Battalion, 79th Brigade Combat Team (BCT), 184th Infantry Regiment had departed their base in Auburn, California at 5:00 AM local time, en route south to help quell the riots in Oakland and restore order. The 19 vehicle convoy had two Humvees in the lead as well as two more as rear guard, with the other four Humvees interspersed among the eleven deuce and a halfs. In all, 152 men and women were heading to the Bay area. Headquarters had told them to expect "civic disturbance" operations and possibly combat against armed gangs, but that the road into Oakland would be quiet. Headquarters was wrong.

"First Sergeant," asked Corporal Cole as he scanned the road ahead, "are we really going to have to shoot civilians? Everyone is saying so…" He was driving with the company first sergeant.

"Hopefully it won't come to that," replied First Sergeant Geoff McDowell. "But you tell me, son, what are you going to do if some of these *civilians* shoot at you? Shoot at us? Our friends in this unit? You've seen the news. The cities are a war zone, and Oakland is one of the worst. Maybe the worst."

"Yes, I know. I did see the reports. But there are thousands of people and criminals out in the streets. Blacks fighting with Hispanics and both of those groups fighting with white gangs. How will we know who's the bad guys and who are the good guys?" asked Private Zamora from the back seat.

"Bad guys are easy. Anyone who shoots at us is a bad guy. Good guys are tougher to figure. Just because someone doesn't shoot at you doesn't mean they are good guys. They could be bad guys who happen to be outnumbered or outgunned for the moment. Or, they may just be waiting for the right chance to shoot at you. I deployed for the 1993 L.A. riots…"

"Yes, we know, Sarge," groaned the other three soldiers in unison. "You remind us of all our operations."

"During the L.A. riots," McDowell continued undeterred, "we saw innocent looking people who later shot at us or were with people who shot at us. The point is you just never know who has a brother or amigo or whatever, in a gang. You never know which one of those brothers was killed or locked up so that their family member or 'homeboy' hates all law enforcement and is just looking for some payback."

"Look at that, Sarge. Should we stop and help?" asked the corporal from his driver's seat.

"Wheew..." whistled McDowell. "That is a *nice* looking Caddy" he observed about the almost new and shiny white Cadillac by the side of the road with its hazard lights on. The fact that the car was stopped just before a bend in the road and there was no one visible with it, made the sergeant feel a bit uneasy.

"Slow up a bit, but don't stop," directed McDowell. "I'll get the license plates and we can call in for help for them."

The Humvee slowed as it approached the luxury car causing all of the vehicles behind them to slow as well. Behind a small embankment 70 yards away on the southeast side of the highway, four members of the Northern California Unorganized Militia observed the approaching convoy with binoculars. Recalling the Indian disguises of the Boston Tea Party, all of the men of Bear Company wore a face covering of some sort. Most wore shemaghs, the Middle Eastern head scarf that many of the militia men had learned to wear while serving in Iraq and Afghanistan. Some wore regular bandanas as coverings, while others wore ski masks. One even wore a paintball facemask with a dark skull painted on it.

"Ok Richie, here they come. Remember, you need to be Johnny on the spot with that RPG as soon as I blow the Caddy. Ron, as soon as the RPG impacts, put a rifle grenade on the second deuce truck." Sergeant Derek Lawson, the fireteam leader, didn't know why he was whispering since it really wasn't necessary. It just seemed like he needed to whisper, so he did. He knew his men knew the plan and how to carry it out, but it helped him to run through it verbally again.

The rest of the militia company was arrayed on both sides of the interstate to the immediate north of Lawson's fireteam. Alpha platoon deployed on the west side and Bravo on the east. As the fireteam furthest to the south, they would be the first to engage the convoy once it was completely in the ambush "kill box." The lead vehicles in the convoy would be attacked first, followed immediately by attacks on the rearmost vehicles. This would effectively trap the remainder of the vehicles so they could be systematically destroyed.

"Almost there," said Lawson to himself under his breath. He needed McDowell's lead Humvee to be abreast of the Cadillac. "Almost there...*NOW!*"as he activated the cell phone trigger for the 500 pound Improvised Explosive Device (IED) hidden in the car. The explosion was tremendous and the glorified Jeep that was the Hummer was shredded. Immediately Richie elevated and sighted his RPG-7D (paratrooper model) and fired. A tongue of flame erupted from the rear as the rocket propelled grenade leapt forward.

The four kilogram warhead impacted the first 2 ½ ton truck with a terrific explosion. Ten of the National Guardsman riding in the rear cargo bed were literally blown to pieces and died instantly. The two sitting furthest to the rear were thrown from the open top cargo bed with minimal injuries from shrapnel. The remaining eight men were alive, but severely wounded.

Then, back on the embankment, Ron hefted his AK rifle to his shoulder and fired his rifle grenade at the second Humvee. The driver had swerved to avoid the exploding vehicle in front of his and this saved his life. The rifle grenade missed.

Along the entire rest of the convoy, vehicles were exploding from more RPGs, rifle grenades, and rifle fire. Each precious RPG was targeted on a truck with its high value target of 20 men. Rifle fire cut down most of those who escaped the deuce and a half trucks as well as those in the Humvees.

Of the 152 men and women of Charlie Company, 1st Battalion, 79th Brigade Combat Team (BCT), 184th Infantry Regiment, California National Guard, only 18 survived and most of them were badly wounded.

The militia rushed down and took the survivors captive. The captain in charge of the Bear Company strode forward with a grim determination.

"Ok people, well done. Very well done. All units report," boomed the captain. His entire unit was present and accounted for and only three casualties. Two men had been hit by what meager return fire the surprised Guardsmen were able to muster. Another had broken his ankle as he rushed down the embankment at the end of the engagement.

"Very well," continued the captain, "Let's get these lucky survivors back to base. Four of them have a video to make."

9

SACRAMENTO, CALIFORNIA,

THE STATE CAPITOL BUILDING

The Governor of the beleaguered state of California stared out of the window of the conference room as he waited for the rest of his advisors to arrive. He could see the smoke from the fires. Like all Californians, he was all too familiar with large fires and clouds of smoke. But those were normally from the forest fires that ravaged his state almost every year. These fires were from burning buildings, cars, barricades, etc. The nearest fires were less than four miles away. Seemingly every major city in his beloved state was on fire, literally and socially. And California was not alone. The entire world seemed to be going crazy.

When everyone was seated around the large conference table, the Governor began the meeting by calling on the Adjutant General of California to brief the situation.

Major General Daniel Brock was something of an anomaly in the state since he was a native Californian. It seemed that the majority of Californians were from somewhere else. He still had the football line-man's muscle mass and quiet strength. But he was clearly concerned.

"Ladies and Gentlemen, we are in a dire emergency," began Brock with his usual blunt manner. "Our great state is in the midst of a soci-etal breakdown. Riots in dozens of cities have been going on for days. All of you can see the smoke visible from where we are, here in the capitol. The California National Guard, Highway Patrol, and local law enforcement have been fully deployed. Yet, despite our best efforts, the situation is not improving, but deteriorating. The anger and frustration of the general populace has now been fully turned on our Guard and law enforcement personnel. Units within the cities are being systematically fired upon and subjected to sabotage attacks. Not only that, several convoys and units on roadblock duty outside of the major cities have also been ambushed and attacked. Most of the incidents outside the cities, we believe, have involved organized or unorganized militiamen. One of our columns was attacked in the Central Valley by militia in what appears to be company strength. We've even had National Guardsmen taken prisoner. The President has offered active duty units from Fort Irwin, Camp Pendleton and Twenty-Nine Palms to help restore order. I realize what a serious step this is. And, I, like you, find the idea of martial law, even temporary, abhorrent. But I feel that at this point, we have no choice," concluded the General grimly. "In fact, the President's 'offer' is not really an offer. More of an ultimatum. The White House asks that we make a formal, public request for active duty federal troops and endorse the enactment of martial law. Illinois is considering doing this and may make an announcement as soon as tomorrow."

"You can't be serious!" exclaimed the Secretary for Health and Human Services. "This simply can't be allowed to happen. There must be another way," said the middle aged former social worker from San Francisco.

"If anyone has any other ideas, I'm all ears," intoned the Governor.

"Can't we wait them out? Won't this all just stop when they lose interest," asked the HHS chief reasonably.

"I don't think it's that simple. At a minimum, food and gasoline supplies would have to be re-established and we know that will take weeks, at best," explained General Brock. "But I don't think this is just about food and fuel," the General continued. "That may have been the spark, but it simply revealed the deep-rooted problems within our state, and country for that matter, that have been growing and festering for years."

"Well, we can wax philosophical some other time about how to fix this in the long run. What we need right now is a plan. A course of action to fix this. And we must fix this quickly," said the Lt. Governor.

"Agreed," answered the General. "Just be aware that any declaration of martial law and confiscation of private firearms will almost certainly lead to a full blown declaration of war on the part of the militias. We know from the FBI infiltrators that the leaders of several units are planning a gathering somewhere in the northern part of the state. We also know that the militia are preparing for a protracted conflict and are in communication with militia units in other states at levels never before seen. Nevertheless, my recommendation stands. The sooner we deal with this the better."

Everyone waited for the Governor to speak next. And when he did, it was not the long monologue the others in the room were expecting. He simply said "Ok, I'm requesting the active duty units and am also formally requesting the legislature's endorsement of a declaration of martial law. As for these so-called militias, they are domestic terrorists in my opinion. And how many can there be? What can they seriously do?"

The response from the militia came the next day in the form of a video sent on a DVD and left outside the capitol. Copies were also mailed, delivered, or emailed to all major media outlets and posted on YouTube.

The video opened with a close up of a heavily armed militiaman, his face obscured with a shemagh. He was wearing old fashioned woodland camouflage BDUs and tactical web gear with four magazine pouches in a row across his abdomen and a holster with a semi-automatic pistol immediately above that. He held a highly accessorized AK rifle in his hands across his chest. Behind and slightly above him hung an upside down United States flag, universally recognized as a signal of distress. Directly underneath that hung the yellow Gadsden "Don't Tread on Me" flag with a coiled rattlesnake crossed with the California state flag with the prominent bear.

The militiaman stared directly into the camera and started speaking in a loud monotone. "We, the people of the great state of California have stood by for too long and watched as corrupt politicians in Sacramento and Washington, who care nothing about the average person, have bankrupted our beloved state and nation. They care more about a tiny fish in a river than putting thousands of families into poverty. They care more about the environment than decent people being able to drive to their work. And now, when their utter failure has resulted in their inability to provide food to their citizens they respond by turning our own brothers in uniform against us. But we the people will not submit. We will not turn over our firearms guaranteed to us by the Second Amendment to the United States Constitution. We will not submit to unreasonable searches and seizures according to the Fourth Amendment. We will fight the Federal Government in Washington and their lackeys in Sacramento for the rights reserved to the people and the states by the Tenth Amendment. The Federal government has been at war with the people for many years. Now, we the people declare war on the corrupt puppet masters in Washington and all who serve them. We implore our brothers and sisters in uniform to remember and honor their pledge to uphold and defend the Constitution of the United States of America. We invite our brothers and sisters all across our great nation to join us in fighting to restore our Constitutional Republic. We are not at all racist. We are a Christian organization and recognize all men and women as creations of our Lord and Savior, Jesus Christ. All U.S. citizens and even legal immigrants are free to join our noble cause. To all civilians, we ask that you remember that we are your neighbors, your brothers, sisters, cousins, co-workers. We are your police officers, your fire fighters, your doctors, your children's teachers. We are not faceless bureaucrats in faraway places doing what is best for them and not what's best for the people, collecting exorbitant salaries while we, the average people, struggle to pay our taxes. We demand the recognition of all of the Constitution, in its entirety, immediately. We demand the immediate cessation of private firearms confiscation and revocation of martial law. We are not opposed to the restoration of law and order, but this should be carried out only by local and state law enforcement with support from the state national guard, if necessary. In fact, we are happy to help and assist with all Constitutional law enforcement activities. We reject all use of active federal troops on United States soil as law enforcement and demand the Federal Government respect the Posse Comitatus Act of 1878. We likewise reject any and all use of foreign armed forces, law enforcement, advisors, monitors, etc. by any title that the illegitimate government in Washington chooses to call them here on U.S. soil. We mean no harm to any peaceful civilian. Until all of the Constitutional rights are observed for all American citizens, we will do whatever is necessary to engage and defeat the corrupt federal forces and their lackeys, wherever they may be found. We sign off with the words of Thomas Jefferson, 'the tree of liberty must occasionally be watered with the blood of tyrants and patriots."

The militiaman then turned as two of his fellow militia brought in two handcuffed men both wearing ACUs. They were seated, and the one on the right began to speak: "We are both members of Charlie Company, 1st Battalion, 79th Brigade Combat Team (BCT), 184th Infantry Regiment, California Army National Guard. We have been treated well. We can confirm that the Northern California Unorganized Militia is very well trained, highly motivated, well equipped and pre-pared for a long conflict."

For the people of California, the die had been cast. Now it remained to be seen how the rest of the country would react.

Riots in the major cities of America continued and spread like water from a broken dam leading to additional deployments of feder-alized National Guard and active duty Army units, and the declaration of martial law in more and more areas. Local militias from Florida to Washington State fought back. Regular citizens took to the streets in protest and demanding food and gasoline. Violence continued to spiral out of control.

The President declared a nation-wide emergency and called for the mobilization of all military reserves and state National Guard units to "restore law and order and ensure public safety."

Phoenix, Arizona, The Governor's Office

Sara Doucet entered her conference room wearing a subdued black pant suit with a purple blouse but not her customary smile. She sat in the seat next to the head of the table (she claimed to dislike sitting at the head of the table although she did end up in that seat more often than not).

"Good morning everyone. Although, honestly, I don't know how anyone can see today as truly good. My goodness, what a mess we as a nation are spiraling into."

All of her staff seated around the table merely nodded in grave agreement. Some even shook their heads.

"So, what is the latest?" the Governor asked no one in particular.

"Washington continues asking when our National Guard units will be federalized," answered the Adjutant General. "What should I tell them?"

"Tell them the truth. Tell them that I have not yet authorized federalization. We still have some unrest in our cities and we need our troops here," Doucet explained.

"Ah, Madam Governor, perhaps we should discuss this further before answering Washington in this manner. Have we considered the all the legalities?" her chief of staff asked.

"I'm not sure what you mean by legalities. Perhaps you refer to whether or not we can supersede a federal request for our national guard?" the governor inquired.

"Yes, ma'am. That is exactly what I am asking."

"I'm not sure about legalities. I'm not a lawyer. But I do know the Constitution. And I know some history. And because I know these things I know that the states created the Constitution and therefore the states created the federal government. Now, it seems a whole lot of people have forgotten or overlooked this very key fact. But I have not forgotten it. In fact, I am always quite conscious of this important facet of the relationship between the state and Washington. So, since our National Guard is needed here, in its home state, I don't care one bit if the President is demanding our units be federalized. But just to be clear, the Constitution does give the federal government the role of providing for the common defense. If, therefore, there was a clear and present external danger to the United States, I would make every effort to federalize as many units as possible, while still maintain a bare minimum to keep order and safety here at home."

"But, your honor, aren't we supposed to defend the Constitution against all enemies, foreign *and domestic?*" the chief of staff persisted. "The President is claiming that this civil unrest, protests, and extremist militia groups are a domestic threat."

"Yes, yes we are. And I am well aware of what the President claims. But do you know who I think is the domestic threat? It's the federal government that is the biggest threat to the United States. So, General, feel free to tell Washington to go to hell. Or, something to that effect. Feel free to be more eloquent or more abrupt. I don't really care at this point. Our Arizona National Guard will not be federalized at this time and will remain under Arizona control."

Around the country governors were having similar conversations were with their staffs. This Federal "overreach" was not well received in many states, particularly those which had already been at odds with the central government over such issues as immigration, health care, Medicare and Medicaid, environmental regulations, gun control voter identification, and a myriad other issues. Ultimately, eighteen governors refused the President's call for federalization of state national guards. Citing the Tenth Amendment of the Constitution's Bill of Rights, twenty-three states passed declarations of state sovereignty and nullification of the International Monetary Stability Act. Twenty-eight states nullified any implementation of martial law by the Federal Government without consent of the governor of the state. In Montana, fiercely independent and with long-standing disputes with Washington, D.C. over federal environmental and land use regulations, as well as gun regulation under the Interstate Commerce Clause and the Montana Firearms Freedom Act, the legislature went a step further and voted to secede altogether by a narrow margin. The state body then sent the matter to the people of the state. After a brief two week long state-wide debate, the citizens of Montana passed the measure of secession by almost a two-to-one margin.

10

HELENA, MONTANA,

THE GOVERNOR'S RESIDENCE

Montana's governor, Byron Sampson, leaned back in his over-stuffed leather chair and chewed on his cigar. He looked out the window over the scenic Helena valley as his best friend and Chief of Staff looked at him intently. Less than an hour had passed since the polls had closed on the special plebiscite in which the people of his state had voted overwhelmingly to declare their sovereignty as a state, to nullify the International Monetary Stabilization Stability Act for Financial Equality and the Federal Government's declaration of martial law. Amazingly, the people had not stopped there. They also voted to secede from the United States.

"What is the first thing we need to do in terms of the feds?" asked the Governor.

"What do you mean?" responded his old college buddy. "That one question has so many dimensions. Are you asking what we do with them or about them politically? Financially? Administratively? Militarily?"

"I don't know," intoned Sampson. "If *you* were the President, what would *you* be thinking right about now? More importantly, what, if anything, would you be thinking about doing with *us*?"

Roger Reynolds's brow furrowed. "First of all, they will be embarrassed by this. He will be embarrassed. Above all, this makes him look bad. I don't know how much he will care that a backward red state full of bumpkins no longer wants to play in the sandbox. He will care about how this may affect his precious legacy."

"I don't know. I don't think the fact that we voted to secede will affect his image or legacy nearly as much as his response, whatever that may be, is," mused the Governor. "But that is what I am really asking. What will be the response from Washington?"

"I may be wrong, but my gut tells me that they will largely ignore it. Act like it's a symbolic vote. 'This is a difficult time and folks are frustrated' sort of thing. And they may truly believe it. They may think that once this current crisis blows over, that we'll forget all about it and say no harm no foul. Of course, they will care about the loss of federal tax revenue, but since we are a small state population-wise, they may let it go."

"You really think they don't get that we are serious? That their declaration of "limited" martial law, whatever *that* means, and giving away sovereignty to foreign entities was merely the final straw? They don't get how onerous we've felt their policies have been for decades? For half a century? They don't understand or care that we feel Washington brought about this crisis by spending our nation into oblivion?" asked Swanson with more than a hint of frustration.

"I think they know we are frustrated, but I don't believe they can fully grasp that this has happened. They can't accept that we truly no longer wish to be ruled by, or even affiliated with the Federal monster. I think they see state secession as truly unthinkable. Heck, we did it and we don't even know what this really means. This is exactly why we are having this discussion," replied Reynolds. "But getting back to your question. I think after they figure out the official spin, they will look at the financial and economic impact. They may try to isolate us and not allow us to export oil or coal to other states unless we relent."

"True, energy is a top concern. But, removing our supply from the national supply hurts them too by hurting other states. Besides, that will probably play out in the long term. What should we be thinking about now, in the short term," the governor asked, getting back to his original intent.

There was silence as both men thought. Finally, the Chief of Staff broke the silence.

"The missiles," he said simply.

"Missiles?" asked the governor.

"Yep, the missiles. If I were the President, I would be concerned about the 150 Minuteman missiles here on sovereign Montana soil."

The Governor whistled as he took that in. "You may be right. If I were him, that is the main thing I would want out of Montana, except for maybe our energy. What do you think they'll do about the Minutemen? What do you think we should do?"

"Well, we may want to deploy the 1-163rd from the Guard to secure Malmstrom and put the 186th squadron at Great Falls on alert. But, if history is a guide, we can work things out with the Feds. The former Soviet republics were able to work things out with the new government in Moscow when the old U.S.S.R. broke apart. Including the security and disposition of nuclear ICBMs. Surely we can do the same or better with Washington."

"Ok, but what about the Air Force security force on the base? Are they going to just turn over one-third of America's nuclear interconti-nental ballistic missiles to us?" asked Sampson.

"Good point. And the answer is, I don't know. I think we should contact the base commander and ask his intentions. Washington may demand we turn them over or even try an airborne assault. Securing an entire Air Force Base is too big a job for spec ops but if I were advis-ing the President, I would think long and hard about a drop by the 82nd and some rangers. Heck, they may even send some Army ground units from Fort Lewis or Yakima."

"Ok, but what are *our* intentions? What do we want from the base personnel? Do we want them to turn over the base and everything in it?"

"Well, yes. That is one option. I don't know that the command would go for that, and even if they did, what about the rest of the men? There is no guarantee they'd go along. Some could try and force a confrontation. Or…" Reynold's thought trailed off.

Both men sat and thought once again.

"What happened back in 1861?" asked the Governor after a while.

"What, you mean with the Union installations in the southern states? I'm no expert, but I think most were turned over to the south without a fight once the garrison commander recognized the unten-able position of being far behind enemy lines, cut off from supplies and surrounded. Of course, not all forts did this. We all know what happened at Fort Sumter."

"Right. I certainly don't want to start a second American Civil War right here in Montana," said the Governor with conviction. "Despite our differences, I am not looking to fight the feds. I just want them to leave us alone. I want Montanans to decide the fate and future of Montana. I don't wish any American ill will. In fact, I bid them the best of luck."

"And, what if Washington is contemplating the same thing, the fate of these missiles, and decides to do something," asked his friend.

The Governor reasoned, "Hmmm…I think you're right. If I were the President, I might try and reinforce the Malmstrom garrison. Probably with airborne. I wouldn't risk sending ground units through our territory, very rugged territory to boot, without knowing what our response may be."

"Right, what about other ground units?"

"Again, we can't be sure, but I doubt any of our neighbors would side with the feds in a move against us. We have friendly neighbors all around us, except maybe to the north, but that's a whole different discussion. In any case, the nearest substantial fed ground forces are in Fort Lewis, Washington or maybe Fort Carson, Colorado. A long and rough way to go to get here either way."

"So then we best figure out what our own position with the feds is and get communication with the Malmstrom garrison commander ASAP. Do you find it ironic that the President's response against us may well be more forceful than what he has allowed against the Iranians?"

"I find it tragic and ironic. In any case, let's get the 163rd moving to Malmstrom. Regardless of what the base commander decides to do, I think we will need them there," concluded the now rogue governor.

Aboard Air Force One over Colorado, en route to San Francisco

The President's Senior Advisor knocked on the door of the President's private suite.

"What is it?" the President's voice answered from behind the door.

"Mr. President, the results are in from Montana and it's worse than we thought," answered Lee Andropolous uncomfortably.

The door swung open and the President stood there in his shirt sleeves. "Worse? We expected them to vote to secede. How can it be worse?"

"The margin was almost two-to-one in favor of secession," Andropolous answered his boss, shifting his feet unconsciously. "This indicates far stronger anti-government sentiment than our emergency polling had revealed.

"I'm still not surprised," snorted the President dismissively. "It's symbolic. A state can't leave the union. The question is, what do we do now?"

"That's the million dollar question, sir."

"Do you have any million dollar answers," asked the President? "Do we respond forcefully or marginalize the 'fringe movement?'"

"I don't think forceful is the correct tact. We are already acting forcefully to quell the riots and restore order. Not everyone feels that we are using force in a measured and appropriate manner. We don't want to give those people any more fuel for their fires," said the senior policy advisor.

"Surely you don't agree with them," the President shot back instinctively.

"Sir, we are not here discussing what I think. We are discussing what the general public of the U.S. thinks. In any case, I think we defuse the situation. We take a very soft tact. 'We understand these are tough times and lots of folks are upset and confused,' that sort of thing."

The President's eyes drifted to the ceiling of the compartment as he considered his subordinate's advice. "Ok, we'll do that, for now. At least, that's our official position on this madness. And that's all this is, you know. Madness. Madness! It is sheer madness for states to *still* think that secession is possible, let alone legal. But regardless, I want this cowboy governor and his legislature to get the message loud and clear that we are not simply letting their state, or any state, break up this union," he concluded with resolve.

"Yes sir, understood," replied Andropolous.

"Oh, and one other thing. We need to get ahead of these cowboys and figure out what concrete steps they plan to take and how we can counter or even, pre-empt them. This includes having a plan for the military to protect our interests should the need arise. Tell General Grissom that I want a contingency briefing on which military units in and around Montana we can utilize if need be."

"Will do, Mr. President, but just remember we are already stretched pretty thin responding to all the riots and unrest, not to mention over-seas deployments," he reminded his friend.

11

PHOENIX, ARIZONA, THE STATE CAPITOL

The riots in Phoenix had been similar to what was happening across all of America's big cities. Shortages of food, gasoline, and then rolling blackouts brought angry people out in droves. But as one of four states that bordered Mexico, Arizona had the added tinder-box of illegal immigration to fuel their social unrest. Hispanics clashed with whites, even as both groups clashed with African-Americans. To make matters worse, a recent spike in the number of pro-amnesty pro-tests and illegal aliens crossing the border had further polarized the divided racial groups. This spike included increasing numbers of men of Middle Eastern descent leading to increased calls from Arizona residents and lawmakers to "secure Arizona now." The Arizona State Police and National Guard were stretched more than comparable law enforcement from other states due to this added role, even as the Federal Department of Homeland Security refused to provide additional help on direct orders from the Justice Department. This odd situation was a direct result of the Federal Government imbroglio with Arizona over the state's continued tough stance on securing their border.

News of the Montana vote of secession and a similar pending vote in Oklahoma within days caused a furor among conservatives in the Grand Canyon State. A spontaneous Tea Party rally gathered in front of the state capitol to call for Arizona to follow suit and vote on state sovereignty, nullification of the IMSAFE Act, and outright secession. A sea of yellow "Don't Tread On Me" Gadsden flags mixed with

Old Glory and the blue and rising sun of the Arizona state flag over one mass of people while the Mexican flag mixed with the Stars and Stripes floated over the other. One man with the conservative group held a large sign which read "By ballot or by bullet, restoration is coming." Another sign read "We came unarmed. This time…" Among the liberal throng, a small group of Caucasians, Hispanics, and African-Americans wore shirts bearing the message "God's Tea Party is Not Racist." Signs also abounded with slogans such as "Surviving is Not a Crime," "Free Aztlan," and "Immigrants' Rights are Human Rights."

The two groups tried to shout each other down and then began to jostle one another where the groups came together. Uniformed police tried to defuse the situation as shield wielding and helmeted riot police stood ready to intervene but hoped and prayed that they would not need to.

Tensions continued to grow. Then the eruption came. Arizona Minutemen in military fatigues noticed a U.S. flag being flown upside down underneath a Mexican flag and became instantly enraged. Five of the minutemen crashed through the crowd intent on removing the insulting spectacle. To the group of young Arizona State University students holding the flag pole, they were merely exercising their First Amendment right of free speech by expressing that their nation was in distress.

The Minutemen reached the ASU students and two of them grabbed the pole violently. The diminutive 19-year old holding the banners tried to pull back but lost his balance. Another Minuteman dragged the flag bearer back two feet and struck the college student in the face with his fist, thinking that the slacker hippy had pulled his friend to the ground. Other college students immediately converged and retaliated and the melee quickly escalated beyond fists to include knives, sticks, and even the flag pole. The riot police moved in, but the battling crowds were much larger and not about to be cowed.

A shot rang out. Followed by another. Then another shot thundered. Suddenly, multiple guns were firing from different locations and people were being hit. The badly outnumbered police were caught in crossfire, being hit from both sides and were forced to withdraw.

Reports and images of the clash, along with pleas for help, went out via television, radio, internet, mobile phones, Facebook posts, Tweets, and Instagram. Both sides received reinforcements. But, the conservative Tea Party, Minutemen, and militia groups were slightly better organized and also better armed and soon they were winning the street battle while law enforcement struggled to muster sufficient manpower to regain control.

Meanwhile, a little over 100 miles away in Tucson, the opposite result had happened. Pima County had greater numbers of liberals, many of them minorities. They outnumbered the conservatives and gained the upper hand. The center of Arizona's two largest cities had joined its southern border area as battlefields.

The President ordered Army units from Fort Irwin, California and the Arizona Army National Guard to quell riots and institute "limited" martial law in Phoenix and Tucson and their suburbs. Arizona's Governor refused to accept the federal forces and declared that the Arizona National Guard and State Highway Patrol would resist any incursion by Federal Army units with force, even as some units were being deployed to restore order. The Arizona legislature called an emergency session and voted to nullify the President's order for martial law. They also voted to submit the issue of secession to the people of Arizona just as Montana had done. The President declared Montana and Arizona to be in rebellion and stated that this "current state of affairs will not be tolerated." Arizona deployed half of its National Guard forces to the northern part of its border with California, as well as its border with Nevada, to block the likeliest routes of advance of Federal Army units. The other half of its units continued the attempt to restore order in its cities and towns. Arizona's Governor sent her adjutant-general staff to the commander of Davis-Monthan Air Force Base in Tucson about the disposition of the three squadrons of A-10 Thunderbolt II ground attack fighters based there, as well as to Luke Air Force Base outside of Phoenix, with its 170 F-16 Fighting Falcons and 18 brand-new F-35 Lightning IIs. The messengers were accompanied by National Guard units to help with "ensuring the security" of such valuable national assets. The Air Force commanders, not sure of what to do, assured the Governor's representatives that they would keep an open dialogue and further assured them that the base's security forces were more than capable of keeping the base and all assets on it, safe. For their part, the representatives of the newly independent state of Arizona remained polite and dropped subtle hints that any attempt by the A-10s or any other aircraft to take-off might be met with .50 caliber rifle and light anti-tank missile fire from National Guard units stationed all around the base's perimeter, during their take-off roll. They also reminded the Air Force General that the F-16s of the Arizona Air National Guard were extremely close by at Tucson International Airport. The base commander, a native of Georgia, communicated the situation to the Pentagon and slightly exaggerated his inability to sortie his aircraft due to the disposition of the Arizona National Guard. Meanwhile, at Marine Corps Air Station (MCAS) Yuma, the situation was markedly different. The Colonel in command of the base tersely informed the Arizona National Guard officers that his personnel stood ready to respond to the President's orders regardless of the "current political climate in this state."

The Joint Chiefs engaged in fierce debate but ultimately did not wish to start a war by committing the Air Force and Marine security forces to a firefight with Arizona Guard units nor did they want A-10s, F-16s, F-35s, AV-8Bs or EC-130s blown up while attempting to take off. The Pentagon brass decided they needed further specific direction from the National Command Authority (the President and Secretary of Defense). Back in Arizona, an uncomfortable stand-off ensued at the federal military bases.

Watching the events all across the nation and the actions of the two break-away states, Oklahoma passed a declaration of solidarity with the "people of Montana and Arizona and all sovereign States of the United States of America." Then, Oklahoma scheduled its own vote of secession. The act of secession passed the Oklahoma House of Representatives 76-19 and passed the Oklahoma Senate by a count of 37-9. Within a week, the Governors of all three newly sovereign states were scheduled to meet in emergency session in Oklahoma City along with key legislative leaders and their adjutant general staffs. Ominously, the governors and key staff from four other states also signaled their intention to attend the meeting.

Phoenix, Arizona, the Governor's Residence

Sara Doucet decided to take a break from reading emails and leaned back in her executive chair. "I do love this chair," she thought to herself. In her opinion, it was an extravagantly expensive chair. But, she had bought in on EBay for a fraction of its worth and considered it one of her best purchases ever.

"Why am I thinking about such silliness when the entire world is going crazy all around me?" she chided herself. "Come on, Sara. Focus!" She was beyond tired. It was almost midnight and now her thoughts were drifting off to her fantastic bed. Her bed was another extravagantly expensive piece of furniture, but one bought at full retail price. "And worth every darn penny!" she thought again to herself while smiling. The thought of sweet repose after such a long day almost overpowering. And then her mind focused again on the upcoming conference. What would the other governors and she do about the rapidly deteriorating relationship with Washington? Would her counterparts be open to negotiations with the president? She knew she certainly was, but she also was not about to give up Arizona's sovereignty in the face of international and domestic pressure. Federal martial law was not the answer, whether the feds slapped the "limited" moniker on it or not. She was definitely not looking for a fight with the feds although the mainstream media was certainly making it look that way.

She thought about the latest text from her old flame, Jake, and smiled again. Then, she thought about Tom. The smile drained from her face. Tom. She hadn't called him back. She was sure he only wanted to wish her well on her trip, but the guilt of her ongoing thing with Jake was growing heavier around her neck. And a thing was all she called it. It wasn't an affair. An affair wasn't conducted entirely through email and phone conversations and text. They had only been physically together twice, both times over dinner when he flew out from Washington. One dinner was in public and the second one in private. Nothing had happened. At least, nothing had happened physically beyond hugs of greeting and parting. But something had definitely happened mentally and emotionally. She was taken by surprise at the butterflies in her stomach on her way to the first dinner with him. It was just like being in college so many years before. The mere thought of a message from him or the prospect of hearing his voice was enough to give her that tingling feeling all through her body. She was a school girl all over again. Amazing!

The sing-song ring tone of her mobile phone chased away her sweet daydream. It had to be Tom. A quick glance at her smart phone confirmed that it was indeed her husband.

"Hi babe," she answered her phone more chipper than she felt. "How are you? How was your day?"

"It was fine, thanks. I'm still waiting for you to call me back after your meeting," Tom answered, sounding less disappointed than he felt.

"I know. I'm sorry, I've been quite busy," Sara replied, trying not to be or sound irritated.

"Uh, it's been four hours…" his voice trailed off. "Anyway, I just want to wish you a good trip and I know you will be leaving first thing in the morning and won't have time to talk tomorrow."

"Thanks, babe. I'm sure it will be interesting, if nothing else."

"Yes, well that is sort of the other thing I wanted to discuss with you, Sara."

"Oh. Tom, beating timidly around the bush is not at all like you. Out with it, babe. What's on your mind?"

"Sara, this conference, or whatever it's being called, may result in some sort of new or provisional government, is that right?" Tom asked.

"I don't know about that. We don't have a firm agenda beyond discussing a joint position and response to the feds threatening to arrest us and put down our so-called rebellion with force. I don't know how far beyond that it may go, honestly. Why?"

"I just want you to please remember our agreement. No job which takes you out of Arizona. And although the possibility of you going to D.C. now seems remote, it seems that some other role for you may emerge. And, this role may not be in Arizona, but somewhere else."

"Tom, I remember our agreement, of course. But I think you are getting way ahead of yourself. Or ourselves," Sara interrupted.

"OK, well whether now or later, I just can't support you taking a position that would take you away, out of Arizona. Two terms as governor. We agreed, OK?"

"Yes, I know we agreed, but like I said, I don't think anything like that is even in the discussion realm yet," Sara assured her husband.

"Well I'm glad babe. I miss you, doll. These years of separation have been hard on me. Harder than I thought. I wish I could be more supportive, but I miss you when we're not together. I miss you terribly. Anyway, have a great trip."

"Thank you too babe. I'll call you as soon as I get back," Sara said and blew him their customary kiss. Tom did the same and they hung up.

12

WASHINGTON, D.C., THE OVAL OFFICE

The President looked at his three closest advisors and shook his head. "Gentlemen, we simply cannot allow this. We have to do something." The statement hung in the air, more of a question than an affirmation of a belief. The tension was as palpable as the silence which ensued.

His chief advisor, Lee Andropolous, finally spoke. "Mr. President, we can't be rash. This is very serious, but we need to carefully consider our actions. I agree that we must act, but if we overreact, it may backfire in a big way. In a very big way."

"Worse than doing nothing? What can be worse than having *three* states trying to leave the Union? I feel like I'm personally reliving a bad dream which this nation has already lived," retorted the President.

"We need to be firm, without seeming to overstep the bounds of federal power. There's a middle road which can work. We can make them see what damage will be done to their citizens by their action while being very clear that we wish to negotiate a resolution by addressing their concerns. But to answer your question, what can be worse is *more* than three states seceding, which is very likely."

"I agree," the President stated, ignoring the last part of the statement. "We start with finances. People always care about their pocketbooks. We let them know that if federal tax revenue stops coming into Washington, D.C., all federal payments to the state and state residents will cease. We will also pull out all federal personnel assigned to those states. In short, we will cut all economic ties with these three states."

"All ties, Mr. President," questioned his Chief of Staff, Joel Miller? "We need to consider what this really means. For instance, does that include interstate commerce transactions?"

The President thought. "Yes, I think it does, doesn't it? Maybe we need to discuss this some more. Thoughts?"

"Hmmm...well, that's probably not going to help the economy at a time like this. It won't make the other states, which do lots of business with these three states very happy, but they are likely to blame the three errant states, rather than us," stated Andropolous.

"I'm not so sure about that. I think some people will blame the break-away states, but others may blame us. In any case, how do we treat trade with these three states? An embargo?" asked Miller.

"No, I don't think so. That is an overtly hostile act. And, besides, what would we do? Send troops to guard interstate crossings between states? No, I think we simply treat them as we would any other foreign trading partner. No special penalties or tariffs, but also no special treatment. They will have to apply to the WTO for accession, for instance," the President opined. "And, we should set up international crossing checkpoints."

"I don't know about *that*, Mr. President. Wouldn't that be a tacit recognition of their status as a sovereign state?" asked the chief of staff.

"So call it a security checkpoint. An agricultural checkpoint like California has had for decades. I don't care what you call it, but they lose the privilege of coming and going into and out of our nation whenever they wish," said the Chief Executive firmly.

"Understood, sir. And what do we do about the situation at the Air Force base in Tucson? Or the Marine Corps Air Station (MCAS) at Yuma? What about the Minuteman nuclear missiles in Montana, for that matter" asked Miller?

"We need to start moving military units out of these states immediately," answered the President without hesitation.

"Sir, the people in Arizona have basically told our commanders there that any aircraft attempting to take off without their authorization will be fired upon. Senator Kelly did communicate to us that he personally was opposed to Arizona's secession, but that his loyalty lay with his home state. He also informed us that Arizona is open to a dialogue about a fair and equitable disposition of the Federal military assets in the state," said Andropolous.

"Fair and equitable?" roared the President. He took a moment to calm down. "Oh, that is rich. All of that equipment belongs to the Federal Government. If they really mean to find a peaceful resolution, they will immediately allow all federal personnel and equipment to depart."

"While I agree that all of that equipment belongs to the Federal Government, to use as we see fit, it's probably not that simple. These state governments are going to be wary of any possible use of force against them, so they are unlikely to simply allow such valuable military hardware out of their control," Miller said. "Kelly made mention of returning most Federal hardware in response for a pledge to take no military action against Arizona or any other state. Besides, we've left those missiles in Montana alone for now. Why not do the same with Arizona?"

"Because, Joel," the President explained "planes that can be flown out of an area with minutes' notice is very different from missiles in silos in the ground. Besides, I don't think it likely that Montana would ever launch those missiles at us, but I *can* see those people in Arizona using our jets against us at some point."

"And don't forget that at least half of all military personnel, probably more, are from red states, many of which oppose us and what we are doing," added Andropolous.

"So?" asked the President.

"So some of those pilots might refuse an order to fly their jets out of Arizona, for instance."

"I'll have them arrested and court-martialed!"

"Really, Mr. President? And how exactly would you do that?" asked Andropolous.

"The base commander is still loyal and obeying orders, right" asked the President.

"Yes, sir, but for every pilot we arrest, it may mean one more fighter that can't be flown out," Andropolous explained.

"And consider this, gentlemen, even if we can manage to work something out so Arizona allows the planes to take off, there is nothing to guarantee that some of the pilots won't choose to fly their planes somewhere else. Just like pilots from the old communist bloc countries used to do when they would defect to the West," added Miller. "That's how the West got its first look at the Mig-25 Foxbat back in 1976."

"And what that Syrian did a while back," said the senior advisor. "Then there is the possibility of pilots turning on each other. A pilot loyal to us may decide to take matters into his own hands if he sees one of his comrades attempting to steal a U.S. Air Force A-10 or F-16."

"Right, we could have an aerial civil war in a flash," agreed the Chief of Staff.

"So what are you telling me," asked the President. "That we do nothing about the military people and equipment? That there's nothing we *can* do?"

"No sir, there's plenty we can do, but I'm saying we should not order any military unit within the three rogue states to move at this time," concluded Miller.

The Senior Advisor agreed with the Chief of Staff. "We need to leave them in place for now and aggressively pursue a resolution via dialogue."

The President walked to his desk and sat somewhat dejectedly. He hung his head in his hands. "So many unknowns. So many variables. How in the world am I supposed to know what to do? Now I really know how Abraham Lincoln felt," he said, without looking up.

"If it's any consolation, sir, you actually have a tougher situation than Lincoln in many ways. We aren't at war yet, and let's hope it never comes to that. But our world and nation are far more complex than in 1860. The first Civil War was about one issue, although it evolved from one issue to another issue, from states' rights to slavery. Today we have at least three major issues causing people to be frustrated and angry to the point of fighting. First are racial issues. We have to face the fact that much of the violence in the cities is blacks and Hispanics expressing their pent-up frustration. Then we have the Christian right and the Tea Partiers angry over 'losing their country', whatever the hell that means. We have both sides angry over immigration, the health care act, growth of government, etc. And, all of these issues are made worse by the explosion of media and communication. The speed and widespread dissemination of information can work for us or against us. We need to ensure that we control the narrative. So, bottom line, we need to consider how any action we do take will be viewed by the masses through that lens." Andropolous could always be counted on to consider and present every side of every issue. While at times helpful, it was also often counter-productive.

"Point taken," stated the President simply. "I will consider all rami-fications. But, I *do* want contingency plans on possible steps we can take with respect to our military equipment and personnel in these break-away states. And maybe on any other states we think may join this madness. Anything else?"

"Uh, Mr. President, I recommend we ask the Joint Chiefs to broaden their scope. I think we also need to consider steps to secure our energy and logistics infrastructure. And, I'm sure we're missing something else we should be considering. We should ask the Pentagon what else we should be concerned about," said Miller.

"Ok, get it done," said the President as he rose to leave.

The dominoes began to fall as the violence continued to spread across the nation and the Federal Government attempted to respond. Soon South Carolina, Alabama, Utah, Mississippi, Idaho, Wyoming, and North Dakota had also nullified federal orders for martial law, the international monetary acts, and draconian gun restrictions. As federal law enforcement in each of these states attempted to enforce federal orders they were met by state and local law enforcement, at times with force.

Within weeks, these state legislatures also voted for their residents to decide on secession and whether or not to join what was being called the Free States of America (FSA). Representatives of the ten states of the fledgling nation met in Salt Lake City and declared it and

Oklahoma City to be provisional, rotating capitals. The two capitals were chosen due to their relatively central geographic position among the states of the newly minted Free States of America. This, and the rotation, would help prevent the lawmakers of the new republic from becoming isolated as had those inside the Washington Beltway.

Salt Lake City, Utah, the Hilton Salt Lake City Center

Sara Doucet entered her suite, dropped her suit jacket on the luggage rack and collapsed on the bed. She immediately kicked off the black pumps and closed her eyes. Her mind was a whirling tornado of thoughts, questions, excitement, and dread.

"Wow," she thought to herself. "What a day! What a past few days! Events were accelerating faster than anyone could have imagined. And what events!"

She was literally participating in the birth of a new nation. She wondered how the delegates in Philadelphia felt in 1776. She knew much of what history recorded about those men and those days. But as always, there was much that history did not record, particularly about their feelings. How many of those men carried the burden of their personal relationships? History did record that almost all of the delegates were ultimately severely impacted by the revolution they birthed. History did record that fact, but most Americans didn't know it or care. What would she tell Tom? What about her "thing" with Jake? There was the contrast. Tom would be very upset about her news. Jake would be thrilled beyond words, just as she was. She didn't want to end her marriage with Tom, despite his indiscretions. But how could she pass up this opportunity? Being nominated for president? That alone was a once in a lifetime occurrence. But being nominated as the *first* president? That situation came along once in a hundred years or more. She could not possibly withdraw her name. She simply could not turn her back on the people of these states, and possibly other states later, at a time like this.

Maybe Tom would understand? These were extraordinary times. The agreement they made long ago was made under completely different circumstances. Tom would have to understand. And if he didn't, well then perhaps it was time their marriage ended. How could she possibly remain with a man so selfish as to ask her to pass up such a calling at a time like this and simply return home? No, she could not. Her kids were grown. She had to follow her calling. Wishing for more time to pray and seek the Lord's guidance, but knowing she had precious little time, she resolved to pray for thirty minutes and then call Tom.

The Utah House of Representatives, State Capitol Building, Salt Lake City

The assembled representatives of the ten break-away states had a long list of items to address. One of the first was the subject of a flag. Some of the men and women present argued that this was relatively insignificant and pointed out that the Second Continental Congress did not adopt an official flag. Others pointed out that these were different times. This was a visual age of 24 hour cable and internet news. Perception was reality, they argued, and the people would need clear visual cues to rally around if they were to garner support for the cause of a new nation. After a long and spirited debate, the delegates chose a design for the new national flag. Dozens of designs were submitted and voted on without a decision being reached. Many of the designs were variations of existing flags, while others were entirely new designs. Representatives from five of the states pushed for the Confederate flag or variations of it. Others thought it might be divisive and send the wrong message and was narrowly voted down. Other candidates included the yellow Gadsden flag with the coiled rattlesnake and "Don't Tread on Me" warning. Yet others included the Bonnie Blue flag with its single star or the U.S. Civil Flag with Old Glory's color palette reversed and the stripes vertical instead of horizontal.

In the end, it was decided that a flag would be used on an interim basis while a committee was formed to determine the best way to design the permanent flag of the Free States of America. The design chosen in the interim as the first flag of the Free States of America was an upside down Stars and Stripes with ten stars in a circle denoting the first ten states of the FSA. At the center of the circle of stars was a larger, single star, to serve as a stark visual reminder that the individual states were central to the new union.

Seeking to stay out of the rapidly expanding maelstrom, Vermont voted to declare itself a free and independent nation once again. The city council of Killington, Vermont, then voted to secede from their break-away state and petitioned to join New Hampshire and thus remain in the United States. New Hampshire approved and submitted the proposed annexation to the U.S. Congress.

In blinding speed, eleven states had formally severed their ties with the United States of America. The number was coincidentally the same number of states as had comprised the Confederacy during the first American Civil War. Whether or not any more states would join this time around, no one knew, but it would have enormous impact on whether a full scale war would erupt once again or whether such a catastrophe could be avoided somehow.

13

THE UTAH HOUSE OF REPRESENTATIVES, STATE CAPITOL BUILDING, SALT LAKE CITY

The newly elected President of the Free States of America (FSA) strode to the lectern looking serious, but trying to smile through her expression. The Chamber was packed with reporters in addition to the representatives of the ten states from the new American nation. Representatives of eight other states were in attendance as well, along with "unofficial" attendees from three more states.

The former governor wore a dark blue skirt suit with a prominent Arizona flag lapel pin. Sara Doucet arranged her notes and took another look around the chamber before beginning.

"My fellow Americans, I come to you on a solemn occasion. Representatives from ten American states that have seceded from the United States have met here in Salt Lake City to convene the Third Continental Congress. We have formed a new nation, the Free States of America. It is with heavy hearts and deep sadness that we have taken this action, to separate from our beloved country. But it has been with even deeper sadness that we have all watched our great and beloved nation slip further and further away from the cherished principles of our founding fathers, principles that they codified in the Declaration of Independence and the Constitution.

These great documents drew heavily from Judeo-Christian principles and formed the framework that allowed the fledgling United States to grow into a great, prosperous, and powerful nation. Indeed, the United States has been a blessing both to its own people and the people of the entire world. However, over the last 30-40 years, some would argue for much longer, as our leaders have gotten further and further away from the principles in the Declaration of Independence and the Constitution, the nation has lost its identity and become, primarily through the Federal Government, a burden to its own people. The Federal Government has bankrupted us, taking us from the largest creditor nation on the earth to the largest debtor nation in little more than a generation. Our most sacred institutions have been trampled. Never ending overseas wars have contributed to our economic problems and continued erosion of our national sovereignty. And now that Washington's failed foreign and economic policies have led to nationwide shortages of food, fuel, power, and healthcare in shambles, the federal puppet masters send in federal troops to kill and arrest its own citizens on a previously unimaginable scale. And when we, the people, attempt to defend ourselves, the corrupt politicians in Washington negotiate with foreign governments to bring foreign soldiers onto our American soil to help suppress Americans who are only looking for food to feed their children and fuel to heat their homes. No, my fellow Americans, the reality is that the fault lines underlying our society and present system have been rumbling for more than a generation.

Today, the people of the Free States of America state unequivocally, 'no more!' We will not submit to tyrants in Washington, D.C. nor from any foreign government. We will no longer stand idly by while our sacred God-given rights are ignored and trampled upon.

But, we wish to be clear. We do not want war or violence of any kind. We wish no harm to anyone, any group, or any nation, including our beloved United States. Yes, we all do still love the United States. We do, however, wish to be given the same right of self-determination which has become increasingly accepted. Since 1990, 34 new countries have been created and recognized around the world, including two former United States territories, Marshall Islands and Micronesia. Thirty-four countries in less than thirty years. We are the thirty-fifth. We strongly desire that the nations of the world, first and foremost the United States, will recognize our right to exist and our sovereignty. We see a future God willing, in the very near future where we can stand alongside the United States as close friends and allies, just as the United States has done with its mother country, the United Kingdom.

Once the United States has formally recognized our right to exist as a separate nation, we will eagerly enter into good faith negotiations to resolve all of the many complex questions that surround such a large and important move. And of course, we welcome the speedy establishment of diplomatic relations and uninterrupted trade with every nation of the world as soon they recognize our existence.

We call upon our brothers and sisters in the armed forces of the United States to honor their oath of office and refuse any order to take military action against the Free States of America. This humble request is not to be construed as a call for active rebellion against the United States or violence of any kind. We do not intend the destruction of the United States, but merely the restoration of its founding principles. Therefore, we do advocate peaceful civil disobedience and non-cooperation on any point in which a government acts contrary to the principles of the Constitution. If the citizens and citizen-soldiers of both nations will simply refuse to attack any other American for simply wishing to live free, we will yet avoid a second, horrible, civil war. However, we, the people, of the FSA, will resist any unauthorized incursion on the sovereign territory, airspace or waters of these Free States.

I leave you with the immortal words of President John F. Kennedy, 'Let every nation know, whether it wishes us well or ill, that we shall pay any price, bear any burden, meet any hardship, support any friend, oppose any foe, in order to assure the survival and the success of liberty.'

May God bless the United States of America *and* may God bless the Free States of America!"

The Oval Office, Washington, D.C.

"Mr. President, there was just a press conference out of Salt Lake City," breathed the Senior Advisor to the President as he rushed into the office.

"And, what's the word," asked the President, looking up from his desk.

"They've declared themselves the 'Free States of America.' Ten states made the declaration but as you know, representatives from several more attended. They also elected a president. It's Doucet."

"Is that so? Are they really that out of their *damn, fucking* minds? What are they thinking? What are they hoping to accomplish?" asked the President rhetorically.

"They also have declared *two* capitals; provisional, of course. And even have a new flag."

"Wonderful. A president and a new flag. *And,* they can't even *agree on a capital or...* " The President stopped himself. "I can't believe I'm having this conversation. This is simply *insane.* "

"That may be the case, sir, but what is the White House's position on all this? What is your position" asked Andropolous.

The President stood up and walked over to the window and looked out. "I don't know what my position is," he thought silently to himself. "This is all just crazy. This can't be allowed to happen. What *should* my position be?"

"Mr. President?" asked his advisor.

"I don't know," he said finally. "I just know this can't happen. They can't do this. No one can break up our country. The United States of America, for crying out loud. Abraham Lincoln was the last person in my situation. He didn't allow this to happen and we can't either, can we?"

"All due respect..." Andropolous started.

"Oh cut the crap Lee," the President cut him off. "Talk to me, it's just the two of us. I need to know what you think. I need to talk this out. I need to figure out what I think and what to do."

"Ok, then you need to wake up, sir," said Andropolous with an edge. "This ostrich in the sand bit is not helpful and won't solve this problem. You need to stop acting like ignoring this or speaking of it dismissively will just make it go away. You keep hoping that 'these people,' as you call them, will eventually come to their senses. Maybe you need to realize that they are in *their* senses. Their senses, not ours. Just because we would never act in this way does not mean that they can't or won't. They went through the trouble of introducing secession in their legislatures, debating it, voting on it, and then sending it to their citizens. They have formed a Continental Congress for crying out loud. This has not been done on a whim. We may completely disagree with them, but they have put much thought and effort into this. Do they know all of the ramifications of what they've done? Do *we?* Probably not. Almost certainly not. But nevertheless, it is what it is and we need to deal with it. Beginning with you."

The President's mouth was visibly agape. Frustration and shock rippled across his face. "War?" he demanded. "Is this what you are suggesting? Is this how I should deal with it?"

"No, I'm not suggesting war. Yet," Responded Andropolous. "What I am suggesting is that we need to consider it a possibility. There will not be an easy or painless solution. We need to take decisive action but we need to consider a wide range, the entire range of options."

"We can't go to war over this. We need to do something, yes, but not that."

"Sir, I'm not saying *we begin* a war. I'm not suggesting that we invade Arizona or Oklahoma or Utah. But we must consider the possibility that they won't return by simply waiting them out. Their statement was very clear about not wanting war and spoke very positively about us. But, what if other states secede and join and then they decide they will go to war against us? What about all of the tax revenue we'll be giving up? What about all of the military equipment in the states which have left or may leave," asked Andropolous.

"I see what you mean. Lots of questions. For the tax revenue, I suppose it's relatively simple. Any state that stops sending tax revenue to us will receive no federal funds of any kind. The military equipment is a far more complex question. What do you think? Any suggestions," the President asked his advisor.

Andropolous thought. "Rather than deal with the theoretical and generalities, let's think about what we are actually dealing with. Montana has 150 Minuteman ICBMs, each with three nuclear warheads. North Dakota has another 150 Minutemen at Minot Air Force Base along with over 20 of our B-52s. This is two-thirds of the ICBM force and almost half of the B-52s. And, North Dakota is the second largest oil producing state. Arizona has Davis-Monthan Air Force Base, Luke Air Force Base and MCAS Yuma. Oklahoma has the Army's artillery center at Fort Sill, as well as Tinker Air Force Base. Are we prepared to surrender control of all of these national assets to this group?"

"No, I'm not," the President said firmly.

"Then these are the sorts of issues we need to address," said the Chief of Staff.

"Alright. And where is General Grissom's contingency plan," asked the President. "I want to consider all options, including flexing a little muscle to send those cowboys a message."

"Yes, sir. Of course."

"Oh, and Lee, one more thing. I want to know everything about the rogue leadership, starting with Doucet. And I do mean everything."

14

AUSTIN, TEXAS, THE STATE CAPITOL

Rep. Roscoe Jenkins ran his hand through his ruddy hair. The three term state representative from the Fourth District of Texas did not feel well. His head hurt and he was nauseous. He had never imagined that it would come to this. He never imagined that he would someday be voting on how to react to states seceding from the Union. While he had long supported turning back the ever growing tentacles of the Federal Government monster in Washington, he did not support doing it through secession, especially when it looked more and more like it would be followed by all-out war.

"Texas cannot secede from the Union. It's as simple as that," said the committee chair, Ron Yorona, the State Senator whose district included Austin. People mistakenly believe that Texas' right to secession is guaranteed by the agreement when we joined the US, but that is wrong. All it says is that we can break up into as many as five states if we ever choose to."

"We are not going to break up Texas!" intoned the state representative from Lubbock.

"I wasn't suggesting that at all. Just pointing out that we can't secede," replied Yorona.

"Eleven states already have," groaned Jenkins. "And isn't this exactly what the thirteen colonies did when we fought the Revolution? Besides, most of our constituents throughout the state believe we can. Many think we should. We have protests in practically every city and town against the bailouts and martial law, not to mention giving away American sovereignty to the U.N., IMF, Chinese, Europeans, etc.,. Violence is spreading. Our job is to figure out how we best serve them."

"But also remember that the New York, Illinois, Massachussetts, and Maryland legislatures have just passed resolutions turning over their National Guard units to the feds, have called for volunteers and are calling for UN and NATO troops to assist the U.S. in putting down this rebellion and restoring 'global economic order.' Thank God the President declined to call for UN and NATO troops," concluded Yorona.

"But our imperious leader added 'at this time' to his declination," snorted the representative from Lubbock. "And he did accept 'advisors'. That doesn't exactly give me a feeling of comfort going forward."

"What if we try and take a middle ground. A strong middle ground. Instead of introducing secession, what if we introduce a Resolution of Sovereignty under the Tenth Amendment? We can also include a resolution to nullify the International Monetary Stability Act. And then, we can really warn off Washington with a resolution that *no* oil, natural gas, or refined petroleum product will be sold to *any* federal agency so long as federal troops are enforcing martial law anywhere without the consent of the governor of the state. We will also not sell to any state that is collaborating with the Federal Government on martial law or the curtailing of the rights of citizens" asked Jenkins.

"That is a middle ground?" groaned Yorona. "How is that a middle ground? Why do we have to do anything concerning Washington at this point? Don't we have enough issues with the economic collapse and food and race riots?"

"If we do nothing, it's a tacit endorsement of the failed policies of the Feds. Some would say unconstitutional policies. Not to mention a rejection of the actions of the FSA states," responded Jenkins.

After considerable further debate, the joint committee of the Texas Senate and House of Representatives passed the measure by a vote of 6-4. The following day, in an emergency session called by the Texas Governor, the measure passed both legislative houses in Austin. A very similar measure passed both houses in the Louisiana state capitol of Baton Rouge as well. Texas and Louisiana had thrown down a joint gauntlet and it was now up to the Federal Government to decide how to react.

The Oval Office, the White House

"Mr. President, we *simply cannot lose Texas.*" Normally, no one spoke to the President so bluntly. The President prided himself on having an open mind and always encouraging conversation on every issue. However, deviation too far from his known biases could at times be hazardous to a career. But these were far from normal times, and the National Security Advisor knew something had to be done. And fast. "Texas is the second largest population and economy of any state, but they're more than that. It is the top oil and natural gas producing state *and* they refine a *quarter* of all the oil in the entire nation. More of our military is based there than anywhere else. Fort Hood and Fort Bliss are the two biggest Army bases and they are *both* in Texas."

"Lose Texas? What exactly does that mean? We can't lose a state. Any state. This is all just madness. And temporary, I'm sure. Like a drunken sailor's haze, this will all wear off soon," the President explained. "Let me tell you, when they need our money, they'll be back. They will have never truly left."

"With all due respect, Mr. President, we have *already lost eleven states...*" The coincidence of the number being the same as the number of Confederate states was not lost on the President's Advisor.

"Texas won't leave. They may talk a big game, like their governor a while back, but that's all it is. Texans puffing out their chest. Everything's bigger in Texas and all that crap. But, deep down, they're not like the other states that are trying to leave."

"What do you mean they're not? How?"

"Well, they're not...they're more...rational. More...sophisticated. Wyoming, Oklahoma, and South Carolina are one thing. But Texas? Dallas? Houston? Big, cosmopolitan cities with educated people. They don't really believe they can do this. They can't possibly. Besides, they aren't discussing secession, are they?"

"Mr. President, I disagree. They may have taken a bit longer than the other states to move, but don't mistake their deliberate nature as lacking resolve or calculation. I think they *believe* they are the key, and they may be right. I think this is a test. They want to see how we react. And our reaction will determine if they vote on secession."

"Right?! Right?! How can they *POSSIBLY* be right?" asked the President, his voice rising.

"No, not right to secede. Or even to consider it. But they may be the key to getting the other states back quickly, if at all."

"You can't be serious," retorted the President.

"Oh, I am. Louisiana will definitely follow Texas if they leave. They already issued that joint "no oil or gas sale for aggression against citizens" proclamation. Arkansas will almost certainly follow, and who knows about Missouri, Georgia, and several other red states. And Virginia and North Carolina are considering joining this madness. Florida may even go. Texas will solidify the legitimacy of the FSA and may prompt 2 or 3 of more states to leave us as well. Maybe more."

"Don't use that term!" Do not dignify these rogue states by calling them the FSA or *any* States of America. There is *ONLY* the United States of America. And, as for Florida, there are mass protests in the streets of Miami and throughout South Florida demanding that the state affirm it's loyalty to us!"

"Yes, this is true, but we believe that is the minority opinion in that state. There are also protests in Tallahassee, Jacksonville, Tampa, St. Petersburg and numerous other cities demanding that Florida either declare sovereignty or outright secede. They may well declare neutrality or decide to go it alone like Washington state is considering and Vermont has already done," stated the National Security Advisor.

"States can't leave. The Civil War settled that question," said the President, mostly to himself. "If nothing else, we know that a few states can't stand against the entire nation, can they?"

"Mr. President, this is not 1861. This is not 11 states against 23 with the Union having great advantage in population and industry. Twenty million people versus 9 million; 4 million of which were slaves. If we aren't careful, we can easily be facing 20 or 21 states leaving and taking with them almost as much population and economic and military strength as in the remaining states. And more states may declare themselves to be independent. As costly and messy as the first Civil War was, despite the North's overwhelming advantages, I believe this may be much, much worse if full blown war can't be avoided. Think the Yugoslav civil war in the Balkans in the 90s, or the Chechen rebels with the Russians. Which, by the way, is a good lesson relative to your question regarding whether a few states can stand against many. In any case, even people who don't want to will be forced to choose sides. And I don't even think we *know* all the sides yet."

15

FORT BLISS, TEXAS,

1ˢᵀ ARMORED DIVISION

HEADQUARTERS

"That equipment belongs to the *Federal Government of the United States* and is under the command of the Commander-in-Chief. That's what the *Constitution says!*" thundered the base Executive Officer (X0), a huge, strapping colonel from New Jersey, to his old friend and boss.

"Paul, you know as well as I do that those *folks* in Washington have not even pretended to follow the Constitution for decades. *We* have discussed this at both of our houses over beers and barbecue on many occasions. What in the Constitution authorizes the Federal Reserve or the huge role it plays in our economy? What authorizes the Patriot Act or big business bailouts? What authorizes the Department of Education, for that matter, or literally hundreds of other regulatory agencies that have been created at the whim of the Washington establishment? Yet, securing the border, which *IS* expressly called for, is not only ignored, but states like Arizona and Georgia are attacked, literally sued in court, by the Federal Government for trying to do so" Major General Parker replied, in an even, reasonable voice.

"It's not perfect, I know," retorted Colonel Antonacci, "but it's our system. It's what we got."

"So, El Paso - Aztlan seceding from Texas is ok, but not Texas or other states seceding from the US?" questioned Parker.

"No, it's not right for *anyone* to secede. The Civil War decided that. But at least the people here in El Paso are only threatening to secede from Texas if Texas first secedes from the US. Totally different."

"Did it? Did the Civil War decide it? If the South had somehow won, or if the North had just tired of the fighting and bloodshed, would that then, and now, mean that secession is legal? Isn't that more of a 'might makes right' view? And isn't it the liberals who decry secession and advocate for the use of force to stop it today but also vehemently oppose the use of force in most other situations? In any case, that *too* can be debated until the end of time, but the question is, what do we do now? What do we do if Texas secedes, which I think they almost certainly will? Most of the men from the FSA states will not simply abandon their equipment and leave, and neither will most of the men from the US states. You've already seen the tensions. Fights in the barracks. Knifing and clubbing one another over political arguments. Black gangs, white gangs, Hispanic gangs, and even Asian gangs. Our personnel have already largely divided themselves along blue and red lines depending on their home states. How do we avoid a miniature civil war right here, on *our* base?"

"Well… every person must be able to decide for themselves? Is that what you are saying? That each man and woman can choose what 'side' they are on and if they want to leave. That's an interesting academic exercise, but in reality the equipment belongs to the government," said Antonacci after some thought.

"*WHICH* government? I thought the people are the government. Did the people create the government or did the government create the people? Isn't it 'Of the people, *by the people…?*'" questioned the General. "The way I see it, the equipment belongs to the people. It belongs to the American taxpayer who paid for it."

"So what do you suggest? Should we divy up all of the base's equipment by 300 million, give or take, and send every household in America pieces of Bradleys, Abrams, Blackhawks, missiles and rifles?" asked Antonacci sarcastically.

"Don't be silly."

"Silly? I'm being silly? We are attempting to have a rational discussion about a new Civil War, for Christ's sake! Silly would be good. This is madness."

"I agree, but we have to do something. Most of the men feel that the split is going to be permanent in some fashion and many feel open, all-out warfare is coming. They feel the need to be close to home and family. We will lose cohesion quickly and they will begin to melt away if we don't come up with *some* course of action."

Antonacci thought long. "Well, if you insist on splitting up the equipment, why not just split it in half? Like when we were kids on the playground. Make it fair."

"Won't work. It's a numbers thing," said the General.

"Huh?"

"We both know that at least 60% of the men will choose the "red" states, including FSA, because that's where they are from. Maybe 65%. Do you really want them squaring off against the other 40% with 120 mm tank guns and artillery? Not to mention that equipment requires personnel to operate it. What are you going to do? Are you going to ask some guys from Georgia or Tennessee to please drive their tanks across the state line to New Mexico and then leave them there so they can later be used against their homes and families? That won't work. The men won't go for that. But, I don't think the men from the red states would begrudge their buddies or former buddies a means to travel out of this place and defend themselves. The ones loyal to USA won't like it, but will accept the compromise."

"I don't know. I certainly do not like it." The Colonel was not convinced.

"And if El Paso votes to secede from Texas, we will propose to the city government of El Paso that we will take those soldiers who wish to leave, along with our equipment. In return for a guarantee of safe passage, we will leave them with 10% of all of our equipment so they can have their 'self-defense' force," General Parker said to his old friend.

"Why do you think we need to ask for safe passage? You think they would try and stop us from leaving?" asked Antonacci. "The leaders aren't stupid. They know they can't hope to match our firepower."

The General looked around the room in exasperation. "I don't know. I always prided myself on reading and understanding people, but it seems that lately, I just don't know what *anyone* might do. We know that in other places, civilians, especially crime gangs, are openly targeting law enforcement and National Guard units. As for the leaders, if they remain loyal to the USA, they may see it as their duty to try and keep us from leaving and taking US soldiers and equipment. And no, they wouldn't try and match our firepower. But they can try and hurt us with IED's, booby traps, ambushes on thin skinned vehicles and soft targets. I just don't know what may happen, but I think we need to communicate with the local leaders about their intentions and ours."

USS George H.W. Bush (CVN-77) in the Western Atlantic

Aboard the Nimitz class aircraft carrier *USS George H.W. Bush* (CVN-77) in the Western Atlantic, news of the two successful attacks on the *Abraham Lincoln* and her subsequent loss were met with stunned disbelief. The continuing riots and secession of the eleven states increased the initial disbelief. The wonders of modern communications allowed the sailors aboard "The *Avenger*," as the ship was affectionately known, to be instantly connected back home and around the world. Nevertheless, being at sea and far from home always imparted a sort of surreal, suspended reality. Thus, it was easy to believe that the chaos being reported from America was somehow exaggerated, or, at least a relative few, disconnected events.

This was far from the case. That very day, the legislature of the state of Virgina, which happened to be the location of their base in Norfolk, was also debating articles of secession. Although Virginia is the state most closely associated with the Confederacy, it was, in fact, only the 8th of the 11 states to secede. It did indeed see the most fighting, and perhaps the greatest devastation of any of the states, although Georgians would argue that point.

Virginia, like many states, had a split political personality. It voted narrowly for the democratic candidate in the presidential election of 2008 and 2012, after having been solidly "red" since the 1968 election.

The northern part of the large state included some of the affluent and very rapidly growing suburbs of Washington, D.C. The dramatic growth of Federal government spending and programs had led to a huge influx of government workers to the area. The other major metro area in the state, the Virginia Beach-Norfolk-Newport News area known as "Hampton Roads" to locals, housed the massive Norfolk Naval Station, as well as Langley Air Force Base. This area had a huge military and ex-military presence, along with a large retiree population and was largely "red" conservative, as were most of the rural western parts of the state.

The ship's CO was Captain Veronica "Archie" Anderson. A Naval Aviator and Naval Academy graduate, Anderson was a petite brunette and all of 5'2" tall, but also all business. And she knew her business. After leading her crew on an initial seven month deployment in the Indian Ocean and Persian Gulf area, she was not about to allow her 5,600 man (person!) crew and air wing to come unraveled now, so close to home. "But if Virginia goes mad along with the other states, do we still have a home?" she thought to herself. Her home was actually western Wisconsin. She was a Midwest farm girl who dreamt of seeing the ocean and sailing off to exotic ports while flying really, really fast jets.

"I will sail this ship to Philadelphia or New York if those on the lunatic fringe succeed in Richmond," she contemplated. "But what will the Admiral do? And what of the other ships in the battle group?" she thought to herself.

Anderson was the Captain of her ship, but her ship was only one ship of eight in the strike group. And her boss, the Admiral in command of the entire group, was a wild card. She would have to raise the possibility of Virginia secession and their subsequent course of action, with him and she did not relish the conversation.

16

THE WHITE HOUSE SITUATION ROOM, WASHINGTON, D.C.

General Grissom, the Commanding General of the U.S. Army, stood up and walked to the lectern. He motioned to the Major serving as his orderly to begin the PowerPoint. Grissom, like many senior officers, utterly hated PowerPoint. But, PowerPoint was the true language of all who served in the Pentagon.

"Good morning, Mr. President, ladies and gentlemen. I would first like to say, with all due respect, that as you all well know, the decision to use military force is a political, and hence, a civilian decision. My staff and I have prepared these contingency plans to the best of our ability, but my presentation here today does not constitute an endorsement of the use of military force.

We have prepared three scenarios, based on an escalating application of force, and on size of personnel to carry out. However, in all three scenarios, the objectives are of the same type. To deny the break-away states three things:

1. Access to military power, namely military bases, assets, and equipment that belong to the national government
2. Access to energy supplies and infrastructure
3. Free transportation of goods, i.e. interdiction of commerce

My staff and I began with a threat assessment to determine the greatest threats from the break-away states and how to neutralize the same.

The first scenario entails dropping a regiment of the 82nd Airborne on Minot Air Force Base, North Dakota, one regiment on Davis-Monthan Air Force Base in Arizona, and another right next door on Luke Air Force Base. Reinforcing these garrisons allows us to ensure control of the nuclear armed ICBM's and B-52s at Minot and similarly ensures we control the air wings at Davis-Monthan and Luke, as well as cut-off Phoenix and the rest of Arizona from Texas, should Texas decide to secede. In addition, it sends a clear message that we will not simply abandon our garrisons, bases, and equipment.

For the second scenario, we also drop a regiment on Mobile, Alabama to secure the naval base and port there and airlift a regiment to Mountain Home Air Force Base in Idaho to ensure control of the F-15Es stationed there. We can also drop a Ranger battalion on Tinker Air Force base in Oklahoma to secure the E-3 Sentry aircraft there. Controlling Mobile provides a base to split Texas from Florida, should that become desirable. We also drop a battalion on Hill Air Force Base north of Salt Lake City to secure the F-16 Fighter Wing stationed there and then reinforce by flying in the rest of the regiment. Same message as scenario two, but on a larger scale.

In the third scenario, we utilize two additional regiments of the 82nd to secure the Strategic Petroleum Reserves in Texas and Louisiana. We also utilize the 101st Airborne to isolate and cut-off Charleston and secure Shaw Air Force Base in South Carolina." The General concluded his briefing and looked around the room with a grave expression as he waited for the questions sure to come.

Jack Darden, the President's National Security Advisor, was the first to speak. "Interesting and also troubling presentation, General. Thank you. Aren't all of these scenarios a massive escalation of military force and inviting similar massive escalation of violence? You also seem to be going way beyond pacifying the cities with the riots. Why, for instance, are you moving units into Texas and Louisiana, even though neither has seceded?"

"Mr. Darden," the General stood up and straightened his uniform, "the President asked me for scenarios on the use of military force against the seceding states. If all he wanted was to move ground units of National Guard into the cities, there's no need for my staff and I to develop those plans. I developed these plans based on the objectives that I outlined at the start of the briefing. Furthermore, the overall strategic objective, as I understand it, is to stop this secession movement dead in its tracks. This means cutting off the ability of those states that have already seceded from hurting us militarily and also stopping any other states from following in or even considering this madness."

"And what of the possible consequences?" asked the President. "How might these states respond?"

"Great question," chimed in Joel Miller. "And I'm no military expert, but don't we run the risk of having these airborne units surrounded by hostile state and local ground forces if we drop them in like you describe? In other words, why are you only proposing to use airborne units?"

The General looked around the room, studying the faces of the civilians, trying to gauge the overall mood. What he saw caused the pit of his stomach to tighten. They were not grasping the potential consequences of what they were discussing. He drew a breath and begin to answer the questions. "The states, particularly Texas and Louisiana will almost certainly respond in a very negative way. In my opinion, they will secede and mobilize all available military force against us…"

"Then why are you suggesting this course of action, General?" the President interrupted forcefully.

"Timing. As we have seen with the eleven states that have already declared secession, once a state breaks away, it is almost too late to secure assets within their territory. For instance, if we wait until Texas and Louisiana secede, we will lose our best chance to secure the Strategic Petroleum Reserves. And this provides an excellent segue to answer the next question. Airborne units are best used for surprise *and* only when they can be re-supplied within 48 hours and reinforced within 96 hours or they do run the risk of being overrun. The airfields can be reinforced by flying in additional forces, including Strykers, Bradleys, and even a few Abrams tanks. The operations into Arizona can be reinforced with Army and Marine units from California, while the ones close to coasts like Charleston and Mobile can be reinforced from naval forces and Marines. But these are high risk operations. We don't fully know the level of the armed response or how quickly it will come together. If we can't or won't get reinforcement to these advance units, they may be in trouble. The only other alternative would be to move combat forces on the ground and this would take days to weeks at best."

"That's not very reassuring," said Darden.

"No, it's not, sir, but I'm not here to be reassuring. I'm giving it to you straight. And there's another wildcard. We don't know the loyalty and reliability of *any* of our units."

"You mean within the seceding states, of course," asked the President.

"No sir, I mean any of our units. We saw it first in California and now spreading throughout the country. Men and women being ordered to move against civilians are starting to balk, and since then, it has become increasingly likely that such an order will lead to firing on civilians. If you were a trooper in the 82nd from Oklahoma or Arizona, would you board a plane to assault your home state? It appears many won't."

A thick quiet permeated the room. Most had not considered this possibility, or at least not as deeply as they should.

"So how do we know? When will we know," asked Miller with exasperation.

"We won't. Not until we give the order to move. But keep in mind, ladies and gentlemen, between 60 and 65% of all active duty personnel are from the red states and we just don't know how they will react."

"So what are you telling us?" asked the President. "That you gave us various scenarios that we can't *even* carry out?"

"No sir. The worst case scenario is that some percentage of some units, maybe as many as half in some units, will refuse orders to deploy against other Americans. So I suggest that we send out direction to our brigade and regimental commanders to ascertain the loyalty of the troops and then, if necessary, form hybrid units of loyal troops and carry out their mission. However, this may reduce our available strength by 20-30%, but that is simply my and my staff's best guess."

"Very well," said the President. "Thank you and your staff, General, for all your hard work. We will take your scenarios under consideration and decide on a course of action for our nation."

Fort Bragg, North Carolina

The alert for the 82nd Airborne Division, the "All Americans," came in from the Pentagon at 9:00 AM. At the staff briefing, the brigade commanders were given the usual orders for such an operation and one additional, strange, almost unbelievable one. Individual unit commanders down to squad level were to ascertain the loyalty of their highly trained and battle-hardened troops. Most of the troops had seen at least one combat tour in Iraq or Afghanistan, or both. The brigade and regimental commanders could scarcely believe that they were now obliged to question the loyalty of their men and women to the Stars and Stripes, the very banner under which most had fought and bled, and even watched friends die. But they knew these were extraordinary times, calling for such measures. The Division Executive Officer, XO, advocated for placing those "disloyal rebel sons-of-bitches" under arrest and charging them with desertion or treason.

Once briefed, just slightly more than 40% of the troopers of the 82nd refused to participate in the mission against fellow Americans, especially when knowing that many civilians might be caught in the chaos and crossfire. And, many of those who did agree to carry out their mission did so knowing that they were no longer loyal to the National Command Authority who would issue such an egregious order. Some went along to ensure they were there to observe the true happenings and be a witness. Others went along to ensure they would be in position to defect and fight alongside those with whom they felt a stronger kinship than just a uniform in these trying times. Among those who refused the mission were two out of four Brigade Combat Team commanders, along with one deputy Brigade commander and ten regimental commanders or deputy regimental commanders.

Those remaining BCT and regimental commanders hastily organized the U.S.A. loyal troops into four smaller, reorganized Brigade Combat Teams and prepared to carry out their mission.

Immediately after the initial assembly and briefing, a young corporal from Arizona with Bravo Company, 3/504th knew he had to get word back home. He called his older brother back home, a former 82nd trooper himself and now a Sergeant with the Arizona Highway Patrol and a company commander with the Arizona Minutemen Militia. After a few inquiries on the well-being of the family, and sibling rivalry good-natured insults, the younger brother casually said that "he and his friends were coming for a visit real soon." Knowing the pervasive scope of big government eavesdropping on every manner of electronic communication, the "visit" phrase and others like it had been pre-set by militia commanders always on the look-out for insider connections with Federal military forces. The older brother immediately notified his superiors in the militia and the Highway Patrol. Similar reports were received by relatives and friends in North Dakota, Alabama, and Idaho. However, the reports went both directions. Personnel at the Federal military installations loyal to the USA similarly phoned friends and family members back home to let them know that the FSA states knew an attack was imminent.

The notification reached the Arizona Adjutant General who notified all Arizona National Guard units to prepare to meet attacks at Davis-Monthan and Luke. The three squadrons of F-16C's and D's went on alert and put up two fighters to serve as a sort of airborne early warning (since Arizona had no E-3 Sentry Airborne Early Warning and Control (AWACS) aircraft) as well as Combat Air Patrol or CAP. Then the Adjutant General remembered that he was also supposed to notify the still-forming National Command Authority of the new nation located for the present in Oklahoma City.

Recognizing the multi-faceted threat, President Doucet conferred with her National Security Council and authorized placing all of the FSA military forces on alert. In Oklahoma, an E-3 Sentry was sent up to watch for the air armada of transports that would signal the coming airborne attacks. Another E-3 was also dispatched to provide watch on the approaches to North Dakota, Montana, Idaho, Wyoming and Utah. On the recommendation of the ranking Free States Air Force (FSAF) General, the President put in an urgent call to the governor of Virginia asking for his help in preventing, if possible, or at least limiting the F-22 Raptors from Langley Air Force base in lifting off to support the air armada tasked with transporting the airborne troops. The Virginia governor agreed to help this time, pending the action of the state legislature on secession. The governor called the commander of the 1st Fighter Wing at Langley, a colonel and himself a native Virginian, and passed along President Doucet's request.

The Colonel had already been agonizing over what he would do from the time the warning order to prepare for action had come in from the Pentagon. He had come to the hardest decision he had ever made in his life. He assembled all of his personnel in one of the large hangars and addressed them.

"My brothers and sisters in arms, we all share a common bond. The bond of love for our country manifested in a desire to serve our country. That is why each and every one of us is here in uniform today. As you all know, this is a time of severe crisis for our nation. Some of our countrymen have decided that they no longer wish to be bound to the central Federal Government of the United States and have acted on their convictions. Now, we have received an order from the Pentagon for us to participate in operations against our countrymen in their home states. I, like you, swore an oath to uphold and defend the Constitution of the United States, against all enemies, foreign and domestic. Incumbent on our oath of office is the obligation to refuse any and all unlawful orders. This order, to take action against Americans who only wish to exercise their right to self-determination, is, in my opinion, just such an unlawful order. I will not obey this order, nor will I ask any of you obey this order."

There were barely perceptible gasps and murmurs among the highly disciplined Air Force personnel. The Colonel waited for a moment as he scanned the sea of grim faces. And then he continued.

"I will not ask any of you to obey this order. However, neither will I prevent any of you from carrying out this order, should your conscience compel you to do so. This means that any action necessary to carry out this order will be carried out on a volunteer basis by each individual. Pilots wishing to fly this mission will coordinate with other volunteers to prepare themselves and the aircraft. Unfortunately, you only have a couple of hours to make your decision on this particular mission. You should be aware that the governor himself called me after receiving a call from the President of the Free States of America, President Doucet. President Doucet requested that no military force based in Virginia be used against the FSA. The governor agreed to relay the request to me but also made it clear that he would not couch the use of violence to prevent such military action on behalf of the USA. It is clear to me that Virginia will vote on secession very soon and you all know that a number of other states are likely to do the same. So, the time to make a decision is upon each and every one of us. May God be with us all."

17

READY ASSEMBLY AREA, POPE ARMY AIRFIELD, NORTH CAROLINA

As the sun began to set against the Western sky, the tarmac was alive with activity. The air was cool and crisp, a welcome respite from the usual oppressive heat and humidity. Row after row of paratrooper was preparing himself and his equipment on the "green ramp" for the upcoming combat jump. A long line of massive, dark grey C-17 cargo transports sat on the tarmac looking like menacing hunched back whales, waiting for the paratroopers to embark. Each could airlift and then airdrop 102 paratroopers and their equipment. Over 20 of the four-engine behemoths were present and more were en route.

The new cobbled together units lacked the cohesion of the previous ones and the men sought to re-assure themselves that they would remain combat effective. They also wondered what sort of resistance they would face from the Arizona Army National Guard, Air National Guard, Arizona militia, and perhaps even plain-old angry citizens. Citizens, after all, who had voted to secede peacefully and would now see their fellow Americans dropping from the sky as part of an armed invasion.

"Sarge, are we going to have close air support?" asked a seasoned corporal with two tours in Afghanistan. "That CAS is kinda nice to have."

"Yes, I know, Rodriguez, but the answer is I don't have the first damn clue what support of *any* kind we are going to have. I know the Air Force and Arizona Air Guard have lots of F-16s and lots of A-10s in the area, and even some F-35s. But we don't yet know if any will be in the air, and if they are flying, whether they will be shooting at us. Fun thought," replied the experienced NCO.

"But Sarge, doesn't the Air Force still control all of the best fighters? I mean, all of the new Raptors, right, so they can clear the sky of any rebel aircraft and make way for aircraft to support us?" responded Rodriguez quizzically.

"Yeah, I think we do still have the Raptors on our side but who can vouch for the loyalty of the individual pilots. Look at how many in our unit are refusing this fight. And what's with this "rebel aircraft" crap? Who says that those who may be fighting against us are rebels?" asked the sergeant.

"Well, isn't that what they are since they are trying to break away from us? That's what the redcoats called us during the revolution and also what the Confederates were called during the Civil War, right?"

The veteran sergeant straightened up and whistled. "Yeah, I suppose you may be right. Let's just pray that we don't get to the point where we are in open rebellion against our fellow Americans," said the older man.

"Isn't it kind of late for that, sarge? I mean, we're being sent into battle," Rodriguez pointed out.

"No, we're not being sent into battle. We are being sent to secure an objective. Mercifully there is no guarantee that the Arizonans or anyone else will choose to fire at us. God willing, cooler heads will prevail and the politicians can work out a peaceful way out of this mess." The older man paused. "Besides, I don't think any American will take to shooting at other Americans too easily. I know I sure don't want to."

Then the "saddle-up" order came down through the ranks and it was time for the men and women of the 82nd Airborne division to board their aircraft and begin their journey into the unknown.

One by one the massive aircraft started their four powerful jet engines until the roar was all that could be heard. Then they lumbered down the taxiway to await their turn for take-off. The first aircraft increased engine power and moved down the runway, picking up speed at a surprising rate for such a huge machine.

Soon the sky over western North Carolina was full of C-17 aircraft and the command and control circuits were full of radio traffic from Washington, D.C. to Salt Lake City and Phoenix and everywhere in between.

In Virginia, 23 F-22A Raptor air dominance fighters lifted off from Joint Base Langley-Eustis to escort the airborne operations against the break-away states.

E-3 Sentry AWACS aircraft operating out of Oklahoma and orbiting over northern Mississippi detected the aerial armada of C-17s and sent out the alert throughout the FSA network. The governors of Tennessee and Georgia sent urgent messages to Washington, D.C. stating that they did not grant over flight rights to the federal aircraft planning offensive operations against United States citizens.

South Carolina and Alabama scrambled their Air National Guard F-16 Vipers to intercept and hopefully turn back the transports. Much further west in Arizona, all of its F-16s and were also placed on alert.

The South Carolina Vipers taking off from McEntire Joint National Guard Base were only 160 miles southwest of the C-17s forming over Pope Army Airfield. They, unlike the Federal U.S.A.F. *had* been granted over flight rights by the governors of Tennessee and Kentucky and flew northwest toward the point where their state borders North Carolina and Georgia. Depending on the route taken by the C-17s carrying the U.S.A. paratroopers, the F-16s would continue northwest, crossing the western end of North Carolina and passing into eastern Tennessee if necessary, all the while seeking to maintain blocking positions on the westward path of the USA aircraft.

In Alabama, their F-16s headed north and slightly east toward the Tennessee border. Crossing into Tennessee from northern Alabama would also put these Vipers in position to block the westward advance of the C-17s.

Meanwhile, the F-22s had caught up with the lumbering transports due to their ability to fly at low supersonic speeds without using gas-guzzling afterburners. The Raptors were receiving tracking information from their own USA E-3 aircraft. Keeping their own radars off was crucial to maintaining the stealth of the F-22s. The two flights of South Carolina F-16s were now 70 miles away and still outside of the maximum range of the AMRAAM missiles carried by the Raptors but the aircraft were closing the distance at a combined speed of Mach 1.8. The FSA F-16s also carried the AMRAAM but USA Raptors still did not show up on the radars of the rebel E-3s. Each of the Raptor and Viper pilots gripped his or her controls and prayed that some way; somehow, they would not have to fire on their countrymen.

The White House Situation Room, Washington, D.C.

"Mr. President we must call off this operation," said Joel Miller urgently. "I've just been on the phone with the directors of the FBI and the CIA and the breakaway states are fully alerted and have deployed ground and air forces to counter our assault."

"We knew this might happen, Joel. General Grissom told us there was a very high chance that moles within our military would notify the criminal states," said the President, unimpressed.

"Knowing that the operation is happening is one thing. Knowing the exact time and fully mobilizing to meet it is something else entirely. And, the Texas governor just announced that we would not be allowed over flight rights and Tennessee, Missouri, Georgia and Kansas did the same shortly after. This means we will have to detour long to the north from the original flight path and go through Kentucky, Illinois, Iowa, and Nebraska, and then back south through Colorado. This will give the rogue state forces more time to prepare and even provide a fairly precise estimate of when our forces would be arriving on target," explained Miller impatiently.

"Over flight rights? Over flight rights? They can't deny us! Are you telling me that Texas or those other states would actively fire upon our military aircraft? Fire on *United States military aircraft?*" demanded the President, incredulously.

"No sir, I am not saying that. As with seemingly everything lately, I am saying we simply don't know what they might do. They might be bluffing. But we can't risk our transports being blasted out of the sky while fully loaded with paratroopers. Either way, this buys the rebels time."

"First of all, please do *not* refer to these rogue criminals as rebels. Second, what are you suggesting we do with this operation now?" asked the President.

"I think we need to call it off," said Miller.

"Call it off?"

"Yes. Call it off. Let's take a step back and think this through some more."

"You want to call this off? Mr. Hawk, law and order?" mocked the Commander-in-Chief. "I thought you wanted to move quickly and decisively and 'nip this in the bud.'"

"Not at the cost of a fiasco. Everything is changing so rapidly that we didn't anticipate having large numbers of moles within our forces being so willing to share information with the other side. Bottom line is that the rogue states are fully alerted and will have their fighters ready. And now, with these other states making noise about 'over flight rights' is a big operational change not in our favor," Miller explained more patiently now.

"They're bluffing," the President almost hissed. "Let me tell you something, they may be a bit crazy, maybe even a little too taken with their own grandstanding but even they understand what firing on our fighters would mean."

"Mr. President, with all due respect, I think you are right, for the most part. But things happen, especially when opposing forces come into close contact during a very tense situation. Things get out of hand quickly. This is often how wars start. Someone panics or is a rogue in the group and fires. Or even worse, someone thinks, truly *thinks* they are being fired upon and fires back, believing it is in self-defense. History is littered with such instances. The Boston Massacre before the Revolution. The Mexican-American War and the Spanish-American War. The Gulf of Tonkin incident before Vietnam. We don't want our transports and fighter escort facing off with fighters from the rogue states with pilots on *both* sides being jittery. All it takes is one twitchy trigger finger or, worse, a true believer in this new FSA cause."

The President sat silently, staring at his long-time confidant intently. "So call it off, huh? And if we do, then what? We simply cave in and allow the states to continue defying us? Submit to the far right lunatic fringe and their anachronistic view of our country? Preside over the break-up of the greatest nation the world has ever seen?"

Miller knew that the aircraft of the air armada was lifting off even as they debated their course of action and therefore time was short. He also knew he had to offer his Commander-in-Chief a viable alternative. Preferably two or three.

"Sir, I think we need to call this operation off and then take a moment to catch our breath and fully assess the situation. We can ask the Joint Chiefs for alternate plans. I'm no military expert, but I'm thinking surgical strikes. Maybe some special ops raids. Arrest some of their key leaders. Maybe arrest lots of them. Or, maybe a cyber-campaign to decapitate the leadership infrastructure and then economic sanctions. We have lots of options and we need to think through them and our objectives. But we need to call this operation off and do it now. The aircraft are in the air as we speak" insisted Miller with urgency.

"No," the President said decisively. "They are bluffing. General Grissom, what is your assessment of the military situation?"

"I'm not sure what you mean, Sir," responded the General matter-of-factly.

"Will these state air guard pilots fire upon US military aircraft? And if they do so, can we defeat them? Can this operation still succeed even if these…these pilots fire upon our forces?" the President struggled to find the right term for men and women whom he considered treasonous criminals.

"Mr. President I think the answer to that depends on what we do. I think if we continue this operation, the men and women of the FSA will fire upon our forces at *some point*. I don't know when that will be. I don't know if it will happen in the air. It may not happen until our paratroopers are on the ground, trying to secure the objectives assigned. It may not happen until days or weeks after our airborne have secured them. But I do think that sooner or later, our forces will come to be viewed as an invasion force, if not from the outset, and met with resistance."

A thick, pregnant silence ensued. The President looked around the room and then up at the ceiling. "How can you be so sure, general?"

"Because, sir," the general spoke in a low, concerned voice, "this is how I would react if our paratroopers were landing in my native Nebraska. This is how many, many of the people I know back home would react, Sir."

18

MUSKEGON, ILLINOIS

The non-descript house in the lower-middle class neighborhood had a brown suburban and an older white diesel dually parked in front. Inside, two militia battalion commanders and their subordinate company commanders met to discuss the dire situation of the nation. The battalion commander of the Illinois Unorganized Militia had never met any of his counter parts in the Illinois Sons of Liberty. In his opinion, the Sons were a bit too open about their views and activity. Captain Rick Weeden was a big believer in operational security (Op Sec) and secrecy. One of his men along with one from the Sons group was on security detail in the front and back of the house. A very discreet security detail.

Weeden's diminutive 5'6" frame belied tremendous physical fitness and strength. A two time Illinois state champion wrestler in high school, Weeden had gone on to wrestle at the University of Minnesota before going to BUD/S training and becoming a Navy SEAL. After only four years a back injury forced him out of the Teams and the Navy. He returned home and obtained a Ph.D. in business from the University of Illinois.

As the years passed, the ex-SEAL grew more and more disgusted with the direction of the nation he loved more than life itself, or even his own kids. After the election of 2008, he struggled with his faith and the direction he knew his beloved nation was taking. His parents had been staunch, working class Democrats. But in college he had come to believe Ronald Reagan's words, "I did not leave the Democrat Party. The Democrat Party left me." He couldn't bring himself to fly the Stars and Stripes for months after. He started to think to himself that he had to do something. He would not let his precious nation go. At least, not without a fight. "But how can I fight this," he thought? "What can one man do?" So, the first thing he did was he started looking for like-minded people. They weren't very hard to find.

He'd heard of the militias, of course, but half-believed the mainstream media's depiction of them as right-wing wackos. He thought he must even know some, given the time he spent at the gun ranges, gun shows, hunting, etc. The ex-SEAL discreetly began to ask around and even look online for militia groups in his area. In time, he found one he felt comfortable with and began to train with them, without fully integrating into their organization. He had to ensure they were a good group and didn't have any anti-government or unstable, Timothy McVeigh types. He simply wanted to be affiliated with a strong, self-sufficient group when the increasingly inevitable economic and societal collapse came.

With time, he regained some optimism. The socialist or at least socialist-leaning policies like universal healthcare were not fixing the economy and making the US and the world in general, a worse place. Surely now, he thought, my fellow countrymen are awake. Or, at least, enough of them are awake to vote out the President and reverse course. The reelection of the President crushed him like it did millions and millions of Americans. And yet, this was a democracy, or rather, a constitutional republic he reminded himself, and the people had spoken. The President won fair and square. The nation had chosen its course.

But now, with the Middle East war, oil and food shortages, economic collapse and exploding unrest at home, it seemed like the right time to act. So, when the Sons of Liberty reached out for a meeting, the Unorganized Illinois Militia responded and sent Weeden, their most respected, if not the most senior, militia officer.

As Capt. Weeden entered the small living room, his attention immediately went to the TV screen. The Fox News reporter was describing how transport after transport was taking off from Pope Army Airfield in North Carolina carrying thousands of airborne troops to points west and southwest in the break-away states. The young, good looking reporter was using the term "rebel" for the Free States of America as he described the impending battle or battles.

"That's right, Jane, I have counted over 20 transports taking off and there seems to be no let up. I'm told each of the giant, gray transports can carry over 100 paratroopers and their equipment. Officials will not say where all these soldiers are headed and will only say they are being sent on security operations. But, speculation is rife all over the blogshere and social media that these soldiers are headed to Arizona, Montana, North Dakota, and possibly, Alabama. And, of course, this means that the military forces of those states, that is, the military of the rebel Free States of America is fully alerted and hence, a battle or battles are likely to ensue."

Weeden looked to his counterpart from the Sons of Liberty. The other militia commander, clad in a dark jogging suit, rose to his full height of 5'11" and extended his hand to Weeden with respect.

"It's a pleasure to finally meet you. I've heard a lot about you. And, I trust that at least *some* of it is true."

Weeden smiled and said, "Thanks, so do I. Not to be rude, but we should get started in the interest of time. I believe the time for cooperation or at least coordinated action, has come."

Both men walked into the kitchen and sat down at the table to discuss how their two groups might collaborate, but without sacrificing OPSEC. Both men were well aware of the FBI, DHS, BATF, and other federal law enforcement's years long efforts to infiltrate and compromise militias around the US, not to mention the efforts of the left-wing media and organizations such as the Southern Poverty Law Center to discredit militias as racist, backward, right-wing crazies.

After a surprisingly brief 50 minute conversation, a loose framework for coordinated operations had been reached. Each group would give the other at least 24 hours' notice of a planned operation. The notice would include the approximate location, within a 10 mile radius and the time, or H-Hour, plus or minus four hours. The other group would attempt, to the best of its ability, to launch an operation at least 10 miles away and within two hours of the first operation. But, with no one person in either organization knowing the details of the other organization's operations, if either organization was compromised by informants or an arrest, the other would be untouched. In this manner, law enforcement and federal military assets would be stretched thin and kept constantly off balance. The area of operations centered on the Chicago metro area and extended for a 100 mile radius all around. The first target would require coordination with the Indiana militia because it would be the oil refinery in Whiting, Indiana. The oil refinery, owned by BP, was the largest refinery in the region and the sixth largest in the United States.

Further degradation of the oil supply in the region would likewise degrade the ability of the state and Federal Government to maintain control. Their oppressive, unconstitutional control over the people, as the militia groups and their rapidly growing ranks of sympathizers saw it, would be greatly affected.

As the two militia commanders parted ways, Weeden shook his counterpart's hand and said, "God speed and God bless."

"Yes, may God be with us all and with our nation," the other man responded.

The skies over western North Carolina along the Tennessee border

The 23 F-22A Raptors from the 27th Fighter Squadron, the "Fighting Eagles" based at Langley Air Force Base in Virginia, had taken position approximately 30 miles behind and 7,000 feet above the mass of C-17s transport planes doing 500 mph at an altitude of 41,000 feet. All the pilots had volunteered for this mission. Most were from "blue" states, loyal to the USA, and felt the rogue states had to be brought back into the fold. Most felt this had to happen at any cost, even if it meant a full blown civil war once again. A few, however, had volunteered as a means to try and ensure that at least some cool heads were in the air to avoid a fight.

The forte of the F-22 Raptors is what is known as BVR (Beyond Visual Range) engagements. By staying 50-60 miles away from any potential enemy, the fifth generation super fighters could maximize their advantages of stealth and speed to fire Advanced Medium Range

Air-to-Air Missiles (AMRAAMs) to destroy their targets, usually without their presence even being known.

However, those advantages of speed and stealth, which every pilot that had flown against the F-22 described as "overwhelming" came at a steep price. Each Raptor cost between $137 million and $678 million depending on whose numbers a person chose to believe and which numbers a person chose to count, such as development costs.

The costly and overwhelming advantages were being limited by the rules of engagement imposed upon the Fighting Eagles. The rules of engagement, in turn, conflicted with the mission of the Raptors, which was to clear a path for the transports carrying the paratroopers to Arizona and Montana. Preferably by intimidation, but by force if necessary, the Raptors were supposed to sweep aside any aerial opposition sent up by the break-away Free States of America.

The flight leader of the USA F-22s, Lt. Col. Wesley "Wes" Williams, listened to the controllers aboard the E-3 Airborne Warning and Control (AWACS) aircraft call out the bearings and ranges to the F-16s of South Carolina's Swamp Fox squadron.

"How exactly do we intimidate those pilots while hiding? They don't really know we're here, but the thought or rumor that we might be here and we *might* fire is supposed to scare off veteran combat pilots," he thought to himself. "I hate politicians more and more every day."

His wingman's voice cackled over the intercom and broke his mental brooding. "Wes, its showtime. I hope the controllers remember to use their command voice and sound very scary," Capt. Martin said.

"Agreed," said Williams. "Our little bit of this madness is making me crazy," joked the Lieutenant Colonel.

The next voice they heard came from one of the controllers.

"F-16 flight on heading 290 True, altitude 47,000 feet, this is U.S. Air Force E-3 flight control. You are requested to turn south immediately and come to a heading of 180. Acknowledge, over."

"U.S. Air Force E-3 flight, this is South Carolina Air National Guard F-16 flight. The governors of South Carolina, Georgia, and Tennessee request that the C-17s you are controlling not enter their air space. Say again, you are requested to not enter South Carolina, Georgia, or Tennessee airspace. Request you turn them back toward Pope. Acknowledge, over."

"F-16 flight, we read you but cannot comply. We have our orders to continue west. Acknowledge, over."

"US Air Force E-3, we are authorized to use force. We prefer not to do so. We do not want an incident. However, our orders are to not allow this force, or any other unauthorized force to enter the airspace of the sovereign states of South Carolina, Georgia, or Tennessee. Furthermore, we have been instructed to remind you, with all due respect, that use of the US military on US soil, other than as part of local and state law enforcement, is against the Posse Comitatus Act of 1878 as well as the Insurrection Act of 1807. Please state your intentions, over."

The squadron leader of the South Carolina Free States of America (FSA) F-16s didn't expect his brief law history lesson to change the mind of the controller or of the course of the C-17s flying west. But, by transmitting on an open channel, in the clear, he knew that every pilot in the air would hear the logic and justification against the federal airborne operation. He also knew it would be picked up and re-transmitted around the country and probably the world. And who knew, it might sway a few hearts and minds and that might be crucial during these crazy times.

Next, the F-16 squadron commander switched frequencies to address his pilots. "Ladies and Gentlemen," he did have three female pilots, after all, "I pray for peace. I pray that Almighty God will return sanity and reason to our nation. But, I also remind you of the words of Captain John Parker of the Lexington Minutemen. Stand your ground. Do not fire unless fired upon. But if they mean to have a war, let it begin here."

By now the FSA F-16 Vipers had closed to where the nearest of the giant USA C-17 transports were becoming specks in the sky.

The FSA squadron commander reminded his pilots to "fly as tight as you dare, or maybe even a little tighter. Our lives may depend on it." He was referring to the fact that each flight lead-wingman pair had been ordered to fly as closely together as possible with each wingman just behind, below and to the right of his flight lead. It was hoped that such a close formation might trick the radars on the USA aircraft and missiles into thinking that the two aircraft were actually only one by merging the radar returns off of each plane. While the deceptive radar returns would not last long, it was hoped that, should the USA Raptors fire AMRAAM missiles at the FSA F-16s, the Viper pairs could split at the last moment and cause the AMRAAMs a moment's hesitation as their computer brains decided which of the two new targets to follow.

The FSA Vipers continued closing the distance with the C-17s as the lead transports in the massive aerial formation crossed into Tennessee air space. Other Globemasters stretched behind for miles back toward Pope. The controllers aboard the USA AWACS aircraft again demanded that the FSA aircraft turn south and clear the westward path. Again the FSA Vipers refused and asked that the C-17s laden with 82nd airborne paratroopers turn back east, toward their base.

Neither force changed direction and the stomachs of all pilots on both sides turned to knots. The Viper squadron commander and wingman detached from the main flight formation to close with the nearest C-17 and warn him off with a burst from the 20 mm cannon located in the wing root of the Viper.

The controllers on the USA E-3s told the Raptor pilots that the rogue state F-16s were now within visual range of the C-17s and that a pair of the F-16s were closing rapidly with the lead transports.

A burst of 20 mm shells erupted in front of the C-17s as the intercepting F-16s fired their warning shots.

"They're shooting at us!! They're shooting at us" cried one C-17 pilot over his radio. Another transport pilot also screamed "My God, we're under attack. Say again, we are under attack."

The flight crew of the second C-17 in formation instinctively dove upon hearing the firing and the radio calls of being under attack. Another transport, further back in the formation saw the change in aspect and altitude of the number two aircraft and mistakenly called out "Simba 2 is hit, say again, Simba 2 is hit."

That was all the tense Raptor pilots needed to hear. The Fighting Eagles squadron leader gave the "weapons free" order only to be interrupted by one of his section leaders, a major from Mississippi.

"Sir, we can *not* fire. We have no confirmation of engagement or damage" said the Major rapidly.

"Secure that, Mustang 4," snapped the Raptor commander. "All ships fire."

Calls of "Fox Three" cascaded over the airwaves as 16 Raptors each fired two AMRAAM missiles at the F-16s, now only 30 miles away. One of the air-to-air missiles failed to ignite and fell away, but the remaining 31 missiles streaked toward the FSA aircraft at over Mach 4.

"Mustang four, seven, eight, and eleven, what is your problem?" screamed Lt. Col. Williams. "Why have you not fired? Fire! Say again, *fire!*"

"Missiles inbound!" the controller onboard the FSA E-3 AWACS warned the Viper pilots.

"Maddog! Maddog! Break now!" screamed the Swamp Fox squadron commander. The FSA Vipers each fired their own AMRAAM missiles in boresight mode as a reflex defensive measure in the direction from which the USA AMRAAMs approached. Then each pair of F-16s split violently as each lead broke hard high and left while his wingman broke hard low and right.

Two of the boresight fired AMRAAMs from the Swamp Fox F-16s struck heavily laden C-17s. One of the massive transports exploded and broke apart in midair. This was a merciful death. The other cargo plane was struck in the left wing by the missile. As the wing broke off, the plane tumbled with paratroopers trying to exit the aircraft as it plummeted to the earth far below.

Despite the splitting tactic, eleven rebel FSA Vipers were struck by the USA air-to-air missiles and exploded. The enraged remaining Viper pilots firewalled their powerful jet engines and raced toward the Raptors which were now just coming into visual range.

In reality, seven Raptor pilots did not fire their missiles as ordered and were in a state of near shock. Shock and disbelief that their squadron mates, friends, had just fired on and *killed* their fellow pilots. Fellow *American* pilots.

The shock was short lived, for five of the conflicted Raptor pilots, as first one and then another and another, yelled, "Cease fire, cease fire!" at their squadron mates even as they took positions behind them.

"Who is that? Who is saying that?" demanded the Raptor commander. "Is that you four? Get the hell off of this channel and return to base you traitorous bastard!" he screamed as he began to shake with rage. "Any man who does not fire will be court-martialed. I promise you."

"I'm sorry sir, but *you* are the traitor. Traitor to this nation and the Constitution you swore to uphold," Mustang 4 answered his squadron commander. Then he squeezed the trigger on his 20 mm cannon and watched with great sadness as his friend's F-22 blew apart in mid-air.

Four other Raptor pilots also fired on their squadron mates. Three USA-loyal Raptors were caught off-guard by their turncoat comrades and were destroyed instantly. The fourth targeted Raptor was lucky and evaded to the right and high just in time. Now all the Raptors began evasive maneuvers as each pilot tried to understand what was happening and who was firing at whom. A whirling furball dogfight ensued.

By this time, the remaining 7 FSA Vipers arrived and joined the dogfight. At this close range, the speed and stealth of the F-22 was negated and the smaller, lighter, more nimble F-16s could engage on nearly even terms, despite the super maneuverability afforded the Raptors by their thrust vectoring engine nozzles. In the mass confusion of the dogfight, two USA F-22s were destroyed by the Vipers along with two of the F-22s which had come to the aid of the rebel pilots. Three Vipers were also destroyed by Raptors before the battle was disengaged.

Radar screen video and audio footage of the first aerial battle fought in US airspace since Pearl Harbor was flashed around the world. People all over the world watched in horror as American fighter planes shot down other American planes. Others watched with amusement and some even with glee.

Images of paratroopers falling among and along with the burning wreckage of destroyed cargo planes was eerily reminiscent of the 9/11 jumpers. All across the United States and Free States, Americans also reacted with rage.

But, not all of those who watched reacted with horror or rage. In several world capitals, including Tehran, Caracas, Pyongyang, Beijing and Moscow, the images were greeted with joy and the raising of glasses in toasts.

The same question flashed into minds around the United States and all around the world. Had the Second American Civil War just begun?

The White House Situation Room, Washington, D.C.

In the White House Situation Room, the live video and audio of American warplanes exploding over U.S. airspace and paratroopers plummeting to the earth were greeted with shock and disbelief. Most of the President's National Security team sat in stunned silence.

The Vice President simply mumbled, "No, no, it can't be. It just can't be," over and over again, to no one in particular.

The President, meanwhile, looked at the screen with anger and then around the room at the faces of his hand-picked team. "This is unbelievable. They are firing on U.S. aircraft. On *our* forces. Are they mad?" the President said with indignation.

"Mr. President we must call off this operation. We must call those airplanes back," said Lee Andropolous, his senior advisor. Then, to add emphasis to the urgent situation, he added, "at once."

"What? Pull back? Tuck tail and run? Like a whipped dog? We are the United States of America. We command the most powerful military the world has ever seen and you want us to run away in surrender?" the President demanded as he rose and with him, his anger.

"I agree with Lee, sir," said Jack Darden, the National Security Advisor. "I'm as big a hawk as anyone when Americans have died, but we have to pause. We can't rush into a shooting war. As much as I want to smash those traitorous sons-of-bitches into smithereens, we need to figure out our next steps. Besides, are we even able to continue, General? I mean, what are our pilots doing now?"

General Richardson, the Chairman of the Joint Chiefs of Staff had been speaking urgently into a telephone when he noticed the question directed at him and abruptly hung up. "Mr. Darden, you raise a good point. Our pilots have turned slightly north, northwest in a big slow curve, awaiting our orders. Langley has scrambled four more Raptors and four F-15s but now apparently some of *those* pilots in the air are saying they will not fire on other American pilots."

"Christ!" exclaimed Darden.

The General and Lee Andropolous both frowned at Darden.

"Sorry," Darden said sheepishly. "Christ, what a bunch of boy scouts," he then thought to himself.

"And what are the rogue aircraft doing? How many of them are left? How many of those criminals?" added the President almost as an afterthought.

"Our AWACS show four F-16s from the South Carolina squadron heading back to their base. They also show the entire squadron of the Alabama Air National Guard F-16s orbiting over southeastern Tennessee in two separate flights. And, it appears that five of the surviving Raptors are not re-forming with their squadron mates nor responding to calls from our AWACS. We do not know their intentions. Some of these pilots apparently fired on their own squadron mates. They may be planning on joining the rebel forces."

"So what are our options, General?" asked the President. "Can we continue this operation? Is there a way, anyway, forward, that you can recommend?"

"Mr. President there are ways forward, but none that I can recommend in good conscience at this time. If we could be certain of the loyalty of our pilots, we could scramble additional fighters and blast a path through any opposition which may materialize. However, this air battle changes everything on the ground if we continue to the point where our paratroopers land at their objectives. Now both sides know shots have been fired and blood has been spilled. Surprise has been lost. There is now no chance of securing any of the objectives without serious bloodshed. In my opinion, the forces of the break-away states will not stand down and negotiate, much less allow themselves to be relieved or removed from the installations we were trying to secure. Continuing now makes no sense. Our strategic objective was to get the rogue state forces to stand down without a major fight. I think we can safely say that is not an option any longer," concluded the General sadly.

"Joel?" the President asked his Chief of Staff.

"I concur with taking a step back and taking a deep breath," the Chief of Staff said.

Another long silence ensued. "All right. Call 'em back. Let's figure this out," the President said, with only a hint of relief but clearly fighting to control his anger.

"Good. Thank God." Miller then took out his mobile phone and called the Secretary of Defense to call off Operation Swiftsure, just as General Richardson began to make phone calls as well.

"And you know, sir, this may well be a blessing in disguise," Darden said.

"Oh really? And how is that?" the President questioned, scarcely able to hide his anger or sarcasm.

"Such a large and overt operation may well have led to more states seceding and may have even sparked a full scale war. Now, we can look at options to avoid both of those nightmares."

19

THE GOVERNOR'S MANSION, AUSTIN, TEXAS

The Governor and his closest advisors were glued to their flat screen televisions just as the rest of the world was. They watched, mesmerized, as were tens of millions, as the air battle over North Carolina and Tennessee developed.

As the first reports of shots being fired were aired, disbelief was the predominant emotion in the Governor's home office. This soon gave way to shock, as the images and audio of air-to-air missiles exploding the South Carolina F-16s were broadcast. The sounds of American pilots screaming, "break now!" and "I'm hit, I'm hit!" were shocking. Fuzzy videos of pilots ejecting from burning fighter jets shook the men in the room to their core. It was for this very reason that the commander of the Swamp Fox squadron had ensured that his aircraft were transmitting video and audio wherever possible. Anger and rage quickly swelled up as the air battle continued and it was apparent that a full-fledged tragedy was unfolding.

"Look at that! Look at that!" said the Governor, fighting to keep his voice below a scream. "This is unbelievable. What more do we need to convince us to act? What more do we need to wait for?" he asked. "Tell me," he demanded from his Lt. Governor and Adjutant General. "What more do we need to wait for to decide the right course of action?" he demanded again. "This administration has declared war on the American people!"

General Westin spoke up. "Governor, I agree with you that this is a tragic turn of events and an egregious atrocity by the Federal government in Washington on its own citizens."

"Atrocity?" asked the Lt. Governor. "Don't you think that's an overstatement? This is a time to choose our words and path carefully. Not at time to throw verbal bombs."

The General regarded the Lt. Governor with a scarcely veiled look of contempt. Westin's disdain for politicians was well known, as was, paradoxically, his masterful diplomacy in hiding it.

"I am considering both our path *and* my words very carefully. I meant atrocity. When your own government, whose central role is to protect its people, orders an overwhelming military attack on you in your own home, in clear violation of existing laws, not to mention the will of the people of the states whom you are serving, and the result is the death of scores of American citizens, yes, I call that an atrocity," retorted the General evenly, fighting to control his emotions.

The men looked at each other but no one spoke. Daggers flew between the eyes of the two men. Finally, the Governor looked at his Adjutant General and asked him to go on with his assessment.

"Sir," continued General Westin, "I do agree that this atrocity must spur us to action. We cannot let this stand. I presume when you refer to our action, you are speaking of secession and or joining the FSA. But I want us to carefully consider what this might mean for our state and the rest of the United States and Free States."

"Go on," prompted the Governor.

I think that our secession will virtually guarantee an all out and prolonged war between the USA and the FSA. Louisiana and at least a few other states will follow us. The feds in Washington, DC will see this as crossing the Rubicon and they will pick up the gauntlet. They will see this alignment of so many states against them as a clear threat and they will move aggressively to preserve the union as they see it. And this war, this new civil war, could last years and kill millions. Millions." The General let that grave prediction hang in the air like a thick, choking smoke.

"I disagree," intoned the Lt. Governor. "I think just the opposite. I mean, I agree with the General that a new, ugly civil war could result, but I don't agree that it is the most likely result of our secession."

"Ok, now you explain," asked the Governor of his second-in-command.

"Our secession will cause Louisiana and at least a few other states to secede. I agree on that. But, I think this makes all-out war less likely not more. Washington moved against the FSA precisely because it is only a handful of states. They see the few Free States as not being able to stand up to the full, combined might of the rest of the 38 states right now. Especially on short notice. So, they tried to cut this rebellion, as it were, off at the knees before it and the FSA gathered momentum and strength. With us and a few other states, the FSA is too strong for Washington to re-take militarily in short order. They can't risk a war with an FSA almost as strong as the USA. No, they simply wouldn't. They will have to accept that the FSA have the right to exist as separate and distinct from the USA. They won't like it and they may impose economic sanctions and seek the same from the U.N., but overall, they will have to accept and accede to the existence of the FSA."

The Governor considered what he had just heard. He had always liked that Texas was such a large and important state. He liked that Texas could always play a leadership role for other states. He now did not like that what Texas did could decide whether a second American civil war happened or not.

"Well, at least this isn't a tough decision," the Governor of the Lone Star State said sarcastically. "This isn't for us alone to decide, praise God. This decision for the citizens of Texas will be a decision of Texans and by Texans. We need to request that the legislature immediately vote on sending a measure of nullification and secession to the people."

The senior man looked at the other two men. Both nodded in agreement.

"Governor, there is one other thing," said General Westin. "I don't know how long it will take to schedule the legislative vote, much less the popular vote. I'm a simple soldier, not a politician. But we need an official policy effective immediately, vis-à-vis Washington. They may well ask for forces here to participate in further offensive operations against the FSA or at least be moved in preparation for future action. How will we respond? The feds are also likely to try something with regards to the Strategic Petroleum Reserve."

"Try something? What does that mean" questioned the Governor.

"I'm not sure. But it seems Washington's options are the same now as when this crisis started, except now they don't have compliant, cooperative state governments in Texas and Louisiana, two of their most important energy states. They may ask that we release some or all of the oil to them. They can't ask for all since there is no other place to store that much crude. Or they may try to secure it by means of a military operation."

"A military operation? You think they would try something this deep into now un-friendly lines?" asked the Governor incredulously.

"I wouldn't rule it out. They may even try something quick, before we can officially act on secession and thus they can claim they are securing their own oil. In fact, that's probably what I would do if I were in their place" concluded Westin.

The Lt. Governor spoke up and asked the question left hanging in the room, "So what do you suggest we do, General?"

"With regards to the SPR? I recommend we move as much state police and other security around the petroleum reserve sites as we can muster, but not deploy military forces overtly. I would put some of our ground Guard forces in positions where they can quickly react to any military threat, but without being overtly provocative. Air defense systems need to be moved into positions to guard against U.S.A. air attacks. They may choose a scorched earth, or in this case, a scorched oil strategy," explained the General.

"What do you mean by that? Since you mentioned air defense I take it you mean that the Feds may decide to try and destroy the petroleum reserves of the SPR if they can't get their hands on it or control it?" the Lt. Governor asked.

"Precisely" responded the General. "But I also mean that we need to do the same for the entire energy infrastructure in our state. We need to protect our oil refineries, tank farms, and pipelines, particularly control and pumping stations. All need to be protected as much as possible against air attack, airborne assault, and sabotage."

While Texas was a decidedly red, conservative state, not all Texans would support secession, much less active resistance against the U.S.A. In the last presidential election, the Democrat had received over 40% of the vote. This represented over 3.3 million Texans. Some of these would actively resist the Texan and FSA cause and even be willing to act as saboteurs on behalf of the Federal Government.

The General took a deep breath and continued to outline the steps he believed his beloved state needed to take. "We also need to formulate our overall military strategy if we do secede, whether or not we join the Free States. Since such a huge proportion of the military power is based here, we need to secure it and ensure we control it. We need to cull all the US forces based here in Texas to see who's loyal to the FSA and allow any personnel wishing to return to USA to do so. We need to prepare contingency plans in the event some areas of this state decide they wish to remain part of the USA."

The Governor leaned back in his chair and interlocked his hands in front of his chest, deep in thought. "I see. We do have much to consider and plan for, but won't the FSA leadership want a role in deciding the overall strategy?"

"Yes, of course they will. But time is short. And, as we've seen and learned today, or relearned, I should say, we must always consider and prepare for multiple contingencies, or events can spiral beyond your control. And besides, there is absolutely nothing wrong with joining the FSA, should our people vote to join them, with well thought out contingency plans. Makes it easy to win acceptance for them."

The three men shared a look and then chuckled. Even in these dark times, the Texas spirit was hard to repress.

CNN Headquarters, Atlanta, Georgia

The attractive African-American host looked down at her black and red dress and smoothed it one last time before lifting her piercing eyes and dazzling smile to gaze directly into the camera.

"Good evening, America. I'm Keshia Carlson and this is CNN. Tragedy and terror over the heartland today is followed by a growing furor across the nation. In the aftermath of the unimaginable, an American versus American air battle over North Carolina and Tennessee, five more states are calling their legislatures to emergency session to take up the issue of nullification of Federal Government actions and secession from the United States. Citing egregious violation of the rights of American citizens and state sovereignty by means of use of federal military force, Tennessee, Louisiana, Arkansas, Missouri, and South Dakota are putting secession on the table. And, it appears that Texas will also convene its legislature, although no official announcement has yet been made. These are truly dramatic developments. As you know, 11 states have already seceded from the union and ten of those formed what is being called the Free States of America, or FSA for short. It is believed that the formation of the FSA led to the military operation earlier today however, the official position of the administration is that the objective of the operation was merely "to secure vital national security assets." Nonetheless, it appears our nation is facing nothing short of an existential crisis not seen since 1860.

With these latest states, the number of states that have seceded or are considering it now number 18. Almost half of the states in America. All eyes of the nation are on Texas. As the second largest state in the union, and with the second largest state economy, Texas secession would be a devastating blow to the administration. In addition, Texas is the energy powerhouse for the nation, accounting for 26% of the total refining capacity and 22% of crude oil production.

The administration, meanwhile, has re-iterated its position that it wishes to find a fast and amicable resolution to the ongoing disagreement with the states that have already broken away.

We are waiting for the White House to make a statement about this morning's aerial clash. So far, the official position of the White House is that this morning's tragic events were nothing more than a misunderstanding that quickly spiraled out of control.

Here in Atlanta, competing massive protests led to clashes and riot police had to be called in. On one side people clamoring for Georgia to take up secession while on the other side, people denouncing what they call "traitors" and "un-American" and insisting that Georgia remain loyal to the USA.

Ladies and Gentlemen, these are truly remarkable times we are living in."

20

THE STATE CAPITOL, AUSTIN, TEXAS

The debate in the Texas State House of Representatives had been ongoing for nine straight hours. In the Texas Senate, it had only been going on for seven. The Senate expected the House to vote first on the measure of nullification and secession from the United States and then send the bill to them. Then, of course, it would be sent to the people of Texas for a special, emergency election if it passed the legislature.

State Representative Roscoe Jenkins, Republican from the fourth district, approached the lectern for the second time in the marathon session. His head was pounding again, threatening to split, and the barrage of aspirin he had been taking no longer seemed to work. Secession was almost sure to pass the House, being controlled by Republicans, 94-56. But the Senate was an entirely different matter. The balance of power in the upper house was only 18-13 in favor of the secessionist-leaning GOP. Informal vote counting kept coming up in a 14-14 tie with three members steadfastly refusing to say how they would vote. If the measure passed both houses, it would almost certainly pass the general election due to the staunchly conservative make up of the Texas electorate. The fate of Texas was therefore in the hands of the 31 souls in the Texas Senate. Nevertheless, everyone realized the importance of the House vote. The larger the margin of passage, the more likely to influence one of the crucial swing voters in the Senate.

Jenkins reached the pulpit and steadied himself. "Mr. Speaker, the time has come for Texas to act. With all due respect to the previous speaker, the distinguished gentleman from Brownsville, I don't believe a single person in this august chamber has not been seriously considering the consequences of particular courses of action every day since the state of Montana first voted to secede. And I also believe that most, if not all, of the members of this body have long considered the consequences of the actions coming from Washington, DC. The actions of the Federal Government have put us, the residents of all fifty states, on a long, slippery slope to ruin and their recent actions have pushed us off a cliff of that slope. I do not wish to rehash all the previous arguments of the past several hours, said much better by my esteemed colleagues. But I will say, once again, that the economic crisis was caused by Washington's ever increasing spending, taxation, and regulation. The energy crisis brought on by the Middle East war would have been a small crisis indeed, if at all, had the Federal Government not strangled the production of fossil fuels in all but a handful of states. Thank Heaven that we and a few other states defied them and developed our resources. Then the tyrants inside the beltway heavy handedly tried to enforce nation-wide martial law and gun restrictions. Now comes this open act of military aggression against Americans. Will we not stand with our freedom-loving brothers and sisters against this aggression? If the Federal Government is not checked now, when will it be? That is the main question. If not now, when? If the monstrosity in Washington is able to reassert dominion over the Free States now, what then will stop their tyrannical thirst for power over every aspect of our lives? Ladies and gentleman, this attempted invasion of sovereign states shows that *they are willing to kill Americans on a large scale to maintain their power.* Allow me to repeat, they have demonstrated a clear resolve and conviction that killing thousands of Americans is justifiable so long as it allows them to maintain power. No, thousands of Americans were not killed as a result of the attempted invasion, due to the steadfast resolve and courage of the FSA leadership, three brave governors, and a few bold pilots. But had the deployed paratroopers reached their destinations, thousands of Americans would have died. If this devouring beast is allowed to endure, it will continue to grow as it always has. And then what will it do during the next crisis? Wholesale dissolution of the Constitution? Surrender of all national sovereignty to the UN, an even bigger monstrosity? Concentration camps? If we, the people, will not stop the Federal Government now, what will it *not* do to us in the future?

No, my esteemed colleagues, the hour is at hand. Louisiana, Arkansas, and South Dakota have just voted to secede and join the Free States of America. Missouri and Tennessee are debating it even now as we speak. This now makes 15 states standing up for liberty and drawing a line in the sand. Can we, the great state of Texas, shrink at this time of need? As the largest conservative state, should Texas not lead? Is Texas not the bulwark? I ardently ask that we vote to secede from the broken union and join the Free States of America."

The chamber erupted in thunderous applause. The feed from the chamber was carried across Texas on the Texas Cable News channel and nationally on CSPAN3.

Next a female, African-American State Representative from Houston took the floor.

"Mr. Speaker, we are in extraordinary times. But, this is not the time for us, for Texas, to join in the madness of some other places. Other states may have seceded, but Texas has not. The so-called treasonous Free States may be at war with the United States, but Texas is not. And let me address this misnomer of Free States. Whose freedom does this refer to? Is it a coincidence that the old Confederate, slave holding states are at the center of this treasonous movement? Is it a coincidence that the rogue states are the very states with the longest, most widespread history of discrimination against women, minorities, and the poor? I think not. It seems the 'free' in Free States refers mostly to the freedom of white males. I urge this body to defeat this measure. I also urge this body to reject the illegal secession of those 15 states, including Washington State. I further urge that Texas throw its full resources and support behind the legitimate government of the United States of America. Thank you."

This time around the applause were more muffled and mixed with grumbling. After another two hours, the secession bill was put to a vote. It passed by a count of 81-66 with three abstentions. The following day the Texas Senate deadlocked at 15-15 with one abstention. Rather than break the tie, the Lt. Governor called another vote. The second vote passed 16-15.

The measures for secession also passed in Missouri and Tennessee. North Carolina's legislature moved surprisingly fast and followed suit the following day in another razor-thin vote, this time passing the measure by two votes. Within days, the voters of seven other states would head to the polls to decide the fate of their respective states, and also the fate of the United States and the fledgling Free States of America.

BP Refinery, Whiting, Indiana

British Petroleum's Whiting refinery was the largest in the Midwest. Stretching from Whiting to Hammond and East Chicago, the refinery was the sixth largest in the US, processing 413,000 barrels of crude oil per day at full capacity. The massive facility also produced 1.7 million gallons of gasoline and diesel fuel per day under normal conditions. However, these were not normal times for the global oil industry. The shortages from the Mid-East war and attacks on Saudi oil facilities had reduced the Whiting facility to processing only 268,000 barrels per day, slightly more than 65% of normal capacity. Nevertheless, it was the primary source of fuel for the greater Chicago area and the Midwest.

The Illinois and Indiana patriot militia groups knew that crippling this facility would make it very difficult for the federal government and their Illinois state government puppets to maintain their "limited" martial law, gun confiscation, and ban on the people assembling for protest.

Like many refineries in the United States, the Whiting refinery was a soft target. An exceedingly soft target. Originally built in the 1880s as a kerosene factory with much open farm land around it, the urban sprawl of Chicago and Gary, Indiana, had grown around the facility and literally up against it. Indianapolis Blvd, 129th St., and Schrage Ave all bordered the facility and much of its infrastructure, including a rail spur, and were not only visible from public roads, but were literally a stone's throw away. There were even private houses, which shared a fence line with the massive complex. As it happened, the owner of one such house had a brother active in the Illinois Sons of Liberty and was herself very sympathetic to the patriot militia cause. The homeowner was only too happy to allow the militia to use her home and backyard to observe the operations of the refinery and develop their plan.

The initial plan to cripple the fuel supply to the Chicago area was relatively simple. Two of the militia members were also truck drivers for one of the companies that hauled products into and out of the facility. A truck with a fully laden trailer of almost 9,000 gallons of gasoline would be outfitted with fertilizer-based explosives to act as a massive truck bomb and detonated once inside the off-loading facility, after the driver had made a hasty exit. The truckers, however, were very concerned that the workers at the plant would not be harmed. A second plan was devised. Four ex-military militiamen would use the adjacent militia house to infiltrate the refinery's perimeter chain-link fence. Certain tank and pipeline valves would be opened and then small time delay improvised explosive devices (IEDs) would be set in a part of the plant far from the off-loading stations. Other militia members would take up secluded positions along Schrage Ave and use improvised Molotov cocktail launchers to fling cocktails into the facility. The improvised launcher was nothing more than one of the water balloon launchers used by children around the country for summertime fun. They also happened to be perfect for launching Molotov cocktails much further than even the strongest man could throw.

The flaming cocktails would be fired first, followed immediately by the IED detonations. This would ensure that most of the personnel would be away from the massive truck blast, which would hopefully cripple the sprawling facility.

At precisely 2:45 am, the first militia team of four men infiltrated the refinery's perimeter fence with very low tech bolt cutters. With the typical lax security at most refineries, the black-clad militiamen quickly set their IEDs and then found their target tank and pipeline valves. The final set of IEDs were set next to the long line of railcars laden with petroleum products and adjacent to the Indianapolis Blvd fence. The infiltration team then exited the refinery as quickly as possible before the second phase. At 3:30 AM, the six-man team began launching Molotov cocktails. Each launcher required three men to operate, and each fired three improvised bombs before the militiamen got on the road to leave the area. Upon seeing the first explosion from the cocktails, the two militiamen from the infiltration team responsible for detonating the IEDs detonated their handiwork. Eight fires were quickly burning and spreading rapidly through the facility. Alarm klaxons wailed and mixed with the sounds of fire suppression systems going off in a vain attempt to suppress the rapidly spreading fires.

The massive truck bomb was detonated five minutes after the IEDs. The explosion lit up the Indiana night sky and was heard for miles. The refinery employee operating the unloading dock control board was in the small control building nearest the blast and was killed instantly. Three other employees received minor injuries, but for the most part, the employees of the facility were spared, just as the two militia truck drivers had wanted. The physical facilities were not nearly as lucky. The fires burned for three full days. By the time the conflagration was brought under control, almost forty percent of the facility had been damaged, including the largest tank farm.

The attack on the Indiana – Illinois border was not the only one. Throughout the region and the nation, militia groups, sensing weakness on the part of the federal and state governments, took action.

In Michigan, one of the largest militia units struck both the Livernois and Junction rail yards, two of the largest in the entire state.

The nationwide shortages of fuel had just been made far worse for the Midwest. And many militia groups were only now beginning to move.

21

FOX NEWS HEADQUARTERS, NEW YORK CITY, NEW YORK

T he three morning anchors sat on the couch and looked gravely into the camera. The two men and one woman each greeted the viewers before the attractive blond woman seated in the middle began to speak.

"The aftermath of the secession votes in Texas and North Carolina, and an attack on a major oil refinery in Indiana are at the top of the agenda this morning. We go first to Washington, DC. Stuart…"

"Thank you, Sandra. Yesterday, the people of Texas and North Carolina voted by relatively small margins to affirm the measures of secession passed by their respective legislatures. In addition, both states voted by larger margins to join the Free States of America. This vote pattern is a bit puzzling, but nevertheless, the die has been cast. The second and tenth most populous states of the Union have now seceded and cast their lot with the other fifteen states of the Free States of America, as they are calling themselves. These are the two largest states to vote to leave the union and join the FSA. The importance of these states can be seen in their size and economic power, as well as the military combat power based there. For instance, nine of the US Army's 41 active Brigade Combat Teams (BCTs) are based in Texas and another four in North Carolina. Thirty-one percent of the Brigade Combat Teams are in these two states alone. Texas, of course, also has a huge role in the nation's energy economy.

The big question now remains, what will happen between the now seventeen state-strong FSA and the USA. Will the USA recognize the right of the FSA to exist or are we looking at a second civil war? Was the aborted airborne operation a signal of future willingness on the part of the administration to use force to compel the break-away states to return? Will the resulting battle, loss of life, and now, the addition of more states to the FSA make Washington more or less willing to use force? We are waiting for a statement from the White House at some point this morning. And, how will the FSA respond? What will happen next? Back to New York."

This time the senior male anchor took the lead. "Thank you Stuart. We will have a panel of military experts on a little later for a fair and balanced discussion on the potential military implications of a possible ongoing confrontation between the USA and the fledgling FSA which just received a substantial boost in support. The impact of the departure of Texas and Louisiana on the nation's energy crisis is even more important in light of the developments in Indiana early this morning.

We go now to our Chicago bureau. Charles?"

"Thank you, Greg. Early this morning explosions rang out in BP's massive refinery just across the Indiana state line in Whiting. Multiple explosions in various locations at almost the same time have led to speculation that this was no industrial accident. An Indiana state law enforcement official who wished to remain anonymous told us that he believes this is the work of one of the militia groups that has stepped up their activity in the region in the wake of the economic and secession crisis. Only one employee is confirmed dead and three more received minor injuries. Two firefighters among the dozens responding to the conflagration have also been injured. Any loss of life is a tragedy, but the few casualties, given the size of the explosions and subsequent fires, is miraculous. The impact on the region's oil and petroleum products supply is sure to be enormous and cause further strain due to the ongoing fuel shortages.

Fort Bliss, Texas, 1st Armored Division "Old Ironsides" Headquarters

The senior staff of the division, the host unit for the entire Fort Bliss military complex, had been preparing for the possibility of Texas secession for several weeks. Now that it was reality, it seemed unbeliev-able and overwhelming even to the hardened combat veterans tasked with dealing with it.

Major General Parker, as the commanding officer, felt the burden more than anyone else. As much as he feared the bloodshed that was now almost certain to sweep across the nation, he also felt he had come upon the right strategy for a quick end to the civil war, if in fact it could not somehow be contained. Or, at least, a relatively quick end. But that was not the immediate task at hand. His immediate task was to implement the plan to divvy up the base personnel and equipment as he and his trusted Executive Officer had devised.

The longtime Army veteran had just submitted his letter of resig-nation to the Chief of Staff of the US Army via email and had also put the old-fashioned, hard copy in the snail mail. Hitting "send" on that email had been the hardest thing he had ever had to do. He suspected that the task would not long hold the dubious honor. The General leaned back in his overstuffed executive chair and reflected on what he had just done. Some, many millions in fact, would consider him a traitor. In fact, he struggled with himself over whether he was a traitor. Thoughts of George Washington and Robert E. Lee had been with him continuously over the last few sleepless nights. Americans adored Washington and considered him the father of their country. Had the British Empire defeated the upstart rebels, as they called their rogue American colonists, Washington would likely have been hung as a traitor and remembered as such in the annals of history. Parker also thought over and over of the words of Robert E. Lee as he declined Abraham Lincoln's offer of command of the US Army at the outset of the Civil War.

When told that the offer to command of the Union army was a huge opportunity to serve his country, Lee observed that he had never dreamed he'd see the day when the President of the United States would raise an army to invade his own country. Furthermore, the inva-sion of the "enemy" territory would include his home state of Virginia, and his greatest duty was to his home. Parker fought back a nauseating feeling in the pit of his stomach and thought of the rich irony of a black man, an African-American, clinging to the words of the Confederacy's greatest hero as he made his most fateful decision. Like Lee, he could not raise arms against his home and native state. He could not fight against Texas. But more, far more than the loyalty to his home, was his loyalty to the founding principles of the United States, which compelled his decision. He simply could not abide the direction which the majority liberal, "blue" states had taken his beloved nation and trampled on the Constitution while doing it. No, he would not serve the US Army any longer. He would offer his services, such as they were, to the fledgling Free States of America, which had at least pledged to return to the principles which the founding fathers held dear.

He shook himself from his melancholy revelry and started crafting his next email. This one was sent to the Texas Adjutant General, General Westin. In it, Parker briefly explained that he had now resigned his commission in the US Army and was available for service in the Texas Military Forces in whatever capacity they wished to utilize him. He also mentioned that he had drafted a paper with his recommendations on how Texas and the FSA might wish to pursue a strategy in the now brewing conflict.

Free States of America (FSA) Provisional Capital, Oklahoma State Capitol Building, Oklahoma City

The conference room contained the Adjutants General of 15 of the 17 FSA states and their senior aides. The senior military officers from North and South Carolina requested to be excused as they dealt with the aftermath of the aerial battle with the USA. President Doucet strode into the room with her chief of staff and senior policy advisor. She wore a grave yet somehow warm look. The generals rose as one and snapped to attention. The President managed a quick smile and then asked them to be seated.

"Gentlemen we are facing the most serious crisis in our nation's history since the Civil War, as you all know. I greatly respect all of you for your service and experience. With that being said, I must cut to the chase regarding my purpose in calling all of you here. We must very quickly constitute the best possible military force. We, as former parts of the United States have parts of the greatest military in the history of mankind. However, if this stand-off with the federal government cannot be resolved peacefully, this greatest military will be facing off against *itself*. We therefore simply must take a hard look at our military situation.

We all know that the military, like every branch of government, has become bureaucratic, overgrown, unwieldy, and inefficient. I take my share of blame in that, having been in government for many years myself. But these are extraordinary times calling for extraordinary measures. I therefore have a series of directives, requests, really.

First, we need to quickly appoint the absolute, very best Joint Chiefs of Staff possible. To my mind, this means we need to largely throw out rank and other artificial obstacles to getting the best possible men or women in each position. I ask you to recall General Dwight D. Eisenhower. He was only a Lt. Colonel at the outbreak of World War II. Yet only 18 months later, he was a three star general in charge of the largest Allied offensive up to that point."

The President paused, almost for dramatic effect, but more to gauge the reaction of the room. To her surprise and relief, the reaction was largely subdued. Perhaps these men and women, who knew they were about to be called to carry out their duty in the most horrible way possible, understood the need for effective action to conquer long held procedures.

Not encountering any challenging eyes, Doucet continued. "So, I would like for each of you to submit to my staff and me the names of the absolute best strategists, tacticians, battlefield commanders, logisticians, administrators, and trainers you have ever served with, be they active duty or retired. As I said, I don't care very much about rank, seniority; time in rank is what you call it, correct? I also don't care about personal vendettas, rivalries, or empire building. We are in a life and death struggle and we need the absolute best and we need them ASAP."

The Adjutant General from Louisiana spoke up. "Madam President, what if the name or names are people who have not yet declared loyalty to FSA and or are from blue states?"

"We need to know those names as well. Know your enemy, isn't this what we are all taught? But you do bring up an excellent point, general. For each person you submit who may remain loyal to the USA, please submit another name of someone you know or think will be loyal to an FSA state.

In addition, as you are thinking of these names, please also keep in mind three committees I want to form. We are calling them fast-action committees (FACs) and they are to be no more than 5-7 top people. Small and agile, I promise you they will *not* be bureaucratic or political. They will quickly make recommendations and if approved by my staff and me, will have the full authority and funding to implement at all possible speed.

The first is a threat committee. From a military standpoint, what are our biggest deficiencies in how we match up with USA? For instance, my adjutant general has pointed out to me that our GPS capability is hugely important militarily, yet the actual GPS satellites are controlled from the Air Force's Space Warfare Command based at Peterson Air Force Base in Colorado. Since we are not expecting Colorado to join the Free States, this may be a severe disadvantage. Again, that is only one example, but I think an excellent example of the types of threats we need to first identify and then figure out how to deal with.

Next is what we are calling the immediate capability committee, for lack of a better name. We obviously don't think we have years to develop new weapons or capabilities. So, we need to know what, if any, equipment is available now, off the shelf if you will, that will help our ability to fight and win this war. As with the name recommendations, we don't care if the particular piece of equipment is civilian or commercial, manufactured here or foreign, high tech or crude, etc., etc. We need to get the absolute best equipment in the hands of our fighting men and women ASAP. If that means trying to buy an APC from the Russians or an artillery piece from the South Africans, so be it. Now, I understand the Army has something similar, a rapid fielding initiative? If that is the right model, we can adopt it. If need be, we can improve it.

Lastly, we need a resources committee. I think the key in this fight is going to be energy, communications, and food. Yes, food. The energy and food shortages were obviously the spark for the civil unrest that got us to this point. This is an area of advantage for us. A big advantage. We need to know how to maximally exploit this area and how to deny it to the USA.

We may also form an 'everything else, outside the box' committee. So, if you have any possible ideas for this, please also submit them. If we get enough legitimate ideas, we will form the committee.

Once we have the names of our best soldiers, sailors, airmen and Marines, we will quickly fill out our Joint Chiefs and staff structures. We will then rapidly determine our overall strategy to win this war and set about implementing it. And just in case you are wondering, we are taking a similar approach in developing our economic strategy and policies. I believe military strength flows from economic strength and we are proceeding accordingly.

Ladies and gentlemen, I firmly believe wars are won and lost on the basis of such key decisions. Let me state again, that bureaucratic wrangling, red tape, politics of any kind, etc. will not be tolerated. America is the last hope for the world. If the embers of freedom completely die out here, where else will they be kindled? And we, the Free States, are the last hope for America. We cannot fail. We must not fail.

Due to the utter need for quick action, we need the first list of names from each of you within 24 hours. You can then submit the names for the committees 24 hours later. Thank you. Oh, and one last thing. Please do not submit your own name. If anyone of us is as good as we *think* we are, our colleagues will have noticed."

The President leaned back in her chair and lifted her cup of coffee to her mouth slowly and deliberately. Many of the eyes around the room registered near disbelief. They had not expected the President to be this forceful or this knowledgeable. While a few of the officers seated in the room had done their homework, most did not know that the President's father had been a World War II senior staff supply officer and an avid, almost obsessed history buff. He had also wanted boys, but instead got three girls. That had made the President also a student of history, even if at times a reluctant one.

22

THE SITUATION ROOM, THE WHITE HOUSE

The President along with his cabinet and national security council, were all seated in preparation for the Presidential Daily Brief. The Secretary of Defense rose and moved briskly to the lectern.

"Good morning Mr. President, ladies and gentlemen. As of 8:00 PM yesterday, another 27 flag officers have submitted their resignation. The breakdown is 12 Army generals, 9 Navy admirals, 5 Air Force generals and 2 Marine generals. This brings the total number of flag resignations since the rogue states began this crisis to 294, out of a total of 850 such billets, and this does not include the Coast Guard admirals who have resigned."

A few grunts and groans escaped those present and even a low but very brief whistle.

"Continuing, the nuclear ballistic missile submarine *USS Nevada (SSBN-733)* was due back at her base in Bangor, Washington two days ago and has not arrived. There has been no communication from the submarine for three days. Similarly, the nuclear attack submarine *USS New Hampshire (SSN-778)* was due back in to Groton, Connecticut, this morning and has also not arrived. The absence of the *Nevada* is particularly troubling, of course, because it is carrying 24 Trident II nuclear missiles, each with 8 nuclear warheads."

"What is wrong with the Navy?" asked the President, more irritated than angry.

"With respect, Mr. President, the nature of a naval ship, especially a submarine, makes it relatively easy for a handful of officers and men to take control and re-route. A general can order a division or brigade to do something, but some of the men can disagree and take their vehicles with them. Similarly, a pilot can only truly control one aircraft at a time. On a submarine, however, only a handful of officers and perhaps 3-4 enlisted men ever know the position or location of the sub. In any case, we are moving assets to search for the *Nevada.*

"Mutiny. Is this what you are telling me Admiral? That we may have mutinies on these subs?" the President questioned.

"No sir, almost certainly not. It's barratry most likely, if anything," the Admiral replied matter-of-factly.

"Barratry? What in the world is that?" demanded the White House Chief of Staff. "Isn't that something like bringing frivolous lawsuits and ambulance chasing?"

"That's the common law usage, yes sir. In admiralty law, it refers to gross misconduct on the part of the Captain and or officers. If these submarines are missing or defecting, it almost certainly is due to actions of the officers," explained the Admiral.

"Do not use that term. Defecting? That term does not apply here!" roared the President, catching everyone present by complete surprise with such an outburst of emotion.

All eyes turned to the Admiral in time to see his face drain of color. "My apologies, Mr. President. It won't happen again."

An uncomfortable silence followed. The Sec Def decided to break the tension by continuing.

"Switching services, 13 of the Air Force's 20 B-2 stealth bombers are effectively trapped at Whitman Air Force Base in Missouri. The Missouri National Guard along with a detachment from Fort Leonard Wood have surrounded the airfield and hangar complex leading to a stand-off with Air Force personnel still loyal to the USA, including the base commanding officer. The other B-2s were away from Whitman on training missions, including three at Andersen Air Force Base on Guam. However, one B-2 on a training mission landed at Tinker Air Force base in Oklahoma and the pilots declared loyalty to the FSA."

"Must everyone continue to call these traitors by that so-called name?" the President interjected. "I don't want to hear that or 'rebels.' When referring to those states or individuals, they are to be called what they are. Criminals and traitors. Rogue at best, but even *that* gives them a connotation that I do not agree with. And furthermore, any officer who resigns over this mess is not merely resigning. They are becoming traitors. And the penalty for treason has never changed."

The threat of the death penalty hung heavily in the air for several moments with no one wishing to break the silence. The President looked around the room, meeting each person's eyes, searching for a reaction. None was to be found.

"Understood, Mr. President. My apologies. Moving along, the situation with our other long range, heavy bombers does not improve. All six squadrons of B-1Bs are based in rogue states. Half in Texas at Dyess Air Force Base and the other half at Ellsworth in South Dakota. Of the 66 Lancers, 19 were away from their bases with 11 on overseas deployment. Of the nine B-52 squadrons, six are based at Barksdale in Louisiana with the rest at Minot in North Dakota. There are 84 active B-52s and of those, 23 are away from their bases. We have just issued orders for all of the bombers to return at once to Dover Air Force Base in Delaware or Travis in California, whichever is closer. We'll know very soon how many will comply. So, as you can see, the situation with our heavy strategic bombers is not very encouraging. On F-22s, it's a bit better. Prior to the battle over North Carolina, we had 189 active Raptors, including seven used for flight testing. Eight were destroyed in the battle. By our best estimate, there are 63 Raptors in FSA control. We retain control of 82 Raptors in New Jersey, Hawaii, and New Mexico. And, there are 36 more in Alaska. However, we can't be sure of the loyalty of the pilots. We may expect some of these on both sides to change sides in the near future.

The Marines at Camp Pendleton, California, have arrested several hundred of their fellow Marines for expressing loyalty to the rogue states. The base commander reports heightened tensions on the base, but estimates that most of his personnel can be reliably counted on. It helps that they are in California, which is loyal to us. However, our intelligence tells us that perhaps as many as three thousand Marines are not fully loyal, but are keeping a low profile after seeing their buddies arrested. My gut is that this is probably true. The Marines in North Carolina may be a different story due to being so deep inside rogue state lines. The commander of Camp Lejeune has expressed loyalty to us, but there is high tension on the base. Many on the General's staff are urging him to declare for the FSA given their location and since he is from red state Indiana. We should begin planning a naval and air evacuation for those Marines as soon as possible. Most of the Marine aviation assets at Cherry Point and New River are probably going to be lost to us. On the other hand, the West Coast Marine aviation is likely to remain loyal.

For the Army, the situation is similar, if a bit worse than for the Marines. For the most part, those units based in the separatist states are in an untenable position. To date, they have been largely quiet on official communications, but the defections of the senior officers are indicative of how many units may not be loyal. Twenty-two of the Army's Brigade Combat Teams (BCTs) are based in rogue states, while only ten are based in loyal states, not including Hawaii, Alaska, and Washington. Eight BCTs are based in those states, with a further six overseas.

With that, I will turn it over to the Director of National Intelligence for the international briefing."

The DNI stood up, straightened his expensive dark brown suit jacket, and took his place at the front of the room.

"Good morning. The global situation is remarkably quiet. Although our domestic crisis has shaken the international markets almost as badly as it has shaken our own, on the security front it is eerily calm. It's almost as if the entire world is holding its collective breath as they watch and wait to see how we react and handle this crisis. The fighting in South Lebanon between Israel and Hezbollah is continuing, but Israeli strikes on Iran and Syria are lessening in frequency as are rocket and missile strikes on Israel.

The NATO Secretary General has once again urged that we request assistance under Article 5."

"I don't know if we can make the case that we were attacked," said the Attorney General. "I hate what these traitorous states are doing as much as everyone, but we actually initiated the operation that led to the battle."

"Secession, riots, attacks on refineries and transportation centers are all acts of domestic terrorism. We are being attacked, even if it is by our own misguided citizens," the President said, with a sarcastic emphasis on 'misguided.'

"That may be the case, sir, but the long standing understanding of both the UN Charter and NATO is to not interfere in civil wars," responded the Attorney General.

The silence fell on the room like a heavy canvass. One of the President's senior and most trusted advisors as well as one of his oldest friends had said it out loud. In his opinion, the United States of America was in another civil war.

But was it?

"One battle does not a war make, my old friend," the President said, trying to lighten the mood by sounding somewhat flippant. "The events of the past few days have been truly tragic just as the last several weeks have been trying. But I do not believe we have crossed the point of no return with respect to civil war."

Furtive glances cut through the room. Now, the President himself had even uttered the words. Civil War.

Palo Cedro, California, three miles East of Redding

The farm had been chosen as the meeting place as much due to its large barn as for its secluded location and surrounding dense vegetation.

Several of the top militia commanders in Northern California, Oregon, and Washington State had decided to meet to discuss a more coordinated strategy. Across the nation, a loose (very loose) network of communication linked many of the larger patriot militia groups, but a unified command structure had always been resisted. The riots resulting from the food and fuel shortages had caused many militia groups all across the country to sense danger and opportunity. The heavy handed response of the federal government, including the arrest of many real and suspected patriot militia leaders around the country also galvanized the multitude of groups to act.

The secession of the first few states, then followed by several more, reinforced the belief that now was the time to act against the hated central federal government in Washington, D.C. And now, with the first full-fledged battle between the FSA and the USA, these militia commanders had come together to decide on a course of action. To what extent it would be coordinated, however, remained to be seen.

For security reasons, the patriot militia groups had sent their seconds-in-command and adjutants, but most remained in secure communications with their superiors. At least, they believed them to be secure. It was impossible to be sure, given the daily rapid advance of technology. But, the militia techies trusted with such things as secure communications believed that the federal agencies normally tasked with monitoring them were busier with far bigger fish.

The physical security was extremely tight as well. No fewer than 16 heavily armed militiamen clad all in black stood guard in two man teams, at two different defensive layers around the farm. Four of the two man teams also had a well-trained dog with them.

The owner of the farm, a member in good standing with the Northern California State Militia, called the meeting to order and then introduced his executive officer as the first speaker. He explained that his militia's commanders felt that further weakening of the California state government in any way possible was vital. Continued trouble in the countryside might well force the politicians in Sacramento to focus on restoring order in the cities. The rural counties would then be able to call elections to secede from the rest of California. Then, they would be free either to petition the FSA for membership or to seek an autonomous state.

Most of the men in the room nodded general agreement, but of course this then begged the obvious question. What was the best way (or ways) to weaken Sacramento's grip on the state?

The first speaker explained that his organization's position was that the two most important steps would be to attempt to isolate the Bay Area and Sacramento by cutting the communication and transportation lines north to Portland and south to Los Angeles. A third objective would be to cut Los Angeles off from its water supply, which came from over 700 miles to the North. Cutting the lines to the north was a logical step for the organizations present. However, given the geography, the Northern California State Militia felt that cutting the lines to the south, including the California Aqueduct which brought water to Southern California, should be undertaken by units in the area. Cutting the Aqueduct further to the south, just north of the L.A. basin would also ensure that the central valley, particularly the farmers there, was not deprived of water.

So, the proposed operation would be to blow up the I-5 bridge over the Sacramento River arm of Shasta Lake, near the town of Lakehead. The other major artery leading north from the Bay Area was Route 101, also known as the Pacific Coast Highway. This road would be cut south of Ukia. Unlike the bridge, which would take time to rebuild, the 101 south of Ukia went over ground and would be easy to re-build. So, suitable sites for ambush would be identified from Ukia south to Santa Rosa and attacked with mines, IED's and militia squads as often as necessary to restrict movement.

To the east of the Bay Area, Nevada remained loyal to the USA for the present, but it was entirely possible that the state would also vote to secede. In any case, Sacramento was over 100 miles from the Nevada state line across mountains and forests controlled by the militia.

The militia units from Oregon would similarly seek to cut off and isolate Portland to the north and south, while confident in their ability to control the eastern part of the state assuming the Army's units from Fort Lewis were otherwise occupied.

CNN Headquarters, Atlanta

"Good evening, America. I'm Keshia Carlson and here is the latest on the Constitutional crisis gripping our nation. The so-called Free States of America have announced that Dallas, Texas, is their new national capital. Also in Texas, several counties along the Texas border with Mexico have voted to leave Texas in protest over its secession and joining with the other renegade states. Fourteen counties in South

Texas have now decided to petition Washington, D.C. to remain in the USA. These counties include the cities of McAllen, Edinburgh, Mission, and Harlingen, Texas. In an ironic twist, the city council of Austin, the Texas capital, has also voted to secede from the state and is petitioning to remain in the USA."

Free States of America Capitol Building, Dallas Texas

President Doucet sat at her cluttered desk in her medium-sized office, overlooking downtown Dallas. She had already taken to referring to her office jokingly as the Square Office. She studied the list of names submitted to her and her staff as the best in their respective fields and competencies. Several names had come up over and over, but one had come up most of all. According to the informal survey, Major General Greg Parker was the best strategist who most had served with, and also one of the better battlefield tacticians. Doucet had been studying his personnel file since the night before and liked what she saw more and more, the longer she reviewed the information. West Point graduate. Near the top of his class, barely missing top 10%. Tank platoon commander initially, before deciding to attend Ranger school. Winner (along with a partner) of the Best Ranger Competition as a young officer. Tours in Iraq and Afghanistan. Executive Officer (XO) of the 101st Airborne (Air Assault) division. Currently commanding officer of Fort Bliss, Texas and the 1st Armored Division. Obvious administrative skills and an innovative thinker, having implemented everything from new social programs to aggressive clean energy initiatives on his base. Everything she read certainly seemed to confirm what all the others who had written his name down also thought. This soldier needed to be an integral part of the defense of freedom and the Free States of America.

The President of the FSA was convinced. She picked up her phone and rang her executive secretary.

"Teri, please go ahead and get me General Parker on the phone."

23

FORT BLISS, TEXAS,
1ˢᵀ ARMORED DIVISION
HEADQUARTERS

G eneral Parker had been sitting at his computer since 6:00 AM. Planning the movement (he refused to call it an evacuation) of over 13,000 personnel and over 1,000 vehicles on short notice was no easy task. But, the still evolving plan called for two columns of vehicles to depart via a road march while a third would be embarked on rail cars. Although rail was the preferred method to move large units with lots of equipment and vehicles within the continental U.S. (CONUS), in this case it was deemed too exposed and thus risky given the crazy situation around the country. Even powerful M-1 Abrams main battle tanks and other fighting vehicles can't maneuver or fire their main weapons while tied down to rail flat cars. Such large trains are very vulnerable to air and ground attack. But, as always, there are trade-offs. Moving such heavy forces over roads, prepared to fight at a moment's notice, burns tremendous amounts of fuel, especially with the gas-turbine (essentially a jet engine) powered Abrams. Every other tank would be taking a second, fully operational and ready, tank under tow. In this way, the formation would save significant fuel and still be able to go into action at a moment's notice with one-third of the force's tanks completely unencumbered.

Nevertheless, due to the security concerns it was decided that the units going via road march would depart the base and follow I-10 East until reaching the junction with I-20. From there, his force would split into two columns, the northern one following I-20 east / northeast as far as Odessa. The southern column would continue along I-10 at least as far as Fort Stockton. Once encamped in Odessa and Fort Stockton, they would be much less vulnerable to attacks from El Paso – Aztlan or New Mexico and could be fairly easily re-supplied from Fort Hood, Dyess Air Force Base in Abilene and Kelly Air Force Base in San Antonio. It would then be decided how much of the force to move to Fort Hood or perhaps other destinations in Texas or where needed. And, the general hoped that at that point, he would be able to again move his forces via rail. For now, though, the general just needed to get his division and attached units away from the now unfriendly surrounds of El Paso and Southern New Mexico.

His concentration was broken by his ringing phone.

"Yes, lieutenant?" the general answered.

"Sir, there's a lady on the line claiming she's calling from Dallas on behalf of President Doucet."

Parker noted that his aide sounded a bit shaken.

"Thank you put the call through, please." The General took a deep breath.

"General Parker?" asked the cheery voice on the other end of the line.

"Yes, this is he. How can I help you?"

"Good morning, General. Please hold for President Doucet."

"Of course" the general said, but the line had already been put on hold.

After two short minutes listening to elevator music, the President came on the line.

"Good morning, General. This is Sara Doucet."

"Good morning, Madam President. I'm honored by your call, and also somewhat taken aback. How may I help you?" asked the general with more aplomb than he felt. Very few people in the world are nonplussed by a call from a head of state.

"Well, general, the pleasure is all mine, but I do hope you can help me a great deal. I hope you can help us all."

"Yes, ma'am. Of course, ma'am. Anything I can do."

"Good. Thank you. Normally I would never have such a discussion over the phone, but I'm sure you understand the remarkable time constraints we are under. Our new nation needs to form up the absolute best senior military staff possible. We've asked around, and several of the top officers feel you are one of the top yourself."

"Thank you, Madam President. It's always good to hear that one's peers have a high opinion of you."

"Don't thank me yet, but you are welcome. Remember, careful what you wish for," the President chuckled. "Anyway, I would like for you to come to Dallas ASAP for consultations."

"Yes, ma'am. Right away. What specific sort of consultations, if I may ask."

"Direct. I like that. We need to know how to proceed, militarily. I think we are at war, or very soon will be, and I need to know how to win it. Or, at least how to end this war as quickly as possible, but without giving in and giving up our new found freedom to that insane asylum that Washington has become. So, it seems reasonable to me to assemble the very best military minds as quickly as humanly possible."

"Understood, Ma'am. As you probably know, we are in the midst of rapid preparations to move most of our units about three hundred miles east. I need to finish overseeing the preparations and then…"

"General," the President cut off Parker. "Pardon the interruption, but if you are half as good as your file and peers indicate, I fully trust you have expertly trained your second in command and the rest of your staff to complete any task more than competently in your absence. Is this correct?"

Parker let out a short laugh. "Now I must beg pardon, Madam President. My executive officer is a loyal US Army colonel from New Jersey. I'm afraid he won't be a part of our march east. He will be leading the USA loyal personnel north into New Mexico. But I do understand. I will be on the next flight I can arrange to Dallas."

"No need General. In the interest of expediency and security, I am sending a plane for you. It will lift off as soon as I hang up. Have a safe trip and I will see you in a few hours. Thanks again and good bye."

The line went dead. The President wasn't rude, just obviously busy. Extremely busy, the General imagined.

Greg Parker sat in disbelief. Each day seemed more surreal than the previous. It's true he had hoped to be given some sort of command in the new FSA Army. Perhaps even a promotion. But to be called on the phone and summoned to Dallas by the President herself? What did she have in mind? Was it something specific, or was she just the "let's get together and brainstorm and talk things out kind of leader? How long would he be in Dallas? He was suddenly very grateful that he had never given up the habit of keeping an overnight / bug-out-bag packed and ready to go.

Michelle, his wife, would probably have even more questions than he had. She sometimes drove him absolutely mad with her barrages of questions. He chastised himself yet again for being so intolerant and annoyed at what was simply his precious wife's attempts to connect and be part of every facet of his life. At the very least this time he could honestly tell her that he didn't know. His thoughts then drifted from his wife to his oldest daughter, away at college at Columbia University in New York City. He still could not believe how quickly she had turned her back on her upbringing and embraced all the liberalism fed at most American universities. And now, with her not returning his phone calls, what would become of their relationship? The General felt the knot grow in his stomach again, and then pushed it aside his mind and rose to begin his journey to the unknown future.

The Pentagon, the National Military Command Center

The Joint Chiefs of Staff had convened to discuss recommendations for the President. The Chairman of the Joint Chiefs, Air Force General Rick Richardson called the meeting to order. Richardson's call sign, "R&R" only described a part of his personality. One of his favorite sayings, "work hard, play hard," did a far better job of capturing his nature. A career fighter pilot, Richardson had commanded the first active squadron of F-22A Raptors. He had fallen in love with the fifth generation "superfighter" the first time he learned about its capabilities while serving as an F-15C Eagle pilot. Once he flew the Raptor, it had become part of his soul. Although R&R was open to ideas for military options against the rebel states, he was certain the remaining F-22s under control of the USA would play a key role in resolving the crisis.

"Good morning gentlemen," Richardson opened out of habit, rather than any feeling of the times being good. "We all know why we are here. So, everyone is fully briefed on the situation of their service. I need to know what we feel we can offer the President in terms of options to bring our power to bear."

"I feel this is premature. We need to know what the President's policy is, vis-à-vis the FSA" said the Chief of Naval Operations (CNO), Admiral Mike Jankowski. "He must decide on a strategy and then we can offer proposals. We don't formulate policy. The politicians do."

"That's right" the Commandant of the Marine Corps said emphatically. General Leon Ezell was always outspoken and insightful, if a bit rash at times. "The President sends mixed-signals. In some ways he refuses to acknowledge what's really happening. He won't even use the right words, choosing meaningless politically correct phrases. Yet, he acts like we are at war with these states at times and at times not. American states, mind you. He orders an airborne assault on three of them, but won't say we're careening toward civil war. In fact, we are there already, unless a rather large miracle happens."

"I don't disagree with you guys," said Richardson thoughtfully. "But I think the President really wants to consider the range of military options before deciding on a strategy. I think he *needs* to consider what can and may happen if we decide to bring the full might of our forces against the rogue states, and also if there is a more measured response that can bring about some desirable resolution."

"More than half of my combat units are deep in red state territory or out of CONUS" said the Army chief, General Grissom. "I can order them to fight their way out or I can order them to stay in place and act as garrisons. But without clear objectives, including providing a means to re-supply these units and relieve them eventually, they can be bled white by guerrilla type attacks by the local National Guard, law enforcement, or even militia units, both organized and unorganized.

And, how long will it be before even the civilian population looks at our personnel as occupiers and join in attacks? We will have a true insurgency operating against our forces in areas we don't even control now. Think about that, gentlemen. Who will be the hunted and who will be the hunters? And consider this, gentlemen. There are over 80 million Americans living in households that own at least one gun. Most, if not all of you know this, and you also know that this is a conservative estimate. Some estimates put the number closer to 100 million. The National Rifle Association itself has almost 5.5 million members. Many of these gun owners have little or no training with firearms. But, several million hunters have scoped rifles and are experienced at hitting deer sized targets out to several hundred yards. Consider that, several million de facto snipers in a sense. Our total military strength today, active and reserve, is 2.25 million, and 460,000 of that are the state national guards. And then there are the militias. No one seems to have a firm grasp of how many there are. But think about this, if there are even 5,000 members in each of the rebel states, again a conservative number that would mean 85,000 heavily armed members. I, for one, think that number is probably over 100,000, just in the states that have voted to break away so far. Furthermore, this all assumes that these military units remain loyal to us. And we know, with each passing day, more and more men and women are declaring loyalty to their home states. Remember the words of Japanese Admiral Isoruku Yamamoto. 'You cannot invade the USA. There would be a rifle behind every blade of grass.'"

"Point taken. No, a ground campaign at this time is not the answer. At least not now. It's not where we start," answered Richardson. "We need to bring our most powerful conventional asset to bear on our biggest threat. The B-2 stealth bombers still at Whiteman need to be neutralized before they can be used against us. As long as the rebels control even a handful of B-2s, they can threaten us anywhere, anytime. I recommend we send half of our remaining F-22s on a strike against the B-2s."

"Risk our F-22s again? Deep over red territory? That didn't work out very well last time, Rick," observed General Ezell.

"Totally different this time. Last time we messed up by giving our pilots overly restrictive rules of engagement. They had to hold fire until their stealth advantage was all but gone. This is an offensive strike. They zoom in at supercruise, launch their JDAMs and exit before anyone in the FSA is even aware."

The F-22 was the only plane in the American inventory that could supercruise, attain supersonic speeds without having to use gas guzzling afterburners for sustained distances. The new F-35 Lightning II could only supercruise for limited distances. Flying supersonically, the F-22 could release a Joint Direct Attack Munition at 50,000 feet altitude and the JDAM would fly 24 miles before striking its target precisely due to its integrated inertial guidance system coupled to a Global Positioning System (GPS) receiver.

Continuing, Richardson punctuated his argument by re-emphasizing the obvious. "Those stealth bombers are a huge threat. They could be on their way here for a decapitation strike on Washington D.C. as we speak and we'd never know it. We simply cannot allow them to remain in the hands of the rebels."

"Then why not a decapitation strike on the new rebel government in Dallas?" asked General Grissom.

"It wouldn't do much good. This movement to nullify and then secede did not come from one person or even a group of people. Remember, gentlemen, every state in the FSA first voted in their state legislatures and also had it confirmed by their voters," explained the Chairman. "Furthermore, a decapitation strike would call into question the Hague Convention against targeting leaders," he pointed out.

"That doesn't apply here," objected the Marine Commandant. "For instance, all throughout World War II military lawyers argued that the Convention, which reads 'treacherous killing' of leaders, is internationally recognized to mean assassination in peacetime."

The Army Chief of Staff, General Grissom, agreed. "We are not at peacetime. In addition, the Hague Convention applies to international relations. It is not meant to apply to internal national disputes such as insurrections and civil wars."

Richardson, along with the other leaders of America's vaunted military paused to think about the arguments floating around.

Finally, the Air Force general broke the silence. "Ok, I think a decapitation strike would probably be viewed as legal, against renegade leaders. We've been using drone strikes to kill terrorist leaders for years, of course. But I also think we need to consider the practical repercussions. At a minimum, this strike will raise the anger of the people in the red states even if it is unsuccessful. At worst, it opens the door for the FSA to undertake similar missions against our leadership."

"Careful R&R. You don't want the President to hear you use that term, or 'rebels' like you did a minute ago," cautioned Admiral Jankowski.

"Well, our illustrious leader is not here at present and I'm simply trying for brevity as we discuss complex issues." Laughter at Richardson's humor with a touch of sarcasm at the expense of the Commander in Chief broke some of the tension.

"We already launched a military operation against the rebels. What's different with this or any other follow on?" asked Jankowski.

"Deploying, or attempting to in the recent case, airborne units to secure DOD assets in areas wracked by riots and other political uncertainty or renegade state forces is one thing. As we discussed, it would have been portrayed as a peacekeeping mission. We don't know whether or not a ground battle would have ensued. And if it had, it could easily be argued that those who resisted were doing so illegally. We were only securing our military equipment and property. Dropping bombs on US soil, on the US homeland, is entirely different, especially when everyone knows that we will have deployed the weapons knowing that Americans, US Air Force personnel *and* civilians, would be killed. This cannot be painted as anything other than what it is. An attack on the FSA states and people," concluded Ezell firmly. "Any attack on Dallas will cause civilian casualties. The so-called capitol building of the FSA is in downtown Dallas. Chew on that before making a decision."

"So, General, you're opposed to any military operation? Is this what you are telling us," questioned Richardson.

"No, that's not at all what I'm saying. I just want everyone clear on what a second overt military operation will mean. We've already put in economic sanctions against the rogue states and are attacking their cyber infrastructure. We've cut off all federal aid payments to those states and we know they are feeling the pinch in that regard. We are taking action. And, we have yet to fully deploy our covert assets against the rebels," said Ezell.

"Excellent point, EZ. The Director of National Intelligence, Attorney General, and FBI Director are refining the covert civilian assets and plans which can be brought to bear. We will submit our recommendations concurrently. He will, of course, decide what plans to implement and in what order," said Richardson. "Very good discussion, but now back to the task at hand. I am recommending an F-22 strike on the B-2 bombers at Whiteman. We can follow that up with additional F-22 strikes against the B-1B Lancers remaining at Dyess Air Force Base in Texas and Ellsworth in South Dakota. Then the B-52s at Barksdale, Louisiana and Minot, North Dakota. As a secondary, wider proposal, we can begin neutralizing remaining FSA air assets. Other proposals? Mike, what can our other brothers in blue offer? Oh, I'm sorry; I meant to say our squid-like brothers in blue."

"The loyalty of many of our assets is in question as well, as we have seen with the submarines that have not reported in. But we still do have enough assets to perform even large missions. We can, of course, enforce an immediate naval quarantine on the FSA ports, starting with Houston, Savannah, and New Orleans, among the busiest ports in the nation. We can also deploy submarine and ship launched Tomahawk cruise missiles in support of a decapitation strike on Dallas or attacks on Dyess and Barksdale. Unfortunately, we don't have the range to hit Whiteman, Minot or Ellsworth. They are too far inland. Remember, that was one reason for putting these strategic assets there. To protect them from Russian submarine launched cruise missile attack or at least provide warning time if the attack was from nuclear sea-launched ballistic missiles (SLBMs). But we do have the range to hit any target within 900 miles of the coast. This includes the Texas-Louisiana oil infrastructure and a whole lot of red state military bases in the South," Jankowski offered.

"Don't forget that our brothers in blue, as you put it R&R, are our ride. They can move my Marines and set them anywhere along the coast, and up to 250 miles inland. We can threaten a whole lot of FSA territory. For instance, we may want to secure the entire Norfolk Naval Complex, in the event Virginia secedes."

"That is an interesting thought, General, but remember that Virginia has already mobilized their Guard and have deployed around the base. And, as Ski just pointed out, we don't know the loyalty of all the naval units. Most of the ships you will need as transports are based at Norfolk unless you propose to bring them all the way from San Diego. Any landing will likely be opposed by the Virginians, at least, and possibly also by naval and naval aviation units. It may just push Virginia over the edge and into the arms of the FSA if they haven't at that point. Just something to keep in mind," said Richardson.

"I think we can all agree that any engagement of ground forces here on US soil will be viewed as a significant escalation of hostilities," the Army Chief of Staff pointed out.

"Yes, and dropping bombs on US airmen and soil will be viewed as a cotillion," Ezell retorted sarcastically.

"Interesting choice of words, EZ," Admiral Jankowski cut in. "But here is a question, should we be focusing on destroying the FSA's military forces or should we be focusing on their economy and ability to wage war? Shouldn't we go after that Gulf oil infrastructure and their electrical infrastructure? Transportation infrastructure? What about the gold deposit at Fort Knox?"

"I think in the short term, we need to focus on defending and protecting against FSA threats against us. Don't we all want more time to work this out politically? I, for one, don't want to see one more American die. Ours or theirs. We are all Americans. We need to give the politicians a chance to end this madness," said Richardson.

"The politicians?" General Ezell practically snorted. "Aren't they the ones that got us into this mess in the first place?"

"Yes, absolutely. But that is our system. And they need to be the ones that pull us out of this mess somehow. Maybe we also need to deliver to the President our best threat assessment from the FSA along with our recommendations. We need to help him and his senior advisors see that the military solution cannot be the way."

24

FREE STATES OF AMERICA
CAPITOL, DALLAS, TEXAS

Major General Greg Parker sat in the lobby outside President Doucet's Office, the Square Office, as she delighted in calling it, waiting for his meeting. The FSA's temporary capitol was located in a newly constructed, if somewhat non-descript office building in downtown Dallas. Parker asked the Presidential staffer who greeted him why the new government was in an office building and not in an existing government building. She explained to him that moving into an existing building would have disrupted the government entity already there and the last thing this new federal government wanted to do was to start its existence by immediately being a burden on the lower levels of existing government or its citizens.

The general marveled at the small but significant point made and that someone had actually thought of that. He felt a touch of nervousness, but had to admit to himself that it was more excitement than nervousness. And, he felt very conflicted over his feelings of excitement, almost angry with himself. No sane soldier is supposed to look forward to battle. And this should be even truer with the prospect of facing off in battle against his fellow Americans, many of whom would undoubtedly be friends and colleagues. Nevertheless, Parker was excited to share his ideas for offensive operations to end the war quickly with the President. In fact, during the entire flight from Biggs Army Airfield to DFW Airport, Parker could not keep a certain scripture out of his mind. Jeremiah 51:20, "You are my war club, my weapon for battle-with you I shatter nations, with you I destroy kingdoms."

But every time the scripture rolled through his mind, Parker also reminded himself of the sin of pride. He must fight that urge for pride as vehemently as any physical battle he would ever face.

"General," the staffer called out. "The President will see you now."

Parker moved quickly to the Square Office, having already been screened by multiple layers of Secret Service.

President Doucet stood from behind her desk and beamed a smile at General Parker as if he was a long lost dear friend. She quickly moved around her large desk and eagerly extended her hand.

"General, it's a pleasure to meet you in person. How was your trip?" inquired the Chief Executive.

"Madam President, the pleasure and honor are all mine. My trip was uneventful, which is to say it was a good flight. I am truly humbled that you asked to meet with me in private," the general saying out loud his reminder to resist pride.

"General, it is my experience that if a person wants to hear what is truly on a person's mind and in their heart, it is better to not have several layers of that person's superiors or wanna-be superiors around. I have heard some very good things about you and I want to get to know you. I want you to feel completely free to speak candidly. I won't be expressing my opinion very much at this point, but if you do sense that you disagree with me on something, I want you to put it out front. Don't hide it. Let's discuss it. You present your ideas and defend them or explain them. I'll listen, whether I ultimately agree or not. Deal?"

The General was immediately drawn to this woman and felt an immediate respect and ease. What was the saying about charm? That charm was the ability to make the other person feel completely at ease? Why was he thinking about this when...

"General? Do we have a deal?"

"Uh, yes, ma'am," stammered the General, scarcely believing that his mind had wondered about charm while being asked a question by his new Commander-in-Chief.

"Ok, well good then. I was worried for a second when you didn't answer," teased the President. "Please have a seat. Can I get you some more coffee?"

Parker declined the coffee and requested ice water instead as he sat in the modernistic chair, which was less comfortable than it looked.

"General, let's get right to this. What do you think about this mess our nation is in?"

Parker was taken aback by such an open-ended question. He took several moments formulating his answer.

"Madam President, I think our nation is in a second Civil War and I think it is absolutely horrible. But I don't think that is what you are looking for. The horrific situation we find ourselves in is obvious to all but extremists, or those completely asleep and watching reality TV shows all day long. I suspect that what you are truly asking is what I recommend you do about it, yes?"

"Go on, General," said the President in a low voice as she continued looking at him intently.

"I've given the strategic situation a great deal of thought. It seems we have two basic options. Each of those options, however, has other multiple variations within them that I will touch on later. So, our two basic options are to wait out the USA or act aggressively against them. I simply don't see another option, broadly speaking, other than forgetting the whole secession thing and re-unification. After all that has happened at the state and local level all across the nation, I just don't see this last option as a true option. Therefore, only two options. Wait or act."

"Isn't this an oversimplification, general?" asked the President, playing devil's advocate to the unknowing general.

"Not at all, Madam President. As I said, each of the two options has multiple possible courses of actions."

"Continue."

"I think the most relevant lessons in deciding between waiting them out or acting can be found in studying the first Civil War and the Revolutionary War. Now I know we are not simply re-fighting the first

Civil War as many on the left and the mainstream media are asserting. Far from it. Very far. As an African-American, I am acutely aware of this. But in terms of strategic decisions, I think the similarities are uncanny. First, however, the ways in which the strategic situation is different. In 1861, one side had overwhelming superiority in population, industrial capacity, technology, railroads, etc. Today, the red states and blue states are fairly evenly split. I think the FSA in its final form may actually possess more military power than the USA."

"Final form?" interrupted the President.

"Yes, I don't think we've seen the last state to secede. Five or six more states are considering articles of secession, as I'm sure you know. Georgia, Florida, Virginia, Kansas, and Kentucky all have large military units based in them and most or all will join FSA shortly, in my estimation. The Federal government is moving personnel out and some equipment as they are able, but the majority of both will remain where they are at present. Fort Campbell's CO has already declared loyalty to us, even before the Kentucky legislature has voted, as has the commanding officer of Fort Riley. In any case, the USA and FSA are fairly evenly matched militarily and economically.

Another difference is the international situation. During the Civil War, the South hoped for Great Britain and France to recognize their independence and intervene on their behalf to secure the flow of cotton to their mills. This obviously never happened unlike in our Revolution when the French did come in on the side of the rebellion. Today, I think the USA will be hoping for European assistance and possibly UN intervention in any drawn out war. And truthfully, they may get it.

Now, for the similarities. In 1861 the best chance the South had to win the war and gain its independence came early in the war, before the North could mobilize their huge population and industry. In 1861 or even 1862, had the South moved the Army of Northern Virginia northeast to attack or even just threaten, Washington, DC, Baltimore, and possibly Philadelphia, Lincoln would have been obliged to respond. This would have probably won the war for the South."

"But Lee did invade the North. Twice. And failed." The President impressed the Major General with her knowledge.

"Agreed, Madam President, but Lee made two grave strategic errors in both of those campaigns. I feel a bit silly for criticizing the legendary General Lee, but first, he waited too long to move North. Had he moved after First Bull Run, for instance, the North would have scarcely had a rag tag band to oppose him. Strictly speaking, he wasn't in command of the Southern Army at First Bull Run, but he was already a trusted advisor to Jefferson Davis, and he did not support moving against the North. Second, on both occasions that he moved north, he moved against Northern strength, their armies in the field, rather than against weakness by threatening the cities, industries, and railroads. He could have brought the pain of war to the northern population while avoiding much of the bloodshed."

"Thank you for the history re-cap, General," the President chuckled to show she was not annoyed.

"My apologies, ma'am. My point is this. We should not make those two mistakes. If war cannot be averted, then I propose that we move ground forces toward Washington, D.C., Philadelphia, and New York as soon as possible. And by ground forces, I am also including airborne and air mobile units. But, we should not seek to engage USA strength as we move north. Moving in a north - northeasterly loop around Washington and toward Philadelphia will threaten these cities plus Baltimore. Completing the loop north of Philadelphia will cut off the eastern seaboard south of New York. If need be, we can quickly swing further north to also threaten New York itself and perhaps Boston. We can occupy or cut off energy and transportation infrastructure as we go, but at all times seek to minimize engagements with USA forces and civilian casualties at all cost.

We also want to minimize damage to the blue state infrastructure, believe it or not, wherever possible. Sun Tzu wrote that the acme of skill is to subdue the enemy without fighting. I don't think we can accomplish this without any fighting or destruction, but our goal should be to minimize fighting and therefore minimize destruction to our countrymen. As Sun Tzu also wrote, 'the best thing of all is to take the enemy's country whole and intact; to shatter and destroy it is not so good.' We don't wish to take the USA whole; we should aim to take their will and ability to fight. And this is the most important part: at all times we include a massive and sustained PR campaign offering peace to the USA in return for recognizing the FSA. I mean truly massive and sustained. We put it on cable, talk-shows, the internet. We blast it from loudspeakers from our military vehicles. We drop pamphlets. We announce it at the UN. We say it over and over to anyone who will listen and also to those that won't. We don't want war. We just want to be left to form our own nation. We want peace. We don't want to 'conquer' the USA states. As soon as they recognize us, we bring our forces home. I have more detailed plans for all of this, of course, should you want to see them."

The President sat in silent contemplation. She looked into Parker's eyes, searching for malice or arrogance and found none. What she saw was a strange mixture of profound sadness and optimism. He truly believed that he had the key to a relatively short campaign to bring the war to an amenable end. But, then again, didn't *every* general and admiral believe that he or she had the key to winning warfare? He also knew that death and suffering on a large scale was inevitable, despite the best plans and efforts to avoid it.

She had to admit, the plan had some merit. She probed further.

"So you think this will minimize casualties? How does this minimize casualties when compared to waiting out the USA and only fighting a defensive battle if and when forced into it?" She asked, again slipping on the devil's advocate veil once again.

"Yes, ma'am. The key is a quick resolution. I'm not saying the FSA can't win a drawn out fight. In fact, I'd say it's almost 50-50. Maybe even 60 – 40 in our favor in a long conflict. But I do believe that the longer any conflict goes, the harder it will be for us to secure victory. At the outset we will control more combat power, but this balance may shift. For instance, the longer this goes, the greater the chance that NATO or the UN will enter on the side of the USA. Whether they do it directly with forces or indirectly with arms and supplies, they will support the USA against what they see as extremist cowboys. In any case, a longer conflict means more fighting, and more casualties, of course. We must endeavor to win this as quickly as possible, for the sake of the FSA *and* the USA."

"I see," the President said dryly. "It doesn't sound like you are proposing to capture Washington, Philadelphia or New York. So what are you saying?"

"We should be mindful of the lessons of Fallujah, Stalingrad, Hue City or Chechnya. Namely, that we should avoid fighting in built-up, urban areas whenever possible. And even more so given that these are American cities we are talking about. No, I think that cutting off their electricity, fuel, and even food, to a limited extent, is the way to go. We make the average citizen understand what a prolonged war will cost them so they demand that the US government recognizes us and enters into peace negotiations," Parker explained. "We will push in as far as possible in the urban areas until we meet with heavy resistance and then we can fall back into strong defensive positions. We can then focus on probes and thunder runs into the cities as a means to keep the USA forces off balance."

"Food. You said food, too, general. We can't be starving Americans on purpose, can we?" the President challenged.

Parker shook his head vigorously. "No, of course not, Madam President. I'm not proposing to cut off food completely. We would allow in basic foodstuffs and even help provide MRE's. The point is to take away what the populace is used to, namely a wide variety of food and conveniences always ready at their fingertips. Push them out of their comfort zone. But no, I don't advocate starving Americans out in a siege. Make life difficult in a quarantine. Now that's a different matter," concluded the General. "And, we allow any civilian who wants to leave to do so once they sign a short document recognizing the right of the FSA to exist and swearing never to take up arms against us. Of course, these are all ultimately questions of policy and would fall under the purview of the civilian leadership."

"What you say does have some merit on its surface. Actually, it has a great deal of merit. I will consider it and talk it over with my staff and senior military advisors. You understand there will be massive resistance to invading the USA controlled areas, and in so doing, becoming the aggressor and giving up the moral high ground."

"Understood, Madam President, but are we looking to win the PR battle or quite simply the battle for the existence of the FSA and the founding principles of our nation?"

"Touché general. And I trust that if I decide to move this proposal forward, you are prepared to defend it to our new Joint Chiefs, and not just to a civilian former governor like me? Are your plans well enough developed to answer operational questions and objections?"

"To a certain extent, yes. I don't have all the details of an Op Plan worked out. But I have thought this through to know the major salient points, objectives, threats, etc."

"Very well, general. I will take this under advisement. I understand you wish to return to your base and your men for the movement. But please be prepared to return to Dallas or anywhere else I may need you at a moment's notice."

"Yes, Madam President, of course. And thank you. But there is one more thing. Actually, three more things."

"Yes, General?" the President asked.

"First, is the issue of the economy. I feel somewhat silly raising this with you, our civilian leader, but as you know, our military strength is largely dependent on economic strength. We must unleash the creativity and productivity of our state economies. I trust you are taking the same pragmatic approach with the economy that you have shown me you are taking with the military."

"I believe we are, general. But if you have specific ideas, please share them now or whenever they come to you."

"My ideas are not about the economy at large per-se, but have to do with efficient use of our resources to field the maximum amount of combat power. To this end, I think we will very quickly deplete much of our first line equipment such as aircraft, helicopters, and tanks. So, I believe we should immediately begin implementing plans to re-activate many of our platforms which are currently in storage, beginning with our aircraft storage at Davis-Monthan Air Force Base.

And if I may be so bold, I would strongly recommend that we begin with the A-10 Thunderbolts stored there. I know from personal experience that there is nothing worse than being isolated and under fire and being told that close-air support is not available."

"I see, general. Being from Tucson, I am quite familiar with our boneyard facility there. I will have someone begin working on this ASAP. What else?"

"Casualties, Madam President. Please understand that everything is relative. The wars in Afghanistan and Iraq have given our nation an unrealistic expectation of war. Namely, in the number of casualties."

"I'm not sure I'm following," the President confessed.

"The first Civil War cost us 600,000 dead Americans at least. World War II, 400,000. In Afghanistan and Iraq, after more than 10 years of war, we lost less than 10,000 total. Now each and every death, or even injury for that matter, is a tragedy. Not only to the individual, but to his friends and family. I personally have seen men die in combat. Men and women under my command. My men. I can see each of their faces. So this is not to minimize any number of deaths. But, Madam President, this war will be very, very different. This will be the first time that peer combatants will engage on a large scale since the 1973 Arab-Israeli war."

Parker paused and looked at his commander-in-chief. She sat quiet, extremely still. She was regarding him intently.

The General continued, "If we cannot end this conflict quickly, I fear the number of casualties from the first Civil War may be far exceeded. And, furthermore, whatever combat does ensue will be far bloodier and more savage than anything we have ever seen."

President Doucet swallowed and nodded, taking in Parker's warning.

"I know what peer means, but I'm not sure how to interpret what you are saying."

"This will be the first time since 1973 that two first rate armies with state-of-the-art weapons and training will be engaging each other. This will not be us against the Taliban, or us against the Iraqi insurgents or even the Russians against the Mujahedin. And on top of all that, it is a civil war, which history has shown us are the most savage types of wars. We simply cannot have this become a long, drawn out conflict."

The President nodded silently. "Understood, general. Thanks again for coming on such short notice."

The General rose, saluted, and did a crisp about face and exited the Square Office. For the first time since the crisis began, President Sara Doucet allowed herself a tinge of optimism.

25

TEHRAN, IRAN

The Supreme Leader of the Islamic Republic of Iran, Grand Ayatollah Seyyed Ali Hosseini Khamenei entered the chamber as the other seventeen men present in the room stood. The Supreme Leader took his seat after nodded greetings. The President of Iran was seated immediately to the right of the Supreme Leader with the 12 members of the Guardian Council taking their places around the table next. The commanders of the Iranian Air Force, Army, Navy, and Revolutionary Guards were seated at the far end of the table.

"My brothers, Allah is striking a great blow against the Great Satan in retaliation for their treachery and complicity in covering for the Little Satan's recent attack on our Republic. He is turning their depraved minds full of lusts, greed, and pride against one another. We have witnessed their aircraft blowing each other out of the sky and falling upon their own lands in flames! Allah Akbar!" the Supreme Leader shouted as he lifted his eyes to heaven.

The room resounded with echoing cries of "Allah Akbar! Death to the Great Satan and the Little Satan!"

"Now, my brothers," the Grand Ayatollah continued more sub-dued, "We must consider what our great calling is now. How do we best hasten the rapid demise of these plagues on society known as the United States and Israel? Our reprisals after the Jewish monkeys attacked us were very successful and, in fact, helped bring about the widespread rioting in America's cities, which brought its internal decay, moral, physical, and economic, to the surface for the entire world to witness. Many of their people are hungry; many without fuel.

They are killing one another in their streets! What actions must our great Islamic Republic take in carrying out Allah's will to see the Satans destroyed?"

"Your holiness, you are wise and inspirational as always. We are humbled that you come to us seeking counsel. I propose that we strike at our mortal enemies now, while they are wounded. The arrogant, unmerciful infidels have a saying, 'kick your enemy while he is down.' This is what we must do. We have been given a wonderful blessing and opportunity. We must not waste it. We must strike at America with every-thing we have. We must use the ultimate weapon which our Russian and North Korean friends have helped us develop. The Hammer of Heaven must strike!" the President said emphatically.

Several of the men seated around the massive oak table nodded agreement. Others, however, did not.

The commander of the Revolutionary Guard spoke next. "I agree with our President. We must not fail to act. With the enemy's eyes turned inward, fighting amongst themselves, it is the perfect time to utilize the Hammer and also our special weapons commando units. We have seven units ready in key American cities as you know. They have been infiltrated into America for a time such as this. Now is the time to strike!"

"Perhaps it is the time to strike. Perhaps not." The Admiral in over-all command of the Navy was known as a thinker and a scholar, as well as ferocious warrior. "I too have studied American culture carefully and our infidel enemies have another saying. 'The enemy of my enemy is my friend.' I agree that America's eyes are turned inward. But if we strike in such a large and overt manner, do we not run the risk of turn-ing their eyes back outward? We have seen how the American rage can be ignited in an instant, especially when attacked in their homeland on a massive scale. The attack on the naval base of Pearl Harbor by the Japanese showed us this anger. As did the glorious attacks of 2001. The Hammer of Heaven will cause far more casualties and damage than both of those attacks put together. Even more so if combined with the activation of our seven special teams. No, my brothers. It is not wise to initiate either of these operations now. Let the infidels kill each other and weaken day by day. Instead, let us search for ways to *help* them kill one another as effectively as possible for as long as possible. May they yet be killing one another when our Twelfth Imam appears and nods to us in approval. Allah Akbar!"

"Compelling arguments, Admiral. I presume you have suggestions on how we can assist the infidels to better kill one another and destroy their wretched, corrupt land?" asked the Supreme Leader.

"Yes, your Holiness. We can increase the smuggling of weapons, drugs, and money through their southern border. Our Mexican cartel puppets are only too happy for the additional business. We can ensure the weapons find their way into the hands of the various extremist groups and racial gangs fighting the government and each other. The drugs we can funnel in larger numbers into the cities. We arm both sides and provide drugs and money as well. We can also activate more of our sleeper cells to kidnap and assassinate leaders of these groups and gangs, and make it look like it was the work of rivals and even the government itself. The sleeper operatives can also destroy targets of opportunity in their infrastructure, particularly their energy and food supplies. Since we have already been utilizing western sayings, 'we look for ways to add fuel to the fire' that is engulfing their wretched land."

The commander of the Revolutionary Guard, eager as always to enhance his image and status, jumped on the Admiral's comments. "Yes, indeed. All wise suggestions. We can also step up our efforts to destabilize the puppet regimes in Saudi Arabia and Iraq. This will continue to put extra pressure on their over-stretched military and the continued interruptions to the flow of oil will continue to hurt world markets, and thus, the Great Satan as well."

The Supreme Leader stroked his long grey beard and nodded knowingly. "Very good. And what of our Chinese, North Korean and Venezuelan allies? Will they also be persuaded to join our campaign of pressure on the Americans?"

"Yes, your eminence. I believe they will. They have very little to lose and much to gain by striking at America's perceived hegemony," answered the Admiral. "In addition, we can now re-assert pressure here in our Gulf. We have detected a noticeable pull-back on the part of American naval forces. This had already started prior to their civil war, due to budget constraints. And now, we believe they are pulling back even more to deal with their own troubles. NATO forces appear to be preparing to increase their presence, but they do not have the capabilities of the Americans and cannot long make up for the absence of their American overlords. We can, once again, close the Strait, comrades," the Admiral concluded confidently.

The Supreme Leader allowed the other men in the room several more minutes of copycat comments and agreement before speaking.

"Very well, gentlemen. We will consider this in prayer and make our decision. Thank you." He rose and glided out of the room feeling content that Allah was working things out just as he had always expected. The Great Satan would soon be completely on its knees and then the Little Satan could be dealt with once and for all to the glory of God...

Antlers Bridge Over Shasta Lake, I-5, California

The recently completed cantilever bridge carried I-5 traffic over the beautiful deep blue-green waters of Shasta Lake. The I-5 was the primary north-south artery on the West Coast. The secondary was Route 101, which ran along the scenic coast, but it didn't carry as much traffic as the I-5, which was further inland. The two eight-person squads of California militiamen had been carefully selected for their skills and knowledge of the surrounding areas. Fourteen of the twenty men were military veterans. Two were from the town of Redding, a few miles south while another was from Lakehead, just to the north of the scenic bridge which was now a target. Each squad also had a woman.

One squad was approaching on I-5 from the north with half the team in a 90s model Chevy Suburban painted dark blue with the rest of the team trailing in black 2001 Ford F-350 dually work truck. Both vehicles carried several hundred pounds of explosives and equipment. The squad that approached from the south consisted of a dark green Ford Excursion SUV and a gray Dodge Ram dually, both vehicles similarly equipped as their northern counterparts. Two women sat in the front passenger seat of each SUV. In the event the vehicles were stopped by law enforcement, a couple would always appear less suspicious than a truck full of men.

The development of the operational plan had seen much disagreement and discussion within the militia leadership. Some of the militia leaders felt it was vitally important that casualties, especially civilian ones, had to be avoided at almost any cost. To accomplish this, massive trees would have to be felled across the northbound lanes on the south side of the bridge and the reverse on the north side, prior to blowing the bridge. Not all the militia leaders felt that the increased time and risk of the tree-felling operation were worth guaranteeing that no one would be hurt when bridge was destroyed. They felt that traffic would be relatively light at 3:00 AM when the spans across Shasta Lake would be brought down, and any vehicles that happened to be on the bridge would be incidental collateral damage.

"Innocent civilians are not collateral damage!" insisted the XO of the Northern California Bear Republic Militia. "This is not Baghdad and we are not an occupying army. We are citizen soldiers and we should not be killing our very neighbors in the process of helping them to wake up about the morally and physically bankrupt governments in Sacramento and Washington, D.C. Like in Vietnam, we need to win the hearts and minds of our fellow citizen patriots."

"The obvious flaw in your argument is that the hearts and minds campaign failed in Vietnam and we lost that war," retorted the militia CO arrogantly. "Our neighbors do need to wake up, and this includes waking up to the fact that we are in a life and death struggle for our freedoms and our republic. Wars, especially 'civil' ones are anything but. The sooner these sheeple open their eyes, the better," concluded the commander while pounding his fist on the table."

Some of the men in the room winced. They didn't like referring to non-aware people as sheeple, even if it was a very applicable metaphor. Others smiled at the reference.

"We are in the early stages of what may be a long insurgency. We will need the local populace to support us and not cooperate with the government. We do not get support and cooperation of the locals by killing their wives, husbands, brothers, sisters and children," said the XO.

"Perhaps you're not understanding the operational risk," the CO said in a not-too-veiled reference to his twenty years of active service as a Ranger in comparison with his second-in-command. The longer we take in messing around with trying to fell large trees across a highway, the greater the chance of detection and compromising the entire mission." The CO was getting increasingly agitated despite efforts to keep it under control.

The XO was highly respected, but had served his time as an Air Force Material Management Sergeant. He was highly respected mainly for his organizational skills and his genius in seemingly being able to obtain almost any type of gear the militia wanted. But, he had started out his career with the Air Force Security Forces, so he was more than just the "wing-wiper" that his comrades like to teasingly call him.

"I disagree," the XO said in his normal, calm manner. "The team working on the trees can begin at the same time as the boat team and bridge team begin their work. The time should not be significantly impacted. And, if the tree teams happen to be detected, it may allow the boat team at least to complete its work while all eyes are elsewhere."

"But if the tree teams are detected, then there will be no way to ensure no traffic on bridge when it is blown. In fact, it will increase traffic. Aren't you now going back on what you say is this very important objective?" the CO asked condescendingly.

"No. War is about calculated risks and not everything will ever be controlled. It is worth the risk to try and ensure we block traffic on the bridge. If, in the end, we blow the bridge and some civilians are killed, at least we know we made every effort to prevent that."

After much more heated debate, it became clear that the consensus was on including the tree felling to block traffic before triggering the bridge explosives.

Both the northern and southern tree and look out teams were in place just before 2:00 AM. Each team had set the female member as a lookout and listening post 1 mile away from where the trees would be felled. The lookouts would report on approaching cars and trucks via clicks, no talking, on small two way radios. By this time, the boat team was also in place on the north bank directly underneath the massive concrete and steel bridge, and the bridge team had stopped their Suburban on the right side of the southbound lanes. Feigning engine trouble, the hood was popped, but no hazard lights were lit. It was hoped this combination would give the impression that the vehicle had been stopped for some time and the absence of a person meant the owner had gone for help.

It had been decided that, in the interest of speed, explosives would be used to drop the trees. The northern team had a logger while the southern team, a former logger. Each logger selected a large tree a suitable distance from the roadway. Then, sticks of industrial explosives were applied to the trunk, just where the face-cut would be. This would still provide a directional fall. While not as precise as using chainsaws, and producing jagged cuts, time was of the essence.

Below the bridge, the boat team had paddled to the third concrete pillar, the one closest to the middle of the river. The boat did have a small trolling motor, but it had not been used due to the desire for stealth. The three men, all with explosive or engineering experience, worked quickly to affix blocks of Semtex in strategic locations. Above them, two of the bridge team had used rappelling gear to descend the approximately forty feet from the road surface of the span to the point where the metal trusses were affixed to the massive concrete column. More Semtex was attached here. When all of the explosives were attached, both teams moved back north and repeated the process on the third column. Both the bridge and boat team reported tasks successfully completed to the southern tree and observation team in overall command of the operation. All other teams began to exit the area and once 20 minutes had passed, the tree teams would detonate the charges to fell the trees.

"Time, sarge," said the southern militiaman – logger.

"Ok, let's blow this and get out of Dodge," replied the sergeant.

"Firing. 3…2…1. Fire in the hole," the logger said barely above a whisper and he pressed the cell phone detonator. The explosion was more muffled than they expected, but then heard a second blast and realized that the northern team had detonated their package a split second before theirs.

Both teams scanned the bridge with night vision scopes to verify no vehicle had come through. Once the southern team received confirmation from their counterparts, they set off the bridge explosives.

Four massive explosions tore at the bridge in an eruption of light and sound. The affected span shuddered and then teetered but did not collapse into the river far below. It was never expected that the operation would collapse the bridge. But the span was blown askew and even untrained eyes would be able to see that the bridge was effectively destroyed.

The leader of the southern team looked on with satisfaction. The damaged section would have to be removed and re-built. And this would take time. Much time. Especially in times such as this, short of money and resources. The militiaman knew that there were also ways to disrupt repair efforts, especially in such remote areas. The primary artery connecting the San Francisco and Sacramento metro areas to northern California and Oregon had been severed. To the west, Route 101 had also been severed in a similar operation against the Healdsburg Memorial Bridge, which carried the historic route over the Russian River.

The militiaman surveying the damage to the Antlers Bridge took great satisfaction in knowing that no one had been hurt during the operation. It also made him wonder. Although born and raised a Catholic, he hadn't practiced his faith since leaving his parents' house. He had looked into New Age beliefs, including the concept of karma. He wondered if perhaps such good luck on this mission meant that their luck would run out on the next. Perhaps it was time to re-evaluate his beliefs. He didn't remember ever being nearly as whimsical. Strong faith might be needed for the long struggle he was sure was still ahead.

26

CNN HEADQUARTERS, ATLANTA, GA

"Good evening, America. I am Keshia Carlson and this is CNN." The pretty African-American anchor flashed her trademark smile at the camera. That smile had served her well during her time as a practicing attorney. So had her ability to immediately put on a gravely serious demeanor as she did next.

"The eyes of America are on Virginia. The Old Dominion is the latest state to vote to secede from the United States and petition to join the so-called Free States of America. This now makes 20 states total that have decided to separate from the United States. In addition to the 18 states calling themselves the Free States of America, Washington State and Vermont have declared themselves independent nations.

Virginia is a large state with the 12th largest population, right behind New Jersey. Virginia is also home to huge military bases. All four services have major bases in the state. And, of course, it is right across the Potomac from Washington, D.C. Will this proximity lead to more military confrontation? There has already been one battle between the rogue states and American armed forces in the skies over the Tennessee – North Carolina border, in what some people are calling the Battle of the Great Smoky Mountains.

And now, on the heels of the Virginia secession vote, word that six more state legislatures may be voting on secession as soon as tomorrow. These states, Nebraska, Georgia, Kansas, West Virginia, Indiana and Kentucky are all red states by their recent voting history, and most political observers expect all of them to vote to leave the Union as well. The only one of those state votes that can even be called close is Indiana. Many of these observers also are now saying that a full blown civil war is all but inevitable. Reports have been surfacing daily of military units segregating themselves along red state – blue state lines and declaring loyalty for the USA or FSA. Dozens of generals and admirals have also resigned from the US armed forces and declared loyalty to the FSA, while others have declared neutrality and retired.

Around the nation, attacks on transportation and energy infrastructure have increased in frequency with each passing day. We now go to our Sacramento bureau. Christina?"

"Thank you Keshia. I'm Christina Espinoza, reporting from Sacramento. Early this morning, massive explosions rocked two key bridges in northern California. The Antler's Bridge, which carries Interstate 5 over Lake Shasta, and the Healdsburg Bridge, which carries Route 101 over the Russian River in Mendocino County, were both severely damaged in what appears to be have been coordinated attacks. In addition, a California National Guard convoy approaching Los Angeles from the north was also ambushed. At least 11 casualties have been reported. The governor of California issued a statement in which right-wing extremist militias were blamed for these acts of domestic terrorism. In the statement the Governor also vowed to continue confronting these terrorist militias until they are eliminated. Back to you Keshia."

"Thank you Christina. Things don't appear to be improving out on the sunny west coast. Militia attacks have not been limited to California, however. Incidents have been reported in Michigan, Illinois, Maryland, New Jersey, and western New York. And in a new development, a National Guard armory was hit with an explosive laden truck in Austin, Texas. This appears to be the first explosive bomb attack in a red state loyal to the FSA. Prior truck or car bomb incidents have all been in states remaining loyal to the US.

Gang violence and civil unrest also continues in many of the large cities around our nation, exacerbated by ongoing gasoline and food shortages. Local law enforcement is struggling to regain control, even with assistance in some places from state National Guard or federal units.

Back to politics, in the wake of Virginia's vote to secede, Arlington, Fairfax and Loudon counties in the northeastern corner of that state will be voting on whether or not to leave Virginia and remain loyal to the USA. All three counties are suburbs of Washington, D.C. and many of the residents work in the capital. Fairfax and Loudon counties share the distinction of having the highest median incomes among US counties, trading places as the highest income county the past few years.

In response to the pending vote by the northern counties, the Governor of Virginia has started moving the Virginia National Guard toward those counties and has also called for, and I quote, 'Virginians to volunteer to secure the borders of our fair state.' The City Council of Washington, D.C. and governor of Maryland have both expressed grave concern over what they call a threatening act on the part of Virginia" and Maryland is moving its National Guard toward D.C. The District of Columbia's National Guard is fully activated and deployed throughout the city.

The Far West Texas Desert

"I forget how much I love watching sunrises" thought Captain Ted Ingle to himself, taking in the brilliant orange and yellow hues as the sun broke over the eastern sky. "Nothing like a desert for sunrises and sunsets" he mused. The air was still crisp and cool, but the day promised oppressive heat. Although he was not from the desert, he had moved to West Texas from Northern California with his parents when he was ten years old. In the years since, he had developed a love-hate relationship with the north Chihuahuan desert which had become his home. He loved the vast expanses and the bright light. He also liked the tactical training opportunities afforded by the isolation. He didn't like the lack of green vegetation or trees. He missed trees. He also didn't like the heat, but the dry heat was much more tolerable than the high humidity heat that blanketed much of the rest of Texas.

He then remembered that he was supposed to be surveying the battlefield below. Or, at least, the potential battlefield. "How did it come to this," he thought, as he looked through his thermal scope. How did the desert of Far West Texas, approximately 60 miles south of the New Mexico border, become the front lines of the unthinkable – a second American Civil War? "Front lines" he half-snorted to himself under his breath. "I don't think there will be traditional front lines in this war," he thought. "And if there are, there will also be lots of fighting behind those lines, all across this nation." And then, for the umpteenth time that morning, he thought to himself again, "How did it come to this?"

He knew, of course, on the surface, just how it had come to pass. The underlying reasons were far more numerous and complex for any one person to truly understand.

It was a little over 2 months since the "trigger" event – the outbreak of a regional war in the Middle East had set the proverbial dominos in motion. With the Middle East going up in flames and the flow of much of the world's oil stopped, oil tripled in price overnight. This had an immediate and serious impact on already weakened state and national economies such as California, Illinois, Greece, Spain, and Italy. It also had a slew of unintended consequences. Collapsed economies and bankrupt governments can't help the unemployed or the poor, can't keep the electricity on, the gasoline flowing, or even feed their citizens. And, as people grew desperate, they began to do desperate things.

Subconsciously, Ingle's gaze drifted down to the subdued pattern Gadsden flag patch on the left shoulder of his Army Combat Uniform (ACU). The flag, with the coiled rattlesnake on a yellow background with "Don't Tread on Me" emblazoned underneath, harkened back to the Revolutionary War but had become the de facto banner of everything from patriot militia groups to average Americans angry about excessive government taxation and spending.

Capt. Ingle was no longer in the U.S. Army. Known to his men as "Knife," he was part of the Southwest Desert Militia, and the flag on his right shoulder was the Texas flag. His nickname came from his almost fanatical insistence that all of the men in his unit have bayonets on their long guns and regular training on using them. Capt. Knife had a few such idiosyncrasies. Another was his insistence that his men not use black rifles. Not in the sense of not using AR pattern rifles, but in the sense of ensuring their rifles were camouflaged. "Boys, there is no sense in having such nice cammies and painting our faces and then having the distinct shape of your rifle stand out all in black," he would tell his fellow patriots over and over. "Especially when you are so often holding it by or across your chest. It makes a nice tempting target for the bad guys."

Ingle had served in the Army in the field artillery first and, later, as a Ranger. He had even once competed in the Best Ranger in the Army Competition with a teammate, a huge ex-wrestler from Michigan. That all seemed like a lifetime ago.

After leaving the Army, he had returned home and struggled to find a decent job during the sluggish economy, which seemed to limp along, but never really improve. He watched with mild annoyance as Washington, D.C. changed the nation in ways he just did not agree with. With time, his mild annoyance became mild anger. Every attack on traditional family values, ever growing trampling on the Constitution, voracious out-of-control spending, and countless other issues transformed mild anger to disbelief in what his beloved nation was becoming before his very eyes. He knew people that he had grown up with that collected disability, had public housing and received food stamps even though they were in their forties and were perfectly able bodied. Some of these people received more money than he earned working an honest job. Sometimes two jobs!

The day came when he realized that his nation was bankrupt and, like a household that lives beyond its means year after, the day of reckoning would eventually come. He could not figure how in the world the federal government would ever be able to pay off the massive amount of debt, let alone fulfill the mind boggling obligations such as Medicaid, Medicare, Social Security, or Federal pensions. Then, the day came when he realized that his nation had reached a tipping point. People like himself, who held traditional American values and who cherished the Constitution, were no longer in the majority. As a result, he believed that no amount of elections or civic activism would reverse his beloved country's slide into chaos and oblivion.

The day came when he began to seek out other, like-minded individuals. At first it was to vent and share ideas. But the more he learned as he dug into the beliefs, assertions, and facts of his newfound friends, the more his talk found ways to become actions. Like many militia units, the Southwest Desert Militia was an independent outfit made up of locals, most of whom were military veterans. It was loosely affiliated with other militia units in Texas and New Mexico, but there was no truly unified command structure. Each unit acted largely as its leadership saw fit.

Ingle wondered once again about his situation. He was only a few dozen miles from his home, and yet he was in the middle between two large approaching columns of Army units; one from the west and one from the east. And he was not at all sure how *his* small unit would be greeted. Depending on where one was in the United States of America, and the parts formerly thereof, the militia were either hometown heroes and saviors or extremist murderers to be hunted down.

He shifted, as if trying to actually merge with the road embankment which was providing cover to his small platoon. "I hope our deuces are hidden well enough," he thought yet again of the three 2 ½ ton surplus military trucks called deuce and a halfs, and half dozen civilian 4x4s on which they had ridden before dismounting to take up concealed observation positions. All of his thirty-four men were in the best positions possible, considering the desert topography. They were a mixed group, down to their mixed uniforms, equipment and weapons. Most were veterans of the armed forces. In fact, some of their missing members were still in the service, National Guard or reserves, but were away on deployment or had been called up for duty in dealing with the civil unrest that had been sweeping the nation for the last six weeks. Since each militiaman was responsible for supplying his or her, own uniform, weapon and equipment, there was variation in what they could afford and spend on all these items.

"Here they come," shouted Corporal Perez, one of the advanced lookouts.

"Remember, hold your fire; weapons tight. These Army units are friendly," intoned the Captain over the radio net, even as his grip on his AK rifle tightened. American soldiers and Marines carried the AR pattern rifles and carbines, known as M-16s or M-4s in the services. But many militiamen, like Ingle, preferred the legendary reliability and durability of the AK. He, like many other veterans of the wars in Iraq and Afghanistan, also liked the greater firepower of the larger cartridge it fired and the fact it allowed every man to fire rifle grenades. He had been on the receiving side of that firepower more than once. How ironic, he thought, that one of the primary rifles of this Second American War for Independence (some would argue it was the third) had been invented in 1947 by a Russian tank sergeant named Mikhail Kalashnikov at the end of World War II.

"And what if they're not friendly," asked another of his men anxiously.

"Yeah, like those Army units out in Cali. They've been *real* friendly to civilians and militia boys like us," interjected Perez.

"Only one way to find out. Besides, those civilians and even some militia in California and some other places are flat out of control."

"Sure, Cap'n, but some of these units fired on civilians in El Paso, right *here*. Not in Oakland or L.A. Not in Chicago. Here."

"Yes, after being attacked by them, in self-defense. And, they are leaving their base voluntarily, to *avoid* spilling any more civilian blood. All American soldiers are sickened at the mere thought of firing on American civilians. All true Americans, anyway. Besides, a lot of those civilians gave up that protection when they decided to choose sides against the very ones who sacrifice so much to protect them," countered Ingle.

Just two days prior, an advanced scout force of the column heading East from Fort Bliss had been attacked by civilians (militia now, truth be told) who believed that the "federal" troops were moving into positions to surround and cut-off their new "nation" of Aztlan. First used by the Chicano movement in the 1960s and 70s, Aztlan was used to designate those areas of Northern Mexico annexed by the United States after the Mexican-American war. This huge area stretched from California to the Gulf Coast of Texas and north to include parts of Colorado, Nevada, and Utah. Aztlan was a term used primarily in areas with large numbers of Hispanic people. And this separatist movement was hardly alone. Various groups had, for years, called for an independent state or states to be formed from the United States. Some counties had even voted to separate from their state and form new states, much as West Virginia had in 1863. To those Americans who felt such separatist feelings, the ongoing chaos and social unrest presented an actual opportunity to do so.

"I don't think most Americans will choose a side. They just want to be left alone to take care of their families, chase the American dream, watch football while drinking beer and cooking out on weekends," said Perez, whose family was still in El Paso. Perhaps it was wishful thinking, but most of his compatriots in ear shot nodded in agreement.

He was wrong. As the storm clouds of civil war and chaos swept over America, no one could know that people everywhere would be forced to choose sides whether they wanted to or not.

The Oval Office, the White House

Lee Andropolous, the President's Senior Policy Advisor, was becoming concerned about his President. The man he had always respected as a thinker and as a person seemed to be increasingly detached. He seemed to have trouble grasping both the severity and the breadth of the Constitutional crisis. Worse, as time went on and developments went from bad to worse, he seemed less interested, not more, in dealing with the crisis. Oh, the President had attended all the meetings, made all the press conferences and was asking for input and plans from his National Security team. And, on individual issues he still was able to grasp relevant information. But as an old friend, Andropolous could tell that inside, the President's interest, his passion, for lack of a better word, in planning the proper path for the nation was just not there. In fact, although the Chief Executive hid it well, Andropolous sensed that the over-riding emotion the President was feeling over the nation's life and death crisis was irritation. This irritation was increasingly manifesting itself as a short temper, even with his closest and most trusted advisors. In classic vicious cycle manner, this was leading his advisors to start being less than honest in their assessments and recommendations. Pulling their punches, so to speak. Such a situation is always dangerous for any leader as it hinders his or her access to all relevant information.

"Lee?" the President asked again. Andropolous had been in such deep thought he had not heard the first time his boss called him.

"Uh, yes? Yes sir."

"So what do you think about the military options the Joint Chiefs sent over?" the President asked again.

"I've been giving this a great deal of thought as I know you have," Andropolous said and reflected grimly to himself that he hoped the second part was true. "I am reluctant at this point to provoke even more fighting and violence. But, the B-2s are a grave threat. With their stealth, range, and large payloads, they can threaten every corner of this nation in a terrible way. I don't think we have a choice. Regardless of what else we may do, I feel we must neutralize this threat."

"I see," the President said as he brought the fingertips of both his hands together in front of his chin. "So you are saying we should bomb Missouri? Is this what you are really suggesting? That we bomb Missouri?" his voice scarcely hiding his disdain for the thought.

"Sir, I realize how repugnant this must be. The thought of bombing American soil and killing fellow Americans. But I just don't see how we can live with the constant threat that, at any time, those stealth bombers could be dropping bombs here on the White House or the Capitol or anywhere they choose."

"I recognize the threat, Lee," the President snapped, now more irritated than ever. "But are you telling me that the only *possible* way to neutralize these bombers is by us adopting the Air Force General's suggestion and bombing our own country? For heaven's sake, I think all he actually cares about is that he gets to show off what his precious F-22s can do."

"Sir, you can't be serious, with all due respect. I know the General is enamored of his superfighter, but they are the best, possibly the only option, to get so far into rogue state territory without being detected and thus any hope of success. We actually based the stealth bombers in Missouri for this very reason. Putting them so far in the middle of the country made it difficult for Russian sea-launched ballistic missiles to reach them quickly with depressed trajectory shots. Now it makes it hard for us to reach them also."

"Oh, for Pete's sake! Don't we have any other weapons? Any other soldiers? Not everything has to be done with aircraft, does it? Why can't we send in a spec ops team in to take them out? Then we won't have to bomb our own country," the President said, clearly exasperated. "Or, what about the new, super-secret and super-fast bomber we have been developing? The one that can go over Mach 5 or something and which has been consuming gargantuan piles of our cash. Can't we use that?"

"We only have seven of the new B-3s. Super Valkryies we call them. They have not yet achieved Initial Operating Capability (IOC). And using those would be the same as using the F-22s. We would still be bombing our own soil. We do have spec ops teams of course. But, no one can vouch for their loyalty. How many men on a 9 or 12 man team does it take to compromise an entire mission and cost the entire team their lives? The answer is one. And, there's the issue of geography."

"Geography?" the Chief Executive asked with a hint of disbelief.

"Yes, sir. Whiteman Air Force Base is at least 150 miles away from the nearest friendly territory in Iowa or Illinois. That's a long way for a spec ops team to move against a high tech and well trained enemy like our own forces now turned against us. The rogue military has continuous airborne early warning aircraft on patrol northeast of Whiteman as well as to the northwest. We may be inviting another failed mission if we go this route."

The President sat silently. Often hard to read, Andropolous could not tell what his boss was thinking.

"What about sabotage?" the President asked.

"You mean sabotage the B-2s?"

"Yes, why not? Can we?" the President asked, suddenly animated.

"That's an interesting thought. We do know that we have *some* loyal folks on the ground. DHS, FBI and ATF agents, for instance, that are in contact with us and still loyal. If we can somehow get them onto the base...or better yet, if we can get them to get word to some loyal Air

Force personnel. It could work. We could damage or at least disable those stealth bombers" Andropolous theorized.

"How do we know we still have loyal Air Force people on the base? Most base commanders have been trying to sort out loyalties and keep the peace on their little base kingdoms." the President observed sarcastically.

"You're right. We don't know for sure, but that is what our agents can find out. What about getting in a small mixed team of loyal spec ops with a CIA spook or two? They can help identify the right Air Force people and even help with the sabotage."

"Good idea, Lee! Now you're thinking!" The junior man couldn't help but think that lately even his boss's praise sounded condescending.

"Oh, and one more thing. I don't necessarily want those planes destroyed. You know as well as I do that the Pentagon's toys are extremely expensive. Two billion dollars apiece...Those planes will be back under our jurisdiction soon. I don't want to destroy them fully. I would prefer that we just disable them so the traitors can't use them against us. After this is all over, we can repair them. I'm turning in for the night, but I want to know first thing in the morning how the votes go in Indiana, Georgia and the others."

"Sir, there is one other tidbit for you. It seems the NSA has turned up an interesting morsel regarding Sara Doucet."

"Really? I thought the rogue states were blocking our surveillance efforts, including the NSA's?" the Chief Executive questioned.

"They certainly are trying, but some stuff still gets through. And this nugget was actually first recorded prior to the start of all this madness. Just before, in fact. Per your orders we've been going through everything, every last bit of intel on Doucet and came across this." Andropolous handed his boss two computer print-outs.

"It's a cell phone record. And?"

"And it's also a record of email messages. It seems that our holier-than-thou, bible thumping all-American girl Sara is having an affair with her old college flame."

"What? Oh my gosh! Are you serious, Lee?" the President gushed.

"Yes sir. This is just a summary. They have been having regular, ongoing communications since before the crisis. He's even flown out to Arizona twice to see her. The best part is her old flame is a highly placed, very well-known lobbyist right here in Washington. Jake McElroy."

"Jake? I know him. He was great for me when I was Senator."

"Yes, he's great for everyone. Great fundraiser. Everyone loves him. Most people consider him the most talented lobbyist around and, he also happens to be the best liked. How do you like that?" Andropolous asked.

"Whheeewww," the President whistled. "I take it there are all sorts of sordid details in the records?"

"Uh, well, no. Not exactly."

"Lee, must I drag every relevant fact from you? What exactly do we have then?"

"They've only met twice. Once for dinner in a public restaurant. The other was in his hotel room, but from the communication, nothing beyond hugs and a little flirting has gone on," Andropolous explained.

"Wonderful. Sounds like we have a whole lot of nothing. Why are you wasting my time with this?" the President demanded, his voice suddenly drained of energy.

"McElroy has only flirted with Doucet. But, he has done a heck of a lot more than that with at least two escorts that we know of. One here in DC and the other in Ohio, who, by the way is at a very tender age."

The President's gaze widened and his eyebrows moved upward.

"She claims to be 21 but probably is 18 or 19. And, the local working girl is known to be a dominatrix, specializing in bondage and humiliation of important, powerful men."

"Ok, well now this conversation is worthwhile, my friend," the President said, with renewed vigor in his voice. "Isn't Jake also married with like, bunches of kids?"

"Yep. He is married and they have six kids."

"Wow, how does he find the time? Or energy?"

"Got me sir, but the point, of course, is that it appears we will very shortly be in control of someone very close to Madam President

Doucet. Now all we have to do is figure out how to best use this new asset."

"There is nothing to figure, my brother. We will very soon destroy that traitor, end this movement and restore order. Nice work. Very nice."

The President's advisor had to resist the urge to lash out. He wanted to ask if his old friend was crazy but he dared not. Gone were the days when he could be so frank and have his opinion actually valued. The President, smart as he was, somehow believed that the crisis – Andropolous knew it for what it was, a war – would soon be over. He thought that, somehow, the break-away states would simply change their minds and hand over all military equipment under their control? And worse, he could not shake the feeling that he was failing his friend and boss, the most powerful man in the world. He knew that he needed to speak to the President plainly and make him understand the gravity of the situation. There was no short or easy road back to the status quo. The only resolutions he could think of, and he could think of several, lay on the other side of a long and bloody road. He hoped and had even prayed that he was wrong. But that is what he felt in the pit of his gut. He could see the same thoughts on the faces of the President's other close advisors, but no one really verbalized their concerns with the possible exception of Joel Miller, the White House Chief of Staff.

He cursed himself. The fate of his nation, possibly the world, was hanging in the balance, and he was concerned about keeping his job and privileged position.

Fox News Headquarters, New York

"Good evening, America. It is 10:00 PM on the East Coast. Another stunning week for our nation. Six more states have now voted to leave the United States. That is correct. Six more states. This brings the total number of states which have left the Union to 26. More than half of the states. Staggering.

Eighteen states have joined together to form the Free States of America with a new capital in Dallas, Texas. It is expected that the 6 states that just voted to secede will ask to join the FSA. Two states,

Washington and Vermont are steadfast in maintaining that they will remain independent and not join the FSA nor re-join the USA.

And this is not all. The legislatures of two more states, Florida and Nevada, are set to vote on secession as early as next week. In anticipation, the city councils of Miami and Hialeah, Florida, along with the surrounding counties of Dade, Broward, and Monroe counties have already voted to break away from Florida and remain part of the USA, in the event Florida secedes. A similar situation is taking place in Nevada, but in reverse. Clark County, which contains Las Vegas, also contains three-quarters of the total residents of the large state. Anticipating that Clark County will tip the balance against secession, every other county in Nevada is set to vote on their own measure to break away from the USA and set up the new state of North Nevada, in effect, expelling Clark County and Las Vegas from their state. In Colorado, eight northern counties with a long-standing effort to break away from the rest of the state, primarily over stiff gun control laws back in 2013, have officially voted for secession from both Colorado and the USA and have requested admission into the FSA as the new state of North Colorado. Lastly, three counties in Northern California, along the border with Oregon, have been joined by two counties on the Oregon side in voting for secession from their respective states to form the new independent state of Jefferson. The provisional state government has not yet requested admission to the FSA, but it has issued a statement which read that they are considering all options for the future of our new state.

How all this breaking up and re-forming of the states will ultimately play out is anybody's guess. And what will happen with the brewing conflict between the USA and FSA given the recent air battle over North Carolina, cyber attacks and skirmishes from both sides and the increase in militia attacks in both red and blue states? There is no way to know.

It has become somewhat cliché to hear, but these truly are extraordinary times. May God be with us all."

27

DALLAS, TX, FREE STATES OF AMERICA CAPITOL, THE SQUARE OFFICE

President Doucet looked over at her newly appointed Secretary of Defense and then back down at the proposal. Doucet and Byron Sampson, the former governor of Montana, had been discussing General Parker's proposal for well over three hours. Sampson had chewed his cigar down to a nub from the start of the conversation while his new boss was well into her fourth huge Diet Pepsi.

"Byron, I respect you immensely. I always have, even before your boldness in leading your state to be the first to throw down the gauntlet of nullification and secession. But I just can't agree to this. I just can't."

Sampson had known it would not be easy to convince the President of the one key piece missing from Parker's bold and innovative proposal. The FSA had to reach out to the militias. Both organized and unorganized. Not only reach out to them, but work with them. Find ways to bring their considerable, though largely unknown strength into the fight on the side of the cause of freedom. The cause of returning the USA, or rather now the FSA, back to its Constitutional roots. As a Montanan, Sampson had grown up around local militias. Knowing that he wanted to someday run for political office, he had been careful to never officially join one, or even be too closely associated with one. But, he had known them and been friends with them, even trained

211

with them at times. Camping, hunting, hiking, and shooting all lent themselves to cover for more serious and structured training with the two militia groups located around his hometown. But, he also knew that many people had serious reservations about anyone tagged with the "militia" label. Some of the suspicions were justified, but most were not, in his experience. The President is reasonable and smart, he thought. She'll come around.

"Madam President, I do understand that the patriot militia movement has not always been portrayed in the best light." Sampson purposely used the "patriot" moniker which had been growing in popularity in recent years. "But you and I both know how the liberal media has allowed its biases to influence their so-called journalism for at least two generations, if not more. It is true that some groups have members with extremist views. But this is true in any large group of people, even Congress, for example. It's also true that many of these groups don't even agree with one another. However, in my opinion, the majority do agree on one thing. The federal behemoth in Washington is out of control and its continuous assault on individual and state freedoms must be resisted or the behemoth will completely consume us all. Many of these groups have already risen up in the blue states and started striking at what they see as oppressive state governments along with the federal monster. We should not ignore this. We should tap into their beliefs on the restoration of freedoms and make contact with them and figure out how to work with them. And, don't' forget that these are folks that live and work in these areas. They will know where and how to cause maximum disruption in their areas. They can be a huge asset for us and a huge headache for the blue state and Federal USA Governments."

"It's not just the blue states that are seeing this rising tide of militia violence. Our red states are seeing it too. We're even having some right here in Texas," the President pointed out.

"Yes, ma'am. That's part of the reason I think we need to enlist the aid of the militias. This civil war may be far nastier than the first one."

"Nastier than the first Civil War? Six hundred *thousand* Americans dead. More even than in World War II. Three hundred thousand more wounded. I don't know that I want to think about a war nastier than that."

"Perhaps I chose my words poorly. What I mean is that the Civil War was largely set-piece battles by armies in the field. Yes, there was some guerrilla –type fighting. Particularly in the border states, like Bleeding Kansas. But this paled in comparison to the conventional fighting, if you will."

"I'm not sure where you are going with this, but go on," the President said with skepticism.

"I'm saying that this war is probably going to have much more citizen on citizen fighting. All of the states, and many, many communities, are extremely divided. Your point about the widening militia and gang violence is already showing this. So rather than allow this to go on piecemeal and possibly spiral out of control leading to more unintended consequences, we need to try and channel it. Use it to work toward the common goal that we do have with most of these groups, namely, throwing off this burdensome Federal yoke which we have worn for far too long."

The President was considering his words, Sampson could see. She was processing. He felt a sliver of hope.

"Even if I were to concede this point, there is no guarantee that we can have any influence with these people, let alone channel them. Isn't this right?" She asked in a demanding fashion.

"To be honest, I'm not sure. But I think we need to try. We very much need to try. If, just if, we could get some of these groups to cooperate with us, it would be a huge advantage for our military efforts. First, just think of the chaos that an active, well-equipped militia group can cause in a state like New York, Michigan, or Illinois. Properly channeled, this could have a huge impact on any operation we might choose to undertake. They are already deep inside the enemy's territory and can make any advance by our forces easier by forcing USA and state assets to react to their operations. They can help protect our long supply lines and flanks or threaten theirs. And, they can rally people to the cause. Every militiaman has family and/or friends. Those are hearts and minds we can win by not belittling the militias or criminalizing them. The left has tried to do that for years. No. Instead, we find these groups and we acknowledge that in some ways we are working toward the same goals. This will rally more and more people to our cause, which is the cause of freedom. The cause of restoring our trampled Constitution."

"So what are the specifics? If you can convince me and the Joint Chiefs, how do we go about working with the militias?"

The Secretary of Defense smiled inwardly, knowing he had won her over. All that remained was the specifics.

"It starts with Parker's plan, or whatever plan we decide to implement. We make contact with the militia groups in an area of operations and we ask for assistance just as we offer assistance. What do they need in order to be good allies of ours? Do they need weapons? Intelligence? Equipment? Fuel? We provide that assistance and we ask them to do certain things in support of our operations. Now in areas where we don't undertake major military operations, we simply figure out ways to weaken Federal ozr state power. This part is more of a classic insurgency against an entrenched statist power. And don't forget, Madam President, many of our spec ops personnel, particularly Army Green Berets, know all about helping insurgents by organizing and training them."

"I don't know. I'm still not convinced. I want to see what Parker says about incorporating your idea along with his baby."

"I understand. Then should we ask for him to come meet with us?"

"Yes, please," the President said. "ASAP."

Fox News Headquarters

The normally chipper looking host of the most popular cable news show in America looked exceedingly somber and decidedly not chipper. He was dressed impeccably in a nice suit as always; he looked down, re-organized his papers, and looked into the camera.

"Good evening, America. The Focus starts now. Tonight, our nation is in flames. Perhaps it's time I begin saying two American nations. The United States of America and now, the Free States of America. Five more states have now voted to petition the Free States for membership.

These states, Nebraska, Georgia, Kansas, West Virginia, and Kentucky represent almost 21 million in population and will bring to 23 the number of states in the Free States confederation. Twenty-three states, ladies and gentlemen. Simply unbelievable. Even more stunning than the actual occurrence is the speed. It is incomprehensible that it was less than three months ago that the Israeli attack on Iran precipitated a global economic crisis that led to fuel and gasoline shortages here in America. Those shortages led to riots and the heavy-handed imposition of martial law, gun confiscation, and food and gas rationing by the Federal government in Washington, not to mention the International Monetary Stability Act for Financial Equality, which some saw as eroding American national sovereignty. Within a month, first Montana and then Oklahoma voted to nullify the Federal acts under the Tenth Amendment and then to leave the Union. Three weeks ago, the Federal government dispatched airborne forces to secure what they termed key national assets. Air National Guard units from South Carolina and Alabama, acting on their respective governors' orders to deny over flight rights to the Federal military resisted and the first American versus American battle since 1865 resulted in the skies over North Carolina.

Since that horrific day, the debate on whether or not we witnessed the start of a Second American Civil war has swept the nation. Or, nations.

And now these next five states join the Free States, with perhaps more to follow. Indiana has also seceded and will vote on whether or not to petition to join the FSA next week. And there's more. Yesterday, all Nevada counties with the exception of Clark County voted to secede from the Union formed the new state of North Nevada. Florida followed suit today in voting for its secession. Since neither issued a declaration of independence, it is thought that both of these states will petition to join the Free States. Alaska is the last remaining state that has not declared loyalty to the USA or scheduled a vote on secession. There is much debate in that state on their future status. They seem to be, once again, the last frontier.

For my part, ladies and gentlemen, I think there is no debate. We are in the midst of a second civil war, as incredible as that seems.

Not only have we had the direct confrontation between the Federal military and the states in the aerial battle, but riots and militia violence continues in almost two dozen states, both blue and red, from California to New York and from Michigan down to Texas. The worst of this rioting and civil unrest has been going on in the large cities of California and also in Chicago, Philadelphia, Baltimore, Atlanta, St. Louis, Birmingham, Houston, Phoenix and others. In many of these places, there is a strong racial component to the violence.

Military units are separating themselves along loyalties to the USA and FSA and skirmishes within the military are being reported with increasing frequency from some bases, despite an official gag order from the Pentagon. I truly hate to say this, but I believe that very soon we will see American armed forces fully engaged in combat against one another, just as we are seeing groups of civilians fighting with one another all across this nation.

Intense diplomatic efforts are underway to avoid this, of course, including on the international level from the UN, the European Union, Britain, Canada, France and Germany. China, Russia, India, and Japan are all calling for restraint and negotiation.

The eyes of the entire world are on America. And, so too are the eyes of Heaven, I believe. I don't have a clue what the future may bring, but I do know that tough times are ahead. Take care of your family, your neighbors and yourselves. And may God be with us all."

The Oval Office, the White House, Washington, D.C.

The President sat at his desk with his top advisor, Chief of Staff, and communications director. They had been meeting for well over an hour. The day had been gloomy and that had given way to a stormy night. Heavy raindrops beat against the special, bullet-proof, distorting glass of the windows.

What an appropriate night, the President thought briefly before turning back to the topic on the table. I can't sit by and do nothing, the President kept thinking to himself. His first and most important job was to protect the citizens of the United States of America. His citizens. He had to do something. He could not allow a few million

Americans to be effectively imprisoned, trapped by the extremist right wingers who had taken over their states. Heaven only knew what other oppression would be visited by the criminal traitors in control of the break-away states on those most vulnerable, without any Federal over-sight to keep them in line.

"Mr. President, it's not that I don't want to do anything, I just don't see very much that we can do," his top advisor, Lee Andropolous said. "I know and sympathize with your concern, but what can we do so far behind FSA lines?" he asked reasonably.

"Damn it, Lee! I am not simply going to abandon all those people! Atlanta, Birmingham, Montgomery, Miami, Las Vegas? Even Austin and those South Texas counties are asking us to protect them from the rest of Texas. How many people is that? Seven million? Maybe eight? And I am just supposed to abandon them to their fate?" the President pounded his fists on the table in anger and obvious frustration.

"Sir, we *can* help some of these areas. Vegas we can obviously help through California. Miami and South Texas we can probably do from the sea, but we'll need the Navy's opinion on that. But the others, sir? Atlanta, Birmingham, and Montgomery are simply too deep in reb... ah, uhh..I mean rogue state territory," Joel Miller, the White House Chief of Staff, barely corrected himself in time. "Rebel" was one of the terms that the President had forbidden from being used in his pres-ence to describe the break-away states.

"At the risk of sounding like a self-help book, aren't we supposed to be saying 'how can this be done' rather than 'this can't be done?'" the President asked, regaining some of his composure and exhaling heavily.

The Federal government could no longer operate throughout the 50 states like before. For some reason, the President can't seem to grasp this, thought Andropolous to himself. Why can't he understand that the status quo is gone? On the other hand, he did know that his boss was asking the correct question. How can we do this? How do we help those loyal Americans trapped by the acts of traitors?

Diana Munoz, the President's Communications Director took the opportunity to jump in. "Sir, we should immediately send in humanitarian aid to these people. The American people will expect us to help them. And we should," she said eagerly.

Miller and Andropolous exchanged glances and rolled their eyes. They both marveled at Munoz's naiveté at times. But, they both had to admit, she always did seem to have the pulse of the electorate very much in tune.

"A marvelous idea," Miller said, with barely veiled condescension. "But even if we did have the capacity to help, after all, the entire nation needs help, what's to say the rogue government in Dallas would allow any aid to enter?"

"Well, that's not really all that important, now is it?" the communications director asked, with almost a playful tone. "We make the offer, in a very public way. If they allow it in, it's a PR victory for us. If they refuse, it's even better."

"Ah, Diana, what's better than a PR victory for us, in this case?" the President asked.

"If they refuse, not only do *we* come off looking compassionate, confident and strong, but they come off looking weak, petty, and not compassionate. Now that's my definition of a win – win," Munoz explained triumphantly.

"That's funny, I thought a win – win would somehow involve actually helping those poor Americans in the rogue states" observed Miller.

"That's enough, Joel," the President chastised. "Diana has a fabulous idea. Let's do it. And what if we do it in conjunction with the UN relief efforts? We show we are still players on the international stage and not just paranoid, xenophobic hicks afraid of the UN, unlike those in the red states."

"Excellent, sir," Munoz beamed.

"Understood, sir, but how does this fit in with our plans to neutralize the B-2 stealth bombers in Missouri? Isn't it contradictory to offer aid and then bomb some areas?" asked Andropolous.

"No, it's perfect. As long as we delay any bombing until after our offer of assistance. If they refuse, it helps convince the people that we had no choice but to use violence. It's justified. If they accept, sending help and then bombing them will still be interpreted as we only use force when necessary. It lessens the impact of us looking uncompassionate as a result of a bombing attack," explained Munoz.

"I like it," the President said simply, settling the matter. "Besides, it's one thing to bomb military targets and another to bomb civilian areas. But Lee and Joel, let the Pentagon know that I do also want some plans on how we can help those trapped people. We don't spend all this money on the military for them to tell me we are impotent. Tell them they start earning their pay as of right now. We are going to act decisively."

The Square Office, Dallas, Texas, FSA Capital

Secretary of Defense Sampson and Major General Parker entered the President's office to find her on the telephone. Parker came to rigid attention and saluted while the Secretary of Defense simply stood and waited.

The President waved them in with a smile and motioned for them to sit. Sampson had used the time waiting for Doucet to be available to get a feel for how the General felt about the militias as a source of help for the Free States' cause.

Parker had remained remarkably poker-faced on the matter. He simply listened to the Secretary of Defense and avoided answering his few questions.

"General Parker," the President began amicably, "so very nice to see you again."

"Thank you, Madam President. Likewise." The General was actually glad for the pleasantries as he tried to ascertain her mood, after largely failing to get a handle on Sampson's.

"General, I must say that I was slightly appalled when I first heard you outline your plan for operations against the USA. The more I have thought about it, the less I like your ideas. The Northeast corridor of the United States is the most densely populated region of the US and you are proposing that we move against it."

"Yes, ma'am, I am."

"Well I still don't like it. What do you think of Byron's idea about incorporating the militias?"

"I don't like to rush to judgment, Madam President, but if you ask me for a quick and dirty assessment now, I will say that we can probably make it work as part of our larger plan, whatever that ultimately ends up being. I do have serious questions and concerns that would need to be answered."

"Well, gentlemen, I have been praying for guidance like I have never prayed before. My knees hurt from the hours I have spent on them. I keep coming back to the words found so often in the Bible's book of Joshua, 'Be strong and courageous, have I not commanded you?' This is what we are going to do. We are going to be strong and courageous. But, we will also be merciful to our foes and may God have mercy on our souls."

Washington, D.C.

Jake McElroy left his expensive gym and strode briskly toward his car, a new BMW 750Li. It was his first import car after always driving American made cars. He felt guilty about it, but the merest, fleeting thought of his new ride brought a wide grin to his face. He truly loved his car. It was just after 9 PM since he had cut his workout a bit short.

Just as he reached for the door handle a black Suburban came up at an unusually high rate of speed and stopped directly behind his car, blocking him in.

Before he could formulate a thought, four men dressed in dark suits exited the Suburban and fanned around him in a semi-circle.

Jake reflexively lifted his hands, palms out, and then realized that none of the men had weapons drawn.

"Mr. McElroy, please don't be alarmed. My name is Special Agent Barnes with the FBI and this is Special Agent Ferguson with the Secret Service," the man gestured toward his nearest companion. The other two men remained silent and ominous. Barnes and Ferguson both showed their identification badges at Jake.

"Um, Ok, what's going on," Jake stammered as he lowered his arms to his side.

"Sir, I apologize for the suddenness, but we need for you to come with us. Please."

"Am I under arrest?" Jake asked, suddenly finding his strength.

"No sir, you are not. But please do not make this difficult. This is for your own good and also a matter of national security."

Jake thought for a second, unsure what to do.

"But I am not under arrest?" Jake asked again.

"No sir, you are not. But if you do not come with us right now, immediately, the next time we come will be under different circumstances. We'd rather not do that. Please."

"If I'm not under arrest, then why can't I come in my own vehicle," McElroy questioned reasonably.

He was met with total silence. After several uncomfortable seconds, Jake relented.

"Fine, all right. I will cooperate, but on one condition. I need to call my wife and let her know."

"That's perfectly fine, sir. You can call her once we are rolling."

Throwing his hands up in despair, Jake stepped to the Suburban's open door. He looked around and for once was thankful for the ubiquitous security cameras. He had heard stories about odd disappearances, but like everyone, always wrote them off to crazy, tin-foil hat, conspiracy theorists.

"Oh well," he thought to himself, "it's too late to worry about that now." Besides, what could he do? What could anyone do? He was an attorney and a lobbyist, not some highly trained spy. As he sat down he realized that the windows were completely blacked out and he was separated from the front seat by a similarly opaque partition. He could see nothing outside. With agents on either side of him, the feeling of being abducted was over powering.

They drove for several miles and arrived at a non-descript mixed-use strip retail center. He heard, rather than saw the roll-up door being raised. He was allowed to exit and ushered to a small conference room. Once inside, he was given a cup of bland, lukewarm coffee. Then he was crushed by the real purpose of the evening's activities. Barnes and Ferguson entered the room and he was shown video of his arrival at most recent visit to Priscilla, the dominatrix to whom he had paid regular visits for the past year and a half. While still in shock, he was shown more video of his visit to the beautiful young escort in Columbus.

His mouth was dry and his stomach felt like clumps of burning sulfur. Not finished, his hosts showed him reams of phone, text, and email transcripts. His head was spinning and felt as if it was also being squeezed in a vice.

"Why are you showing me this?" he struggled to speak. "What do you want with me?"

"It's simple, Mr. McElroy. We want what you have always provided. We want you to serve your country at this hour of need," Barnes replied.

"I, uh, I…I don't understand," Jake stammered, still not fully in control. "What does this have to do with anything?"

"Come, come, Jake," Barnes used his first name for the first time trying to soften the mood and re-assure his captive. "We don't care about your extracurricular activities, no matter how bizarre they may be, right? I mean, young, barely legal girls and a dominatrix are your business."

Jake swallowed, his eyes tearing up.

"We don't care, but your wife. Ah, your pretty wife and all your kids. They might care, am I right Jake?" Barnes asked in a low, soothing voice.

"What do you want? Just tell me what you want," Jake asked, his voice cracking.

"We know all about your little relationship with Sara Doucet."

"But I haven't done anything with Sara! I swear!"

"We know. We know you haven't, Jake. But you have done plenty with your other two friends. And if you don't want your family and career destroyed, you will tell us everything you know about Sara and, more importantly, everything she tells you from now on."

Jake swallowed again. His mouth was so dry, he thought.

"We don't talk about anything significant. We just reminisce and talk about non-political things. I never meant to have an affair with her. I just thought she could help my career someday."

"Ah, Jake, I wish you hadn't told me that," Barnes said with a hint of anger. I can empathize with a guy that still has feelings for his college sweetheart. But to know that you are just a greedy bastard using Sara to further your career? That's pretty slimy. I suppose there is a reason for all the attorney jokes people make. Anyway, whatever. You will tell us anything and everything you discuss with Sara. In fact, for now, don't even press her on anything. Have your normal conversations just like you've been doing and report back to us. We will decide what's important. We may at some point need for you to press her on certain things, but for now, just keep on as before."

Jake simply nodded.

"Are we clear? Don't change a thing with her. Of course, it goes without saying that if you breathe a hint of this to anyone, so much as a crumb or a sliver, we will be back and your family and life will be destroyed. Are we clear?"

"Yes. Yes, we are. I never meant to hurt anyone, honest," Jake explained.

"Fine, Mr. McElroy. You now have an opportunity to be of significant service to your country."

Ferguson opened the door and stepped out. Barnes started to follow him out but stopped at the door and turned back to Jake and said "You have yourself a fine evening. One of my colleagues will take you back to your car and explain how we will be in touch with you." Barnes gave Jake a last, thinly veiled look of contempt and left.

28

THE OVAL OFFICE, THE WHITE HOUSE

"**D**amn them!" the President cursed as his fists crashed viciously against the Resolute Desk. "Damn that insolent little we…" the President trailed off before using the sexist and derogatory term. His eyes glanced around the room, as if suddenly aware of himself. All those around the President knew that the first couple never allowed women to be referred to in demeaning terms. Despite being dressed in his usual slacks and shirtsleeves, the President looked somewhat disheveled.

"Who do they think they are? Who does she think she is? Denying offered aid to the American people? Denying help to hundreds of thousands of people suffering from food shortages and without electricity. Without even sufficient clean drinking water in many places? And then the nerve to offer to have them send aid to areas outside the rogue states. It's preposterous and insulting at the same time! We have to teach them a lesson. We have to show them and the whole nation who is really in charge. This sham has gone on for far too long."

Joel Miller gazed at the floor and grimaced, carefully considering his words.

"Mr. President, with all due…"

"Oh cut the crap Joel!" the President thundered. "It's just the two of us in here. Tell me what you think. Out with it."

"Fine. Whatever we think of the red state leadership and their views and actions, this was a political and public relations master stroke" Miller explained.

"Oh really, and how is that?" the President inquired sarcastically.

"Well first, they didn't reject our offer of aid. By eagerly accepting our offer of assistance they put the onus back on us to show that we are truly offering aid with no subtext."

"They demanded that any aid convoys or shipments be supervised by rogue armed forces within red state territory and denied entry to our armed forces. You hear that. *Denied* entry to US armed forces."

Miller was surprised to hear his boss say "red state territory." He never had heard him say anything other than "rogue", "break-away", "renegade", "traitors" or "criminal" to discuss the FSA states. Interesting. Perhaps the President's view of the true situation was evolving in the correct direction finally.

"Well Joel? What do you say about that?"

"I also say it was brilliant. Why would we or any relief effort spend extra resources for security when it is already being provided by the host states? What could possibly be our justification for sending in substantial military forces with relief workers and supplies? And then them offering to send us help, particularly fuel from the Gulf region while observing the same security rules of transit is absolutely brilliant. In our areas where gasoline can even be had at all, it now costs $6-$7 per gallon as opposed to $4 in the FSA states. So now they are in the position for one of Diana's "win – win" situations. If we refuse, we look defensive and uncompassionate. If we accept their aid and terms we are granting them tacit recognition as a legitimate government."

"I am doing *no such thing!*" the President's fists again met his over-sized desk. "I think some of our Pentagon friends are right. I think we take the gloves off. We need to hit them hard and hit them smart now. Sooner rather than later. They grow in strength with every passing day and..."

"Oh I disagree. I think..."

"Excuse *me!* I believe I was still talking. Look I said speak freely but I am still the President and you should not just interrupt me, Joel."

"My apologies," Miller said while struggling to not roll his eyes. "Please go on."

"They grow in strength and legitimacy with every passing day. It has been our unwillingness to act decisively that has allowed this to go on and on and on. And now, refusing to return our gold from Fort Knox or the oil in the Strategic Petroleum Reserve until we negotiate a settlement on dividing the national debt? Then there is this business of them conducting foreign policy. Declaring that Israel's eternal capital is Jerusalem and that they will open an embassy there as soon as Israel recognizes the rogue states as a legitimate government? Sending emissaries to the UK, Canada, Australia, New Zealand, Japan, South Korea, Mexico, Brazil, Poland, Ukraine *and* declaring that they are unilaterally approving the completion of the Keystone XL and a follow-on project? Announcing that they will copycat observe any existing US free trade agreements, and offering to fast track approval of all other pending free trade agreements? Preparing to issue new government backed bonds, tied directly to oil and natural gas production? You know that many analysts are saying that these bonds may be very well received and raise lots of money for these criminals. And do we need to talk about the volunteers? The crazies in those criminal states are flocking to volunteer for military service by the hundreds of thousands. By most estimates it's a rate two or even three times more than what we are seeing in the loyal states. I can go on and on, Joel. No, this must stop. I think we need to consider all options including some of the military options laid before us."

"We both know that refusing to return the gold is nothing more than grandstanding. In a $14 trillion annual economy, $265 billion in gold and $90 billion in oil is not that big a deal," said Miller reasonably.

"It's the principle of the thing, damn it! That is all property of the Federal Government that they are holding illegally. Stolen from the American people, in fact. And, let's not even get into the millions of other American citizens that they are holding virtually hostage and oppressing in those states. Not to mention the energy shortages we are all experiencing while they sit on all that oil that rightfully belongs to the American people. All of the people, not just the ones that happen to live in the states where *we* chose to store it. Our economy is being slowly strangled by the lack of oil."

"Ok, but to your other point, having hundreds of thousands of so-called volunteers is one thing. Training them and equipping them is very different altogether. The rogue government doesn't have the finances to pay for that. As for the international community, we have far more support. The UN condemned the rogue states actions as have China, Russia, Germany, France, and the EU government at large. Japan and South Korea have refrained from open condemnation, but have sent us clear support through back channels. Nations won't enter into free trade agreements with them for fear of angering us. Our position will grow stronger over time, especially vis-a-vis the international community while theirs will weaken. The UN's sanctions will hurt them and they will not be able to pay for anything. We can still just wait them out."

"No, you're wrong," the President retorted flatly.

"In any case, which military options in particular are you thinking?" asked Miller, not wishing to try and engage in any further debate on the President's points.

"The decapitation strike against that trumped up school teacher, for one. Then we also need to begin neutralizing their strategic military assets like the B-2s and strike at their oil infrastructure down in the Gulf. Maybe also close the Port of Houston by sinking some ships in their channel too. Teach those damn obnoxious cowboys a lesson." The derisive term about the FSA president's former career caught Miller off guard. The one for the Texans did not. "Crippling their oil will severely hurt their ability to issue bonds based on oil and gas revenues. Taking out their leadership will hurt their ability to resist while taking out the B-2s levels the playing field. Those stealth bombers are the biggest threat to us militarily."

"I see," was all Miller said.

"I know you don't agree, Joel, but I think it's time. The media is starting to call this Sitzkrieg 2. The second phony war."

"So you are going to undertake wide-scale offensive operations against our fellow Americans to appease the media? So they won't use terms like this anymore?" Miller asked in disbelief.

"Don't be silly. Of course that's not why. But I do think that our inactivity has emboldened the rogue government and I think it is time to act."

"But we have discussed this multiple times. A decapitation strike on Dallas and aimed at their President, uh, so-called President, will open us up to retribution in kind. Are you prepared to see rogue forces attack Washington, possibly with the intent of killing you? What sort of danger does this put your family into?"

"Now Joel, you know better than to bring my family into any policy discussion," the President scolded icily.

"Well, you better think long and hard about this. If you try to kill their President they will likely try to kill you. And, you will do well to remember that your office happens to be part of the same home where your family lives."

The President just looked back at his trusted friend and advisor silently. Processing the implications, Miller knew.

"Look, it's like we've been discussing. If we launch large scale cyber-attacks on the FSA, they will likely launch them on us. If we go after their energy or infrastructure, they will do the same. If we bomb their capital or key cities, they may also do the same. If we try to blockade their ports, they will do the same to us. Whatever we do, we should expect them to try and reciprocate in kind, if not escalate. All I'm saying, is we need to carefully consider the consequences. I don't think we should just do any kind of escalation, even measured, gradual ones, without an overall strategy on how we intend to end this conflict."

"We end this conflict, Joel, by bringing those states back into the fold. All states. This union will not be shattered. Especially not under my leadership." The President was extremely determined.

"I agree with you, in principle, but I don't feel we have a coherent strategy," Miller objected.

"Our strategy options have been laid out and now I intend to act. We will bring all financial, political, cyber, and military force to bear if necessary," the President said emphatically.

Miller thought he detected a hint of excitement, but shook it off. "What about the reports that the rogue government has deployed Patriot and THAAD missile batteries in Dallas and other key areas?"

"Good point. We'll have to look for another opportunity or discuss with the Joint Chiefs their ability to neutralize those missiles. And now that we have moles inside Doucet's staff, we should have plenty of information with which to plan a strike."

Miller realized that his old friend was absolutely set on this course of action. Over all the years, he could tell when he was still academically debating something in his mind and also when he had decided, even if it sometimes seemed that the decision point was apparent to others before it was apparent to the President himself. He shuddered internally but the point had come. So, he relented. "Perhaps we can do this while she is visiting some other high value target. Kill the proverbial two birds with one stone. Avoid killing civilians if at all possible."

"Excellent thought, Joel! That's why I pay you the big bucks!" exclaimed the President.

"Really? Well it's not enough, trust me."

The President chuckled.

"In any case, we will only have one chance at surprise once we begin air raids and cruise missile strikes so we really need to make it count. Let's get Richardson back in here to go over the simultaneous strike on multiple targets options."

Miller simply nodded grimly.

"And yes, Joel, your point about me and my family's security is well taken. We will take all necessary precautions and defensive measures once we begin to go after these traitor bastards."

The Chief of Staff's Office, FSA Capitol, Dallas, Texas

President Doucet's Chief of Staff, Laura Hearn, was going over the itinerary for her boss's trip to Houston with the head of her Secret Service detail. The Chief Executive was going to visit with the heads of five of the largest energy companies in Houston to discuss ways to quickly ramp up the production of strategically critical oil, natural gas, and even electricity. In fact, production of oil and natural gas for the Free States of America had already been increasing. As soon as Texas, Louisiana, and Mississippi threw off the yoke of Washington, they also threw off the yoke of EPA regulations which had been limiting production in the Gulf and onshore. The new FSA government also immediately approved the stalled Keystone XL pipeline project to bring Canadian heavy oil from its vast tar sands in Alberta and Saskatchewan. Oil and natural gas were proving to be potent leverage in the FSA dealings with both the USA and the international community. The FSA was preparing to issue government bonds backed directly by oil and gas revenue, and this was already gathering significant interest from domestic and international investors, despite the fragile geopolitical situation of the entire world.

So, it was judged important that the FSA and various state governments be very vocal and visible in its support of the expansion of the industry at a rapid pace.

"Does she really need to fly out to the oil rig? Aren't the visits to the headquarters, the refinery, and the SPR site enough?" David Samuels asked. "The rig visit is extremely risky in my opinion and difficult to protect."

"Our Navy friends are detailing one of their destroyers to be there to provide protection," said Hearn.

"I know, but there are other ways to go after a rig. What about swimmers? Or even torpedoes or cruise missiles fired from a submarine."

"Torpedoes? Seriously?" asked Hearn.

"Yes, seriously. Torpedoes can be fired at the deep sea supports and destroy them, thus crippling or destroying the rig while the President is there. Heck, I'm no expert, but the heavy torpedoes may even be strong enough to blow the whole rig, depending on how many are fired at it. They can sink big ships, after all. Anyway, I will feel much better if the Navy can also send a fast attack sub to guard against an attack from a USA boat. In fact, I would feel better if they could send three, given the amount of coast we should be covering."

"*Three* subs?" Hearn thought Samuels was messing with her. "And I thought Navy ships were never to be called 'boats.'"

Samuels chuckled. "Sharp as always, Ms. Hearn. *Only* subs are referred to as boats. It's a historical thing...anyway, yes, subs can also launch cruise missiles with a thousand mile range. That's a huge chunk of coast for the bad guys to lurk and try and hurt us."

"Well let's talk to Sec Def. I'm sure he will provide a submarine if one is available. I wouldn't hold my breath for three, though. Besides, we are keeping the visit secret until she is there. So doesn't that make it difficult to plan an attack?"

"Maybe," grunted Samuels. "We know from the abortive airborne assault the USA attempted that individuals on both sides are passing information to the other side, at the very highest levels of the military and the government."

"But it's been over a month and the USA hasn't attempted any kind of attack. If they were going to, wouldn't they have already tried?"

"Maybe," Samuels repeated. "Dallas is several hundred miles inland and inside FSA territory. Makes it a bit difficult for air or sea attack, including submarines, due to the possible warning time we would have. But in Houston, or worse, on the coast or on the rig, we may have virtually no warning. This would be the perfect time to strike if they were so inclined."

"I'm glad we have you to be paranoid for us," Hearn chuckled and playfully punched Samuels in the arm as he walked out of the room.

Samuels liked Hearn but still couldn't help rolling his eyes. Was he the only one taking the President's safety seriously, he wondered?

CIA Headquarters (Temporary), Fort Meade Maryland

After the secession of Virginia, the CIA had hurriedly if reluctantly vacated their headquarters in Langley, Virginia and re-located roughly 40 miles northeast to Fort Meade, Maryland, already the home of the infamous NSA. In the days leading up to the secession vote, and partly due to increasingly bellicose but secret threats from the Federal Government, the Governor of Virginia had defiantly ordered the 116th Brigade Combat Team (BCT) to deploy from its base in Staunton to

Arlington and the surrounding areas just across from Virginia's border with Washington, D.C. and Maryland. The 116th was none other than the famed "Stonewall Brigade" and also the unit which spearheaded the 29th Division's assault on Omaha Beach on D-Day. In addition, the Governor asked the FSA military command in Dallas and the Governor of North Carolina to send help in the form of the 252nd Armor Regiment of the North Carolina National Guard, based in Fayetteville. Dallas approved but asked North Carolina's Governor if he felt he could spare the regiment. With his major cities relatively quiet, the Governor readily agreed to help his neighbor to the north, noting that the forces were likely to be needed on the new frontier between the FSA and the USA.

Several tense days then followed as the Governor of Virginia "politely" asked all federal personnel to vacate Virginia territory within 72 hours of the secession vote. The President refused and it seemed as if the first major ground battle of the Second Civil War would take place for control of the Pentagon and other federal installations around Northern Virginia. Maryland had already mobilized its National Guard, the Maryland Line, but refused to allow their troops to participate in offensive operations, especially outside of the state, unless federalized. Even then, the Maryland governor made it be known that he vehemently opposed the use of Maryland as a base for launching offensive operations as it might then open up his home state to attacks from Virginia or West Virginia.

The Joint Chiefs and the National Security Advisor had also lobbied the President against going on the offensive into Virginia so hastily. So, the President refrained and also ordered the District of Columbia National Guard to be put on full alert, being the only National Guard unit in the nation that reports only to the President, and not to any governor. But this was also primarily a defensive posture since Virginia was making no sign of ordering its Guard units to cross into D.C.

In fact, the Governor of the Commonwealth had already offered to federalize Virginia National Guard units to the new FSA Federal Government. President Doucet was very appreciative of the offer, but declined on the counsel of her advisors. Federalizing FSA National

Guard units would be viewed as overtly threatening by the USA, they reasoned. In addition, General Parker had lobbied vociferously against federalization on the grounds it could jeopardize the element of surprise in the event President Doucet adopted his military plan.

One of the dirty little secrets about the Washington, D.C. region was that despite the huge concentration of military installations and personnel in the area, there was very little actual ground combat power based there. Ground combat power resides with massive tanks, armored personnel carriers (APCs), howitzers, rocket launchers and the men and women to operate them.

With the exception of the Aleutian Islands in Alaska during the Second World War, no foreign army had set foot on US soil since the War of 1812 so the primary threats to the area had always assumed to be from the sea and then later, from the air. The vast majority of military personnel in the region were assigned to administrative or support commands.

Eventually, the USA President's military advisors convinced him of the folly of engaging in an offensive foray into Virginia on such weak terms until far more Federal and USA Guard units could be mobilized and deployed to the area. So, in the short term, the President was forced to abandon the Pentagon and CIA Headquarters in Virginia along with countless other installations after the FSA offered to allow federal personnel to take "personal property" with them, to include laptops and desktop computers. This took place under the watchful eyes of 116ᵗʰ soldiers and Virginia State Police, to ensure that no acts of sabotage were attempted. No real property or large equipment was to be removed from any installation on sovereign Virginia soil. USA loyal Pentagon and CIA personnel were not happy about leaving their facilities. The troopers of the Stonewall Brigade, on the other hand, observing the evacuation of the Pentagon by federal personnel from their Strykers, M-113 armored personnel carriers (APCs), Bradley fighting vehicles (IFVs), and MRAPs began to cheer as the first convoy of trucks departed. Their commanding officer silenced them and reminded them that the departing men and women were "brothers and sisters in arms and still our countrymen."

The director of the CIA was not happy about the report he was about to make to his boss, the Director of National Intelligence, known as the DNI for short. While the CIA director did not support the traitorous actions of the break-away states, he also knew what his report would mean. And he definitely did not support an offensive attack on his fellow Americans no matter how misguided they may be since he knew the bloodshed that would follow. The DNI's secretary showed the director into the DNI's office as soon as he arrived.

"Sir, we know Doucet's itinerary for her upcoming trip to Houston. I think this is the information the White House has been looking for."

"I think you may be right. Nice work. Let's let General Richardson and Joel Miller know. We'll all need to get to work on this ASAP. When is she going?"

"Next week, sir."

"Hot damn!" was all the DNI replied.

The Oval Office, the White House

The President hit the speaker button on his phone. "Yes, Dolores?"

"Mr. President, it's Mr. Miller."

"Ok…yes, Joel."

"Mr. President, I think we've got her. She's going to Houston at the end of next week to, get this, visit the energy industry there and our inside source just gave us her itinerary."

"How interesting," the President said slyly.

"It appears that two of our birds will be together soon. We will see to it that the stone is ready."

"Nice work, Joel. I want to be briefed ASAP."

"Of course, Mr. President."

29

FSS (FREE STATES SHIP) MINNESOTA (SSN-783), 120 MILES SOUTHEAST OF CAPE HATTERAS, NORTH CAROLINA

The crew of the *Virginia* class fast attack nuclear submarine was made up of 120 enlisted and 14 officers. The *Minnesota* was on a routine peacetime patrol in the North Atlantic when the news that states started seceding from the United States came in through their burst transmission communications with fleet command. The officers had earnest discussions among themselves about how they would handle the new situation. Those with loyalties to the U.S. of course argued that the $2.7 billion submarine was the property of the U.S. government and should be returned to Naval Submarine Base New London, Connecticut. Some of these crewmembers thought that any shipmate wishing to leave US Navy service, whether to serve the FSA or simply go home, should be allowed to do so. Others thought that anyone not re-affirming loyalty to the USA was a traitor and should be arrested or at a minimum, discharged from the navy. The internal debate continued as the patrol wore on and more and more states left the Union.

Regardless of constitutional or legal arguments, numbers were hard to ignore. Of the crew, 78 enlisted sailors were from states which had seceded and joined the Free States of America. All but nine had also declared their loyalty to the new nation. Among the officers, eight were from FSA states originally and seven declared loyalty to the rebel cause. The lone USA hold-out among the officers, however, was the sub's commanding officer. The sub's Executive Officer (XO) reluctantly ordered the Chief of the Boat, the senior enlisted man aboard, to place his commanding officer effectively under house arrest in his stateroom while they decided what to do. The other USA loyal personnel were confined to quarters under the watch of the masters-at-arms, responsible for security aboard all Navy warships that did not have Marine detachments aboard.

The FSA loyal personnel were not about to return their boat to its base in Connecticut and risk getting arrested for their trouble. Instead, the crew decided to put into Norfolk Naval Base in Virginia and there disembark the USA loyal crewmembers. These crew members were detained in the base brig while the base commanding officer decided what to do with these Americans.

While there, the sub was hastily given replacement crewmembers and the former XO was made the new CO and given a new mission along with a new, female Executive Officer.

Although open hostilities between the USA and FSA had not broken out, the USA's numerical superiority in fast attack submarines had given the new FSA government cause for concern. This advantage was due primarily to the submarine bases in New London, Connecticut, Kitsap, Washington (the former Bangor base), and Pearl Harbor, Hawaii. Although Washington State had declared independence, it had made it clear to the USA Federal government that they would in no way interfere with US armed forces based in the state. Some sort of lease for the land would have to be worked out, of course, but in the meantime, operations could continue as before. However, in order to remain neutral, active military operations against the FSA and staged out of Washington territory would not be allowed. Naval ships could sail from bases in the state and aircraft could fly, but any unit engaging in combat operations against any entity would not be allowed to return. Any such unit which did return to Washington under these circumstances would be detained and become property of the independent nation. As for the naval units based in Pearl Harbor, the US

Navy had ordered half redeployed immediately to San Diego. It was felt that proximity was important, if the ships were needed to deal with the rapidly escalating crisis.

For its part, the new FSA national command authority had decided it would be prudent to pro-actively guard the critically important Atlantic ports (the only ports available to them) in the event of the USA beginning naval operations against them. So, the *Minnesota,* newly re-christened as Free States Ship (FSS) *Minnesota* had been tasked to patrol the approaches to the Port of Savannah, the fourth busiest US port before the secession crisis and now the busiest in the FSA. Other subs were deployed to guard the other major ports, from Norfolk-Newport News, Virginia in the North, all the way to Brownsville, Texas, in the South.

The previous two weeks on patrol had been largely uneventful. They had tracked two USA submarines, one a *Virginia* like herself; the other an older improved *Los Angeles* class. The former were the most advanced fast attack submarines in the American navy or now, navies, while the latter were one generation removed, but still highly capable. *Minnesota* had also tracked one Russian *Akula II* submarine only 14 miles from the Georgia shore. Interestingly, a French submarine, believed to be the *Emeraude* had also been found patrolling close to the Atlantic coast. Apparently, the Russians weren't the only naval power interested in keeping a close eye on developments on the North American continent.

Lieutenant Commander Jesse Eckerd thoroughly enjoyed being the Operations Officer of the deadliest submarine in existence. He loved standing watch as Officer of the Deck (OOD) as he was now. The OOD oversaw the operations of the submarine while underway as the Commanding Officer's representative. He relished the challenge of matching his wits and training against any and all threats, while leading the watch crew on their elaborate dance of cooperation for effective operations.

Originally from Morgantown, West Virginia, Eckerd had wanted to be a naval aviator until his eyes failed to qualify him for flight training. He had then decided to "fly" under the waves as part of the original stealth craft.

Like most from the Mountain State, Eckerd had long felt that the growth of the Federal government was unsustainable, both financially and politically. And then after the September 11 attacks of 2001 and the financial crisis of 2008, the central government had simply gone out of control. The signs and evidence were everywhere and it seemed that each passing month brought another major assault on traditional American freedoms, values and views. He was saddened and angered by the events that led to the breakup of the United States. The submarine officer had been horrified to learn that American pilots had fired on fellow Americans over North Carolina. He had been even more horrified to later learn that his fellow submarine officers and sailors onboard multiple submarines had fired upon one another, fighting miniature civil wars for control of their vessels. Two submarines had actually sunk as a result of these undersea battles. One, an *Ohio* class ballistic missile submarine was believed to have been willfully scuttled by die-hard FSA loyal crew members including the Chief Engineer (the senior-most engineering officer) and the Chief of the Boat (the senior-most enlisted sailor) after USA loyal crew had gained control of the boat following a firefight lasting several hours. The other loss, the *USS Seawolf* (SSN-21) was thought to have succumbed to damage sustained during its own internal power struggle. Automatic weapons fire and pressurized hulls and sensitive equipment do not typically mix well. Other submarines in the area reported hearing prolonged gunfire coming from the sub before hearing equipment shattering and then the breakup noises of the sub herself. So much loss of life. Two hundred and ninety-five sailors never to see their homes or families again.

Eckerd came out of his reflection since it was time to communicate with fleet headquarters in Norfolk. "Diving officer bring us to periscope depth."

"Sir, aye aye, sir," came the crisp response.

Eckerd barely smiled. The crew remained crisp despite being at sea for more than four weeks.

The ship's captain soon joined Eckerd.

"What do we have Jess?" asked the CO. "Anything interesting?"

"Actually yes, sir. We are to depart for Houston immediately."

"What? Houston?" asked the Captain.

"Yes sir," Eckerd replied, showing the Captain the print-out. "We are to assume station 180 miles southeast from the entrance of Galveston Bay ASAP. We are to patrol the approaches to the Houston Ship Channel and surrounding areas, paying particular attention to Gulf oil drilling platforms."

"Oil drilling platforms?" the Captain questioned.

"Yes sir. Apparently the brass is expecting some sort of move against the oil infrastructure and / or against Houston itself" answered Eckerd.

"Wow," breathed Eckerd's boss. "What's that Chinese proverb which is actually more of a curse? 'May you live in interesting times?' We are definitely living in interesting times. And they may be about to get real, real interesting. In a cursed sort of way."

Both men looked at each other and shared a serious chuckle.

The Square Office, FSA Capitol, Dallas, Texas

The President sat at her non-descript, but oversized desk looking over General Parker's proposal for a combined arms offensive against the USA for what seemed the umpteenth time. She was in complete internal turmoil over it. As she had been telling her senior advisors, she clearly saw the logic in both the reason for and the manner of the offensive. Obviously clear. But also painfully clear. As much as she saw the logic and even the need for such a prompt and bold move, she just could not bring herself to set into motion plans that would set American versus American and lead to the deaths of thousands, if not hundreds of thousands. Yes, thousands had already died in the aerial battle over North Carolina, in the urban riots, and even in the clashes on military bases and onboard Navy ships. But those thousands of tragedies would be greatly multiplied by her authorization of Operation Octopus. And yes, Parker was also probably right that, in the long run, Octopus had the best chance of averting a protracted war with ever spiraling casualties. In fact, it may be the only chance of avoiding such a long and very bloody civil war. Of course, she wished with all her might and every part of her soul that additional fighting could be avoided.

She also knew that this was likely an impossible dream. Conceding the almost certain inevitability of full scale war, part of her almost wished for the USA to attack her fledgling nation so that they would be the aggressors and the FSA could remain in the moral high ground.

"But they have already attacked us. Those big government types in Washington, D.C. have been attacking Constitutional Liberties for years. It was their actions that finally backed so many states against a wall where the people felt they had no choice but to vote first for nullification and then secession," she reminded herself as she put her head down on her desk. "Ugh. A person can go round and round on the morality and legality of all that's happened. I am going round and round," she thought to herself. Her mental merry-go-round was mercifully interrupted by a buzz from her personal administrative assistant.

"Yes, Mary?"

"Madam President, the Vice President and Chief of Staff are here," the assistant informed her boss.

"Ok, thank you. Please send them right in," the President replied as she lifted her head off the desk and cleared her eyes.

The former governor of Texas strode in along with Laura Hearn, the President's Chief of Staff.

"Bud," the President exclaimed enthusiastically, getting up and quickly moving around her desk to greet her Vice President with a hug. "Hi Laura," she also greeted her Chief of Staff warmly. "How was your trip? I sure have been keeping you on the road."

"Yes, Madam President, you have," replied the Vice President with his light, easy manner. "If I had known this was a traveling salesman gig, I think I would have passed," he added with a chuckle.

"Yes, you did know, and no, you would not have passed on this job for the world," replied the President, also chuckling.

The lean Texan chortled heartily as well. "Sure, sure. I suppose you're right, Madam President. And we definitely do need someone out there, with all the states, building support for volunteerism and shared sacrifice for our new nation. Things are going well. At least, as well as can be expected under the difficult circumstances."

"Yes, we are all very grateful for your efforts and especially for the support and volunteers that are streaming into the recruitment offices."

"Madam President, I wish I could take more credit for that. It's the people. They get it. They understand what is at stake. Well, most of them do, anyway. They know that we have all been forced into a corner by the feds and now it's time to defend our liberty, by force of arms if need be."

"Yes, well, we all hope that it won't come to this. By the way, I've come to a decision on General Parker's proposal. Well, a partial decision. I know you're here to discuss the trip to Houston, but let's cover this quickly," the President said.

The Vice President and Chief-of-Staff exchanged glances and sat down.

"First, I have not decided to authorize Operation Octopus. But I have decided to authorize our military to begin those preparations, which can be carried out in secret. I want the military units positioned to carry out this offensive and quickly, should the need arise. However, I cannot stress the need for secrecy enough. Moving large units from Texas, Kentucky, North Carolina and Georgia all the way into Virginia will be viewed as extremely provocative by the USA, if not an outright declaration of war. So, if we need to move the units more slowly or in parts, we will do so. I do not want this, our mobilization of forces, to be the proverbial attack on Fort Sumter. This is my decision and I will meet with General Parker and Sec Def ASAP to inform them."

The two visitors to the Square Office simply nodded gravely and look down at the floor before lifting their eyes once more to their Commander –in-Chief.

"What, no comments?" the President asked and then smiled broadly.

"Madam President, I am happy to discuss this with you as we have been doing over the last few days, of course. But it seems like you have made your decision. I know you have given it much thought. So, no, at this point, I have no comment or question," Hearn responded matter-of-factly.

"I see. Very well then. On to our real purpose. I'm glad the agenda for my trip to Houston and the Gulf oil facilities is finalized. I know some of my staff have serious security concerns, but this show of support for the oil and gas industry is critically important. And, I refuse to live in fear. Whether or not we are at war or will be, I must govern in the way most effective for the Free States of America."

"Boss, I just don't like the intel reports we are getting. Our sources in the USA federal government are hearing that they may move against certain strategic targets *and* you," Heard said, voicing her concerns once again.

"Yes, I know. But we've been over this. First, the sale of the oil and gas backed bonds is absolutely crucial, vital, in fact, to us raising the money we'll need in the short term. Our national economy is really going to start to chug along due to our reforms, but we need this initial infusion, especially if war comes in the face of the international sanctions. This visit is very important to the success of those bonds. We must be very clear to the markets that we will not allow environmental or bureaucratic roadblocks to fully developing our national resources. Second, I don't believe for one minute that they would come after me, personally. Our military sure, they may take action against us there. Maybe even go after our economic assets, but I think they won't risk international condemnation by the specific targeting of a head of state. Not to mention that we would then be morally justified in taking the gloves off against the USA leadership. No, no, he won't come after me personally. Lastly, we are taking every precaution. The details of the itinerary are being kept confidential are they not?"

Both Hearn and Ricks nodded.

"Right. And are we not also taking military precautions? We have AWACS and Patriot batteries deployed to protect Houston. We have two submarines patrolling the ocean approaches, correct?"

The visitors nodded again.

"So, then, we have done all that we can. We will not cower in fear. I am going to Houston and to the Gulf oil rig. Bud, you will be in a secure location and all is in God's hands."

The Vice President and Chief of Staff nodded gravely once again and then both smiled at their leader.

"Tough as nails. Just like everyone says," said Ricks with a deep chuckle.

"Actually, Bud, my husband affectionately describes me as a 'bag of hammers,'" chimed the Chief Executive as all shared a hearty round of laughs.

"And, no, don't ask me exactly what that means."

30

101ˢᵀ AIRBORNE (AIR ASSAULT) DIVISION HEADQUARTERS, FORT CAMPBELL, KENTUCKY

Upon hearing from President Doucet that he had received approval to begin the initial phases of the movement and disposition of forces for Operation Octopus, Greg Parker made preparations to convene the division commanders from the chosen units in Fort Campbell. Due to their unique air mobility, the attack, should it ever be launched, would be led by brigade combat teams (BCTs) from the 101ˢᵗ Airborne, 82ⁿᵈ Airborne, and the 75ᵗʰ Rangers, based at Fort Benning, Georgia. On the Marine Corps side, the 22ⁿᵈ and 24ᵗʰ Marine Expeditionary Units (MEUs) from Camp Lejeune, North Carolina would also be among the lead units. Other, heavier ground units would also be heavily involved, but Parker's idea was for the highly mobile airborne units to be the tip of the spear, utilizing their mobility in ways never seen previously in warfare. This first briefing was only for the Airborne, Marine and Ranger commanders and staff. A later briefing would bring in the divisional commanders of the other units to participate.

Once his audience was seated, his adjutant stepped to the edge of the platform and called, "Attention on deck!" As one the men and women rose crisply from their seats and snapped to attention with a thunderous clap. Lieutenant General (Select) Greg Parker strode to the lectern, looked around and took a deep breath.

"As you were everyone," the General's voice boomed. Everyone was seated once again and the PowerPoint lit up the huge screen behind and to the left of Parker.

"Ladies and gentleman, what do ancient Greek trireme warships, Hittite chariots, Mongol horsemen, steam powered trains, World War II tanks, airplane transports and helicopters have in common?" Parker questioned.

Among the seated officers several muttered responses.

"Yes, I heard it. Someone said it. A couple of you said it. Mobility. Mobility, ladies and gentlemen. The mobility of these weapon systems proved revolutionary to warfare in their day. You are all here today because you lead combat units that can rapidly move to their objective via air mobility. While our nation has used airborne forces since World War II, I believe that we have only scratched the surface of what large-scale air mobile forces can do. With all due respect to the giants upon whose shoulders we stand, innovation is not nice and linear, but rather comes in fits and starts. Men such as Lieutenant Generals James Gavin and Hal Moore gave us a foundation upon which to build. Our ability to airlift entire brigades and move them hundreds or thousands of miles and then re-supply them is simply revolutionary and still at the cutting edge of what is possible in a modern force. And while we have successfully used our air mobility many times over the years, we have yet to fully realize the full potential. Yes, it is true that we have successfully landed our airborne forces behind enemy lines, cut off enemy forces, and even effectuated vertical envelopment.

However, we can and will do more. Far more with our ability. I will get more into this in a bit.

The situation we face is grave, as you all know. It is also highly sensitive. I was asked by the President to submit a plan for the military defeat of the USA."

Silence greeted his comment. All present had felt that in all likelihood, this was the crossroads at which they found themselves. But it was still extremely hard to discuss it in real terms rather than as some future nightmare scenario.

"In short, I am proposing that we use our unmatched mobility to threaten and put extreme pressure on as many schwerpunkt of the USA as possible. We will not merely make one airborne operation and then sit and wait to be reinforced and or relieved by heavier forces. We will strike, seize an objective, force the USA loyal forces to react and then move once more to threaten or seize another objective. With our mobility we will put pressure on the full three dimensions of the battle space, length, breadth and depth. The forces opposing us should have very little chance of effectively countering our maneuver. I believe that modern precision guided weapons make mass assaults of large units suicidal in most cases. So, we will move to excellent, defensible positions and dare any USA forces to attempt to dislodge us. If we somehow make an error and get flanked or outmaneuvered, we still have the option of using our airlift to pluck out our units and redeploy them to once again threaten USA positions.

No unit loyal to the USA and currently located within CONUS can hope to match our mobility, with the possible exception of one or two brigades of the 10th Mountain at Fort Drum. One or two brigades to counter our 11 or 12 airborne and air assault brigades, ladies and gentlemen. This is an overwhelming advantage for the Free States of America and one that I plan, with your help of course, to exploit fully."

The General paused once again and took a sip of water.

"With our mobility we will conduct a campaign of violent maneuver. Violent, aggressive maneuver while making every attempt at minimizing violent encounters. All of you, I'm sure, are students of 'The Art of War' and so I remind you of what Sun Tzu wrote, 'Supreme excellence consists in breaking the enemy's resistance without fighting.' This is what I am tasking all of us to do. We will break the USA's will to fight with a minimum of fighting. Our campaign of maneuver will place the USA in an untenable position."

Parker clicked the PowerPoint to advance from the Sun Tzu quote slide to the next slide showing thrust arrows on a huge map of the Northeastern United States. "We will cut off Washington, D.C., Baltimore, Philadelphia and New York from energy, food, and most other goods. We will seize or cut-off key nodes of their energy and transportation infrastructure. At sea, our squid buddies will help in enforcing a quarantine of the major ports to include Boston. We may not be able to close off the ports completely due to naval and political considerations, but even if half of the normal maritime traffic can be blocked, the cities will be in very bad shape. This will hopefully cause the leadership of the USA to decide it is simply not worth it to continue the fight and recognize the right of the FSA to exist.

The biggest threat we will face are USA fighters, but we will have our own fighters flying cover. Furthermore, we will use deception to try and ensure that US fighters are caught off guard or out of position. The other big threat, of course, are anti-aircraft systems. Here again, if we use our maneuver ability properly, we will put immense pressure on the relatively limited AA to defend the whole of the battlespace without knowing where or when we will strike next. We will take losses. This is war, after all, ladies and gentlemen. But we can and must use our advantages creatively and aggressively to minimize those losses.

Moving on, each of you needs to consider if your current brigade commanders are the right leaders for this job. We are not a peacetime bureaucracy any longer. We are a wartime Army. My apologies to our Marine brothers. We are a wartime military and we need to get the absolute best commanders and staff in place regardless of time in rank. Your brigade commanders need to select the very best regimental commanders, battalion commanders, etc. I leave that your discretion, but just know that from my standpoint, you have wide, wide latitude. Similarly, after you have reviewed your respective warning orders, please do let my staff know of anything you feel you may need to carry out your objectives. I am cutting out all the bureaucratic crap to give you all what you need to succeed. Take advantage of it. Anything we have in the inventory or that we can get, you can have. Don't be shy about asking. Dream big. Let my staff and I be the ones to say whether or not it's simply impossible to get you what you need. That being said, I have one request and one suggestion in this area. First, I would like for all of you to equip your units with the maximum ability to move fuel. Bring as many bladders, tanks, and trailers as possible. We will opportunistically seize as much fuel as possible wherever we go so as to both limit our logistical burden and to deny that fuel to our adversaries. Next, you should all consider increasing your sniper and countersniper ability as much as possible. We should have as many .50 cal and new 25 mm rifles with our troops as possible, in my humble opinion.

Now, I don't think I have a monopoly on good ideas. If anyone has an idea or even an inkling of an idea of how we can better meet our overall strategic objective of making the USA give up the fight as quickly and with as little spilled American blood as possible, then let us know ASAP. Any questions?"

The Executive Officer (XO) of the 101st stood and asked, "What is our timetable, sir?"

"Your lead elements need to be ready to move to their assembly points in 48 hours. The remainder of the units for this operation can then follow within 48 additional hours, but the sooner the better," Parker answered. "Of course, this is not to say that you will be moving that soon, but we need to be ready. I've stressed to the President that surprise is vital to our success."

"Sir, if we are not counting on reinforcement or resupply from heavier ground units, doesn't that risk some of our units being cut off or left short of supply?" asked the Commanding Officer of the 82nd Airborne division.

"There's always a risk, General. 'He who will not risk, cannot win,' correct? Heavy ground forces are going to be coming behind us, in large numbers. But that will merely allow us to leapfrog and maneuver deeper and deeper into USA territory. Once our heavy armored columns arrive outside of Philadelphia and New York, we will move north again to threaten or isolate Boston as the case may be. Or, depending on how things play out on the international level, we may need to move to cut off the cities from help coming from Canada or further north in New England. In any case, we can and will use our mobility to resupply, reinforce, redeploy, or even retreat as needed."

A civilian standing in the back of the room raised his hand and then took two steps forward once recognized by Parker.

"General, my name is Francis O'Mangan. I am ex-Navy and now a civilian in the employ of our new government. Have you considered what to do about the large concentration of nuclear submarines based in New London, Connecticut? As you know, our leadership considers those submarines a major threat."

"Yes, Mr. O'Mangan, I am aware of the threat. However, as you can plainly see, my forte is land warfare. I do plan to confer with my naval counterparts as soon as possible."

This drew a few good natured chuckles from the crowd.

"Yes, General, your forte is plainly visible," replied O'Mangan, drawing additional laughter. "You are in luck because naval warfare is my forte and I have some ideas about those submarines in Connecticut."

"Well Mr. O'Mangan, then you are one of my new best friends. Let's chat after this briefing is concluded."

"You buy the drinks, general and I'll do the talking," O'Mangan offered with a sly smile.

"Deal," the General replied simply with a large grin.

USS New Mexico (SSN-779), submerged, 200 miles south of Galveston, Texas

The *Virginia* class nuclear submarine had arrived on station eight hours later than expected after its transit. Based at Naval Submarine Base New London, Connecticut, the sub had been patrolling off the approaches to Philadelphia when it received orders to make best silent speed of 23 knots for the Gulf of Mexico. In a massive allocation of naval resources, the USA had ordered a total of seven submarines to move to the heart of the Gulf oil industry, with an additional two submarines ordered to provide security behind them further out in the Gulf. Three of the subs, including the *New Mexico*, were to concentrate on the Galveston / Houston area and the other four were to concentrate further east, along the Louisiana coast, from off of Grande Isle State Park in an arc roughly toward Gulfport, Mississippi.

"Officer of the Deck, we are on station, depth 750 feet," came the report from "Nav" as the navigation watch station was known. Station was an area in the Gulf of Mexico known as the Perdido Foldbelt, an area extremely rich with crude oil and natural gas in waters almost 8,000 feet below the surface of the ocean. The foldbelt was at the extreme edge of the United States' (now the Free States') territorial claims and on the border with Mexico's territorial claim. Their orders had instructed them to take station 25 miles from a massive oil platform known as the Perdido Spar and, in exactly 12 hours, to destroy the $3 billion dollar facility owned by Royal Dutch Shell and partners.

The Spar was emblematic of all things hated by those who hated "big oil" and sought to limit or even eradicate deep-sea drilling. It was the biggest manmade object in the Gulf and also the deepest operating offshore oil rig in the world. Over 150 workers lived and worked on the massive facility for 30 days at a time before being relieved by another crew for 30 days. Over 130,000 barrels of crude oil per day flowed from the platform into the lines that carried it to all the way to the mainland. Being fairly new, to others it was emblematic of the progress and potential of the domestic oil and gas energy. It was for this very reason that President Doucet had chosen this rig for her visit.

The crew of the *New Mexico* was not aware of the FSA presidential visit, however. Their orders received via burst transmission, merely read that the oil rig had become a high value, high priority target to be attacked as part of a much larger campaign against the rogue states. They were to a fire a spread of four Mark 48 Advanced Capability (ADCAP) torpedoes to strike the platform at precisely 9:30 AM local time. Then two Tomahawk cruise missiles would be launched from their vertical launch tubes in the bow of the sub to hit the rig immediately after the torpedoes. Eight additional Tomahawks were then to be launched at oil refining targets in Texas. Then another four ADCAPs were to be fired. Both the timing and composition of the attack seemed strange to the submariners. There seemed to be no need to use Tomahawks on a platform full of oil, fuel, and other flammable materials once hit by four Mk 48s, each weighing 3,695 lbs and carrying 650 lbs of high explosives. Unbeknownst to them, the reason for the unique composition of the operation was driven by two considerations. First, the torpedoes could strike with no warning, thereby achieving surprise. Second, the cruise missiles would destroy President Doucet's helicopter or at least prevent it from taking off.

The call "Captain's on the bridge" went out as the commanding officer of the sub entered the control center.

"What's the tactical picture, ops?" he asked the operations officer.

"We have one contact 17 miles to the southeast. Contact designated Sierra One. This is a *Virginia* class, possibly the *Minnesota*, which is FSA. Second contact, designated Sierra Two is approximately 22 miles away, to the northeast. Sierra Two should be the *Toledo*, based on her orders."

"Very well. Thanks Ops. Let's just sit here, make like a hole in the water and wait until show time. Obviously, we need to stay vigilant, especially on Sierra One. Carry on."

Along with the submarines, the USA military plan called for an aerial component using the best arrows remaining in their quiver. The stealthy and fast F-22 Raptors and the few B-2 stealth bombers still under their control. In one fell swoop, the government of the USA would seek to kill the president of the rogue FSA, neutralize a large proportion of the FSA's heavy strategic bombers, and cripple their crown jewel and cash cow, the massive energy infrastructure that stretched for hundreds of miles along the Gulf, but concentrated between Houston and New Orleans.

Simultaneous with the attack on the oil rig, F-22A Raptors flying from the closed Air Force base in Carmi, Illinois would attempt to destroy the B-2A Spirit stealth bombers based at Whitman, Air Force Base in Missouri. After the aerial battle of North Carolina and the secession vote in Virginia, the USA had ordered all USA loyal Raptors based at Langley Air Force Base to move to Andrews Air Force Base in Maryland and McGuire Air Force Base in New Jersey. From there, they would be well positioned to provide combat air patrols over the Washington, DC – Baltimore area, as well as Philadelphia and New York City.

With the decision to go on the offensive, twenty-four of the precious air superiority fighters had been moved, one pair at a time and by night, to the old abandoned base that had been secretly re-activated. From Carmi, Illinois, the F-22s would have a short 300 mile flight before launching their JDAM (Joint Direct Attack Munition) bombs from 50,000 foot altitude for the bomb's 40 mile flight to their targets at Whiteman. Sixteen F-22s would each carry two 1,000 pound JDAM bombs in its internal bomb bays while the remaining eight Raptors flew escort, armed with air-to-air missiles. In reality, JDAMs were not technically bombs, but rather add-on guidance kits that converted unguided gravity bombs (known as "iron" or "dumb" bombs) into precision guided munitions (PGMs). The kits were comprised of aerodynamic control tail fins, body strakes (winglets), and a combined GPS receiver and inertial navigation system. With such an advanced navigation system, a JDAM could fly for many miles after being released by an aircraft and hit its intended target with a circular error probably (CEP) of 30 feet in all weather conditions, and often less than twenty feet in ideal conditions. Even if the GPS receiver were jammed, they could still hit within 100 feet of their intended target.

Whiteman AFB had 21 hardened aircraft shelters, one for each of the B-2s originally built, along with the low observable restoration maintenance facility with two bays to house two bombers at a time. The 32 JDAMs carried by the Raptors would target each of the 21 shelters, both bays of the restoration facility, the main runway, and the control and support facilities. In short, the USA would attempt to end Whiteman's role as the only permanent base for the most advanced bombers in the world.

In the final piece of Operation Unitary, three of the six B-2s still under Washington's control would bomb the B-1B Lancers based at Dyess Air Force Base in Texas and the remaining three would attack the B-1s stationed at Ellsworth, South Dakota under the cover of darkness the night after the attacks on President Doucet and Whiteman. Each element of three Spirits would carry 90 JDAMs with which to target the B-1 bombers and their bases. The USA Joint Chiefs would have preferred to also attack the B-52s stationed at Minot Air Force Base, North Dakota and Barksdale, Louisiana but did not have enough B-2s or B-1s. Spirited debate then ensued as the Joint Chiefs of Staff debated whether the B-1s or B-52s were the more important target. Some argued that since the B-52s retained their nuclear capability, they were more of a threat. Others insisted that while the B-1s were no longer nuclear capable, overall it was a more capable platform and could easily be restored to nuclear status. Furthermore, it was argued that not even the rogue government in Dallas would ever dream of using nuclear weapons against fellow Americans, on American soil. The President also insisted on the political value of sending such a strong message to Texas ("those hick cowboys" as he called them) by striking three targets in the renegade state (Dallas, the Houston area oil installations, and Dyess AFB).

A broader air attack also involving F-15s and F-16s (of which the USA retained control of hundreds of each) was considered so as to strike more targets, but was nixed due to the much higher number of aircraft that would need to be committed and the risk of higher losses due to the loss of surprise with the non-stealthy aircraft.

Thirty minutes before the attack was to commence (marked by the launch of the Raptors and Tomahawks with the B-2s already en route) the US Cyber Command (USCYBERCOM) was to launch the most massive cyber attack by far in the relatively short history of cyber warfare. Every major FSA government and business system would be targeted for shutdown or disruption. This included the FSA military, federal and state systems, major utilities, transportation systems, and banking and financial services systems.

The USA had truly taken off the proverbial gloves.

For their part, the military forces of the fledgling FSA had not been standing pat. The new SIA (Strategic Intelligence Agency) apparatus had quickly realized that the most likely course of military action from the USA, should it come, would be an aerial bombardment campaign targeting the large force of strategic, nuclear capable bombers and missiles now controlled by the new nation. E-3 Airborne Warning and Control System (AWACS) had been assigned to patrol the vicinity of Whiteman and the new capital of Dallas continually. However, there were not enough E-3s to continually patrol every vital installation such as the strategic bomber bases, naval bases, Army bases, Marine bases, nuclear power plants, port facilities, bridges, major rail yards, – the list of potential targets went on and on. Similarly, the FSA did not possess sufficient fighters and Patriot surface-to-air (SAM) missile batteries to protect the very long list of potential targets in the young Free States of America. So, like most decisions in life, compromises had to be made based on guesses, themselves in turn based on assumptions.

The most important targets in the FSA were allocated E-3 aircraft along with both a fighter squadron and either a Patriot or THAAD surface-to-air (SAM) missile battery for their defense. Due to the E-3's long radar detection range of 250 miles for low-flying targets and up to 400 miles for high flying targets, in places where a single AWACs could provide coverage for multiple high value targets protected by multiple fighter squadrons, the practice was quickly adopted by the new FSAF.

The vital task of guarding airspace around the B-2 bomber base was assigned to the F-15E Strike Eagles of the 333rd Fighter Squadron, the *Lancers* moved to Whiteman from their base at Seymour Johnson AFB in North Carolina. Similarly, the F-15 Eagles of the 122nd Fighter Squadron, the *Bayou Militia* of the Louisiana Air National Guard, had been detailed to protect the Gulf Oil Industry from Houston to New Orleans from Naval Air Station Joint Reserve Base (NAS JRB) New Orleans, while the 182nd, the *Lonestar Gunfighters* squadron, would defend the Dallas / Fort Worth Metroplex capital region in their F-16C and D model Fighting Falcons, called Vipers by their pilots.

From California to Massachusetts and from the Gulf to the Canadian border, the military leadership of both the USA and FSA moved air and naval assets to the best defensive posture possible, given the situation. Interestingly, no meaningful ground combat forces had been moved.

When the Joint Chiefs and National Security Advisor had suggested moving ground units, including the federalized National Guard units of various states, the President of the USA had firmly rejected the idea.

The Armed Forces of the two American nations would continue to eye each other uneasily across the various state borders.

The Oval Office, the White House

"First, I have no intention of invading the rogue states, as much as I'd like to. This is not 1861, people," he had said. "And since I have no intention of invading, won't moving ground forces and then *not* invading make us look weak, or worse, indecisive?" he asked rhetorically.

"Mr. President, this is not about perception. Moving our ground forces into a better defensive disposition is simply prudent," pressed his NSA.

"Do you really think the FSA would invade *us,* Jack?" the President asked forcefully. "Do any of you believe this," he asked his entire National Security team, looking around the room to each of them.

"Mr. President, we've been through this before, while…"

"Do NOT speak to me in that tone, General Richardson," the President thundered. "I will not be condescended."

Everyone froze with their eyes flickering between Richardson and the President. While no one had verbalized it to anyone, several of the President's inner circle of advisors had begun to wonder if the stress of the global and national situation was starting to weigh on the Chief Executive. Increasingly, he displayed irritability and even a quick temper that had not previously been part of his character. He seemed to be withdrawing. Changing.

General Westin, the Vice Chairman of the Joint Chiefs spoke up to take some heat off of his Air Force superior. "Mr. President the rogue states have far more tanks, APCs, artillery pieces, etc. than we do, by virtue of our largest bases being located in several of those states. We are about to launch a large air attack on the rebels. While they probably wouldn't risk a ground offensive in response, we can't be sure they won't. If they do, we should do everything possible to mitigate their numerical superiority on land by moving as many of our forces into ideal defensive positions."

The President leaned against the Resolute Desk and thought silently. Then he began to shake his head slowly. "No," he finally said simply. "Moving forces make us appear as the aggressor, or worse, weak. We would look to be the ones initiating ground combat. And besides, we need the National Guard units to continue maintaining the peace in the towns and cities, not to mention assist with the food and fuel distribution."

"That is true, especially since the militia attacks in several areas seem to be picking up, rather than tapering off. Homeland Security seems to be in need of additional assistance," Darden agreed. "Can we get an update on this, Madam Secretary?"

The Secretary of Homeland Security looked uneasy. "Uh, um, yes, Mr. Darden, of course. Mr. President, I'm not fully prepared with an actual briefing, but we have seen an increase in what we deem domestic terror attacks perpetrated by various extremist militia groups. Activity seems to be particularly heavy in southern Ohio, central Pennsylvania, central and northern California, eastern Washington state and southern Illinois. We have had two fusion centers and three other DHS installations attacked in the last three days alone."

"Why are we having such a hard time rounding up these criminals? I'm especially concerned that this is getting worse and not better. Why is this so?" the President asked. This was the same question he asked every time militia attacks were discussed.

"Mr. President, we believe that at least some of the militia units are being aided and abetted by Special Forces possibly sent by the FSA."

"Yes, Madam Secretary, we've known that the militia units include lots of veterans, including former special operations personnel."

"No, Jack. I'm referring to something different. Our local informants have reported men not formerly known to the areas as operating with locals. In addition, one of our informants in the FSA military has reported Presi...ah, I mean Doucet has approved the infiltration and use of active duty special forces within the USA."

"Could this mean that they are preparing for wider ground operations?" the Vice President asked.

"The consensus is that it does not mean that," the DHS secretary answered.

"Then why would Doucet take such action?" the President questioned.

Again it was General Westin who spoke up. "Mr. President, we can't say for certain. But if it were me making recommendations to President Doucet, one of my recommendations would be to utilize the local militia, and any group, for that matter, to destabilize as many areas as possible. One goal of an insurgency is to convince the people that their government cannot protect them. Cannot provide the necessities of life such as food, water, and power even, on a reliable basis. If this happens, the people begin to switch sides or at least become opportunistic and back whichever side seems to be winning at the time."

"This is your opinion, General?" the President inquired.

"It is my opinion, sir, but I saw it while serving in Columbia in the late 80s and early 90s," the General replied. "And it is part of various theories on insurgencies."

"Interesting. I would like a briefing tomorrow from my military staff on what to do about this use of rogue special forces in our states," said the President.

The Secretary of Defense didn't acknowledge the President's response due to being engrossed with his pad computer. As the room looked at him and waited his face suddenly lit up and he looked up to his boss.

"Mr. President, my apologies. I was just reading a communiqué. Our naval assets are all in place for Operation Unitary. The Air Force reported being ready yesterday. Now all we need to do is wait for Mrs. Doucet to make her little visit and we can begin to put an end to all this madness."

The President's beaming smile was his only response before adjourning the meeting.

31

ABOARD *LIBERTY ONE* EN ROUTE FROM HOUSTON TO THE PERDIDO SPAR OIL RIG

The President was visibly excited to be taking her first trip aboard the newly commissioned *Liberty One*. *Liberty One* was the gleaming, brand new FSA Presidential helicopter. In reality, it was not a helicopter, but a tilt rotor, a brand new MV-22 Osprey. Built in Amarillo, Texas, by Bell Boeing with many parts manufactured in Fort Worth, the MV-22 was chosen for both symbolic and practical reasons. Symbolically, it was good "PR" to have a locally built aircraft. The FSA Air Force Chief of Staff had recalled the uproar when the USA President's administration had selected a European made helicopter to be the new Marine One. The outcry over the selection of foreign made machines, especially in a time of deep economic recession had forced the administration to backtrack and continue upgrading and using the aging Sea Kings. The practical side of the decision was that as a tilt rotor, the MV-22 could fly at more than double the speed of a conventional helo at comparable or even greater ranges. The name had been chosen to differentiate from the USA aircraft and to show greater inclusivity in a time of national crisis.

Similarly, the President's new flying command center was named *Freedom One*. But, instead of a jumbo 747 like *Air Force One*, *Freedom One* was a hastily modified E-6B Mercury TACAMO (Take Charge and Move Out) airborne command and control aircraft, itself a modified

Boeing 707. Although both Southwest Airlines and American Airlines had offered to lend-lease an airplane for use by the new President, Doucet felt the need to be as frugal and practical as possible. So rather than accept the airlines' offer and have to do extensive and costly modifications to a civilian aircraft, she asked her military staff to suggest a cheaper, faster alternative that still met the extensive communications and control requirements for a presidential airborne command post. The TACAMOs already possessed all the enormous capabilities necessary due to their mission of communicating with the Navy's strategic nuclear submarines and the Air Force's ICBM's and nuclear bombers. All President Doucet requested in the way of modifications was the addition of a small, private office and a minimally appointed sleeper compartment.

The President sat looking out of the right side window as the waters of the Gulf of Mexico whizzed beneath *Liberty One.* The crew chief's voice came over the PA system, "Madam President and guests, ten minutes out; please prepare. Thank you."

USS Minnesota, 210 miles south of Galveston, Texas
0930 (9:30 am local)

"Con, sonar, contact Sierra One has settled at 850 feet and has slowed. I can barely hear her, skipper. Computer says probably the *New Mexico.* Sierra Two has faded out again. Last contact was on a bearing 055 degrees true. Best the computer can do is that it is an Improved *Los Angeles* Class. Can't identify the specific hull number."

"Very well Johnny. Stay on top of Sierra 1 and if Sierra 2 pops up again, we'll hear her," the commanding officer of the sub replied to his sonar operator. "What about the surface picture?"

"Only our two friends to the north and northeast, skipper." The two friendlies were both FSN (Free States Navy) surface combatant ships. The larger ship, the *Ticonderoga* class cruiser USS *Vicksburg* (CG-69) was also the closer of the two and was approximately 30 miles to the north. The smaller ship was the USS *Rafael Peralta* (DDG-115), a new *Arleigh Burke* class destroyer and it was 50 miles to the northeast.

The Captain looked at his tactical display screen pensively. "XO, what do you think," he asked his second in command.

The executive officer chuckled and then replied sarcastically, "About anything in particular, skipper?"

The captain looked back at his XO without smiling and then broke out with a grin. "Why, about our friend and neighbor the *New Mexico*, of course, and the overall situation."

"Well, first, I don't think *New Mexico* knows we're here. That's the advantage of us laying here in wait. I wish Fleet had given us more info. They obviously knew he would be coming, but it would be nice to know more about his intentions. Even if just an educated guess. Beyond that, I think their CO is sweating it out just like you, boss."

"All good points," the captain observed. "Continue."

"Fleet is obviously expecting trouble. They send lots of firepower to this area and then we have one, possibly two, potentially unfriendly subs show up. I don't much believe in coincidences," the ship's XO concluded.

"I agree. I don't like coincidences."

"If things heat up, it will get ugly mighty quick, skipper. I don't even want to think about it."

"Are you still talking about our tactical picture here in our little corner, or the rest of the country?" asked the CO.

"Both. I'm talking about both. Open warfare against our own Navy? Or parts of it? Americans against Americans on a wide basis? Killing and destruction on an unimaginable scale. Just too awful to think about. I don't know. I really thought that after the big aerial battle over North Carolina when no other big incidents happened, that this would somehow simmer down. I thought that after some bluster, threats, and maybe sanctions, or I don't know what, that the USA would accept our existence as our own nation rather than fight another civil war."

"No other big incidents? You don't consider what happened at Camp Pendleton or Fort Carson, Langley, or Norfolk big incidents? What about what is *still* going on in the cities, with the shortages, rioting, and outright urban fighting between groups we can't even be sure of anymore. You don't consider thousands and thousands of dead Americans big incidents?" asked the Captain incredulously.

"Yes, of course I do. But what I mean is there have been no other large military engagements between the FSA and the USA. What's happened on the bases and in the cities is bad, but it has not involved armored vehicles shooting at each other with artillery and large numbers of aircraft dropping bombs and shooting missiles. That sort of thing."

"I see. Well, I agree that all that would be horrible. Let's hope that this is precautionary and that Fleet is wrong and we have nothing to worry about."

The Perdido Spar, the Gulf of Mexico
That Same Time

Liberty One and her back up / decoy approached the landing pad on the enormous structure and flared slightly as their twin wing-tip rotor pods swiveled from full horizontal to straight vertical as the aircraft transitioned from airplane mode to helicopter mode. The back-up came in first for a touch and go before *Liberty One* came in and alighted on the oil platform. Overhead, a flight of two F-15s of the Louisiana National Guard's *Bayou Militia* orbited on Combat Air Patrol (CAP). The Eagles were being controlled by an E-3 AWACS radar airplane orbiting over Houston to provide radar coverage. After a great deal of cajoling, the President had also agreed to have a SEAL team onboard the massive rig to assist with security and have a Navy special boat detachment with two boats patrolling the waters in the immediate vicinity.

Dignitaries and employees of Royal Dutch Shell and local, regional and state of Texas government were on the pad to greet the President along with her Secret Service detail. A smaller than normal contingent of media were also present. A few select correspondents had been allowed to ride in the Presidential back-up, but others had to agree to travel to the rig on short notice without full knowledge of where they were heading or why.

The President strode smoothly and confidently to the receiving line and shook everyone's hand with a warm greeting. The Chief Executive beamed and positively gushed charisma. As she had repeatedly enjoined her staff, the importance of this event could not be overstated. The formal announcement of the first sale of the new Hydrocarbon Backed Bonds (HBBs) on the international bond market was a monumental event that virtually ensured that the nascent Free States of America would be on a better financial footing than its struggling mother country. In addition, the head of the FSA was also going to announce a massive program to open up federal owned lands in the FSA states for lease, purchase or other development. This would also help the financial standing of the new nation. President Doucet was extremely excited to make such important announcements in such a stunning setting with the waters of the Gulf of Mexico stretching behind her.

USS Minnesota, 16 miles South – South East of the Perdido Spar
0950 (9:50 AM Local)

"Con, sonar. Sierra One is flooding tubes. Say again, Sierra One is flooding tubes."

"Sonar, con. Sierra One flooding tubes aye." The captain responded, fighting the urge to tense up, but not being entirely successful.

"Captain, I recommend we compute firing solution and flood tubes one and two," the XO chimed in.

"Negative on flooding tubes, old buddy," the XO's boss said in a conscious effort to lighten the mood, primarily his own. "They're just trying to spook us into moving and revealing our position. They must have picked up a hint of our trail and want to know who's out here."

"If so, and I pray you are right, that's a hell of a bluff," the sub's second in command replied. Flooding tubes for a submarine was tantamount to locking radar onto an aircraft. An extremely overt and threatening prelude to an actual firing of weapons.

"Con, sonar."

"Go ahead Johnny."

"Captain, Sierra One is opening forward missile tube doors *and* torpedo tube doors."

"Oh shit! Are you sure? Both sets of doors opening?" the Captain demanded.

"Yes, sir, Cap'n. No doubt about it. He's fully locked and cock… wait. No! Transients, transients! Torpedoes in the water!"

"How many, Johnny? Heading?"

"Four fish in the water. ADCAPs. Not heading our way. Bearing 290 true. Heading directly for the oil rig."

"Captain, recommend firing tubes one and two," the XO echoed.

"Agreed. Flood tubes one and two. Open outer doors. Generate matched bearings."

"Con, sonar. Missiles ejecting. Say again, missiles being ejected from Sierra One."

"Damn it! Damn *it*!" the Captain's swear was barely under a full yell.

"Con, sonar!" the senior sonar operator was also struggling to keep a calm voice, just like the senior officers. "Sierra Two is launching missiles."

"Talk to me, Johnny," the CO said with a measure of control returning to his voice.

"I count 10 missiles launched from Sierra One and now hear missiles launching from Sierra Two, approximately 22 miles away."

"Damn! What's the status on our tubes?" asked the Captain.

"Tubes one and two ready, sir," came the response from the torpedo room.

The Perdido Spar
That Same Time

The first two of the ten Tomahawk missiles launched from the *New Mexico* headed straight for the massive, $3 billion dollar oil rig. The E-3 AWACS orbiting over southeast Houston picked up the missiles as soon as they emerged from the wave tops of the Gulf, as did the patrolling surface ships. The call immediately went out over the secure net, including to the President's detachment on the spar. But, with the missiles being launched at just under 30 miles from their target and covering over 8 miles per minute, the Secret Service agents had less than four minutes to react.

The two cruise missiles targeted on the Spar were both armed with conventional, unitary 1,000 pound warheads. The first was programmed to detonate a few feet over the helicopter landing pad where President Doucet would be giving her remarks. Next, the second missile would burrow deep into the structure itself before detonating among the complex maze of oil lines, fuel lines, machinery, chemical storage and the myriad other explosive and flammable materials found in any modern oil operation.

The remaining eight missiles headed toward two different targets. The first, and closer target was the second largest refinery complex in North America (and sixth largest in the world), the huge ExxonMobil facility in Baytown, Texas, just east of Houston. The other four cruise missiles headed further east, to the largest North American refinery, the complex in Port Arthur, Texas. Located 69 miles east of the Baytown refinery, this facility was owned in equal shares by Royal Dutch Shell and Saudi Aramco. With an expansion of an additional 325,000 barrels per day (bpd) capacity completed in 2012, the 600,000 bpd refinery was also one of the most advanced in the world. Between the two targets, they refined almost 1.2 million bpd. The Tomahawks slated to attack the refineries were all TLAM-Ds (Tomahawk Land Attack Missile, D variant) with 166 BLU-97/B Combined Effects submunition bombs. Each of the bomblets separates and falls independently toward the ground, being slowed and dispersed as they fall by an inflatable bag on their top. Each bomb has a combined fragmentation, shaped charge and incendiary effect on anything they happen to hit. Normally very effective against personnel, material, and lightly armored vehicles, they would have great effect on the highly flammable and explosive liquids and solids found in the refineries.

Over 1,200 people worked at the Port Arthur facility, while another 1,300 people would be working at the Baytown site. All of them were now directly in the line of fire, as were many of their neighbors. The Patriot surface-to-air missile (SAM) battery deployed in Texas City, to the south, would be their last line of defense.

The sky fifty miles east of Tipton, Missouri

The twelve F-22A Raptors of *Bull* flight were screaming through the air 70 miles south of their compatriot flight. Eight Raptors carried two 1,000 pound JDAM bombs and two AIM-9X air-to-air missiles in their internal weapons bays, while the remaining four F-22s carried the maximum stealth air-to-air load out of six AMRAAMs and two AIM-9Xs. Maintaining total radio silence and full EMCON (Emissions Control) the stealthy super fighters had launched from the old (and defunct) Air Force base in Carmi, Illinois. Quickly climbing to 50,000 foot cruising altitude, they also accelerated to their Mach 1.5 "super-cruise" speed.

"Five minutes to release point," the pilot of *Bull Lead* thought to himself. He keyed his mic twice and waited to hear responses from the other eleven pilots of the flight.

Just after the eighth set of "beeps," his radar warning system alerted him. The radar energy they were receiving from the E-3 AWACs orbiting east – northeast of Whiteman was increasing rapidly. Although separated by almost 150 miles, the AWACs and Raptors were closing on one another rapidly, at almost 800 miles per hour, despite the fact that the early warning aircraft was at present angling slightly away from the F-22's current course. The Colonel knew that, sooner or later, enough of a radar return would reach the AWACs to enable it to detect his jets. And to add to his concern, his pre-flight intel briefing had told him that somewhere out there would be a flight of F-15Es patrolling the skies over Whiteman. In addition, there was a Patriot battery at the B-2 bomber base, but he was not worried about that. They would not come within 50 miles of the base and he doubted the Patriot's radar could acquire his stealthy birds from that distance.

Meanwhile, at Fairchild Air Force Base outside of Spokane in the newly independent state of Washington, three B-2A Spirit stealth bombers were being readied for their night time raid against the B-1B Lancers at Ellsworth Air Force Base. Similarly, another three Spirits were undergoing final preparations at Holloman Air Force Base in New Mexico. From here, the stealth bombers would cross the southwestern desert and enter Texas to strike at the Lancers at Dyess, outside of Abilene. Intense closed door negotiations had ensued before Washington State (in the process of considering a name change to Olympia or Cascadia) agreed to allow the Federal US Air Force to fly an attack mission from its soil. Washington State officials feared getting dragged into the burgeoning civil war, but under immense pressure from Washington, DC, finally agreed, provided it would be a one way mission and would not be repeated.

In Maryland, at the NSA's Fort Meade headquarters as well as at several other massive facilities in Pennsylvania, Colorado, New Jersey, and New York, a legion of cyberwarriors prepared to launch the most massive cyber attack in history. The audacious goal of the cyber offensive was no less than the crippling or serious disruption of every major federal and state network, both public and private, within the rogue states.

From the Pacific Northwest to the Midwest to the East Coast to the Gulf of Mexico, surprise seemed fully on the side of the USA.

USS Minnesota, 15 miles South – South East of the Perdido Spar
0955 (9:55 AM Local)

"Match generated bearings and *shoot!*" came the call from the Captain.

The sub's 7,800 tons shuddered as the high pressure compressed air ejected two ADCAP torpedoes into the water, bearing down on the USA sub that had just fired its weapons. Just like the previously fired torpedoes, these warshots also quickly accelerated to their maximum speed of over 60 knots, screaming through the water at slightly more than 70 miles per hour. As the cylindrical killers cleaved through the water they also unspooled long, thin control wires back to their mother ship, allowing them to be precisely controlled.

"Con, sonar. Sierra One just accelerated to flank and is diving hard to port, sir. She's fired noisemakers and is sure to fire fish back at us. I think we'll get her, but that rig is going to be hit hard."

The hisses and thumps clearly preceding the eruption of multiple false submarine acoustic signatures marked the deployment of the decoys intended to draw off the *Minnesota's* homing torpedoes.

"Sonar, con. Roger. Four ADCAPs and ten Tomahawks is an awful lot of firepower to put on one rig..."

The Captain's thought was interrupted once again by a report from sonar. "Transients! Transients! Torpedoes in the water. These are sure to be the reverse axis shots, Cap'n."

"Right full rudder! Twenty degrees down bubble! Diving officer, make your depth 1,200 feet. Launch decoys!"

The undersea warship experienced more hisses as its own countermeasures deployed into the erupting battlespace. The USA torpedoes, having not been given a proper fire control solution were easily deceived by the countermeasures. The USA sub *New Mexico* was not so lucky on this day. The *Minnesota's* torpedoes locked on the hapless vessel and tracked mercilessly like the cold, unfeeling killers that they were designed and built to be. The first ADCAP struck the *New Mexico's* port side midway between the sail and the prop. The massive blast blew an enormous hole in the pressure hull allowing tons of ocean water to rush in. The luckiest sailors were killed instantly by the blast or by being crushed as their compartment collapsed by the pressure of the sea. The unlucky ones were in parts of the submarine forward and aft, which took several minutes to collapse as they sank to their watery grave.

Onboard the *Minnesota,* all of the crew could hear the sickening sounds of metal being torn asunder and being crushed. The sonar techs could even hear some of the stricken sub's men screaming as they died.

Despite the death of the *New Mexico,* the four torpedoes she fired continued their relentless charge toward the Perdido Spar.

"Skipper, does this mean we are officially at war with the US?" asked a young Lieutenant (junior grade).

"I don't know son, I hope not. But let's keep focused on the tasks at hand. We still have at least one more hostile sub out there that just fired missiles at our side."

The Perdido Spar

Meanwhile, above the waves, the Tomahawks settled in for their final low level run to the Spar as well. Flying barely fifty feet above the waves they were extremely hard to detect by sight. However, the sound of the approaching missiles soon filled the air. Luckily for the FSA, they were not entirely devoid of luck on this day. President Doucet was not, in fact, giving remarks immediately upon her arrival on the oil rig. Instead, the President had accepted an offered "in-depth" tour of the facility. Her party and escorting dignitaries were three levels below. Upon receiving the report of missiles inbound, the Secret Service detachment scrambled to begin the evacuation of President Doucet. But, the maze of passageways and relatively few stairways ("ladders" in the parlance) made it virtually impossible to move quickly in either direction.

Therefore, only a handful of people were still topside on the helicopter landing pad when the first Tomahawk arrived and detonated a few feet over *Liberty One,* even as her pilots spooled up her dual tilt-rotors for immediate take off. Fragments and jet fuel exploded in every direction in a rapidly expanding fireball inferno. *Liberty One*'s pilots were incinerated where they sat in the cockpit, along with the crew chief in the main compartment. The other people on the pad were cut to ribbons by jagged pieces of metal or engulfed in flames. One oil rig worker was blown off a catwalk only to die after hitting the water hundreds of feet below.

Upon hearing the explosions above, the Secret Service agent in charge of the President's detail immediately changed directions and began to head toward the launching platform for the Spar's rescue boats.

"Madam President, we must assume that *Liberty One is* destroyed and we are heading toward the rescue boat per our briefing," was the last thing the Secret Service agent said to his charge. The last thing anyone in the party heard was the low scream of the Tomahawk's turbofan engine. The missile impacted the second level and burrowed into the maze of pipes, platforms, and steel grating. The detonation of the 1,000 pound warhead created a second, much more powerful inferno than the one already engulfing the top of the platform. Diesel fuel, crude oil, hydraulic fluid and other flammable liquids fed into the massive fire and drove it ever larger and fiercer. President Doucet was thrown backward and down a stairwell like a rag doll. She blacked out momentarily before regaining consciousness. She looked around, dazed, and realized she was completely deaf. She also found that she could not move. At that moment, the level above her erupted in a terrific secondary explosion. Her thoughts turned to her children and her husband as she began to pray silently for them. The last thing she saw was a huge, burning metal beam falling directly at her...

In addition to the Presidential party and visiting dignitaries, over 150 people lived and worked on the oil rig. The vast majority of them would also die there.

On board *Liberty Two,* the back-up to *Liberty One,* approaching the Perdido Spar at an altitude of 2,000 feet, President Doucet's Chief of Staff, Laura Hearn looked on in disbelief.

"Nooooo..." she heard herself scream as she saw the multiple massive fireballs engulf the oil platform. "The President..." but her voice trailed off as she heard the folly of her statement. She shook herself inwardly. "Think Laura, think!" she screamed at herself silently. She looked up to see the expectant eyes of the crew chief. "Dan, we need to get to Houston ASAP. And we need to ensure that the Vice President is evacuated from Dallas to safety ASAP. Next, we need to radio for search and rescue and fire teams to deploy to the Spar ASAP. I want every available asset. There are almost 200 people on that platform and we have to try to extinguish the fires and help them."

She knew it was too much to hope for anyone to survive the hell on earth she was observing below, but she struggled to maintain faith. Besides, even if no one survived, they would make every effort to search for survivors. At that instant, the massive oil platform was rocked once again and two massive plumes of water erupted from either side of the Spar as the *New Mexico*'s torpedoes found their mark.

The next second, another realization rocked her to her core once again. "My God! We are at war! The President is dead and we are at war. God help us all."

The war that all sides had hoped to avoid had now begun.

www.ingramcontent.com/pod-product-compliance
Lightning Source LLC
Chambersburg PA
CBHW071308170626
46809CB00001B/379